Flight Of The Revenants

By

Jeffrey P. Wilcox

authorHOUSE™
1663 Liberty Drive, Suite 200
Bloomington, Indiana 47403
(800) 839-8640
www.AuthorHouse.com

First published by AuthorHouse 04/13/05

ISBN: 1-4208-1926-7 (sc)

Printed in the United States of America
Bloomington, Indiana

This book is printed on acid-free paper.

CHAPTER 1 Evasion of Fate

No light could be seen, no sound could be heard. Darkness had engulfed the unseen landscape, and the stagnant, humid air hung as a thick blanket of choking fog. Several muffled shots pierced the abyssal silence, followed by much louder thundering roars. Again the sharp reports of weapon's fire echoed through the blackness. Flashes appeared briefly to illuminate the dark and dusty terrain only to be hastily swallowed up by the fog.

Emerging from the darkness, a man appeared, running for his life. As he bolted through the void, he heard the sounds of heavy footsteps coming from the darkness behind him. Beyond him was nothing; the utter blackness yielded no clues as his feet stumbled over the unknown surface. His mind was filled only with his determination to escape; pain was ignored, fear was ignored. Had he the time to stop and reflect, he would be astonished that he had survived thus far.

It was then that he heard a growing whistle of turbine engines. The fog began to illuminate around him and he looked back to see a bright white beam of light slice through the thick haze from above and sweep the terrain in search... of *him*. He could now see the illuminated surface before him, keenly aware that he had lost his cover of darkness.

The searchlight thankfully swept off in a direction perpendicular to his position, and as he watched over his shoulder as it disappeared he collided with one of *them*, both of them falling and rolling down a steep rocky hill.

He shouted as he and his assailant embraced each other in a mortal struggle. His attacker was unusually strong, and its head was covered in a metal helmet that protected its face. It had seized the man by his throat when he noticed the shadows of three more of them, partially illuminated by the spotlight, and closing on his position. Not wasting any time, the man blindly fired a short burst from his weapon, a Heckler and Koch MP5 submachine gun, into the attacker. It made gurgling sounds but refused to release his throat. The man fired another burst into its trunk and it finally rolled off of him. Quickly jumping to his feet, he fired the remainder of his magazine into the illuminated fog, and saw one of the shadows drop to the ground. He then spun around and began running again, gravely aware that the remaining shadows were in close pursuit.

Another one immediately appeared in front of him. With incredible reflexes, the man swiped it across the face with his MP5, knocking it to the ground, while he sprinted by. Just for an instant the fog flashed with a red glare, and he heard a shot, then quickly saw an explosion of sparks just ahead of him. Before he could begin to imagine what to make of it, another shot went off and he was able to see what looked like a straight neon light fly out from his hip and into the darkness. He threw back his head and screamed in pain, while continuing to run.

At first, he thought he had been hit with a tracer round, but as he ran, he looked down to see a charred and cauterized wound. Whatever it was, it had thankfully only grazed his hip.

"What the hell are you?" he yelled in fear-tainted rage.

The man continued to run, disregarding the wound in his hip. Another shot went off, this time missing him completely and impacting a rock beside him, sending a shower of sparks into the air once again. As he passed the rock, he could see a bull's eye shaped mark where the beam had hit; it was glowing red hot.

The terrain had become increasingly rocky and difficult to negotiate. The man knew that a sprained ankle or stumble would mean his death. As he ran, he heard their footsteps close behind. He looked back, but could see nothing, as the spotlight was too distant to illuminate them. He knew *they* were back there. As he turned his head forward, he became aware that through the darkness was a large black void directly in front of him. It was a large rift in the ground, at least fifteen feet wide, and he knew it was an impossible jump to make, but found himself leaping into the air anyway. He sailed through the darkness and slammed into the opposite rocky cliff wall, dropping his MP5 into the darkness below just in time to grab the top of the ledge.

He heard the footsteps draw closer. The man looked back just in time to watch one his pursuers try to stop before falling over the edge. Its feet stepped in a frenzy, desperately trying to slow down, but it was too late. Diving head first into the darkness below, the unfortunate being let out an inhuman scream unlike anything the man had ever heard. The horrible shriek ended abruptly with a loud thud as the being hit the ravine floor.

The man wasted precious seconds trying to look for some foothold on the rocky face of the ravine to which he clung. Finding a small rocky protrusion to use to climb up, he began to pull himself up. He was almost out of the crevice when the fog lit up, and he instantly felt a bolt of pain surge through his right arm just as his ears registered the shot. The man slid back down the wall and was now hanging by one arm. Not even looking at his wounded arm, he turned his head around and saw a lone gunman, crouched on one knee with an unfamiliar weapon in its gloved hand. Another shot went off this time, piercing his right shoulder. The sound the weapon made was unlike any weapon he had ever heard. When discharged, it sounded more like a loud camera flash accompanied by a hiss.

"Bastard!" The man yowled.

He looked back again and saw the thing that was firing at him; silhouetted before the luminous fog, its humanoid form was evident: It had two arms, two legs, and a head on its shoulders. It wore a gray uniform, mostly obscured by a dark silvery metallic chest plate, and a helmet with what appeared to be an antenna sticking out the top. The two eyes of its helmet protruded about two inches and contained lenses that glowed an eerie shade of green.

He heard footsteps and saw more shadows closing just as he noticed the creature was taking aim again. It was obvious that he would be shot to pieces if he stayed there.

"Okay, pal. You want me? Come get me!" He let go of the cliff wall and quickly slid down the smooth rocky wall into the abyss below. He felt the temperature drop as he descended into the darkness. As he slid down, his fall was slowed by several violent collisions with outcroppings of rock along the way down. His descent finally came to an abrupt halt on top of the body of the dead being that had fallen down before him. As he hit, he rolled off of the body and came to rest a few feet away, stunned.

For a moment, a minute, or perhaps longer, he didn't move, but then suddenly opened his eyes and let out a cry of terror. He found himself looking into the large black eyes of the creature that had fallen. Its helmet had broken open and milky white fluid was covering the ground. As he, of course, already knew, they were *not* human. Jumping to his feet with a shout, he immediately started looking for his MP5. He was sure that he had broken some ribs on the fall down, but miraculously his legs were still operational. Only the light from the fog above reached into the darkness at the bottom of the crevice. He could not find his weapon, and began to search the body of the creature just as he was showered by beams of red light like the ones that he had been shot by.

He dodged out of the way and withdrew his Berretta 9mm semi-automatic pistol. He fired several shots up into the air, clipping one of his adversaries in the side of its helmet, causing it to spin around before falling into the crevice. The man stared at the fallen being as he replaced his clip, and saw it move slowly before the bright red beams from its own comrades perforated it.

"Jesus!" he shouted as he expended the last clip for his Beretta, catching another creature somewhere in its chest. He pulled out the clip and searched desperately for his spare, but in horror, realized that he had already used it. The man watched, defenseless, as they slowly lowered cables into the ravine and began to descend. Just then, he stepped on something. He frantically reached down to pick it up, only to find that it was the dead alien's weapon! It was about the size of an Uzi, and with its silvery appearance resembled a toy.

He quickly pointed the end with the hole at one of the beings repelling down into the ravine and squeezed the grip. The crevice lit up with a red flash, and the creature was hit in the back by two red beams and fell from its cable onto the rocks in front of him. The enemy's weapon was almost weightless and had only a slight recoil from the exhaust gases that hissed from a vent in the sides of the muzzle. He fired a few more shots at some of the other beings whose heads were visible, hitting one square in the face and throwing it on its back.

He saw them getting ready to return fire when, without thinking, he pulled his only grenade off of his desert camouflage fatigues and threw it upwards. With a thundering blast, it detonated. For about five seconds, as the ringing in his ears subsided, the man heard inhuman moans of pain as well as the sound of small rocks raining down from above. Soon all was quiet, except for the dreaded turbine engine sound above. The man's gaze instantly fixed on the cable in front of him.

Despite the wounds to his arm and shoulder, he climbed the cable to the surface to find four beings mutilated by the grenade writhing upon the ground while emitting sickening moans. The man quickly surveyed the area and, thankfully, could not see any other shadows closing.

He ran alongside the crevice for about fifty feet when he came across a metal bridge spanning the dark rift. He heard the gravelly noises of more footsteps behind him as he crossed the bridge and again broke into a sprint. As he ran, his right arm hung limp by his side, but the pain never registered in his brain. He could barely see the sun through the fog, coming up on the horizon. He knew he was going in the right direction. The fog was clearing, and the lights appeared behind him again, and he heard the deafening whine of a turbine engine grow ever louder.

"No! " he shouted, dropping his strange weapon, grinding his teeth, and sprinting harder. Despite the years of training, and despite his excellent physical shape, the man was nearly depleted of any remaining energy. But somehow, he tapped a last hidden reserve, and sprinted as if his life depended on it... which was the case.

It was then when he heard the sound he had been praying for: waves of water crashing into the cliffs below. More shadows were approaching from behind, and the whining sound of the flying vehicle following him was directly overhead. In front of him, he noticed that the rocky surface disappearing rapidly, and a dark blue void beyond. He heard a loud thundering sound coming from above and saw a red glare.

"Adios, motherfuckers!" he cried just as he jumped off the cliff, through the wall of fog, and out into open air beyond him. The vast horizon of the Pacific yawned before him as he descended over the cliff. At once, the ridge behind him exploded in a giant red flash. The pursuing aircraft had fired a rocket and it exploded exactly where he had been standing mere seconds before. The man yelled all the way to the water below, just less than one hundred feet down, before smashing into its surface.

The salt water stung his wounds as he struggled against the undertow while swimming to the cliff wall, where he scurried into a small concavity in the rocky, algae-covered cliff. Seconds later the hovering craft had lowered down above the water. Although the man couldn't see it, he could hear it, and could see its spotlight scanning the water, searching for him.

Pounding thunder rung out as the water was violated with beams and explosions. The roar was deafening. The man screamed, squeezed his eyes shut, and covered his ears to escape the din. As quickly as it had begun, the onslaught came to an abrupt halt. The spotlight continued to search, finding only dead fish that floated to the surface. The man removed his hands from his ears and waited. After what seemed like eternity, the spotlight was shut off and the unseen flying vehicle left. All was quiet. He waited for what seemed like half a lifetime, then looked at his watch and realized his last chance for extraction was in thirty minutes...

. . .

The sun was setting. Beautiful hues of purple and fiery orange were cast across the endless ripples of the Pacific Ocean. With no warning, a periscope shot up from the surface and began to scan the beach nearby.

"I still don't see anything, Sir," the chief operating the periscope said.

The executive officer, a commander, turned to look at the captain. "They must be gone..."

"...I sure as hell hope not, stay on it." the captain mumbled.

In the periscope, all that could be seen was the barren beach, most of which was covered by fog. The chief suddenly saw a bright blue light emanating through the fog on the beach.

"Contact! Captain, I see one of them," the chief reported as he saw a lone blue signal flare wavering on the beach.

"Bring 'em home, XO," the captain said.

"Aye captain. Deploy the rib!" the Commander ordered.

The captain then turned to the chief at the periscope. "Keep an eye out for the rest of them, chief. He can't be the only one..."

When the rigid inflatable boat returned, it brought back only one man. He was remarkably battered but was still alive. The spent flare was still clutched tightly in his fist. He was now aboard the nuclear submarine USS Amberjack; a corpsman was carefully dressing his wounds as the captain was debriefing him.

"Where is the rest of your team?" the captain asked.

The man didn't answer; he only closed his eyes and shook his head.

The captain frowned. "Dead? Wounded? I need a definitive answer."

Then the man pulled out a small black object, an optical video cartridge in a zip-lock plastic bag. With a trembling hand, he dropped it on the deck at the captain's feet.

"They're not human..." the man mumbled.

"What?" the captain said.

"He's delirious, Sir," the corpsman said.

"...Not even *human*..." the man mumbled as he passed out.

CHAPTER 2 The Reckoning

Washington D.C.
Monday, October 21st, 2033

In one of the many chambers beneath the Pentagon, a meeting was held. Most of the top players of the U.S. military were gathered as the emergency meeting of the cabinet of the Joint Chiefs of Staff got underway. Today was a special meeting.

"Wars don't end like this," an Air Force general said to the Commandant of the Marine Corps, who was seated next to him.

"That's even if you could call this a war, Phil... more like the mother of all standoffs in my opinion," the Commandant said, chuckling.

"Nothing but an arms race, and a standoff. The media's found a name for it... *Cold War II*, clever." an army brigadier general said.

The Commandant laughed again. To him, a war wasn't a war unless there were battles. His name was General Maxwell. He was the only combat veteran of the last declared *War* in the room. He was an infantry private 1st class during the Terror Wars of the early 21st century over two decades ago. During his career there had been many small skirmishes and UN police actions, but never another declared war.

"Why have we been called here, Admiral? Is it about the anomaly in China?" the Air Force general asked the admiral at the head of the table.

The admiral spoke up. "We'll wait until everyone is here. Mr. Sheridan."

The Air Force general nodded, and went back to his discussions.

The conversations continued for few moments until the two double doors leading into the room opened.

A man dressed in an army uniform with four silver stars on his shoulders walked in, carrying a briefcase. As he approached the table the men began to stand.

"General Sterling. Glad you could make it on such short notice," the admiral said, while standing with his hand extended. He was the Chief of Naval Operations, Admiral Chuck Bruin.

"That's why they pay me the O-10 pay, Admiral," Sterling said, as he shook Bruin's hand.

The Chairman of the Joint Chiefs of Staff spoke up. "All right, now that we are all here, let's get this show on the road," he said. The chairman was Admiral Brandt Fox, known only to his peers as *Bud*. He was a four star admiral in the US Navy, and had seen the country through the US - Asian Confederacy standoff until its abrupt end.

It had been a war of numbers, statistics, threats and incidences. It was the Cold War again; only nuclear weapons had not been at the forefront of the conflict. The United States possessed a ballistic missile defense network consisting of laser-armed satellites; two fleets of AL-52B airborne lasers and ground interceptor missiles. The Chinese and Russians worked together to design their own space-borne anti-ballistic shield and it was operational shortly after, though no match for the US nuclear triad, which the allies were unwilling to use.

The standoff and following arms race materialized not in nuclear weapons but in that of sheer conventional military numbers; it was raw military might that was built up. On October 12th, 2023, the Chinese, Cambodian, Russian, Laotian, Vietnamese and Korean people had united together to create another union of far greater power than the Soviet Union, known as the Asian Confederation. The A.C. began to mass up weapons and an army unparalleled on the planet that threatened the stability of the entire globe.

In spring 2026, the A.C. declared the United Nations a puppet of the West, and withdrew. A year later, the United Nations was dissolved, and NATO became the only binding alliance the U.S. maintained. As the political fallout heated up, both NATO and the A.C. began to acquire more and more neutral countries into their alliances until nearly the entire world was on one side or the other. Both NATO and the A.C. had begun a rapid arms buildup as it seemed inevitable that World War III was going to break out between the two superpower alliances.

But war never came. There was the Aleutian Incident, where an A.C. aircraft carrier was supposedly sunk by a mine off the coast of Alaska; the Hong Kong Massacre, where the U.S. ambassador in the Hong Kong embassy and his staff were slaughtered by Chinese *freedom fighters;* and the South Korean Missile Standoff where it was discovered that the U.S. had armed the South Koreans with several nuclear weapons, and both they and North Korea were poised to blow each other up. However, none of these horrible events were enough to spark off the impending war. Due to the overwhelming anti-ballistic missile coverage on the U.S., and the formidable conventional armies massing on the Asian continent, no military strategist could predict how this standoff would end. None had ever dreamed the tides would take the unimaginable turn they did.

On 30 September 2033, after years of low intensity conflict, a crushing blow had been delivered to the Chinese. An atmospheric anomaly, never seen before, began to form a pocket of mist over Shanghai. It grew rapidly, gaining several square miles an hour, and grew until it was over one hundred miles in diameter. Those who did not flee from the advance of this fog were never seen again. Millions of Chinese citizens who did not evacuate simply vanished. Amid sketchy reports of fighting within the fog, and suspecting this to be some kind of NATO preemptive attack, the Chinese deployed most of their massive army into the anomaly. Fully prepared for a chemical attack, they launched a series of offensive skirmishes against what they claimed was an invading NATO army using the anomaly as a smoke screen. Reports were sketchy, but apparently in less than three days; over half of their army had been wiped out while fighting whatever was in the fog. Without China, the A.C. was thrown into shambles... the war was over before it ever even started.

Until this day, nothing was known about the nature of the anomaly.

"Gentlemen, I've called this emergency meeting to discuss the outcome of the recent operation to investigate the *anomaly.*" Fox didn't need to call it the *Asian Anomaly* or the *Chinese Anomaly*; everyone in the room knew just which anomaly he was referring to.

Everyone was quiet as the admiral spoke.

"We've only been able to piece together details about the anomaly from reports from the Chinese and what our satellites can tell us."

"The truth is, we don't know what it is," General Sheridan interrupted. Muffled chatter began among the rest of the joint chiefs.

"Until now," Admiral Fox finished.

The men quieted down. Admiral Fox removed a brown folder from the table.

"This report appeared on my desk only twelve hours ago. I'll read you some," Fox said, opening the file.

He began, "The extraction of SEAL Team 9 was incomplete. Only one survivor was recovered, a lieutenant named Michael Gates. He was wounded and in shock. Wounds were inflicted by an unknown method." He looked up at the generals, admirals and administrators. The expressions on their faces were that of curiosity.

"Here's where it gets good," he continued. "Lieutenant Gates' only statement was that the enemy forces he encountered were not human. No further statements could be taken."

At first no one spoke.

"That's a crock of shit, Admiral," General Maxwell chuckled. His outburst invoked a grin from Admiral Bruin, who sat next to him.

"The man who wrote that report was obviously traumatized in battle," one of the CIA specialists remarked.

"This Lieutenant Gates will be here in this room in a few days. We will get his report personally," Fox finished. "Are there any questions?"

No one said a word.

"I'd also like to say that if this turns out to be true. If this anomaly is the result of some kind of..." the admiral paused. "...non-human organization, then we will need to act immediately."

Several of the joint chiefs scoffed at the admiral's last statement. The thought of *little green men* being responsible for the atmospheric anomaly was preposterous to most of them. But Admiral Fox knew something they didn't: He had seen the video footage taken from the survivor.

. . .

Thursday, October 24th, 2033

Lieutenant Gates awoke to find himself alone in a hospital bed; the room was small, with white walls. He was almost completely immobilized, with splints on his arms, and multiple bandages all over his body. As he tried to talk, he realized he had trouble breathing, then found that he had a tube inserted into his throat; a machine was breathing for him.

Despite the bad wound on his shoulder, he reached over and pulled the tube out with his right arm. He could barely breathe, and it hurt to try. There were no windows in the room. There was only a large glass mirror. Gates guessed it to be a one-way observation window. There was also an oval doorway next to the window. The door was the only exit from the room and looked airtight, indicating to him that he was in some kind of containment room.

"Hey... Hey let me out of here!" he strained to say.

Just then, the door hissed and opened, and a woman in what looked like a full-encapsulation biohazard suit walked in, closing the door behind her.

"Oh, you're awake," she said casually. Gates could see her face through the clear plastic visor. She looked as if she might be in her early thirties or late twenties. What he noticed most were her two greenish-blue eyes. Although he could only see her face, he knew she was absolutely beautiful.

He tried to get up, but his head was spinning. The woman put something down on the stand next to his bed. It was a metal tray, with something not resembling food on it.

"Now you try and eat something and get better, all right?" she said with a smile, and before he could respond, she was walking away towards the airlock. Gates, with some degree of difficulty, sat up in his bed, and looked at the tray. On it were four pieces of green Jell-O, and a pile of white slime that could have been rice once. Gates picked one up with his fingers and began to eat one of the Jell-O cubes. The green gelatin laboriously slid down his throat.

Gates leaned back. "Imitation lime... they're trying to poison me," he said while spitting what he had left of the Jell-O in his mouth onto the tray.

The airlock hissed again, and opened, this time a man walked in, wearing another bio-suit.

"Good evening Lieutenant Gates," the man said. "I'm Doctor Green."

"Where am I?" Gates replied weakly.

"You're all right, you're at Bethesda Naval Hospital."

"How long have I been here?" Gates rasped.

"This is your sixth day,"

The man began to change his patient's IV solution. "How do you feel?" he asked.

"I don't know," Gates said, "How do I look?"

"Not too bad, I would say you're going to make a full recovery,"

the doctor said optimistically.

"What's with the space suits, Doc, am I diseased or something?" Gates asked, looking at the bio-suit.

The doctor scoffed, "No, we don't think so. It's just standard procedure, when our patients have contact with something that could be a biological hazard."

It was Gates' turn to scoff. "Biohazards, huh? You could call them that." He then squeezed his eyes closed hard.

"What's my condition?" he said bluntly.

The doctor sighed. "You've sustained some of the strangest burn wounds I've ever seen. Bone has been grafted into your hip and shoulder. You have a fracture to your right knee, probably due to a sharp impact, you have a minor concussion, you also have a hole..."

"I guess I should just ask you how long," Gates interrupted.

"Until you recover? Probably at least two months," the doctor said with his Hippocratic optimism.

Gates started coughing. "Why does it hurt to breathe?" he asked.

"You've been treated for smoke inhalation. You really should let us put your tube back in and try and relax. We're still running tests."

"Well, it was nice chatting with you Doc." Gates started to sit up.

The Doctor eased Gates back onto the bed, "I told you, Lieutenant. You'll probably be in here for at least two more months."

"Months? I've got to get back and give my report."

Just then another man in a yellow biohazard suit walked in. "It's good you feel that way Mr. Gates, we have a lot to talk about. My name is Special Agent Hoffman," he said while pointing to his laminated badge, which had CIA in big bold black letters.

"Not now you don't!" the doctor said while running between the bed and the man in the yellow suit. "Not until this man is fit for questioning."

Hoffman gave a smile through the window in his suit. "Well, there may not be enough time, Doctor, so please get this man in a wheelchair."

The doctor didn't smile. "You can't order me to..."

"It's okay, Doc," Gates interrupted. "He's right, there isn't any time. I don't think this can wait."

The doctor shook his head, "This man may have still have an infection or..."

"We've been monitoring him for a week. Blood, heart, brain activity... all normal. He's healthy," the agent argued, still smiling.

In the end, Gates was taken from the room. From that experience, he gathered the impression that this Hoffman was a powerful individual.

Gates was escorted down the main hallway, out of the building, and into the fresh air by Hoffman, two security guards, and three other men in suits to a black van escorted by two black sedans.

Hoffman appeared to be the classic secret agent type. He was dressed in a gray suit, had a full head of slicked back black hair, a black earphone in his left ear, and was wearing black sunglasses. Gates was surprised that his name was Hoffman, and not something like Johnson, Jones or even Bond.

"You're going to meet some important people today, Mr. Gates," Hoffman said. "Try and get some rest before you get there."

. . .

The fog flashed again, and he saw a red beam of light heading for one of his shipmates. It was Marcus. Marcus's leg nearly exploded on impact; he dropped to the ground, the video camera flew from his hands and struck the ground as began to scream in horror and pain.

"Oh my god... Marcus!" Gates yelled as his best friend fell to the ground.

"Run, you asshole, RUN!" Marcus yelled.

Gates didn't listen, he ran up to Marcus and grabbed the video camera, slung it over his back, and picked up Marcus and tried to run for cover.

Gates opened his eyes, and saw the interior of the van.

He had fallen asleep. "Marcus..." he murmured.

. . .

"This is probably some kind of ploy by the A.C," General Sterling said quietly to the Commandant of the Marine Corps, General Bert Maxwell.

"Maybe, but what would be the purpose? What possible advantage could they hope to gain with this?" Maxwell responded.

Sterling raised his eyebrows. "I don't know. Throw us off balance, maybe."

"Perhaps this anomaly is an attempt to hide a new weapon of some type. Remember that Shanghai was where they were building their own prototype rail gun system," General Sheridan interjected.

"Hell, I wouldn't doubt that it's something they were toying with that blew up in their faces," someone said.

Admiral Fox remained silent throughout the discussion.

Two double doors opened into the room, and several CIA agents entered. Behind them was Gates in a wheelchair.

"Ah... Lieutenant Gates, it's nice of you to come, how do you feel?" Admiral Fox asked as he was pushed towards the table. Hoffman closed the doors and stood in front of them with his arms folded.

"I'm sure you already know most of us, Lieutenant, but I'm going to introduce us anyway." Gates was introduced to everyone at the table, most of whom Gates knew already.

Among them was General Sterling, whom Gates had read a lot about. Sterling was arguably the best strategist in the world; some of his tactics were legendary. His biggest achievement, however, was to push for the Army and Navy to begin refitting their arsenal with what is now the cornerstone of the U.S. strategic initiative, the sky carrier.

Essentially, the sky carrier is an airborne nuclear-powered aircraft carrier run by the Navy, used to support the Army, and paid for by large parts of both of their budgets. In the opening years of the 21st century, it was recognized that the United States' dependence on permission from fickle allies to use their countries airspace or bases during the Terror Wars was a crippling shortfall. The Navy proposed reviving the airship, a class of aircraft used in the 1930s and was a cousin of the famous German

Hindenburg airship. The technology was over 100 years old, but may well have been ahead of its time: new lighter and stronger materials now existed and allowed for a sturdier and larger hull, while computer modeling offered engineers opportunities to optimize and streamline the designs.

Gates was in awe of the man who shaped the modern U.S. military.

Also among them was Admiral Bruin, the Chief of Naval Operations, his boss. Like Gates, he wore on his uniform the gold eagle with the musket and trident, the badge of a SEAL.

"It's a pleasure to finally meet you, Sir," Gates said to him.

"Likewise, Lieutenant," Bruin said.

"All right, let us begin," Fox said. "Lieutenant Gates, I want you to tell us what you saw from the moment you arrived at the beach."

Gates' stomach was churning. He asked for a microphone because his lungs still hurt and he couldn't speak very loudly. He was given one promptly, and began his story...

"I can barley remember what happened, it's like a blur..." he began.

"Well... we went in on an MC-130 and did a HALO to the water. We cut our chutes, and as my team and I swam to shore we... well we didn't really see the shore, as soon as the water stopped the fog started. And the air around the fog was like ice, when I stuck my hand into it, it was as if I stuck my hand into water a few degrees above freezing, but once about a foot in, the temperature rose to about ninety-five degrees and it became one hundred percent humid."

Gates painfully swallowed.

"One by one we crossed into the fog and onto the beach. We could barely see anything once we were on shore, and radio contact from you was cut off, and our radio headsets hardly worked; voices were full of static. We made our way about half a click from the beach to our first waypoint without sighting anything alive. We checked our maps, but with no landmarks, and no GPS, we began to doubt if we were really at a human city. There was no city, no concrete foundations in the ground, no roads. It was as if the city never existed," he finished.

"Did you see any hostiles? Any A.C. troops?" Sterling asked.

Gates sighed, "No, there were no people, no bodies, no grass, no weeds, no Shanghai, only sand, lifeless sand, a few rocks, and random pits and trenches dug everywhere..." the memories were rapidly becoming vivid in Gates' imagination as he spoke. It was now as if he had been there an hour ago. The green glowing eyes of the things that had chased him were burned into his memory.

"...then we walked in deeper, and the moonlight disappeared, the mist was so thick no light was penetrating it. At first we thought we were off course, and that we should have someone go back out into the ocean, away from the mist so we could communicate with our GPS and get a fix."

Gates stopped talking, he just looked down at the table and said, "None of us were prepared for what happened next..."

"What did happen next Lieutenant?" Fox asked politely,

"We got lost, the Chief sent Miller with the satellite-phone back to the shore outside the perimeter of the fog, but I can see now that he didn't make it. The compasses didn't work, they just spun around and around. Even though it was supposed to be dawn in four hours, the fog was still dark, we couldn't see the sun, and the infrared goggles were useless, the temperature was constantly shifting, we were forced to turn on the lights on our MP5's and randomly explore. We had been searching for three and a half hours straight when Wallis found the road,"

"A road?" Admiral Bruin asked.

"A black strip with eleven segmented gray lines going down the center. Just like a highway, only this one was a hundred feet across! Some of the lanes had huge regular gouges pressed into them, like something very big and very heavy had driven across them." Gates paused reflecting. "It was the God-damndest thing I ever saw," he said while fidgeting with one of his many bandages, "It was our corpsman, Marcus that suggested we walk down it, he said it would be our best bet in finding some sign of civilization." Gates began to sadistically chuckle, "Well, we sure found it." his grin abruptly disappeared.

"We were all walking along the road, Wallis, Marcus, Crow, Navarrete and Chief Benning and myself. Then something came out of the fog, down the road...", Gates coughed a couple of times and then cleared his throat, "It was some kind of vehicle, it even had tail lights, blue ones, naturally we all jumped from the road and hit the dirt. It drove right on by, in one of the rightmost lanes, and disappeared."

Gates paused again. "Something big came after that. I couldn't see all of it, but I tell you it was massive... bigger than anything except maybe a sky carrier. Its hull was up in the fog, too high to see, but I could see its lights as it thundered by. It was huge..."

"You say this was a ground vehicle?" General Sheridan asked.

Gates nodded quietly and continued, "Crow said we should follow it, and continue down the road, but Chief Benning said we should try to get back to the shore and find Miller so we could report to you what we've found. But to tell you the truth, I could feel that we were out of our league. And I'm sure my guys did too."

"I decided to turn back, but before we could make any distance, the Chief noticed a dim light to our left, roughly north of our position. We approached the position where the light seemed to come from, and that's when we heard the noises."

"How do you know it was north if you couldn't use your compasses or GPS?" Hoffman asked sternly.

"Because when I came back the other way running for my life, I ended up in the ocean south of where we entered." Gates explained, with a touch of annoyance at Hoffman's question.

The room was dead quiet.

Gates continued, "We walked closer and as we did the fog began to clear. The light got brighter, and brighter, and the air got fresher and clearer, we were going up a hill when we walked into a gigantic clearing in the fog. And we were shocked to see a hundred foot pillar of steel rise from the ground below. The area was circular, with a radius of about two hundred feet. The tower's base was in a big pit. In front of us was a thirty foot drop off to the reflective metal floor at the bottom, and as we got closer to the edge we saw... *them*. About fifteen creatures, roughly five foot six, in gray suits and colored metal helmets and chest plates, some with pick-axes and some with shovels, clearing away more off the cliff on the opposite side. In front of the tower's entrance was the smaller vehicle we had seen on the road, the creatures were offloading some crates. Navarrette kept asking me what the hell they were. I could see it in his eyes that he was terrified now. Hell, I didn't know how to respond."

All of the men in the room, including Hoffman were silent, their foci locked on Gates.

"I heard a couple of weird sounds, they sort of sounded like belching, or a growling stomach." Gates attempted to imitate what he heard, "*Minaminamina!!*" Sterling almost thought the sound was comical until realizing the gravity of what Gates was trying to convey.

"Then one of the creatures caught my eye. It seemed to be directing... you know, giving the orders. It was the only one not working. I grabbed my binoculars and got it in view. This thing was a little different then the others: the workers had two legs and two arms, they had two little glowing green eyes in their helmets, but the commander had four thin metal covered legs, four thin metal covered arms, and it had a big ass. I knew then, without a doubt that they weren't human. On its head, it had two curved horizontal strips, bulging out of its helmet, they were for its eyes. Sticking out of the top of its helmet, was what appeared to be a blue Mohawk. It kind of reminded me of the old roman soldiers' helmet."

Gates took a deep breath.

"I was frozen, It seemed to look in my general direction. I knew it couldn't possibly see me from this distance without binoculars, just then it took a couple steps towards our cliff, no one else noticed it but me. It seemed to look at me, but it couldn't possibly have seen me, not from that distance, not as dark as it was..."

Gates paused again, and gave a hard sigh, "As I watched, I noticed it was reaching for its helmet. I watched it remove its helmet, and as it slid off of its face, I became terrified. It was the scariest thing I've ever laid eyes on, its skin was gray, it had two fangs, a blue Mohawk, and had four red eyes. Its eyes dilated and fixed in my direction... my heart stopped, and my binoculars lowered." Gates had turned pale.

"I realized it was looking directly at me."

CHAPTER 3 Marathon

"I didn't have any time to even blink before it raised one of its arms, pointed at me and gave the loudest, most spine-chilling hiss I've ever heard. All of the alien workers stopped working, and I heard an alarm sound. The next thing I knew the four-eyed creature that was standing a hundred feet away was now only twenty feet from the base of the ridge, and closing fast... I had no chance to think, no chance to react," Gates explained.

"I heard several shots, and saw flashes from below. I gave the order to return fire." Gates paused.

"Could I get a glass of water please, my throat is killing me." At first no one moved, no one seemed to even blink. He noticed that he had everyone's apt attention.

Gates sipped from his glass of water and continued.

"Chief Benning was firing his weapon at every moving thing below and encouraging the rest of the men. One of the men - Crow, I think, threw a grenade that landed next to the vehicle parked down there and took it out of action. Navarrete had hit the dirt, next to Benning on the ledge, and began firing down at the workers. Marcus was filming all of this with his shoulder-mounted camera. He was crouched on one knee, also firing into the pit. I began to concentrate my fire on the running workers. Something was terribly wrong, and I guess Benning knew it too because when he caught my eyes, I could see he was terrified... something I didn't know Chief was capable of feeling." Gates sipped his water again.

"Well, it looked like we were winning, six workers were on the ground and not moving, and one of their vehicles was in pieces and on fire. That's when it happened. Benning stopped firing and began to replace the magazine in his MP5, when that four-eyed thing reached up from the ledge and grabbed him by the throat. Crow fired two or three rounds from his pistol into the creature. Crow was suddenly covered in blood, I think from Benning's throat. The thing threw Benning over the edge and advanced to Crow. He fired a few more rounds and hit the creature in the chest every time. I then fired my MP5 at it, emptying my clip." Gates paused for a moment then continued.

"After at least ten rounds the creature fell back down the ledge, out of sight. With one man gone, I yelled for my team to retreat and Crow, Navarrete, Marcus, Wallace and I all began to fall back. Just before I finally left the ledge, I noticed that several of the worker creatures were in pursuit, climbing up the ledge behind us. I don't honestly know how long the battle lasted. But it felt like maybe sixty seconds."

"My God..." one of the men said.

"How did you escape?" Hoffman asked.

Gates nodded his head while staring intensely at the table before him, and slowly collected his thoughts. "Navarrete was shot down by some hovering aircraft in the fog with a spotlight; Wallace was too but I don't think he died right away because I heard somebody screaming over the radio for a few seconds before it went dead." Gates paused.

Gates' voice took the tone of anger, "It was only Crow, Marcus, and I, and we took out about ten more of those... things... before... before..." Gates paused again.

"Please continue," Bruin said in an apprehensive voice.

"Crow was bringing up the rear. He was right behind me when I looked back just as he was hit by the bastards chasing us. They were shooting at us with lasers or something."

"Lasers?" General Sheridan interrupted. "Laser systems aren't small enough to be man portable..."

"Please allow Mr. Gates to continue," Admiral Fox said patiently to the general, who looked at Gates with stubborn disbelief.

"Sir, I have burns on my body that sure as hell weren't made with a cigarette!" Gates said angrily. "They were bright red beams, brighter than tracers, and they exploded on impact. Would you like to see what they do to human flesh?" he almost shouted while holding up his arm in a cast.

"Please, Lieutenant Gates..." the Admiral said. "Please go on."

Gates swallowed and took a deep breath. "Only I and Lieutenant Junior Grade Marcus were left. We stuck together and ran what seemed like a half a click before I heard a scream." Gates was clearly upset, his voice quivering. "Marcus was hit. And I wasted the bastard that shot him."

Now Gates' voice turned to rage. "I grabbed the busted camera, pulled out the video-cartridge, and while I was running with Marcus over my shoulder, put it in a shock proof bag."

Gates was now clearly agitated, his voice now almost screaming. "You know, they train us to run while carrying a man, but in that fog, I was winded before I had made it one hundred yards. He screamed at me to leave him behind... I couldn't leave him. We don't just leave our people behind. But kept pleading with me to just drop him! I couldn't do it. Right when I spun around to make a stand, he kicked his way out of my grip and hit the ground."

Gates spoke quietly into the microphone, almost too quiet to hear. "My eyes caught his for one last time, I knew it was over for him, and so did he. I ran away into the fog, to make it back, to survive."

Gates' eyes were fixed on the glass of water on the table. "I heard weapons fire, and then nothing. Marcus was dead. I just kept running, and put some good distance between them and myself, but when I got near the shoreline, it got real hairy real fast; They started catching up with me, and I was being followed by the flying thing in the air that got Navarrete and Wallace. I fell into a deep trench, got shot to hell, jumped off a cliff, and by God's will, I survived."

Gates inhaled and exhaled loudly. "Just me..."

"Are you sure about that?" Hoffman asked in his monotone.

Gates grit his teeth. "What?! Are you asking me if I intentionally left one of my people behind?"

Hoffman shrugged, "No, Lieutenant. I'm just asking if you can confirm the death of Petty Officer Navarrete or even Lieutenant Marcus..."

Gates slammed his cast onto the table so hard it echoed, visibly startling a few of the joint chiefs.

"They're dead! You don't think I could tell? The sounds I heard... the sounds of my men dying," Gates glared at Hoffman, "I *know* they're dead... There's your confirmation!"

Admiral Fox raised his hand to stop the conversation before it deteriorated further.

"I don't think the status of the rest of SEAL Team 9 is in question," Fox said, staring at Hoffman. "If the lieutenant says none of his men made it out, then none of them made it out."

There was another long silence.

"Lieutenant Gates, the ones that chased you, how do you know they weren't human?" Sheridan asked, with a combined look of disbelief and curiosity. His skeptic expression nearly sent Gates over the edge.

"Because human beings don't scream like they did... human beings don't bleed white when you bash their heads open..." Gates stood up from his wheel chair. "...and human beings don't shoot people with Goddamned laser beams!"

"Thank you, Lieutenant, that will be all for now," Admiral Fox said.

Gates fell back in his wheelchair, frustrated, and also pleased that he no longer had to speak. "Good day, gentlemen," he said respectfully.

He was soon wheeled out of the room by one of Hoffman's men. The doors closed behind him.

Hoffman began to speak, "I think we should take Gates' emotional state into account when we decide..."

"That won't be necessary, Mr. Hoffman. Lieutenant Gates is a man who just lost his entire team, but I guarantee his testimony here is not clouded by emotional burden. He's a professional."

Hoffman shrugged again and remained silent.

"By the way, General," Admiral Fox began to say to General Sheridan, "I have the reports on the wounds that man received in China. He has burns that are believed not to have been caused by a laser, but by plasma."

"Plasma?" Sheridan repeated with a confused look.

"Plasma systems exist only in labs. We're not even close to making weapons out of them. That technology is at least thirty years off, assuming we even spend the money on it," Sterling said thoughtfully.

Admiral Bruin spoke. "We have the video cartridge with us here, gentlemen, and I think its something you all must see." Bruin pushed a button on the table and on the wall directly in front him two doors slid open to reveal a large flat-screen monitor. With a push of another button, the video began to play.

. . .

High above the western Asian continent, a vaporous white trail streaked through the sky so high that it was practically invisible from the surface to the naked eye. The streak was heading for the center of the evaporating atmospheric anomaly.

Captain Riggs could see the facility now. The fog was almost completely dissipated.

"Eagle's Nest, Thunder Bird: I can see the facility now," he said into his helmet-mounted microphone.

"Thunder Bird, Eagle's Nest, we copy you. Reduce speed and proceed with caution," a voice crackled back to him.

"Roger. Reducing speed," Riggs said casually to himself as he pulled back on his throttle, bringing his spy plane, an SR-84 Wraith, down from mach four to mach two. Riggs knew there was danger; not more than twenty four hours ago, an old E-3 Sentry reconnaissance plane, carrying a crew of twenty, was shot down by God-knows-what near this same position. However, Riggs felt safe as he was in the single most advanced spy plane the United States owned: a spy-plane equipped with a scram-jet engine. This revolutionary Supersonic-Compression-Ramjet engine was capable of hurling the plane at hypersonic speeds in excess of mach twenty if pushed. He was flying the fastest plane in existence, exceeded only by a reentering space shuttle or a meteor.

He began to turn past his final waypoint into the target reconnaissance zone. His seven billion dollar aircraft banked sharply to the left, as he turned into his search lane and began his high-speed electronic-photography run.

As he made his first pass over the facility, he could see several buildings, most of which were under construction. Although not briefed about the existence of an alien threat below, Riggs had heard the rumors that wildly circulated throughout the military. His own suspicions were confirmed as he observed the enormity and oddity of alien structures. He could see several small square dots scattered in front of a large patch construction work. Several miles further he over flew a massive dome. But, as he continued, he could hardly believe his eyes as he over flew an absolutely massive central tower that he judged to be at least three thousand feet high.

"My God! What the hell is that thing?" he asked out loud as he stared in awe at this physical enigma. The tower itself was by far taller than any skyscraper in existence. Even more unique was a silver globe mounted atop the structure at least two hundred feet in diameter. Its purpose was a mystery, as were all the structures observed so far. His camera equipment snapped continuous photographs and video as he flew above.

Riggs was searching for only a few seconds when his sensors began to pick up high electromagnetic radiation levels emerging from the facility below.

"Eagle's Nest, Thunder Bird. I am picking up extremely high radiation emissions from the facility," Riggs reported, with a high degree of excitement in his voice.

"Copy Thunder Bird, stay within your pattern and m.. s..re ..ot tr.." Eagle's Nest was suddenly cut off. Riggs had a very bad feeling about this situation.

Bright flashes could be seen below through the fog. Riggs began to feel the tickling sensation of a bead of sweat rolling down his brow behind his visor. *Is this what the Sentry saw before...*

"Eagle's Nest, Thunder Bird! Do you copy? Over," Riggs begged the radio but met static. His counter-electronic-countermeasures system reported that he wasn't being jammed, it was as if something had simply taken Eagle's Nest's signal out of the air.

Trying to reestablish contact, he turned on his sensitive electromagnetic monitoring equipment. Suddenly his radio crackled to life with voices. Riggs couldn't make anything out - the noise sounded almost like a grumbling stomach. A tight grip of fear began to choke Captain Riggs as he realized that he was receiving these signals from the base below, and they didn't sound human.

The remnants of the fog flashed with a red glare.

"The hell with this," Riggs said as he banked sharply to the right, to pull out of his search lane. Just as he did this, the cockpit was lit up by a red flash, as a considerable large red beam of light blinked past the left side of his plane, missing it by only ten feet and left a white vapor trail in the sky behind him.

"HOLY SHIT!" Riggs shouted as he banked sharply left as another red beam pulsed past his right side. He pushed his throttle forward before diving as another shot missed the tail of his craft by less than a hundred feet. His craft slowly accelerated to mach three. As suddenly as they had started, the red beams had ceased.

Riggs reached down and grabbed his crotch to make sure he hadn't urinated in his flight suit.

"Those..." he wheezed, breathing heavily, "were lasers..."

The facility was behind him now. Before Riggs could count his blessings, his radar picked up something. A small flying object, not more than two meters long, had emerged from the facility and was now coming straight at him.

"No, no, no..." he said aloud as he locked his plane's Target Recognition & Identification Module onto the closing object. TRIM classified the object as a flying homing projectile, but could not identify it.

The unknown projectile was closing very fast. Riggs began to climb as he increased throttle. The G-forces pulled Riggs' cheeks back as he climbed. The scramjet engine could not be engaged under mach three because of design constraints, so Riggs kept increasing the throttle.

As his altitude increased, the air became thinner and less friction restrained his aircraft. Slowly, he leveled out only a mile below the perimeter of the planetary atmosphere, which was as high as he could go without being the first man to fly an SR-84 into space.

Riggs checked his radar once again. The object was still closing. It was now only about a mile away.

"OK, you bastard. You want to race? I'll give you a race..." Riggs said, gritting his teeth. He pushed the throttle forward as far as it would go. The entire plane began to vibrate as Riggs was sucked back into his seat. The SR-84 was capable of reaching mach three safely using its conventional jet engines. It was now at mach two and holding.

Riggs smiled as the object began to drop back. "Yeah! Take that, you bastard!" Riggs jeered. The SR-84 rocketed through the Earth's atmosphere at an incredibly high speed, the strange object right behind it.

"Come and get me now, you chicken shit!" Riggs howled. He almost didn't notice his TRIM system showing the object releasing another smaller object from the front. Riggs looked at the readouts in confusion. "No way... Another stage? This is *not* happening!" The larger object disappeared off the screen, and smaller one gained speed at an alarming rate.

The TRIM read the speed of the smaller object as over mach three and was gaining speed. Riggs pushed his throttle to its absolute maximum. The object was not more than six thousand feet in his wake.

Riggs depressed the small blue switch that armed the scramjet, and without wasting any time, hit the ignition. With a thundering roar, the hypersonic jet engine roared to life, only to sputter and die a second later. Riggs frowned.

The plane was at mach three and the enemy projectile was still gaining. It was now only four thousand feet from the rear of the plane. He looked in his rear view camera and could actually see it as a little black dot on the horizon.

His plane reached mach three and a half, which was faster then his plane had ever gone before on its conventional engines. The missile closed to two thousand feet and still gained quickly. He frantically tried to start the engines again, and again they flamed out.

"Dammit!" he shouted.

Riggs' fuel was burning away too rapidly, and his scramjet was still not igniting. He suddenly veered up to try to catch the missile in his punishing jet wash, but it dodged out of the way. He tried this once more, but the missile dodged again. The SR-84 began to vibrate vigorously, and at mach three and a half, this was a very bad sign that the conventional engines were not taking the abuse well. Riggs knew that if he slowed down he would be a dead man, so he had little choice but to maintain his airspeed.

Riggs began to pray. Then he depressed the ignition again, and heard the scramjet thunder to life, sputter for a moment and then roar. He had done it.

"Let's see if you can do twenty..." he muttered as he turned the throttle control for the scramjet to its maximum setting. The SR-84 stopped vibrating as its conventional engines were shut off and inlets closed as his speed began to increase. Steadily, the scramjet increased its thrust and the plane gained speed.

The missile dropped back. Buried in his seat from the horrendous G-forces, Riggs was elated, "Yeah, eat it! Eat it you..."

With a flash of white light that burned out his rear view camera, the missile detonated. The Wraith pitched in the air uncontrollably as the aircraft was blasted from behind by a massive pressure wave of super heated atmosphere. Riggs was lucky the stress didn't tear his wings off. His aircraft was tossed around the sky violently as he fought to keep control. The blast wave eventually faded, and Riggs became free of its wrath. His jet shook violently and he could hear metal bending and his heart beating. Then, all was quiet. He was still alive. It was over. He had survived.

"A nuke! That was a God dammed nuke!" Riggs shouted. "Who would use a nuke on a single plane?"

Riggs glanced down at his computer readout. It was dead. It was a miracle he still had hydraulic control of his aircraft. He was now flying hypersonic over the Pacific Ocean at sixty thousand feet and dropping. His fuel gauge was broken, and he had no idea how much fuel he had left. He began to reduce altitude in the hopes of ditching the plane and surviving or possibly reducing speed enough to eject. He re-ignited his conventional engines and could only get one to light. Just as he did, his airspeed dropped to the point where his scramjet flamed out with a loud bang.

"Come on... come on..." he mumbled, fighting the controls as his airspeed drastically slowed.

As his crippled aircraft headed towards the ocean below, he became aware of something on the horizon. It was land. The beach didn't appear to be too far away when his last engine flamed out because of lack of fuel. He had no idea how long an SR-84 could glide for.

Not long, he found out.

CHAPTER 4 Eyes of the Unseen

The lights in the room automatically dimmed. The video screen displayed a garbled mess of colors and then a black screen as the digital video began streaming from the cartridge. Aside from video, the cartridge also displayed neutron radiation levels, temperature, day, and time. It also recorded audio, though none played yet.

"Aliens, Goddamned aliens," General Maxwell said aloud.

The video was surprisingly clear, and began while the SEAL team had just penetrated the fog.

"There's nothing... nothing here," the room heard Lieutenant Marcus whisper.

The video ran for several minutes while revealing nothing to the men except endless dark fog.

"Mac, conserve your video," they heard a voice, probably Gates, say.

The video went black, as it had been shut off. A second later, it came on again and displayed a small four-wheeled vehicle race by. Its blue taillights disappearing into the mist within seconds.

"That looked like a hummer," Sheridan said.

The whining sound of the vehicle's engine faded off into the unseen horizon.

"I hope you got that?" a distant voice called to Marcus.

"I got it, Boss," Marcus replied.

The audio of the cartridge was poor at best, but it still picked up the growing low-frequency rumbling. Suddenly, a massive tank appeared on the screen, and lights were moving overhead. As it rolled by, another one followed about eighty meters behind it. Massive armatures protruded from the tops of both tanks into the fog and out of sight. It took the men in the room a few seconds to realize that the tanks were merely two of the four treads of a massive vehicle whose hull was suspended so high in the air that only its lights could be seen through the fog. It was moving at approximately thirty miles an hour.

"My God! It's huge!" Bruin said almost whispering.

The video followed the lights of the vehicle until they were obscured by growing volume of fog between it and Marcus's camera. The rumbling slowly faded away.

"That was no hummer, General," Admiral Fox said, looking directly at Sheridan.

The video recording was corrupted for a moment, showing static and partially formed images. The sound was also garbled. After five seconds it cleared up, and the men were staring through a clearing at a large tower that disappeared into the fog above. No one in the room spoke as the SEAL team slowly made its way over to the ledge. Marcus had just pointed the camera down when the four-eyed creature Gates had described pointed and hissed. The entire battle was recorded in perfect clarity.

"Look at it! What is it?!" one of the men asked as the four-eyed creature sprinted at the ridge the SEALs had taken position on.

"Some other form of intelligent life..." Hoffman said, stunned.

"I'm betting *those* things aren't human, either," Sterling said, gesturing at the workers, who looked similar to a man while clad in armor and helmets. "Look at how low their knees are jointed. They may look physiologically similar to us, but they are definitely not human."

The four-eyed creature's claw reached over the ledge and seized Chief Benning's throat, and one of the generals jumped. The audio was poor, but had enough quality to give every man in the room a deep chill. Even the sounds the creature made as Gates and Crow emptied their magazines into it were horrifying. Its hiss was like a cat hiss and a bird whistle combined.

"Fall back!" Gates could be heard shouting.

Just as the team began to fall back, Marcus's camera picked up several new figures emerging from the base of the tower. They looked similar to the worker aliens only larger, and appeared to wield large gatling-style guns. Sterling assumed that they were soldiers. Six or seven of them stood at the base of the tower before the camera panned away. Sterling noticed one of them was larger and taller. He only saw it for a split second, but what it was carrying caught his eye.

"Hey, back it up!" Sterling shouted, gesturing with his hand while getting to his feet.

The film backed up to when the alarm went off. Sterling watched intensely; he saw Benning killed again, everyone beginning to retreat; the soldier aliens came out...

Sterling pointed. "Stop right there!" The film froze instantly.

"There, do you see it?" Sterling started gesturing at the lower left corner of the screen, at a large but distant silvery figure.

"Can we get a close up of the lower right corner?" someone asked.

The screen flickered and then displayed the lower right quadrant four times as large. Now everybody saw it, and everybody knew what it was holding.

"Right there..." Sterling said sitting back in his chair. "What the *hell* is that?!"

On the screen, was an image of a large two armed, two-legged creature that looked just like the soldiers, only much bigger. And in this thing's clutches was the biggest, meanest gun Sterling had ever seen, meaner than anything he had even conceived. It was a large mass of twisted metal with pipes and hoses that resembled nothing portable. From the top was a handle where it held on to with its right hand, and where shoulder straps hung it below the creature's right arm. On both sides there were two red cones within small metal tubes, perhaps rockets. And in the front were two multi-barreled turrets with six barrels each. This weapon must have weighed at least eight hundred pounds, but the creature didn't seem to have a problem carrying it.

"Now that is one big fucking gun!" General Sterling exclaimed.

The video became corrupted again right after the retreat and no further video was recorded. The screen went to static and then went black. The room was silent.

"Jesus, what are we up against?" an air force general asked in a hopeless tone. The room suddenly broke into a mumbling roar.

"What does the public know?" Admiral Fox asked, his calm voice louder than the collective rumble of voices in the room. They all quieted down.

"As much as we did before today, Bud. I'd say most Americans believe we hit the Chinese with something new," Sterling said.

"CNN quoted an anonymous CIA official as saying the same," Hoffman followed.

"Well, that's not going to hold forever... we'll have a panic of epic proportions if we let this leak out," Sterling said.

"We'll leave that up to the President. What I want from all of you is your solemn oaths not to let any of this leave the room. Understand. You tell no one, not your wives, not your kids, no one!" Bud Fox said with a very severe expression. "Consider this matter... *beyond* compartmentalized."

It was very unusual for Fox to ever have to remind the rest of the joint chiefs to respect their top-secret/compartmentalized security clearance.

"What if *they* leak out word?" Sheridan asked. No one responded.

"Does the President know?" Sterling asked.

"He saw the tapes yesterday morning. Gates' report should be on his desk in an hour or so," Fox responded.

The room broke out into a rumble of conversation again.

"Time is of the essence, gentlemen," Fox said. "We need to figure out a plan of action."

"We need to gather more intelligence. What satellites do we have on this?" General Sterling asked.

"No good, General. That fog interferes with all of our sensory. My copy of Gates' medical report here says that the mucus he's been coughing out of his lungs is full of nano-colloids," Bruin said, flipping through pages of the report in front of him.

"English please, Sam," Fox grinned.

"Uhh, it says here he inhaled billions of little carbon bucky-balls full of... neon, xenon... inert gasses, Admiral. They call these things nano-colloids," Bruin explained, flipping through a few pages.

"Toxic?" Sterling asked.

"No, but apparently in the right conditions, they'll mask infrared signatures and are perfect at absorbing radio waves. Our satellites can't see them. Those that haven't disappeared, that is..." Admiral Bruin said.

"Disappeared?" General Maxwell asked, raising his eyebrows.

"Five of our satellites have already been lost. As far as we can tell they've been destroyed or blinded or overheated by an unknown force, possibly from the facility below," Admiral Bruin explained.

"Or from something in orbit that we can't detect," General Sterling said quietly.

"We've already lost one AWACS over the facility earlier today. Whatever took it down was so quick and effective that the pilot never even had the chance to radio that they were under attack..." General Sheridan explained. "She simply vanished from radar."

"So that's it? We're being blinded?" Sterling asked, disbelievingly.

"Systematically," Bruin confirmed.

"Not entirely," Sheridan began. "We are now conducting another flyby using our new SR-84; it's a much faster bird than the E-3 Sentry. If all goes well, we should have the data in a few hours at most," General Sheridan said, folding his arms.

A buzzer rang out. One of the men picked up the black phone set into the table. "General, it's for you, Sir," the man said, handing it to General Sheridan.

General Sheridan slammed the phone down after only talking for about a minute.

"What has happened, General?" Sterling asked.

"Operation Gander is a failure. The SR-84 was destroyed," Sheridan sighed. "The pilot survived, though; he ditched his plane in shallow waters off the coast of Maui, and nearly wiped out a couple tourists on jet skis. We're checking to see if his reconnaissance data is intact."

. . .

Deep in the bowels of the Pentagon, within the vast network of ventilation shafts, a single electric fan was running. Its motor sang with an electric hum as cold air was rushing by at a fast pace. Suddenly, there was a loud click, and the fan fell silent, slowed, and came to a halt. Two wires dangled down from the electric motor, their ends cut. Under the blades, something emerged from the cold darkness.

. . .

Hoffman turned to Admiral Fox.

"Sir, perhaps we should discuss a diplomatic solution..." he began.

Sterling suddenly showed a look of shock. "Make peace... on their terms?"

Everyone stopped and looked at him.

"Take a look around, Mr. Hoffman. These... *things*... have destroyed everything around them so far. I think it's clear they're not interested in peace!" Sterling shouted.

"Come on, John, be reasonable! If these beings are indeed from another world, then we should make every effort to make peace with them, rather than provoking them," Hoffman retorted.

"Provocation?!" Sterling stared at Hoffman with a combination of disbelief and laughter.

"Yes. Provocation. For all we know *we* may have cast the first stone... their first impression of us was the Chinese, for Christ's sake!" Hoffman explained.

"They came here to fight... it's clear as day to me," Bruin said quietly.

Sterling paused and said to Fox, "Bud, it's apparent, at least to me, that we need to capture some of their technology, then maybe they'll be in a chatty mood... because right now I haven't heard a word, and we need to know what we're up against."

Everyone nodded, and Hoffman sat back down in his seat and regained his stoic composure.

"I think another team needs to be sent in. Better armed and better briefed," General Maxwell suggested.

Admiral Bruin spoke up. "I agree. Only it needs to be done soon. It's obvious that they are building a base, and it's still under construction. If we delay until it's completed, who knows what kind of defenses they could have waiting for us."

"I'd like to point out, too, that President Benton has embraced the A.C.'s truce. After being briefed yesterday and seeing the tapes, he has also given us the authorization and responsibility of removing this threat from our surface," he said. "And he stresses that we need to act now."

"All right. We all can now see that this isn't an A.C. ploy..." Fox began, "But I'm recommending we still don't turn a blind eye to those scheming bastards."

"Trust me, General, without Chinese support, there is no A.C., and China just got a hard kick in the nuts. They're out for the count. It's all up to us," General Maxwell said.

. . .

Something laboriously crawled up the sheet metal, and it was hard work. There were no footholds on the smooth metallic wall except for an occasional rivet or seam. The air was dry, cool and constantly breezed by. The dryness of the air had dehydrated the glands that secrete adhesive fluids on its feet, making it very difficult to climb. For a second it looked down, and saw another electric fan spinning below; its blades were spinning so fast they looked partially transparent. To fall would have been sure death.

The small creature started climbing again, the wind blowing into it from above. After what seemed like eternity, it reached the summit, and the sheet metal tunnel turned ninety degrees, running parallel to the ground. The voyage was an easy, albeit long walk in the cold and dry air to its objective.

. . .

"This makes little sense... Why build here? With this technology of theirs they could have secured the whole planet in a day... obliterated us from orbit," Sheridan argued.

"Invasion? Maybe this is how they do it where they're from," Maxwell said.

"If they wanted to have a planetary invasion, they would have done it already; we are no match for their technology. They could at the very least destroyed our satellites in orbit without any more reprisal from us except for a middle finger," Sterling said.

"Yes, but why travel millions of miles to fight with us? With not even a word?" Maxwell asked.

"No, no. Isn't it obvious - they don't want war. They've only attacked us when we've invaded their space. It's possible they want to avoid war. But if we start poking around, we might change their minds," Hoffman interjected.

"Our space..." Sterling muttered, staring at Hoffman.

"Look, none of us can do more than guess what their motives are. What's important is how we either get rid of them or get them to leave. They've not attempted any communication with us, and have destroyed everything we've sent over to study them," Admiral Fox said. "They are a threat that needs to be neutralized. Period."

There was a long pause.

"I say we go with General Sterling's idea, Admiral, and acquire some of their technology. We need to rise closer to their level," Maxwell said.

"What do you have in mind, Bert?" Bruin inquired.

Maxwell began to explain. "I'd like to send in a much larger group of force recon Marines. Their mission would be to expedite..."

"No, no, no... this can't be done in numbers... it's got to be a surgical hit," Hoffman stated.

"Excuse me, Mr. Hoffman, but I think I know what I'm talking about," Maxwell rebutted angrily.

"Gentlemen, please..." Admiral Fox interrupted. "I'd say that I'd have to agree with Mr. Hoffman, General Maxwell. Too many lives have already been lost. We'll use stealth and precision, not brute force and numbers... not until we know what our boys will face."

Maxwell sat back in his chair and crossed his arms with a heavy sigh.

"Please explain your proposal, Mr. Hoffman," Admiral Fox said.

"Well, I know of a specialized group who would be perfect for the job. A special operations team I've been funding over the last five years," Hoffman said.

"The Screaming Demons?" Sterling interrupted. "A little pricey, aren't they?"

"Who cares as long as they get the job done, right?" Bruin remarked under his breath.

"And what if they fail? Then we've just wasted more lives, and taxpayer money!" Maxwell exclaimed.

"If they've failed, that means they're dead, and the dead don't come back to collect their pay..." Sterling quietly said.

. . .

The journey was easy now; it was walking instead of climbing. The creature ran into many forks in the smooth tunnels ahead, but every time it came to a fork, voices would tell it which way to go. The voices were from its *family*. The end of the journey was at hand. Directly in front of it was a metal grate. From behind this grate were the natives. It walked closer and peered through the metal bars. Its lone cyclopean green iris contracted as it studied the room behind the grate. It saw them: the bipedal creatures, with hair on top, just like the images it had been shown.

This was its mission. It quickly communicated its arrival at the grate to its family. Seconds later, they communicated back to it, to stay there and transmit what it saw and heard.

It did so with perfect clarity.

CHAPTER 5 Take Two

Rogers raised the binoculars to his eyes and looked in wonder at the great pillar of metal towering before him. With no fog left, his visibility was now limited to the moonlit horizon.

"I'd say, sixteen to seventeen more meters and we're at the base of the tower," he whispered into his headset. The man was dressed in a desert camouflage blouse and trousers with standard dessert combat boots. Slung over his back was a satchel pack of high-powered semtec-X explosives. Developed only a year ago, they represented the next generation of explosives and were only used by the U.S. government for demolition.

On the man's shoulder, a small camera and transmitter housed in hardened plastic transmitted everything around him.

With little effort, Rogers jumped off the rocky terrain down to the sand below. With movements similar to those of a reptile, he crawled along the ground until he reached the crest of a large pit surrounding the tower. Looking down, he could see dried human blood on the dirt next to him.

"I've reached the ridge," he reported as he crept forward to the edge and looked down.

Rogers found himself looking at the metallic floor at the base of the tower. The area was no longer well lit, as it had been when Gates' team had arrived there, but the moon did an adequate job illuminating the area. Upon further inspection of the tower base, he noticed a human body. It was lying on the metallic floor, his head nearly completely detached from his neck except for a thin piece of tissue. Rogers recognized him as Chief Benning, formerly a SEAL, not long before he had discovered the mangled, dead remains of Petty Officer Crow, who they could only identify by his dog tags. His skeleton looked as if it had been picked clean... by what? No one knew.

"Confirmed. This is where the SEALs bought it. I'd say we're at the right spot," Rogers said again to his headset.

"Copy, Rogue," A voice replied into his earpiece.

One by one, six more members of the Screaming Demons special operations unit arrived, each with a shoulder-mounted camera.

. . .

Back at a hidden underground room in the Pentagon, a group of men was assembled. Before them were seven monitors, each receiving an image from a different channel, from a different satellite encrypted up-link, transmitted by the different cameras attached to the men's shoulders. In front of these seven monitors were nine people. Two technicians, five members of the Joint Chiefs of Staff, The President of the United States, and his National Security Advisor.

"So this is your little dream team, Mr. Hoffman?" President Benton asked.

"Yes, Mr. President, these are the guys. Unconventional, unpredictable, reliable in every sense," Special Agent Hoffman smiled with confidence.

"I hope so," General Sterling said quietly.

. . .

All soldiers of the Screaming Demons were of different nationalities. Rogue and Scum were American, Chop was Chinese, Scarecrow and Merc were British, Lord was Canadian and made sure everyone knew it, and no one knew what Spike was; a big ox of a man, he could speak six languages, bench press four hundred pounds and was in command of this operation, secretly funded by the U.S. government.

The Screaming Demons were a group of highly skilled mercenaries, the misfits from all over the world. They were the best of the best at their profession: destroy, kidnap, hijack, observe, and escape alive to collect their large pay. Hoffman had been hiring them to carry out special operations for the CIA for the last two years against the A.C. Some of them had even been in China before, though none of it looked familiar.

Their record of accomplishment was flawless, and because of Spike's extreme perfectionism and professionalism, they had lost only one member since the team's creation five years ago. In this mission, they were to raid the tower Gates' SEAL team had discovered, and gather any artifacts or equipment that could be brought back for study. Engaging the enemy was discouraged if it was not necessary.

"All right gentlemen, lets earn our keep," Spike ordered.

Rogue and Chop began to skid down the ridge to the metal floor at the bottom of the pit. Simultaneously, Spike and Scarecrow ran around to opposite sides of the pit to take up offensive positions. Lord and Scum set up the heavy fifty caliber machine guns on their tripods and aimed at the small metal door where the alien troopers had come out on the video that Gates had brought back. Merc set down his large backpack, and began to remove pieces of an expensive and very deadly *Talon* rocket launcher, which he began to rapidly assemble.

When Rogue and Chop reached the bottom of the cliff, they could go no further. Rogue tapped the muzzle of his Beretta against the nearly invisible bluish barrier blocking his path. The barrier started exactly where the metal floor did. Chop looked at

Rogue in confusion. At the same time, Scarecrow slammed face first into another invisible wall blocking off the area behind the tower. Spike, however, saw the faint blue light and stopped just short of it.

"Spike! We've got a major problem here, there is some kind of... glass barrier... protecting the entire installation!" Spike's headset relayed.

"Yeah, man, here too. I can't go around. It's not glass, though..." Scarecrow said, rubbing his sore mouth in pain.

"Shit! How long does it run for, eh?" Spike asked.

"I'm no MIT here, but I'm guessing this is here to keep people out, Spike. It probably goes all the way to the next towers downrange," Scum said while pushing on its frictionless surface. He noticed that it was neither hot nor cold, and when he tapped on it with his fingernails, he could hardly hear the tapping, as if the barrier absorbed all of the shock.

Spike heaved a large sigh. "Well, gentlemen, if we can't do the job, we can't do the job..." Suddenly, the hair stood up on the back of his neck. He heard something.

"Maybe we could punch a hole in it. I got the *badda-booms,*" Rogue said, referring to his satchel charges. Spike didn't respond; instead, he felt a cold sweat cover his body as he heard the noise again. A very deep rumbling, very close. It suddenly occurred to him that there were no patrols, no guards, and no resistance. Spike gulped... *he realized it was a trap.*

"Chop! Get your oriental ass up here; you too, Rogue!" He voice boomed over the radio.

"Are you calling my ass Chinese?" Rogue laughed, not realizing the urgency in Spike's voice.

"I'm not dickin' around! Something's not right. Retreat!" Spike said, and just as he did, he noticed something rise from the sand behind Lord, Merc and Scum.

Merc had just finished loading the rocket launcher when he turned to see that he was not alone. Standing quietly behind him was a large figure, wearing dark silvery armor and carrying a very large multi-barreled gatling-style weapon. Merc screamed and raised his rocket launcher. Blue flames erupted from the front of the gatling gun, and Merc rolled away just as several hundred projectiles shattered the sand where he had been.

Chop raised his head as he heard the scream, but before he could even turn to face the cliff wall, the dirt and sand above him exploded as several bluish projectiles, missing Merc, penetrated the ground at an angle, slicing Chop into an unrecognizable condition against the force field. Rogue found himself wedged between the force field and most of Chop's perforated body.

Lord turned his fifty caliber around and fired a burst at the enemy. The Molluskan soldier was thrown back as the explosive-tipped fifty caliber shells detonating against its armor rocked it, but recovered quickly enough to drop to the ground. Scum began to fire his fifty caliber next, but not before the alien soldier opened fire on him tearing him to a red spray. Merc finally fired the rocket at the soldier. Fire spewed out the rear of the launcher as an anti-tank rocket was catapulted at the silvery armored soldier. Upon impacting, it exploded, ripping the creature apart into organic and metallic shrapnel.

"Holy shit!" Merc screamed aloud, while white fleshy debris rained down around them.

"Everyone get out of here! " Spike yelled.

Scarecrow was advancing on Lord and Merc when he saw a green glow appear in front of him. He watched in awe as another alien soldier began to rise up from the sand. First its head, then its body, weapon, and legs. Its glowing green eyes in its helmet glared at him. Scarecrow raised his Russian Saiga-12 assault rifle and fired. With a bright red flash, the small red cone on the side of the trooper's gatling-weapon streaked towards Scarecrow and exploded mid-air next to him. The blast was enough to melt patches of the sand together, and a charred Saiga-12 was all that remained of Scarecrow.

Spike, Merc, and Lord all ran in different directions. Merc looked back just in time to see four more aliens appear. "Chop! Rogue!" He shouted as he realized that he had no choice but to leave them behind. Merc continued to run without looking back, his reloaded Talon rocket launcher slung over his shoulder with the bore pointing to the sky. In his left hand, he had drawn his personal side arm, a Glock/USP. He could hear gunfire behind, and someone screaming. Suddenly he stopped in horror.

Standing before him was another alien. This one was unlike anything he had ever seen, even on the videos. It was tall, mostly mechanical, with white patches of skin. Its head had tentacles where its mouth should have been. Half of its head was mechanical, with a glowing red lens where its left eye should have been. Its right eye was large and black and glimmered strangely in the moonlight. There were two legs, and two arms, although one wasn't exactly an arm, it looked like some type of weapon. It was a long complex tube with an opening at the end and it was pointed at him.

Merc slowly held out his Glock, which he knew was useless against their armor, and dropped it to the ground. The alien raised its left arm and pointed a silvery-gloved finger at the mercenary, and made a strange noise. He slowly raised his hands.

Merc gulped, and with as fast as his muscles would allow him, he reached back and swung the rocket launcher over his shoulder, dropped to one knee and flicked off the safety. He aimed at the alien creature knowing he only had one shot.

The creature let out a grumble and began to drool. Its finger still pointing at Merc.

There was an eerie silence as both beings started across the moonlit darkness at each other.

Merc understood the silent message: *Go ahead, take your best shot.*

Amid the sounds of weapon's fire, another human scream was heard in the distance.

Merc grit his teeth, held his breath and depressed the trigger on the top of his launcher. The rocket hurled at the alien. The laser designator on Merc's rocket launcher painted a small red dot on the alien's chest. A searing blast blinded Merc for a second as the rocket detonated, and after the smoke cleared he was not entirely shocked to see the alien standing off to the side and a large crater and glowing bits of debris in a rocky cliff behind it.

"Oh my god! It dodged the rocket!" Sterling said, watching the video screen.

"*What is it?*" One of the technicians asked, not expecting an answer.

The President shook his head, "Run... just run Soldier!"

Merc dropped his launcher and resumed his running. He ran for only a few seconds before he heard a thundering high pitched whistle and in a flash of light was consumed by an explosion. Not even the metal eyelets in his boots survived the intense heat of the alien rocket.

Lord and Spike ran the way they had come, hoping to reach the beach, where a refitted yacht was waiting off shore for them. Lord was suddenly hit by a hail of glowing shells from behind, and fell to the ground. The attacker who pursued them was only twenty feet behind, and was carrying a gatling-weapon. With a roaring thunder, a stream of glowing blue projectiles swept across the sand and grazed Spike's left leg, ripping part of his calf out. Spike fell to the ground, shouting insults in pain. He fired at the alien soldier, but it dropped to the ground and out of sight over the crest of the hill.

"Lord, are you hit?" Spike shouted back to Lord, whom he had not seen go down.

Lord coughed up a large volume of blood. Spike crawled over to him.

"Just grazed me. Now be a good chap, and don't keep the boys on the boat waiting," Lord pulled the pin from his grenade and clutched it in his hand. Spike was without words.

"I said go, you stupid git!" Lord shouted. "I'll make sure he doesn't follow."

Spike began to crawl away, as he did he looked back to see Lord jump to his feet and charge over the hill. Spike heard more alien's weapon's fire, an explosion, and then total silence. Only his breathing and the sounds of his left foot dragging across the dead soil were audible.

"Who's still with me?!" Spike asked his headset, grunting as the pain from his calf jolted through his body. There was nothing but a quiet hiss of static. Again, the cold sweat returned to Spike as he heard heavy footsteps in the distance approaching from the black night beyond the crest where Lord had died.

"You seein' this? I know you're watching!" Spike shouted into his headset at the men in the Pentagon.

Two soldiers in black armor had approached from over the crest. Although they appeared unarmed, they were sprinting straight at him. He began to fire his .50 caliber machine gun at one of them, and after an entire chain of fifty rounds hit it, it exploded into a great inferno, knocking the other soldier down. Spike dropped the empty machine gun and withdrew a 9mm Berretta. The second soldier got to its feet and bolted at Spike as he emptied his magazine into the rapidly approaching alien without even slowing it down.

"They knew we were coming!" He yelled into his radio, and pulled out his machete.

Knowing he was going to die, Spike raised his right arm and extended his middle finger. "Fuck you!" he shouted. The soldier tackled Spike a second before exploding into a magnificent ball of flames, leaving only a black crater where he had once been. It was all over.

. . .

Monitor #1 flashed white and then displayed static.

"He's dead," Bruin said with a look of disbelief on his face. "There all dead!" he said loudly, staring at the six monitors displaying only static.

President Benton just stared... he didn't even seem to blink.

"Not all of them..." Sterling pointed out, pointing to monitor #5, which showed a bloody mess of flesh, rather that static.

"Whose camera is that?" Bruin stood up, while a glimmer of hope ignited within him.

. . .

Rogue heard another explosion, and then silence. *Were they all dead?* he wondered.

"Is anyone left?" he asked into his headset, but all it revealed was endless static.

Rogue was pinned between the cliff wall, the force field, and Chop's mangled, bloody corpse. With considerable effort, he heaved the body away from him.

Rogue was sure that his comrades were dead and he wasn't, and he wanted to keep it that way. After removing his useless pack of high explosives, he got back to his feet.

With extreme stealth, Rogue climbed the wall back to the surface. He cautiously poked his head up over the ridge, and nearly vomited upon seeing Scum's crushed face staring back at him. Scum was obviously dead; his crumpled skull was the most intact part of his body. Rogue realized that whatever hit him was not a normal weapon.

Not seeing anything that could jump out and kill him, Rogue climbed up the wall and on to the ridge. He began to sprint back the way he had come, and soon heard the high-pitched sound of a jet turbine. He could see the hovering craft approaching with a spotlight searching the ground for survivors. Without a second to think, Rogue dropped to the ground near a rock formation protruding from the sand. He saw a hole in the formation and quickly backed into it.

Rogue was now as far in the hole as he could get, the mouth of the small cave about four feet from him. He waited patiently, and after a couple of minutes, the sound faded in the distance. The blood-soaked mercenary remained in the crevice for nearly an hour, while the men back at the Pentagon all were intensely watching monitor #5 like mindless robots.

After what seemed like an eternity, Rogue heard a sound. It wasn't a threatening sound, but it was enough to make his heart race. It sounded harmless, and yet unnatural, like a cricket happily chirping, then a mouse squeaking. These noises became louder and louder until Rogue was certain that it was originated just outside the mouth of the formation. He was terrified, for he thought the loud thumping of his heart would give away his hiding place.

Suddenly, Rogue was aware of a presence. He had the feeling that he was being watched. Raw terror struck Rogue like an the windshield of a fast moving car strikes a bee flying in the opposite direction, for in front of him was a little round creature.

It looked like a human eyeball, only a little bigger, with a central yellow iris, which was contracting and dilating as it studied the human before it. The creature had little gray arms and legs that were about the width of toothpicks, and tiny springy antennae that were swaying back and forth, ever so slightly.

Rogue instinctively drew his Beretta handgun, and pointed it at the little creature. The creature began to make squeaking noises at him, and slowly, Rogue's fear evaporated a little.

"Your not so bad, are you," Rogue asked, more to himself than to the eyeball. However, he kept the gun pointed right at the center of the creature. Slowly, the eyeball began to walk in the cave towards Rogue, prompting a further elevation of his heart rate.

Rogue tried to shoo it away, but it just looked up at him, squeaking innocently. He didn't want to touch it, and shooting it was out of the question; any shot would give away his position. The eyeball trotted towards his left arm, which was laying elbow down in the sand.

Rogue tried to back his hand up, but his elbow struck solid rock. All he could do was watch helplessly as the eyeball walked closer to his hand. Now only an inch away, Rogue thought it must only be curious.

The eyeball gave Rogue a look, and made another chirping noise, then without warning, it began to growl and a small slit opened up, beneath its iris, exposing two rows of needle-point teeth. Before Rogue could react, the eyeball had bitten a morsel of flesh out of his left index finger.

Rogue yowled in pain, and then in rage as he looked at the little eyeball, with a mouthful of his flesh. It seemed to smile at him, cheeks bulging, as it made more squeaky noises.

"You little bastard!" Rogue barked as he raised the butt of his gun and brought it down on the eyeball. It squealed for a split second before popping, all its internal organs splattered on the ground as it was crushed under the mass of his pistol.

Rogue stared at the bloody wound in his index finger in horror, realizing it went to the bone. He then heard another squeak. He looked up and saw two more eyeballs.

"Shit!" he muttered, as he pointed his gun at one of them and fired, turning it into a yellow spray. Rogue had expected the other one to run away, but instead it charged at him and leapt on his neck. It tore away a large piece of flesh before Rogue pulled it off and ground it into a yellow paste with his bare hands. He looked up just in time to see six more rushing in.

He fired at them, and after six more shots was out of bullets. Scores of eyeballs poured in and began to chew holes in the mercenary. He yelled and thrashed about, but soon was covered in scores of them. Before long he would end up as Petty Officer Crow's body had: a chewed skeleton.

"Oh my God!" Hoffman gasped.

The men all watched the monitor #5; nobody spoke. They all watched as Rogue's arm was slowly being turned into nothing more than a skeletal wreckage, filled with gnaw marks and holes.

Then one of the eyeballs walked up to the camera itself. It seemed to stare directly at all the men in the room through monitor #5, as if it knew they were watching. It tapped on the camera lens with its tiny claws. Eyeballs could be seen carrying pieces of plastic away as they began to tear the camera apart. The image on the monitor began to flicker and then went to static like the others.

"That's it..." Sterling said.

No one spoke. No one even breathed.

CHAPTER 6 Mastermind

It was dark. The muffled sounds of electrical transformers and motorized servos droned in the background as the sound of approaching footsteps grew louder. In an instant, a swath of white light cut across the dark floor as a door opened. Within the light stood a figure, which promptly walked inside the vacant room and was followed by another, shorter figure carrying Merc's rocket launcher.

The second figure's red artificial eye glowed in the darkness as it waited patiently to speak with its master. It was almost too dark for the first creature's cyclopean eye to make out the small green button set in the wall, but upon locating it he quickly slammed his fist into it.

The lights in his new office flickered on, instantly bathing both creatures in white fluorescent light. The pale tentacled creature with the glowing eye began to make synthesized sounds, forming words that would be unpronounceable by a human.

The taller creature nodded, and replied in the same language of clicks, hisses and sharp guttural vocalizations.

"They arrived exactly when they were expected," the semi-mechanical creature said.

"What losses, Rycon?" the taller creature asked.

Rycon's tentacles twitched slightly. "One soldier dead, two wounded, and two sprinters destroyed, Sir."

The taller alien bared its teeth. "Unacceptable. We can't afford to lose any soldiers even at a ratio of fifty to one."

"Sir, they were better armed than we anticipated," Rycon retorted, handing the rocket launcher to the tall alien.

The tall alien took the tube and examined it. "Well, well, well... this is remarkable craftsmanship." It began to pace the room. "Yes."

"Their primitive arms are nothing compared to ours." The tall alien dropped the rocket launcher at Rycon's feet. "So I am assuming it was their superior tactics... or was it one of my officer's blunders."

Rycon stood perfectly still, its partially mechanical face not moving a millimeter at the accusation.

"Admiral Krewtek. With respect, the humans are no fools," Rycon stated.

Krewtek smiled, an expression both his species had in common with man. "Of course they are not, Lieutenant. But neither are we. Do not fail me again."

Rycon stared, emotionless.

"Get out of here," the alien admiral ordered.

The cybernetic creature scooped up the rocket launcher and departed the room.

Krewtek grunted a few times and looked around for a switch, which he found on the wall opposite the light switch. He pressed it.

For a second, nothing happened. Then all at once, the wall before him, made up of sixteen flat monitors, flickered to life. At first, they only showed static, but in a flash of brilliance, there appeared a symbol. A yellow triangle with an inverted black triangle inside. It was the Eye of Kroyce, the symbol of the Trexian Empire.

He stood in the exact center of the room, raised both of his arms high and behind his head, and closed his single eye in the Trexian position of ultimate respect.

Admiral Krewtek was not nervous. He knew the routine; he had done this several times in the past. However, he was the only Trexian on the entire planet and felt that the time to appear professional was at hand, since all eyes would be on him.

Normally, using a standard radio transmitter and receiver, it would take several weeks for a signal from Trexia to reach Earth, and the same time for the signal from Earth to reach Trexia because of the sluggishness of the electromagnetic spectrum, which only traveled the speed of light. Krewtek, however, was privileged enough to use an extremely expensive and fragile system using more advanced concepts such as quantum entanglement. He really had no idea how it functioned at all; however, he knew that it allowed him to talk to anyone with the same system at any distance with zero delay.

Although he couldn't see it, the yellow, triangular Eye of Kroyce symbol disappeared, and was replaced with Grand Admiral Clu Hotches. The same race as Krewtek, Hotches was the commander of the Trexian Navy, which had absorbed all operations involving space travel and conquest. He was of abnormal stature and had undergone many surgeries to ensure a long life in service to the Trexian Empire. Clothed in brilliant red robes, his many mechanical augmentations gave his figure a bloated unnatural look through the fabric.

"Speak, Admiral Krewtek," Hotches said indifferently.

"Thank you, Grand Admiral Clu Hotches," Krewtek said, opening his eye and returning his arms to a more comfortable position at his sides.

"His Holiness will see you now. Don't screw it up, Krewtek,"

With that, Hotches disappeared, being replaced by a ghostly white figure, dressed in a bright red robe.

Like a human, the figure had two legs and two arms. However, it had little else in common with a man's physical makeup. Its skin was tough and leathery, and in some parts was covered by exoskeletal-armored plates, with no color but dark gray. Its head was a large white sphere, riddled with dark green veins. Two obscenely large deep blue horns protruded from the top of its brow. One large central eye bulged out of the center of its face. Its yellowish iris showed only a small triangular star of dark green pupil. Under its eye, several folds of skin were visible, giving the figure a very ancient look. Below the eye was a large mouth, filled with twenty-four bluish, razor sharp teeth. This was the living Trexian god: Mentra Kroyce.

Krewtek's arms shot back up to the position of respect as he spoke, "Your Holiness, I exist only to serve..."

"Enough, Admiral... You will speak plainly to me," Kroyce interrupted with his raspy voice.

Krewtek smiled, exposing his own set of bluish, razor sharp teeth, and lowered his arms.

Kroyce smiled. "What is the status of the facility?" he asked patiently.

"Up and running. But the Rao Lok is providing shielding power for now," Krewtek reported.

"The reactor?", Kroyce raised the fleshy fold above his eye.

Although Kroyce loathed his next words, he showed nothing but confidence on his face, "My lord, half of our construction forces have not rendezvoused with us yet. We have only the materials brought by the Rao Lok. The reactor cannot yet be started."

"Were they lost to the enemy?" Kroyce asked.

Krewtek again looked stoic, "We don't know my lord."

"What vessels have arrived?"

"None yet Sir, but the MegaKore is due in tomorrow, followed by the Batteckery." Krewtek said immediately.

"Interesting... disturbing... and no word from the other three ships?" Kroyce asked with a concerned tone.

"None my lord."

Kroyce was silent for a moment and then spoke,

"I sent our finest ships away from the front to protect this vital mission, there is no room for error Krewtek. You have established the base... this is good. You must keep it protected until the fleet arrives. Failure is will be lethal."

"I understand, my lord," Krewtek said, it was the first time in his career he had been directly threatened by his God.

"When can the reactor start?" Kroyce asked.

"The MegaKore carries most of the coolant we need in her hold. The rest can be substituted with water, which we have absorbed from the land we have taken."

"Very good." Kroyce commended.

"The MegaKore is our largest battleship. When she arrives, use her help defend the base." Kroyce advised.

Krewtek nodded.

"Who is commanding her?" Kroyce asked.

"A Thalkaloid by the name of Kimbett. Admiral Kimbett actually... just promoted," Krewtek explained.

Kroyce's swollen eye squinted, "Thalkaloid? You promoted a Thalkaloid to admiral?" He rasped.

"Yes, my lord. You approved it several months ago before we left port," Krewtek stammered.

"Did I? How interesting... didn't we exterminate all Thalkaloid?" Kroyce asked.

"Yes, my lord, all but him and a few others for research," Krewtek explained.

"Strange that I remember a report that all were dead," Kroyce said, his greenish, bloodshot eye showing not the least bit of regret.

"Almost true, my lord. All of the others are all dead, he is the only survivor of his species," Krewtek said.

"One of your subordinates, I assume." Kroyce's voice seemed to grow raspier than ever.

"Yes. His rank was upgraded from lieutenant to captain only two years ago when he defeated his former captain in the Trexian Spearax Arena. I offered him a promotion and command of the MegaKore if he agreed to aid the Earth Point operation," Krewtek's smile disappeared.

"It isn't often an inferior makes it so far up our chain of command, is it, Admiral?" Kroyce rasped in more of a statement than a question.

Krewtek gulped, "His victory in the area was legal by our laws, my lord."

"Can he be trusted?" Kroyce asked.

"Yes, my lord. His species is nearly extinct, and he has nothing left but us." Krewtek assured.

"Let us hope so," Kroyce paused, "And what of the natives of Earth?"

"The *humans*?" Krewtek chuckled slightly, "Well, they seem to be a little beyond where our spies led us to believe. It seems they have discovered electricity, rocketry and even nuclear fusion."

Kroyce raised the folds of skin that served as an eyebrow. "Interesting... The reports I read stated that they hadn't made any significant advancements in the last two centuries."

"Well, my lord, that's simply not the case. As soon as we got within their solar system, we started picking up digitized transmissions... you wouldn't believe how much information about themselves they carelessly broadcast into the void around them," Krewtek smiled. "It's fairly entertaining to listen to reports from our radio-intercepts."

"Is their military going to be a problem?" Kroyce asked.

Krewtek was silent for a moment. "I've been considering a preemptive strike against their continents to reduce the military threat, but don't think it's necessary. They'll never make it past the front gate."

"If need be, you have my approval to level the native cities if it will command their respect. But remember, you will not destroy their planetary resources. I will not accept any error on your part, Admiral. You carry full authority; therefore, you carry the burden of responsibility."

Krewtek nodded. "You have nothing to worry about, my lord. They have already made several attempts to breech the perimeter and failed miserably," Krewtek paused. "With no survivors," he lied.

The Living God Kroyce and Admiral Krewtek continued their conversation for half an hour. In the end, Krewtek again saluted his god and the screens went dark.

A sigh of relief escaped Krewtek's thin scaly lips.

Krewtek was happy that the conversation was finally over. As much as he liked talking of his success on Earth, he loathed telling his leader the truth. This was because all Trexian officers have learned through watching the unfortunate actions of others that the truth can kill.

Although he had lied when telling his god that there were no survivors when he knew that in fact a small handful of humans had escaped the initial battle within the fog, and one human narrowly escaped from a recon mission days later, he also believed that a thousand humans couldn't alter the fact that the humans would never breach the shielded perimeter, so therefore the lie was acceptable. Perception was reality, and as long as his god perceived that he was in control of the situation, he would be victorious in his eyes. The fact that he was horribly understaffed and was extremely low on resources would not have benefited him.

Krewtek walked over to the wall and pressed one of the silver keys imbedded in a keypad. Two large floor panels sunk into the ground and slid aside, as a large steel desk rose from between them; the desk was littered with several plastic slates, as well as a Trexian oil-painted portrait of the Living God. The screens suddenly flickered to life, and began to show different sections of the facility and an aerial chart of the facility appeared on the wall just above the button. Krewtek picked the portrait up from his desk and attached it to the opposite wall. A tiny door, set low in the left wall, opened, and a small, yellow-irised eyeball scurried out.

Krewtek sat down in a large chair that had been resting in the corner. He pulled it closer to his desk and put his hands on the computer keypads in front of him. The eyeball climbed up his desk and jumped onto his shoulder.

From here, Krewtek would control the world.

CHAPTER 7 Better Late Than Never

Sand lazily blew over the dunes. The thick artificial fog that once smothered the landscape was completely gone, and the sky was crystal clear and the once-fertile area of Shanghai known as Pudong was dried and picked clean of any metallic or organic material.

Conspicuously out of place, an eagle soared in the sky above, peacefully gliding through the thermal updrafts.

Even more out of place was the wide strip of black material that bisected the dusty landscape. One end of the strip stretched off west into the horizon and eventually crossed the dry Huangpu riverbed into eastern Shanghai; the other end terminated at the maw of the largest metal monstrosity seen by human eyes, a gigantic metal barrier nearly six hundred feet tall. Set in the bottom of this barrier was an opening where the oversized road terminated. Inside this opening was a gate, which was currently shut. The gate was at least three hundred feet in height, and looked as if it was one continuous piece of metal.

This was the front line, commonly referred to as *The Wall* by the crowd of intelligence gatherers who stared day and night at photographs, thermal spectrographs and various other data sets to attempt to figure out just what, if any, weakness *The Wall* possessed. The only way into or out of the alien station, they determined, was through the gate, since every other inch of the massive base was encapsulated by the looming force field.

In the exact center of *The Wall* was a huge trapezoidal cutout, sealed off by massive metal doors, assumed to be an aircraft hanger. Below that was a large yellow triangle with an inverted black triangle in the center, a symbol seen marking most buildings beyond. Set on either side was two gigantic portals. With circular doors that closed off into swirls. What lay behind them was a mystery. Above them were two smaller, rectangular doors, which also concealed mysteries. On top of the barrier were three pillars that connected the wall to the force shield above. An unbelievably large dish was quietly sweeping back and forth on the right side. The top was also studded with various weapons and what look like oversized spotlights. Every other foot of the top was studded with large spikes, their purpose also unknown.

As the Chinese eagle came within range, a small blue beam appeared between the bird and one of the small instruments atop the wall. The bird burst into flames and fell to the surface. As its charred body hit the sand, there was little left but bones, smoking flesh and an occasional feather. Death was instant.

Mere inches from where the bird had landed, the sand began to move. Suddenly, the heap of sand had eyes and they stared at the dead smoldering bird.

"What the hell?" a voice murmured.

The sand pile grew an arm, at the end of the arm was a hand, and in the hand was a pair of U.S. Army issue Clairvoyant digital binoculars. The soldier peered through the binoculars at the top of the wall. Nearly six hundred feet above the desert floor, he could make out a large pod with a central aperture, attached to rotating turret. A curl of smoke was rising from the bore of the weapon.

The soldier spoke into his headset. "Fox, Coyote. I think I just saw this thing fry a bird. Over."

"A bird? With what, Coyote? Over," Fox radioed back.

"Some kind of laser. Should I fall back? Over," Coyote asked calmly.

"Negative, Coyote, continue to feed us on-site into..." Fox was suddenly cut off.

"Say again, Fox. Over," Coyote waited.

All that came over his headset was a soft hiss.

"I can't make anything out, Fox. Over," he said patiently.

"If you can hear me, switch to alternate frequency now. Over," Coyote said as he turned the dial on the right side of his head set until it clicked. Coyote suddenly heard noises, inhuman noises. Then his headset went dead.

Coyote waited quietly, not daring to talk into his headset anymore, for fear of what might be listening. He realized that he was shaking slightly, then violently. In the distance, he could hear a soft rumbling sound. Then it became a thundering barrage. The sun suddenly went black as if eclipsed by the moon. Coyote strained his eyes through the dying glare of the sun to see something coming down from the sky at him. He kept calm, although he was scared out of his mind. Winds began to blow sand around him.

The Wall instantly came to life, the circular doors dilating open to expose enormous gatling guns, only each barrel was forty feet in diameter. The giant Gatling guns pushed outward and aimed at the horizon. The spotlights came on and swept across the sand, sweeping over Coyote's hiding place several times. Coyote's mind did not fully comprehend what his eyes were trying to report to him; the ship was larger than anything he had ever seen, it was bigger than two of the U.S.'s largest sky carriers put together... or even three. As it came down, its blurry shadow over the desert focused. Coyote watched helplessly as the shadow passed directly over him. The vehicle descended quickly, but was slowing down. Mounted on its under carriage were rows of white flames spewing from rocket thrusters. The winds whipped around him at gale force, causing sand to sting his body, and heat was pouring down on him from above. He watched the alien ship descend to the desert floor, the front of it a measly two hundred feet away. Before it landed, four massive circular cowlings that housed twenty thrusters apiece rotated ninety degrees outward to become massive wheels.

As the wheels met the sand, the ground left Coyote as the shock wave hit and the thrusters terminated. It was like being on an oversized trampoline, and Coyote fell flat on his back as he landed. In awe, he gazed up to see the front end of a gigantic vehicle. He could make out weapons of every imaginable type on its bow. With a powerful rumbling, it began to drive in his direction. Coyote tried to dig himself back into the sand, but gave up and resigned himself to let it pass over him as it relentlessly approached. Seconds later, it thundered overhead, its undercarriage at least fifty feet above him. The red-hot rings of the rocket thrusters and countless small blue lights colored the dark sand under the ship with unearthly hues of violet. It passed completely over his position made its way towards *The Wall*. After rolling onto the black strip, its wheels suddenly stopped turning and it came to a thundering halt.

It waited there for a long five minutes. Coyote could make out small turrets lining the rear of the ship, but the most stunning feature was the giant turret mounted on top. It housed a lone gun. An unusual gun, considering you could park a Winnebago in it sideways.

"These guys like to build things big..." Coyote mumbled to himself. He imagined that the captain inside the ship was giving security codes and protocols to open the gate.

The inner gate of the wall began to screech open. Instead of rising, it lowered into the ground. Coyote watched, transfixed. After the ship rolled in, the gate closed, the spotlights shut down, the giant gatling guns retracted and the doors constricted back into swirls. All was once again quiet.

Coyote's headset began to crackle. "...m in Coyote. Are you there? Come in Coyote. Over."

"Yeah, I'm here," Coyote said, still stunned.

"What happened? Where did you go? Over," Fox asked, concerned. "What happened? Over."

"...Over," Coyote said quietly.

. . .

In China, the state-run media at first reported the mist anomaly as a new chemical weapon that was destroying entire populations, then it was reported as a smoke screen to hide an invasion in Shanghai. Mere hours later, panic-stricken soldiers, civilians and rescue workers emerged from the mist raving about the horrors they had seen, but the government had squelched the reports, and immediately requested a cease-fire with NATO after realizing the horrific truth.

In the U.S. and most of the rest of the world, it was reported that the Chinese mist anomaly was the cause of some kind of explosion of a weapon they were secretly working on. President Benton immediately accepted the Chinese's proposal as they learned the truth as well.

In the efforts of preventing widespread panic, the knowledge that the Earth had actually been invaded was known to a relative few groups of people, but the secret would not stay hidden forever. The area surrounding the alien base was restricted, and enforced with both Chinese and NATO aircraft.

Around the globe, ordinary citizens carried out their normal daily tasks, oblivious to the danger that was now brewing in Asia.

A young woman in New York City walked down the street looking for a birthday gift for her boyfriend when she noticed people gathering around a television in a store window. In a grade school in Indiana, while a twenty-seven year old man was explaining division to his students, a fellow teacher burst into an adjacent classroom and told him to turn on CNN. In an auto-plant in Detroit, Michigan, production stopped as the workers drifted to the nearest radio or television they could find. All around the world, people stopped what they were doing and tried to accept the incomprehensible truth.

"You're now... this is it! You are looking at recorded... at the first alien ... vessel to visit Earth," The CNN anchorwoman said, stuttering, "This is simply incredible."

The footage was from a new weather satellite. It clearly observed the massive ship barreling by and descending into the Earth's atmosphere, directly over the Asian continent.

"...we have unconfirmed reports that they landed at the site of the Chinese Mist Anomaly."

Many people were excited and thrilled at the prospect of contact with an alien race, a feat only existing in the dreams of mankind since the first human being looked up at the stars and wondered if we were alone. Others, however, were stunned and afraid.

"President Benton has announced that he will be addressing the nation..." the anchorwoman droned on while additional footage taken by a observatory showed the craft streak down from the star-filled sky like a giant meteor.

The president did not smile.

"Ladies and gentlemen of the United States of America... citizens of Earth. Today we have witnessed an unprecedented event in human history. We have been visited by an advanced alien race. Many of us have dreamed of such a day, the day that visitors would come to our great home in peace, wishing to learn and to share. Many of us would expect this from such an advanced culture."

The President paused.

"Unfortunately..." He let out a sigh, "This is not the case thus far."

"They arrived on the 23rd of September this year under the cover of the mist anomaly, and proceeded to murder and destroy anything within the perimeter of the mist. Peaceful contact with the aliens has not been made after numerous attempts, but we *will* keep trying. "

"But if it comes to it, my fellow Americans... my fellow citizens of Earth..."

"...We *will* defend ourselves."

CHAPTER 8 The Dogs Of War

Major Brobyn lifted his infrared binoculars to his eyes. He could see heat plumes of what he suspected were several vehicles heading towards his position from the abyssal darkness of the night.

"Bring it," he muttered as the convoy itself came into view.

He couldn't believe how arrogant his enemies were. From a tactical standpoint, the way in which they deployed their forces appeared to leave them wide open for an ambush from the flanks, or even from head on. He began to wonder if they had a good reason to be so arrogant. An eleven-year veteran of the U.S. Marine Corps, he'd thought he'd seen everything until being handed the orders to this top-secret operation. Officially listed as an exercise, the top brass called it *Operation Junkyard*, but his Marines and himself referred to it as *Operation Grand Theft Auto*, considering what their objective actually was.

As the vehicles came at them from almost eight miles away, Brobyn gave what was left of the Chinese city of western Shanghai one last visual sweep to make sure that everything was set up the way he had intended. It just didn't feel right that he was about to ambush a *greatly superior enemy* as his colonel had explained.

Western Shanghai, known as Puxi, was west of the now dry Huangpu river, which had once bisected the city, and was now one of the few patches of land once within the perimeter of the fog that wasn't yet a barren wasteland. Since the dissipation of the fog that once blanketed the area surrounding the alien base, what few spy satellites were left were able to monitor regular forays by alien convoys into some of the remaining deserted sections of the city. Thousands of tons of former human civilization was stripped from the land and taken back within their shielded base across the riverbed into the eastern section of Shanghai known as Pudong. The aliens had a particular taste for metal especially, and always harvested it first. The reason for the pilfering was unknown.

"Blue Team, Blue One. Get ready..." he spoke into his radio headset. "Three minutes," he added, looking at his wristwatch. Selected for his outwardly bold heroism and competency during the Terror Wars, Brobyn was the only real logical choice for an operation regarded as a suicide mission such as this one. He commanded nearly seventy men, separated into four platoons. His mission was intricate, yet simple: he was to board the largest vehicle in the group that now approached, commandeer it any way he could and return it to friendly space. In addition he was to shake off any enemy resistance in pursuit. Neither the latter nor the former had been done before, and appeared remotely possible at best, and therefore presented a challenge that Major Brobyn could not pass up. He was to lead the the Blue Team, who were the main ground assault force.

While surveying the scene from his position on the third floor of a gutted Chinese four story hotel he reached into his pocket and retrieved a flat metal can of Skoal chewing tobacco, which was illegal back in the states and stuffed a wad of it under his lower lip.

"Green One, Blue One, move your unit to the back of the restaurant and make sure they don't see you until we're ready," Brobyn whispered into his headset. "Copy Blue One," a crackled voice replied.

. . .

A lone Marine crouched behind a twisted metal wreckage that was probably once a car. After only being in the Marine Corps for two years, Lance Corporal Milan had been praying to get a piece of the A.C. Now he found himself in the heart of the dead A.C. wasteland.

"Who's next?" he thought to himself fearlessly.

Milan felt the ground rumble, and quietly peered over the obstacle to see nothing but complete darkness. He raised his infrared binoculars to his eyes, and saw approaching vehicles in the distance. One was very large; he saw that the bulk of it was suspended above four tracked feet by a set of massive hydraulic trusses, each foot wrapped in tank treads. The hull, which was suspended in the air by the four mobile legs, looked like a car crusher with teeth. In the center front he saw a somewhat large compartment where the drivers would be stationed. He found it amazing that something so large could be driving at *fifty-five miles an hour!* Because of its appearance and obvious function, it was nicknamed the *Tortoise* or, more commonly, *Metal Crusher*.

Two other vehicles were big six-wheeled vehicles. Inside, Milan could make out the heat signatures of at least twenty individuals. His superiors unimaginably designated this vehicle *Troop Transport*. One very small four-wheeled vehicle was traveling at least one mile ahead; it had a big radar on top and what looked like little guns mounted on the front, obviously a scouting vehicle.

The entire parade was escorted by four sleek, mean looking smaller craft. They had what appeared to be a rack of jet-black missiles with red tips on one side and a multi-barreled gatling gun on the other side; and above that, there was an assembly of antennae. These were nicknamed Brawlers, for their obvious firepower and maneuverability. The last vehicle in the parade was one large heavily armored vehicle with a gatling gun on top and large cannons on both sides. Its nickname: *Antlion.*

"These guys are coming stronger than they told us," Milan whispered to himself. As he watched, he noted that the front of each of the vehicles bore an insignia, a yellow triangle, with an upside-down black triangle in the center. He pondered the meaning while he patiently waited.

Milan didn't expect to win this one; he had seen the videos. He knew that the ones Gates ran into were just construction workers. But the ones the Screaming Demons ran into were the soldiers, and that team didn't come back. Now he was going up against the soldiers, the *big boys*. The hair stood up on the back of Milan's neck as he lowered the binoculars and looked out into the darkness and saw the lights. He figured that win or lose, the aliens weren't walking away from this battle without a bloody nose.

" Blue-One, Blue-Twelve. They're here, Sir..." he said into his headset.

There was an unusual calmness in the air, there was no breeze, no temperature change at all, and no noise. The sky was clear, yet the moon was but a feeble, thin crescent surrendering little illumination to the dark landscape. Milan ducked behind the metal mass in which has had partially concealed himself. One by one the vehicles arrived and parked.

After all vehicles arrived, Milan began to get psyched up for the inevitable blood bath. He began to wonder if this was what it must have been like to face Omaha Beach on D-Day. He controlled his fear like a well trained Marine and felt ready for battle, but to his surprise, the radar equipped scout vehicle turned around and drove off at high speed, followed by two of the four Brawler-class vehicles, one of the transports carrying twenty soldiers, and the Antlion.

He watched as they drove to rendezvous with another metal crusher and another transport at least twenty miles away.

"Looks like our boys are cutting corners," Milan mumbled.

This left only the large metal crusher, one troop transport, and two of the Brawler-class vehicles.

A ramp extended from the back of the troop transport. All twenty of the strange beings, clad in silvery armor, exited the vehicle and began to spread out. The metal crusher began to lower down to its treads. The ground shook as its underside met the surface. A hatch opened up in the back, and two small forklift-vehicles drove out followed by a dozen workers who began to swarm over the remains of Puxi like ants on a piece of candy.

One of the small brawler vehicles rested as if the vehicle itself was bored, not long after, the canopy opened, a soldier in silver armor climbed out and began walking towards another one of the larger, gatling-toting creatures.

. . .

Major Brobyn, crouched on one knee, observed one of his corporals through the glass of a large window from the second floor of the hotel. Mounted next to him were four large black cylinders, which contained large guided missiles. The new M-63 Halo missile system was designed by the U.S. Army to counter the recent invention of absorption armor by the A.C. Although untested against the new enemy's hardware, Brobyn was *assured* they would be effective.

"Blue-Twelve, Blue-One. What the hell are you doing?" Brobyn asked as his lance corporal bolted from behind his cover and dove behind a half-buried blue garbage dumpster. Miraculously, none of the alien troopers noticed him.

The worker aliens began to furiously dig up the metal wreckages of cars, trucks, tanks, dumpsters, and anything metal. The tower in the rear of the metal crusher tilted diagonally and lowered a cable with a magnetic disk at the end, revealing itself to be a magnetic crane. It quickly began pulling wreckages from the sand and dropping them in its crusher.

"This is Blue-Twelve. Sir, with your blessing, I'd like to perform a miracle," Milan whispered, while craning his neck to peek over the dumpster, which was only four feet from the vulnerable brawler.

Brobyn looked at his watch briefly and made his decision.

"Blue-Twelve... Very well, try not to get yourself killed," Major Brobyn said reluctantly.

Blue-Two, a captain, looked at his commanding officer with a look of astonishment.

Brobyn returned the stare and shrugged. "Hey, he's got good timing. I was about to give the go-ahead to attack anyway. Let's see what he's got in mind..."

"All Teams, Blue-One. All right, wait for my signal," Major Brobyn ordered over his headset.

Milan wasn't interested in simply attacking; he had a much grander idea. He sprinted from the dumpster to a small pile of ashes a mere fifteen feet from the two aliens that appeared now to be talking.

. . .

"Crazy son of a bitch, he's gonna hijack the damn thing!" Brobyn thought to himself aloud.

"What? He's crazy, he'll never make it. Should we distract them a little?" Blue-Two suggested.

"No. No... I think he just might make it, Captain." Brobyn stared in awe.

. . .

Milan didn't have a death wish; he didn't want to die. In fact, he had a lot to live for. Milan had a family, and he had a classic 1956 Chevy Nomad, but he also had a strange urge to do things that others thought were suicidal, but were not enough of a rush for him. He had gone skydiving, bungee jumping, base jumping and drag raced more times than he could remember, but the ultimate rush perpetually eluded him. In fact, he had joined the U.S. Marine Corps simply to quench his thirst for excitement. With almost no sense of fear, the lance corporal ran out into the open, only a split second before jumping into the brawler.

Milan literally dove into the cockpit. After a few seconds, he found himself sitting at an alien helm, looking at controls he had never seen before. He poked his head up over the dash and looked around. To his total astonishment, he hadn't been seen. He began to try to figure out the controls. In the center of the board was a hole with a larger black ball in set beneath it. Milan guessed it to be steering. A lever was to the left; it looked like a throttle control.

"Great, so how do you start this thing?" Milan asked himself. He then noticed a small metal plate with the strange yellow triangular symbol on it. Milan cautiously pressed the plate.

As the engines roared to life and automatically revved up, all creatures stopped working and all turned to stare at the brawler with the human driver in it. Milan wasted no time; he pushed the lever as far forward as it would go. To his shock, the brawler shot backwards in reverse instead of forward. The two talking aliens behind it were run over. Milan, while trying to find the button to close the canopy, pushed a red button that looked like it might be the one. Brilliant yellow fire erupted from the rear of his missile pod as a small rocket spat out. It veered at and impacted one of the loading vehicles, blowing it to pieces and sprayed the workers with shrapnel.

"Jesus Christ! He's crazy," Brobyn yelled. "All teams, Blue-One. Hold your fire! Hold your positions!"

"Blue-One. Come in Blue-One," Milan said casually over the radio.

"Go ahead, Blue-Twelve," Brobyn answered.

"You go after the metal crusher, Sir, I'll take the second brawler," Milan said casually.

"You're a crazy son of a bitch, Marine, you know that?!" Brobyn asked while gesturing for his men to move out.

Most of the alien soldiers began to pile into the troop transport to chase down the stolen brawler that was now driving around backwards in the desert. Some ran to the metal crusher. The second brawler's engines howled to life.

Milan felt that he was getting the hang of driving. He slowly pulled the lever back, and as he did so, the brawler slowed, stopped, and then finally drove forward. Milan heard high pitched buzzing sounds coming from all around him as sand exploded mere feet from his captured vehicle. He was under fire.

. . .

The metal crusher's main hull began to rise from its treads, off the desert floor, and up onto its tracked feet in preparation to move. Its engines thundered to life. The smaller troop transport began to move. On the roof was an alien with a very large gatling gun. It was sending waves of bluish glowing bullets at Milan's brawler, which was dodging unpredictably.

"Fire for effect!" Major Brobyn shouted.

The glass window of the hotel shattered as one of the large black cylinders launched its *halo* rocket at the troop transport. To Brobyn's elation, the transport disappeared in a white ball of vaporized metal and organic debris upon impact. The explosion shook the Earth as the shock wave radiated from the large crater where the transport had been. *They actually worked!*

"Blue-Two, " Brobyn tapped the captain's shoulder. "You waste anything that tries to interfere. You copy? Any new ship that enters the battle you fry! Got it?"

"Hurrah, Sir!" Captain West said enthusiastically, patting the fire control console.

"All teams, Blue-One. Fix bayonets! Expect to see ET up close and personal in the next few minutes."

Brobyn nodded and ran down the spiral staircase to the ground floor. "All teams, Blue-One. Green Team will defend the HQ, all other teams commence attack on the metal crusher!" He yelled into his headset, "Let's get the bastards! Move!"

Shrieks, howls, explosions and gunfire filled the air. Tracer rounds and man-made shoulder launched rockets converged on the seemingly dazed alien soldiers and workers still in the open. Blue points of light and red streaks arced back out as they began to return fire. In a short moment, the Marines from all four platoons, who now emerged from their concealed positions from within the partially collapsed buildings and rubble, cut down any aliens that could not get to the metal crusher.

"Hold the fort, Green Team, we'll be back soon..." Brobyn muttered into his headset while gazing at the metal crusher. Its rear ramps were closing. He chewed on his tobacco and moved out.

Milan continued to struggle with the canopy. After only three minutes, he had accidentally run over four aliens and vaporized another, all while trying to close the canopy. He finally found the right lever, and the canopy lowered and sealed. At this time, the sand in front of him exploded in a ball of super-heated sand and fire. He shielded his eyes from the bright light, and turned sharply to the right, missing the ten-foot deep crater by less then a yard. As he looked in his rear view camera, Milan saw the second brawler in pursuit. It was still far off, but closing alarmingly fast.

. . .

Several grappling hooks sailed through the air until hooking onto the railing of the metal crusher's deck or heavy equipment nearby. The deck of the metal crusher was twenty feet above and rising, and a difficult climb. In less then four minutes, however, twenty-four Marines had scaled the lines and were storming the vast deck of the metal crusher. It was as large as an aircraft carrier with the central crusher pit. Behind the pit loomed the enormous crane. At the bow was the pilot's pod. There was not an enemy soldier to be seen.

"I'm going for the pilot! Kill anything you don't recognize," Major Brobyn yelled to his men, who were fanning out across the deserted deck. Without warning, several aliens poured out of hatchways and doors and a full-scale firefight erupted on the deck of the metal crusher. These weren't soldiers, however, but mere workers, for they wore minimal armor. Brobyn dove behind a large mushroom-shaped metal exhaust stack as hundreds of short, pink plasma bursts and even more bluish glowing bullets filled the air. Two aliens were tossed overboard when hit by the blast wave from a grenade. One of the creatures sprang around the corner and ran at Brobyn, weapon in hand, but was tackled by one of his men and both rolled off the deck at each other's throats. Brobyn stared at the small four-barreled gatling-gun left behind. Under a hail of bullets, he made a dash for it.

. . .

Milan flipped the blue switch and heard several crackles. His cockpit seemed to glow with a soft bluish haze. Seconds later, his cockpit was filled with red light, and he was thrown hard to the side. "*That was a damned missile!*" he realized. He didn't know why he had survived a direct missile impact until he realized he must be covered in some kind of shield. He turned to his attacker and began pushing the largest of the buttons on his left panel. Plasma, missiles, and blue projectiles poured out of his weapons array. The other brawler, blinded by the explosions against its shielded canopy, cut left to avoid further punishment and collided with a section of what may have been part of a concrete overpass. It careened on two wheels for moment before flipping upside down. Milan, wasting no time, faced the disabled brawler, and relentlessly pressed buttons on the left panel. The disabled brawler was torn apart by the hail of projectiles and was later vaporized by the missiles. Milan smiled an evil smile.

As the second enemy transport came within range, Captain West noticed that it had brought friends. A flying craft with a spotlight sweeping the sand was in escort. West almost felt fearful of the transport with its threatening gatling-turrets and missile pods. But that didn't stop him from depressing the rectangular red button on his halo fire control console. The second rocket blazed down to meet the unfortunate transport. It was vaporized instantly, but the flying craft emerged from the white flames with a glowing shield around it. It began flying at West's position in the hotel.

The rest of the windows shattered, and large holes began to appear in the flooring around him. He quickly dove at the stairwell and rolled down to ground level just as the entire second story exploded as a missile from the flying craft impacted the one of the remaining two rockets, causing them to detonate.

. . .

Brobyn had problems of his own; the alien troopers continued to pour out of hatches and doorways covering the deck of the metal crusher, and his men were being overrun. Although the outnumbered and surrounded Marines were engaging the workers in vicious hand-to-hand combat, Brobyn had at least one advantage: As he depressed the trigger of the smaller four barreled gatling-gun, his entire body shook as it fired several hundred bluish, glowing bullets into an incoming group of armed aliens, cutting them down in one burst. He continued to fire at every non-human thing he could see. Everywhere bodies dropped. He heard a hiss, and then he was thrown back as a missile destroyed a vehicle that three of his men were hiding behind, killing all of them.

Brobyn turned around to see what had fired the missile. As his eyes fell upon the flying vehicle, he noticed the burning hotel behind it, *a hotel... the HQ!* He knew the tide of the battle was turning. The flying craft was heading straight at the metal crusher when it suddenly blew apart, sending shrapnel into the air. A curl of smoke rose from the rocket assembly on Milan's stolen brawler before it sped away and engaged another enemy craft.

Brobyn jumped up to his feet and ran for the pilots pod. "Damn it, Marines! We're just warmin' up! " he shouted over his shoulder. Several others jumped up to join him, while others stayed in their positions and held off the enemy. As he reached the pilot's pod, he noticed the silver door, set deep into the wall on the side.

"Open this door," Brobyn ordered the Gunnery Sergeant beside him.

The Gunny slapped the shoulder of the muscular private next to him, "You heard the man, Carmichael, kick it in!"

After three hard kicks, the metal door wasn't moving.

"Sorry Gunny, this door isn't going to budge," the private apologized.

"Do we have any explosives?"

The gunnery sergeant shook his head. "Simpson went over the side with the satchel charge. Sir."

Brobyn grit his teeth and spit out tobacco laced saliva. His mission's success hinged on them getting through this door.

"Wait for my signal, then start kicking this sucker in again," were the only things he said before climbing the pipes lining the wall to the top of the pilot's pod.

"What's your signal, Major?" one of his men asked.

Brobyn looked down and shrugged. "Just wait until you hear screaming and gunfire from inside of this room..." With that he disappeared over the top.

Captain West had survived. His left arm didn't work, and he assumed it was broken. Smoke and fire was consuming most of the hotel. Lying next to him was Green-Two, a staff sergeant, and explosives expert. He was dead. As he looked around, West could see the rest of the Green Team, either firing at the endless aliens that were pouring out of the three troop transports that had just arrived on scene, or dying on the sand. With Green-Two dead, and Blue-

One on the metal crusher, West realized that he was the only one left to arm the *device*.

West ran for the basement, where they kept this device. As he staggered down the steps, he heard another thundering explosion from above. He turned on the flashlight that was hanging on the wall and looked around. Standing in front of him was a small metal cube with several radioactive warnings on it. Plugged into it was a small laptop computer.

. . .

Milan looked around furiously, he had seen the radar vehicle a second ago, but now it was nowhere to be seen. Milan broke a hard left as an explosion rocked the side of his craft. "So you're *behind* me you little shit?" he growled through gritted teeth.

The radar vehicle was designed to be the eyes and ears of the vulnerable metal crusher. With minimal weaponry, it was merely an irritation to the brawler; a persistent irritation, however.

. . .

As the captain of the metal crusher watched the radar vehicle keep the Earth native in the stolen craft busy, it turned its attention to *The Wall* only thirty-seven miles away. It knew if it could make it halfway there, it would meet up with the rest of the reinforcements. It stood behind the pilot who was the same species as it was. It had yellow rubbery skin with tentacles protruding from just above its mouth. Its two eyes were large, black and devoid of any other features. Next to the pilot on both sides were a navigator, and a crane operator. The captain pointed out the window and was about to say something when an explosion of glass threw it back as something flew through the windshield and landed on the dashboard. *It was a native!*

With a well-placed punch to the face, Brobyn knocked the pilot out of its chair, then jumped down to the floor. The alien sitting at the crane controls reached for its side arm. Brobyn blasted it to a pulp with his stolen weapon. He turned his weapon on the navigator, but with an agitated snarl, it kicked it from his hands as it pulled a small handgun from a holster in its belt. Brobyn grabbed it by its cloth uniform and threw it into the opposite wall. As he turned, the captain, who was back on his feet, it hit Brobyn in the face. When Brobyn smiled at it, it stared back in a blank expression of terror. The Marine major kicked it where its testicles should have been and as it doubled over, he slammed its bald yellow head into the dashboard five or six times and then heaved it out through the shattered windshield where it screamed all the way down to the sand.

Brobyn turned around and stopped dead in his tracks. In front of him, was the navigator, holding the strange handgun it had reached for earlier. As it pointed, the hatch leading into the pilothouse swung inward and crashed into the creature holding the gun, it fell to the ground unconscious. Four of Brobyn's men rushed in and looked over the scene while another guarded the door.

"Great timing... how did you get in, I thought the door was locked?" Brobyn said to one of his men.

"We knocked, and one of the yellow morons opened it up for us," one of his men said, kicking the gun from the unconscious alien's hand.

Brobyn shook his head in disbelief. "Now let's figure out what we've got here," he said while pushing the unconscious body of the former pilot out of its chair and jumping behind the pilot's controls.

. . .

More shots chipped away at Milan's draining shields as the infinitely more maneuverable scouting vehicle stayed directly behind his brawler. Milan gave his vehicle full throttle and tried to open up a gap between himself and the scout but it stayed right on his tail.

"Stop riding my ass..." Milan suddenly realized the solution.

The pilot of the scout had no time to react as Milan suddenly locked his brakes and the scout collided with the heavier brawler, shredding the front of the vehicle and causing it to flip up and over the shielded brawler and come to rest on its side forty feet in front of Milan's stolen alien gunship.

Milan accelerated and slammed his fist onto the left keypad. Several lights flashed as two missiles and several bullets raced at the crippled radar vehicle. It exploded with such force that it nearly flipped the stolen brawler onto its side as it raced by. Milan yelled as his canopy was lit up with in intense glare. The craft jerked hard to the left, and then back to the right with a hard jolt and he found himself lying on the dashboard. Through the canopy, all he saw was sand.

"I drove into a crater?" he thought aloud. Throwing the throttle into reverse, he tried to back out of the crater, but his rear tires were off the ground. He looked in his rear-view screen to see the Antlion closing in on him. Lance Corporal Milan began to fidget with buttons and levers, careful not to hit any he knew that launched weapons. The craft refused to budge.

As the Antlion closed on the stranded Brawler, it opened fire. Milan saw several bright flashes at the corners of his canopy as the shield around the Brawler dimmed. Just as escape seemed impossible, he saw something slam into the roof of the Antlion, then watched in even more amazement as it was lifted off the dessert floor by a magnetic disk attached to a cable, which was connected to a large crane. Milan watched in amazement as the metal crusher lifted the paralyzed alien vehicle high into the air.

. . .

"What should we do with it, Sir?" the Marine corporal sitting at the crane's station asked.

"Throw in the crusher," Brobyn said flatly.

The Marine smiled. "Yes, Sir."

As the Antlion was dropped into the metal crusher, the walls began to close in. Panicked, four of the yellowish creatures abandoned the vehicle along with one of the four-legged spider-esque creatures with four eyes. Before they could scale the walls, Brobyn's men appeared over the edges and captured the Antlion undamaged. They took all five of the aliens captive as well.

While Milan was frantically playing with the controls, the brawler shuddered as the front tires caught the sand. With the four-wheel drive now engaged, it easily climbed backwards out of the crater. Milan spun the craft around towards the metal crusher just in time to watch the metal crusher swing its magnetic disk into a flying craft, pulverizing it into flying metal scraps. He began to drive towards the burning hotel where Green Team was.

. . .

The basement echoed as Green Team managed to destroy one of the many transports that continued to offload alien soldiers. With no time to communicate with the rest of the team, West set the device for its fifteen-minute countdown. With that, he ripped the cables from the device and smashed the laptop against the charred linoleum floor. Only after he completely destroyed the computer did he leave the basement. The device began a slow rumble. "WARNING! WARNING! YOU HAVE T MINUS 15 MINUTES

UNTIL DETONATION!" The device's computer radioed its death cry to all remaining teams.

. . .

"Did you hear that? Staff Sergeant Hill must have activated the device!" the Marine at the navigation center said.

Brobyn gasped, "Dammit, Green-Two! We're way too close! Turn this sucker around and let's get the hell out of here!" He reached for his headset. "Blue-Twelve."

"I heard for myself, Sir. I'm already on my way to cover Green Team's escape," Milan said confidently.

. . .

As Milan reached the hotel, he came under heavy fire from many silver armored aliens. They had apparently overrun all of Green Team for Milan could not see a single Marine left standing. He did as much damage as possible before retreating, but just as he began to pull out, he noticed a lone human running for him. He recognized him as Blue-Two, Captain West. Milan heaved forward on the throttle and hit the brakes, and then changed course to intercept. As soon as he was close enough, West jumped onto the tires and scrambled up the shielded canopy, his hands leaving behind blue handprints on the shield. In a moment, he had climbed between the missile rack and multi-barreled alien machine gun.

"Drive!" West shouted, pounding on the canopy just as glowing blue projectiles ricocheted off of the brawler, inches from the captain. Milan put a large distance between him and the alien soldiers and stopped. Before he opened the canopy all the way West jumped down and began to shout wildly.

"They're all dead! All of 'em!" he screamed.

Milan raised his hands as if to tell the captain to calm down. "Who's dead, Sir?" he asked.

"Captain Pratt, Sergeant Hill, their men! All of Green Team!" West raved.

Before Milan could continue his conversation, the metal crusher thundered by them.

"Blue-Twelve, come in Blue-Twelve," Brobyn's voice came over the headset.

"Copy, Blue-One. I have Blue-Two. Green Team is gone, Sir."

"Just get your ass in back! We're pulling out!" Brobyn shouted.

"The ramps are down lance!" Captain West pointed furiously, "Hurry!"

Milan drove the brawler into the rear bay of the metal crusher with West riding shotgun. They both jumped out and after an adventurous moment trying to figure out how to close the ramp, they finally sealed the rear door.

"We're in, ramp's closed, and door's closed, Sir!" Milan said before West pawed the headset off of his head.

"Sir! This is Blue-Two! All of Green Team is dead! I barely had time to set the device!" West shouted. "We only have about ten minutes before it goes!"

Outside the pilot's pod, looking back, Brobyn looked off in the distance through his binoculars and gasped. "And not a moment too soon..." was all he could say.

Behind the metal crusher was a fleet of enemy craft, most of which he had never seen before. Some were tracked cylinders with giant multi-barreled gatling-guns protruding from them. Flying vehicles, weapons hanging from their wings. All were coming straight at him.

"Let's go! Let's go! Put this bucket in gear!" Brobyn yelled as he ran back into the pilot's pod.

At the crushing pit in the deck of the metal crusher, seven Marines from Red Team held five aliens at gunpoint. All of them glared at their human captors.

"All teams. Blue One. Get inside now!" Brobyn shouted over the radio.

"Come on, ugly! That's you! Move it!" Red-One, a first lieutenant, motioned with his OICW rifle to one of the aliens, one of the yellow skinned ones, which had removed its helmet. Without warning, it jumped up and ran for the edge of the deck. Another one jumped up to follow and Red-Four opened fire on it.

"Hold your fire!" Red-One shouted. "Let him go."

The alien leapt off the edge to the surface twenty feet below.

The spider-like alien just glared at Red-One, its four eyes glistening.

"Yeah, you're smarter than that, aren't you? You bastard," he glared back with no trace of fear.

. . .

"DETONATION IN T MINUS 10 MINUTES." The computer's voice boomed over the radio.

The metal crusher began to rumble as its mass gained momentum. It had reached thirty miles an hour when Milan reached the pilot's pod with West following behind.

"What is the minimum safe distance?" The soldier piloting the crusher said. Beads of sweat rolled down his forehead.

"Five miles," Brobyn said with a stoic tone.

"We can make it!" Milan said quietly.

Two miles behind the metal crusher was a giant armada of alien machinery. They were gaining on the slow metal crusher.

"We've just passed forty miles an hour. We're one point six miles away from the nuke!" the Marine at navigation said with a fierce tone.

"WARNING! WARNING! T MINUS FIVE MINUTES," The computer droned.

The enemy was close enough to see without binoculars now. There they were, hundreds of them, most were land craft, but the flying ones kept pace with the land vehicles. They were now past the smoldering hotel of gaining fast.

"They're on our ass, Sir!" one of the Marines shouted into the pilot's pod.

"Fifty miles an hour! We're three and a half miles away!" the pilot reported.

"WARNING! YOU NOW HAVE T MINUS ONE MINUTE," said the computer.

Brobyn put some more chewing tobacco in his mouth.

"Four miles! We can make it!" The pilot gripped the controls.

Milan ran outside the pilot's pod and looked back.

"T MINUS 10...9...8...7..."

Milan sucked in a large breath of air.

"Oh dear God!" someone said.

"Four point five miles!"

He could see the enemy craft less than one mile away.

"...4...3...2...1... ZERO" was the last thing the computer would ever say.

Milan was nearly blinded as the horizon lit up with an intense white glare. Although a nuclear bomb had detonated, he heard nothing. Time seemed to slow down. He opened his eyes and saw the alien vehicles for only a second, before they were overtaken by the wave of fire heading straight at him. At first, some seemed to accelerate as the wave pushed them, some simply disappeared behind the curtain of light, and some exploded into a short lived blast of fire. In less than five seconds, there was no more enemy fleet, just a firestorm heading relentlessly at him. Somebody pulled him inside the pilot's pod and slammed the door as it hit...

. . .

All was quiet. Lance Corporal Milan was dead.

He felt nothing, he heard nothing...

"Wake up, boy!" was all his brain registered before Brobyn slapped him in the face.

Milan opened his eyes to see the smiling face of Major Brobyn.

"We're alive?" "Sir," he added.

"Yes, Marine, we are." Brobyn helped him up.

Milan looked around to see the interior of the pilot's pod of the metal crusher. Through the busted out windshield, he could see two roads ahead, with grassy meadows on either side.

"You know you are one crazy son of a bitch!" Brobyn said, patting Milan on the back. Milan was too dazed to respond.

"What about the enemy?" he asked.

"Fried! All of 'em. They were just a little too close. Lucky for us, these alien bastards know how to build a dump-truck... heh," Brobyn said slapping the metal wall of the now captured tortoise metal crusher. Milan limped outside and looked back towards the rear. He could still see the smoke plume of a mushroom cloud. The sun was rising behind it. It suddenly hit him:

Major Brobyn, his men, all of them...

...they had not only cheated Death, but they had made off with his scythe.

CHAPTER 9 Weird Science

General Sterling hated being behind schedule. From the day he was a 3rd class cadet at West Point, to this day, he had demanded steadfastness, accountability and honesty from his subordinates. Those who had worked under him had learned to revere his standards and expectations. During the tumultuous years leading to the collapse of the United Nations and build up of NATO and the A.C., then-Major Sterling had earned a reputation for ripping up and rebuilding any unit he was assigned to into a smooth running machine, a talent that gained him rapid promotion and the respect of those he left behind.

Unlike the soldiers whom he had lead, he reluctantly accepted that civilians were far more difficult to motivate. One would have to be careful not to *light a fire under their ass* too fiercely, as it often slowed work, rather than speed it up. The current situation demanded tact, which was something Sterling knew well.

The general walked into a shiny, metallic hallway towards a featureless silver door. Although unseen, many cameras were tracking him. From his left breast pocket he withdrew a black plastic card and slid it through a crack in the wall panels. After several clicks as a hidden computer analyzed the card, the door opened and he was met by four heavily armed escorts. Wearing black masks that concealed their identities, the escorts also wore flak jackets and toted chrome Mossberg 770 shotguns.

"This way, Sir," one of them said in a monotone that would frighten most, but not Sterling. After a retinal scan, fingerprint, and voice analysis he was finally led to an elevator. Before the escorts left him, one nodded to him, gave him a new black card and confiscated his old one. The door slid shut.

"Welcome to Wonderland, General Sterling," a female computer voice quietly said to him as he slid the new black card through the slot below the keypad. He then he pressed the buttons for level twenty-eight, which, of course, didn't exist.

. . .

Doctor Rick Tieseler sat at the controls of one of the world's most powerful weapons, the Groom Lake's mainframe computer, also known as Cid. A gigantic custom-built parallel cluster with 1,150 individual over-clocked eleven-gigahertz processors working together and more than 150 terabytes of data stored in its own database. The cluster itself was a tower of ten rings, each of which had 115 processors and was bathed in liquid helium. Cid's computing speed was unheard of, and up until the invasion, was the most powerful computer on Earth.

Doctor Tieseler wasn't using Cid to study the recently captured alien technology, nor was he cracking the alien genome and unlocking the secrets within their complex DNA. On the big screen usually used for presentations, he was busy playing an old PC game called Doom II, which barely used a fraction of the computer system's full potential.

"Rick," Sterling said calmly. Tieseler was too engrossed in his game to notice that one of the most important men in the country was standing behind him. Sterling reached his hand out and shut off the huge screen.

"Hey, what the hell?!" Tieseler blurted out angrily before turning to see whom it was he had shouted at. Upon seeing the general, he bit his tongue.

"Uhhh..." he said, "...hi, General! What's up man?" he added.

Sterling stared at him with a poker face that would make Maverick fold. Suddenly, with a light grin, he chuckled a little bit. "I can see the taxpayer's money they unknowingly pay you is well spent."

"Come on, General!" Tieseler stood up. "It's okay, man... your pills."

Although Sterling was in a hurry, he remained calm. One of the unknown jobs of his profession was to put up with the brilliant and erratic minds of the Wonderland Technology Consortium, or the Tecksters, as they were nicknamed.

"It's all right, Rick, I got your email..." Sterling began.

"Oh yeah! Dude! I almost forgot, good thing you reminded me," Tieseler, sitting back down, gestured for Sterling to sit down as well.

"I wrote to you so you could see what I've been able to find." As he talked, his hands were busy at the keyboard. "The metal they use, isn't normal metal, it's like... it's an alloy... kind of."

He handed a piece to the general. Sterling was surprised at how light it was.

Tieseler continued to explain. "It is made up of multiple layers of different metals, some are only one atom thick. Some layers are set up as honeycombs, and are half empty space."

Sterling nodded as he studied the shiny rectangular piece.

"The result is a metal that is a little under half the weight with twice the strength." Tieseler concluded.

"What's its weakness?" Sterling asked inquisitively.

"Watch this..." Tieseler snatched the piece from the general and produced a hammer.

"You can beat on this flat side all day," Tieseler set the metal scrap on the floor and savagely beat the metal with the hammer and Sterling could see the metal flex momentarily with each blow.

After several hits, Tieseler picked up the metal and held it up to the general.

"See, there are no dents, no scratches. It is very good at taking direct impacts." Tieseler explained before setting it back on the floor, this time on its side.

"Watch this, though," he said before hitting it once.

The side of the metal that sustained the blow deformed as the tiny layers separated. After a second hit, the metal flaked apart, with large cracks appearing. A third hit pulverized the entire piece.

Sterling raised his eyebrows. "Impressive."

"I'm glad you liked it. We can't make this metal, so I wasn't supposed to do that," Tieseler explained, getting back to his feet and dusting the alien metal flakes off of his lab coat.

"So as long as we can hit these metals perpendicular to their layering, we can destroy them?" Sterling asked.

Tieseler shook his head, "You can destroy anything if you hit it hard enough, man. This metal was flat; most of their stuff is curved. The curved stuff can't be hit from the sides. Straight on, this metal here was about twice the strength of titanium, so conventional missiles and tank rounds would have trouble getting through anything usin' it, but their own weapons could rip through it like tin foil."

"Tin foil... so why is it that one of my men driving one of their vehicles was hit by an alien missile that melted the sand, and he lived?" Sterling asked.

"Ah ha, dude. You ever watch Star Trek?" Tieseler asked, smiling as he began typing again. "Shields..." he said as he brought up an electronic profile of a Brawler. Surrounding it was a blue aura.

"These alien dudes use a technology that lets them use high-energy fields to absorb or transform kinetic energy. The field and the opposing energy will cancel out, leaving a void. Only drawback is, every time the field is hit, its power draw increases until the void is filled," Tieseler scratched himself.

"...how does it work?" Sterling asked, before predicting it was beyond his comprehension.

"Uhh, how?" Tieseler's face lit up, "Well the field is actually many fields, all with their magnetic lines of force overlapping at exactly ninety degrees. Now at a really high frequency..."

"Could we replicate this technology?" Sterling interrupted. He was right; too technical.

"Yes and no." After a long pause Tieseler finally finished.

"Their shields hug the surface of their vehicles, and that's where we're hung up. If we made shields of out own, they would probably have to be sphere-shaped or some ellipse. In any case, they wouldn't be too aerodynamic."

After hitting a couple more keys, an image of a Brawler began to rotate. Sterling could see the smooth surfaces of the protective shields encapsulating the vulnerable fuselage.

"These force fields are the basis of their technology." Tieseler looked at the general with a huge grin. "They can deflect or cancel light, heat, electricity, radiation or even a kinetic impact. Any kind of energy! But only at the expense of equal energy."

"Energy can neither be created nor destroyed... Einstein," Sterling muttered.

"Newton... the apple guy," Tieseler corrected.

Sterling scowled slightly.

"Other applications of these fields can be used, too." Rick began typing on the keyboard again; this time, he brought up a picture of a strange looking gun. It was silvery gray, with four barrels protruding from a metal turret in front.

"We call this weapon the *Hellion*..."

Tieseler pressed a few keys as another larger six-barreled version appeared.

"...this is the Viper..." he said pressing more keys.

A massive gatling-style weapon with six thick barrels and what appeared to be rocket tubes on its sides dominated the screen.

"And this beauty is the *Decimator*." Tieseler said with a chuckle.

Sterling just nodded, unmoved by the clever names.

"This thing fires small conical bullets," Tieseler explained.

"So what? It looks like a big minigun to me." Sterling shrugged.

"Yes but the bullets aren't made of matter. I mean, they're like..." Tieseler looked up, trying to think of the right word. "Force-bullets... or force shells."

"Force shells? What the hell is a force shell?" Sterling began to pick at his mustache.

"Like a cross between a force field and a shell? It's a conical piece of a shield. And it's fired like a bullet." Tieseler stood up. "The need for ammo magazines has just disappeared."

Sterling stared at the screen, stunned, as he realized the possibilities.

"Incredible," was all he could say.

"Wait until you see some of the other things these fields can be used for." Tieseler logged off the computer and led Sterling through two double doors opposite the computer. They began to walk down a large hallway lit with blue light. It had a slight slant downward, and as they walked, they went further down.

"What do you mean, other things?" Sterling asked inquisitively.

Tieseler smiled. "Propulsion," he said excitedly.

"You mean... like an engine?" Sterling asked, trying to figure out Tieseler's cryptic response. As they reached a silver door at the end of the blue hallway, they both had to wait as the door's computer scanned the thermographic heat signature of both men and recognized them as high clearance personnel.

"Welcome to Hangar C5, General Roger S. Sterling and Doctor Richard G. Tieseler," a computerized voice droned from a hidden speaker. After several metallic clicks, the smooth metal door slid aside to reveal a gigantic room at least fifty feet high, with catwalks everywhere. Several scientists were operating computers and equipment. Parked at one side of the hanger was the captured *tortoise* metal crusher, in a state of disassembly. Sterling and Tieseler walked in as the door slid shut behind them and locked itself.

The hangar was bustling with activity. Over on one side, sparks were flying as workers took apart the metal crusher, on the other side, engineers were busy constructing something large and silver. The trilling sounds of air ratchets and the pounding of riveters echoed in the vast underground facility. Sterling walked over to where the men were working, Tieseler followed behind.

"What in God's name...?" Sterling's jaw hung open as if it was broken.

"...Is this?" Tieseler finished with a smirk. "This, General, is the F-202 Lakota."

Resting on a metal cradle elevated six feet into the air was the strangest ship he had ever seen. It had a smooth aerodynamic hull, its length was about twenty-five feet long. The long, silvery, cylindrical engines were held about four feet off the hull on pylons attached to the sides of the frame. Below the pylons were a set of stubby wings with weapons mounts on the under sides. In front was a black canopy and below that was a six barreled twenty-millimeter gatling gun that looked exactly like the alien weapons he had seen in Gates' video... in fact, it *was* the same. At the rear was a huge engine, with no visible air intake, and Sterling imagined it was some kind of hybrid rocket engine. The landing gear was not yet installed, but he could see the slots for them in the wings and body.

General Sterling gaped at the craft in awe. "How can it fly without a tail?" he suddenly said, surprised.

"Who needs a tail? This thing hardly needs wings," Tieseler said boastingly.

Sterling just looked at him, confused.

"First off its extremely light weight, 'cause we're using their metals. I know I said we can't make it, but I didn't say we can shape pieces they've already made for us." Tieseler gestured to the captured tortoise.

"Second off, I told you earlier that there were many applications for these shields, right?" Tieseler gestured for Sterling to agree.

"Yeah..." Sterling said, trying to keep up.

"One of the many forms a field can take is a what we call a flow-sensitive field, or one-way field. What that means is that matter can only pass through one side. This creates a vacuum on one side and higher pressure on the other."

Sterling nodded.

"So..." Tieseler gestured to four reflective metal domes on the under side of the ship. "Those are what keep it in the air. We call this setup the *magic carpet drive*."

Sterling listened silently.

"Before takeoff, these will open and expose four field emitters. They create a kind of subduction field under the ship. It pulls air from around and thrusts it below those four bubbles, which causes the craft to hover. The thrust can be controlled by the power given to the subduction field, and attitude and orientation can be controlled by varying the ratio of thrust per each emitter..."

"But why build a jet like this?" Sterling interrupted.

"Because aerodynamic lift is a thing of the past! These things are effectively aerostatic only!" Tieseler continued. "This thing could maneuver circles around anything we've got today. It can hover, fly backwards, strafe... all by manipulating the carpet field. And because we're so light, we can carry one hell of a bomb load."

Sterling looked at the black canopy in front. "What about fuel?"

"We use a special type of ethanol-based fuel. But the engines are almost completely run by electricity; the fuel is just for that little extra kick. It gets great mileage too."

Sterling raised his eyebrows. "Electrical engines?"

"The engines also use the one-way force fields instead of turbines." Tieseler handed Sterling a schematic of the engine. We call it the *comet engine*, and all three of the new craft will have them. There are only two turbines in each engine, the compressor turbine is in front. Behind it lie four one-way fields. Behind the second field is a combustion chamber where the fuel is aerosoled, compressed and combusted. The air is heated over ten thousand degrees and jetted out the exhaust through the two remaining fields, one of which can constrict the flow. The final turbine is mounted before the last field, and is on the same shaft as the compressor... so the faster it spins, the more air it sucks in, and the more thrust you get."

Sterling always felt dumber after conversations like these, but he found himself keeping up.

"How do you power such an engine? Surely this engine uses a lot of energy. Is your super-alcohol enough?" Sterling asked as he thumbed through the blueprints for the Lakota that had been lying on a nearby table.

"Ahh... like their metals, they also donated a couple of lightweight power sources..." Tieseler walked over to the blueprints and flipped through them a few times.

Sterling stared at the diagram of the alien power source, "Nuclear?" he asked while reading some of the small print.

Tieseler nodded, "Yes, but not like ours. They're using elements we've never encountered... 125, 127 and 129. Now we figure the 125 and 127 are just products of the decaying 129..."

"Wait a second. The short version, please." Sterling said.

"Uhh... they are very small and light, but give off a lot of power... We recovered them from their largest gatling weapons... the *decimators*. Each reactor produces almost four hundred megawatts if cooled properly. Otherwise, as the unit heats up, the performance is greatly decreased." Tieseler, upon seeing a nod from the General proceeded in more detail, "The coolant they use is remarkably efficient and using it would allow us nearly enough power to fly these engines to the moon and back."

"So what's the catch?" Sterling asked.

"The problem is the ethanol. If conserved, these engines can keep these craft going at high speeds for more than one dogfight, but after several, the craft will be forced to run on electrical only, which will be much slower," Tieseler said.

Sterling merely nodded.

"This also carries the latest in computerized hardware, for damage control, navigation and defense," Tieseler added.

"I read your preliminary reports on some sort of cloaking device," Sterling said, his eyes not leaving the blueprints.

"Oh yes!" Tieseler's face lit up again. "I call it the *chameleon system*. It's very loosely based on the data collected from the Eldritch experiment in 1943. It uses Tesla's unproven research in electromagnetic harmonics." Tieseler chuckled. "It's proven now!"

"Is it safe?" Sterling said, turning the page of the blueprints.

"Oh yes, Sir, it won't cause any... *side effects* like those seen on the Eldritch. Using a thin permiable field, we can create a magnetic bubble that will bend and redirect any low frequency electromagnetic waves around the ship. Any radar and other electromagnetic energy waves will pass around it rather than reflecting," Tieseler explained.

"Can it still be seen?" Sterling asked.

Tieseler shook his head. "Oh yeah, man. We don't have the technology to redirect higher frequencies like visible light... yet, not without serious power consumption, and dangerous levels of EM radiation."

Sterling was silent.

Tieseler spoke again, "Dude... this is brand new stuff, I doubt our enemy even knows about this technology or they'd be using it. We may have an edge, man."

Tieseler's words echoed in Sterling's head as he read through the plans.

"This is only one bird. Where is the other two?" Sterling finally asked, putting the clipboard containing the plans on a metal table. His eyes were not friendly as before.

"The Lakota is the fighter version. The bomber and interceptor classes have been designed but are only half completed. We need to cannibalize the metal off of that thing parked over there first. Give me at least another month," Tieseler said disappointedly as the mood of the conversation changed.

"We need those three aircraft soon, Rick; not a week, not a month, but soon, which means no more computer games," Sterling said coldly. Tieseler felt offended that the general suggest he wasn't working hard enough, and flinched as he mentioned the old PC game he had been playing.

"I'm working as fast as I can, but it's hard to know how to implement this stuff! Do you realize that this is the first time this technology has been used by a human being? Man, there is no research to be reviewed! No documents to be read! We are making this shit up as we go! The reactors, the metals... we had to learn how they worked first... now we're looking at their power cells..." Tieseler's voice was raised just high enough to qualify as shouting, but he kept his composure. "Look, I'm not lazy, but this will take time, dude. And there's nothing I can do about it," he said simply.

Sterling sighed, "I know, Rick, but time is not just something you and I don't have. It's something the Earth is running out of."

"The Earth... You want to fill me in on what's going on up there? Why is it my time has been cut from four months to one?" Tieseler asked, point blank.

"All right. You want to know? You really want to know?" Sterling wheeled a metal stool out from under the nearby table and sat on it. Tieseler sat on a workbench.

Tieseler nodded.

"The looting, the mass hysteria... it's the least of our problems if this gets out... nothing I say here can ever leave this hangar," Sterling stated.

"So tell me," Tieseler said, nodding.

"Six months ago, the James Webb telescope snapped pictures of a black space orbiting above the enemy facility. Eighteen hours ago, it revealed itself to be an orbiting platform at least six miles across. After studying the pictures and infrared shots of the platform we discovered an energy beam carrying gigawatts of electromagnetic energy transmitted to a large tower at the center of the enemy facility."

Tieseler stared at Sterling in disbelief.

"We also have read seismic vibrations and heat signatures in China that lead us to believe that they are attempting to start a nuclear reaction below the facility. Our guess is that they are preparing to start a reactor that will power them on their own... they're digging in like a tick, Doctor."

Sterling looked at the Lakota and continued. "Our plan is to somehow block this energy beam for a couple of hours. At the same time, we attempt to destroy the shield covering the gate to the facility. When the shields drop, our new aircraft will blast through into the facility. And that's all I can tell you. If the enemy reactor starts, we'll have no chance. We are out of time, Doctor."

Tieseler stood up. "You'll have them, General. I promise, man."

Sterling stood and nodded. "All right... We're counting on you."

Tieseler smiled awkwardly and walked off.

Sterling inhaled a huge breath of air. "All we need now are pilots who are crazy enough for the job," he said without humor.

CHAPTER 10 Heroes

Sasebo, Japan:
December 26th, 2033

$160 lay on the table between two bottles of Miller Genuine Draft. Next to this table was a pool table. A tall, built man of about twenty-eight, with blue jeans and a white Stetson hat was making a shot while a much larger, dark-skinned and muscular man watched. He had to weigh at least two hundred pounds, and was wearing a green pixilated camouflage fatigue that said U.S. Marines over the right pocket, matching camouflage pants, and sported a buzzed haircut. The Marine was currently waiting impatiently, beer in one fist, and his stick in the other.

"Never been beat," the man with hat drawled in a heavy Southern accent.

"Just make the shot, cowboy," the Marine said, replacing his beer bottle on the table with the money.

"Why? You ask... " the cowboy continued while leveling the pool stick with the cue ball, "...because to be beat, means you have to lose." He finished as his stick prodded the cue ball into the solid red 4, which bounced into two striped balls, knocking one in.

The Marine smiled and gave an audible chuckle. "Have yourself another beer, redneck. Only two balls stand between me and that one sixty."

The cowboy swiped his beer off the table and took a big swig, then slammed it back down. The Marine made his shot, knocking the last striped ball into the corner pocket. He looked over at the man with the cowboy hat and laughed. The cowboy just stared at the ground, and then drank the last of his beer.

"Hell, if I were to lose a game of pool after all of these years to a Marine...." The cowboy said.

The Marine shook his head. His stick was leveled with the cue ball that was in direct line with the black 8-ball.

"I think I'd have to shoot myself," the cowboy continued.

"8 ball, corner pocket," the Marine said irritably.

The Marine tapped the cue ball lightly. It glided down the table, hit the 8 ball, and as the 8 ball rolled towards the corner pocket, the cowboy reached down and picked it up, and watched the cue ball roll into the pocket. "Looks like a scratch to me. Bummer..." he said happily.

The Marine laughed a little. "Very funny, cowboy," he said before chugging the rest of his beer. "We'll see how funny you look with this pool stick shoved up your ass!" The Marine approached the cowboy.

Everybody in the bar stopped and watched the two men. All wore Marine camouflage utilities, except for the short Japanese bartender who looked at Ford with annoyance.

"No fight in my bar!" he shouted, but no one listened.

With one arm, the Marine grabbed the cowboy by his shirt and lifted him off the ground. The Marine stood a full foot taller than the cowboy, and they were now looking eye to eye.

"I think your making I huge mistake, jarhead," the cowboy said with no trace of fear.

"Is that right? What the hell you gonna do about it, cowboy," the Marine blustered.

"Well," The cowboy started, "first I'm going to do this." He threw the 8 ball off to his left and shattered the large plate glass window. The Marine removed his attention from the cowboy for a fraction of a second. "Then I'm going to do this!" The cowboy said as he swung his beer bottle into the side of the Marine's head. Shattered brown glass sprinkled against the Marine's boots, but he didn't fall. He was standing, dazed. "And then this!" the cowboy said, while grabbing the Marine's bottle and smashing it into the other side of his head. The Marine still didn't go down. The cowboy gave a push, and sent the Marine falling backwards. Before he hit the floor, the entire bar was coming straight at the cowboy.

"Here we go! Come and get it, ladies!" the cowboy said as he dodged a chair.

Fists, beer bottles, and chairs flew from all directions, but the cowboy dodged most while delivering his own punches to the mostly sober mob. From the side, a chair shattered into wooden splinters upon impact, sending him to the floor. Eight muscled Marines kicked and beat him to the ground, but the cowboy fought his way back to his feet and began to fight with a fury none would expect from a human being.

"Now you gone an' pissed Dusty off!" the now bloodied cowboy shouted. At the same time, the doors swung open and more Marines ran in. They wore armbands that said SP on them, designating them as Shore Patrol. Most of the Marines backed off of the cowboy, and those that didn't were pried off by the SPs. The cowboy jumped on top of the pool table and beckoned them to come back and fight.

A Marine captain in charge of the squad of SPs walked into the bar and looked around. Instantly, his gaze fixed on the cowboy, who somehow had managed to keep his white Stetson on his head.

"Ford!" the captain yelled.

The cowboy looked over at the captain. "Howdy there, Joe! Nice night, isn't it?"

"This is the last time, Ford!" the captain yelled. "You hear me, you bastard?"

"What are you talking about?" Ford asked, looking at his torn shirt and ripped jeans. "I'm good for at least twenty more bar brawls!" he said while wiping the blood from his lip.

Ford jumped off the pool table and began to rummage through the broken wood and glass on the floor. He finally recovered his money.

"Look what you did! My bar! My bar!" the Japanese bartender was shouting, while standing amid the broken glass and wooden splinters.

Ford smiled and dropped the one hundred and sixty dollars on the floor. "That's for the mess. I kicked that guy's ass for free," Ford said, smiling.

"Let's go, hero," said the captain as the SPs hand cuffed him and dragged him out of the bar.

. . .

Ford awoke to find himself in a familiar place. *The Cooler*. Actually, the cooler was slang for the Navy's drunk tank. Ford knew this place well; it was a home away from home. And also too familiar was the intense hangover he had. He felt as if a grenade had exploded inside his head.

Normally, he would have been discharged for conduct unbecoming an officer, as it was so poetically stated in the Uniform Code of Military Justice. But he wasn't worried. He had been through more bar fights, dogfights, firefights and fistfights than John Wayne. He knew they weren't going to get rid of him. Not with his medals, not in these dark days.

After a few minutes, he got to his feet and began stretching, waiting for someone from his squadron to come down and bail him out. Just as he began to envision the inevitable speech from his commanding officer about his bad behavior, he heard the door down the hall open.

Footsteps echoed down the hallway.

Ford sat back down on his small cot and waited patiently for the men to stop at his cell, and they did.

Ford was confused. He had expected his someone from his squadron to come down there, but instead there stood a tall skinny man dressed in a black suit with sunglasses. Two other men dressed just like him escorted him.

"Lieutenant Dustin Ford?" the tall man asked.

"Yeah?" Ford replied.

The man blinked, "You are *the* Dustin Ford? The *Flying Ford*? The man who shot down nine MiG-102's in the Adak Incident..."

"Yeah! That's me. Why? Who the hell are you guys?" Ford asked, clutching his head.

The man grabbed the bars of Ford's cell and said quietly, "I'm a salesman, and I'm here to sell you a chance of a lifetime."

Ford stared at the man, intrigued.

Sanford Lake, New Mexico:
December 31st, 2033

One hundred and fifty-four men and women filed into the gigantic, well lit, trapezoidal amphitheatre. The amphitheatre was extremely bright, with white floor, walls, and ceiling; at the longest wall were rows of chairs, in which the men and women sat in no distinguishable order. Ford walked in and took a seat near the front. The rest of the people found seats and sat down quietly. He recognized uniforms from all branches of the military. Army, Navy, Marine, Air Force and even Coast Guard officers of varying ranks were all present. Of all of the naval officers present, he was the most junior of the men there, being a mere lieutenant.

Most were spreading gossip about why they were there in chattering whispers. Ford spoke to the female Army major next to him.

"Any idea what is going on here, Ma'am?" he asked.

The major looked at him and shrugged. "All I know is I was told to get on a plane and fly here to New Mexico with less than two days' notice."

"Attention on deck!" An officer's voice echoed from the large speakers hanging from the ceiling, as a general walked in from a door opposite the men and women. Everyone rose to their feet.

"As you were," the general said as he reached the small podium. As soon as all doors to the room were closed and locked, the general spoke.

"Good morning, ladies and gentlemen. I am General Sterling. Time is short, so I'll get right to it. Sorry for the short notice, but for those of you who've been in the business for a while, you know that's sometimes the way it works." He began quickly. "First off, I'd like to say that this briefing is perhaps the most important briefing you will ever attend."

"You men and women have been chosen to undertake in an operation that will decide the survival of the human race," he said bluntly.

The crowd murmured with intermittent conversation at the general's statement.

"As I'm sure most of you have already heard, either on the news or from friends who forgot what the word *classified* is all about... we are not the only intelligent life on this planet, you all no doubt saw the footage of the unidentified vessel descending over the Asian continent a month ago and I know the tabloids and networks are running with it. But that's only the tip of the iceberg." The general continued, "Four months ago, an unidentified structure appeared in the eastern Chinese city of Shanghai." A picture of the facility appeared behind Sterling.

"Our attempts to recon the area have been met with lethal opposition." The screen then displayed an aerial map of the facility. "It occupies nine hundred square miles of Chinese territory and is encapsulated in a barrier of energy that we have found to be utterly impenetrable."

The men and women in the room watched and listened in silence.

"The purpose of this structure and who occupied it was a mystery up until our first recon team, made up of Navy SEAL Team 9, was able to penetrate its barrier while it was still under construction and gather critical... and terrifying, information. All of that team was destroyed while attempting to leave with the data, with exception of one survivor." Sterling paused.

The screen revealed a clip of the battle at the tower, where Gates' men attacked the alien workers.

"Our new enemies are *not* human," Sterling said, the screen freezing on the four-eyed creature reaching at the SEAL's throat from over the ridge.

There were a few gasps in the crowd.

"A week ago, we captured several of their vehicles, and are now in the process of replicating their advanced technology." The screen showed a picture of the tortoise metal crusher.

"We also managed to capture samples of two of the enemy species." The screen showed pictures of the yellow skinned, bipedal creature. "This one has been called a Molluskan because of its resemblance to Earth mollusks, such as squids, or octopus."

Ford stared at the screen, tantalized by the first glimpse at something from another planet. No one in the room spoke.

"The *Molluskan*, when tested, showed intelligence equivalent to that of a six year old child, and it is believed that this species is subservient to a higher, more intelligent race," Sterling said.

The screen then displayed another creature. A four legged, four-armed creature with fangs, four red eyes, and a large protruding abdomen. Ford recognized it as the same creature that had grabbed the SEAL in the picture earlier.

"This creature we call an Aracteroid, because of its distinct resemblance to an Earth arachnid." Sterling paused for a second, letting everyone digest what he had just said.

"This creature was far too violent to accurately test its IQ. After repeated attempts to communicate with it, it committed suicide by self-mutilation. Although we were unable to test it, we believe it has intelligence equal to or higher than an average human. However, it is still believed that a third, yet more intelligent species is in control of this installation."

Ford laid back his head. "Jesus," he said, still shocked.

"Just under five hours ago, we received our first message from the enemy compound. It was broadcasted in sixty four human languages world wide over short-wave radio," The screen displayed the English message. It said simply:

"Natives of this planet:

It is not our intention to harm you,

If you assault, harass, or wander within the operating area of Grantex,

you will be destroyed the nation(s) responsible will face retaliation.

Consider your safety, and those of your people."

"As you can see, we are dealing with an enemy that knows our languages and has a foothold on our territory. It is very probable that they have a great deal of intelligence gathered on us, and we have next to nothing on them."

"General... that message... that's their first message to us?" An Air Force colonel stood and asked. "No demands, no ultimatum, no *take me to your leader?*"

"We are as confused as you, Colonel, as to the logic behind that message," Sterling continued. "The message refers to Grantex; we believe that this is the name of the enemy compound. We have since attempted to contact them, but have again met silence. It is clear that they have nothing more to say to us."

"And they only want us to just stay away..." Ford said to himself, trying to imagine what they could possibly have in mind for the human race.

The briefing continued for an hour, and the general laid the proverbial cards on the table.

The enemy's army was discussed and, to Ford, it appeared that enemy was severely short on troops and equipment. Most of the compound was empty space, with few buildings standing. Sterling surmised that the base was only half completed. He also talked about a giant satellite powering the facility from above, and a non-functional reactor below the surface.

"You and your men are responsible for operation Hail Storm. The objective is to capture or destroy the facility. You will each be briefed on your individual roles in this crucial and complex mission."

The general sighed. "Their biggest advantage is the shield surrounding the facility, for no attack can be made unless we can breach it." The screen went blank, and Sterling walked around to the front of the podium.

"I would like the following officers to remain here: Commander Drummond, Captain Tobias, Lieutenant Bishop, Captain VanDuinwyk, Captain Cochran and Lieutenant Ford. The rest of you men and women are dismissed," Sterling said.

Almost everyone in the room stood and began to make their ways to the exit. Ford didn't recognize any of the names of the other officers, nor could he imagine his apparent role in this mission. One thing was for certain: he knew he'd be in the air.

Ford got up from his seat and walked towards the general. The five other officers who remained in the room all made their way to the podium as well.

"Well, well, well," Sterling began, "you men are the ones that will truly decide if the meek really shall inherit the Earth." As he said this, another man walked in and whispered in the general's ear.

"Where is he?" the men heard Sterling ask.

"Appendicitis, Sir," The other man said very quietly, but loud enough to hear.

"Damn," Sterling said and he then turned to men, who were patiently awaiting orders. "So it looks like we're one short," he said with a tone of annoyance.

The men were lead into another, smaller room, with a large view screen occupying one wall. The general walked in and stood next to another man. Ford recognized him instantly as Admiral Bruin. After all five men were inside, the huge pressure door closed and sealed. The room was actually a heavy-duty radiation shelter.

"Have a seat, gentlemen," Sterling said.

There were six chairs laid out and the men sat. Ford sat in the third chair, to his left was a huge black man with large meaty arms, and to his right was a dark skinned man with a head of whitish blond hair. One chair was left open.

Admiral Bruin clasped his hands together, "First of all, I'd like to thank you all for volunteering for this mission. I want to stress for the last time, that this is an extremely vital and exceptionally perilous operation. Once I begin this briefing, you will be committed to this mission. There is no shame in deciding you're not the guy for the job."

No one said a word.

"Anyone?" Bruin asked, and was met with continued silence. "Alright then."

Sterling spoke. “For security reasons, you are being briefed separately because of the sensitivity and importance of your mission. Our enemy has shown that it is capable of listening to us through unknown means, but we’re sure nothing can penetrate these walls. Admiral.”

Admiral Bruin began again, “You have been chosen to make up a new squadron called VFX-187, and will be taking part in the most crucial element of Operation Hail Storm. This particular mission is called Operation Locksmith. Its objective is to knock out the enemy shield generator by destroying its power station. You will be flying in three specialized aircraft; one interceptor, one fighter, and one bomber. The first part of this mission is...”

The screen turned itself on and showed an aerial map of the facility. “...to penetrate the main gate of this compound.”

The screen switched to a close up of the main gate.

“We call it *The Wall*. It is their main line of defense, and therefore, the first hurdle,” a red arrow was shown moving through the wall. “Next, you must proceed to the inner gate, where you are to blast your way through and finally reach the power sub-station,” the arrow went through the inner gate, and ended with an explosion at a small cylindrical building, next to the large tower. “...and blow it to dust.”

The screen changed to show a side view of the sub-station. “This is the most important part of the mission: the bomber is the only ship that will carry the BLN-88 Atlas bomb. It is a nuclear tritium-deuterium fusion bomb, and is the only thing we believe will destroy the sub-station. It is the primary role of both the fighter and interceptor to defend the bomber at all costs.”

“BLN-88... I’ve never heard of it,” Ford recklessly mumbled aloud.

All of the officers sitting with looked at him with annoyance.

"You've never heard of it, Lieutenant Ford, because it didn't exist until last week," Bruin said. "We're playing for all the marbles, gentlemen, and Uncle Sam has written us a blank check."

"What are we going to be flying, Sir?" The tall, blond Air Force officer asked.

"The aircraft are the FB-177 Nightshade designated Meridian One, F-202 Lakota designated Meridian Two, B-100 Revenant designated Meridian Three," The Admiral answered.

"What the hell is a Revenant?" Ford whispered to the man on his right.

"Who will be flying what, Sir?" A large black man with a deep voice, four chairs down asked.

The admiral looked at Sterling, and Sterling spoke up. "The first man is the pilot, and second is the navigator..."

Ford was amused at how gently the general stated that.

Bruin spoke up again. "Drummond and Tobias are the FB-117 Nightshade. Bishop and VanDuinwyk are the F-202 Lakota. And Ford will pilot the B-100 Revenant."

"The Bomber's a single man bird, Sir?" Ford asked, excited at the prospect of flying solo.

"No. Captain Cochran was supposed to navigate, but he was taken out with appendicitis. A replacement will be forthcoming."

Ford tried to hide his disappointment.

The admiral continued to explain the finer details of the mission, and gave the positions of the known enemy bases within the compound. They were *The Wall*, *Molluskan Barracks*, *Garden Barracks*, *Inner Gate*, *Cryo-Plant* and the *Shield Tower* itself, *which* contained a large hangar.

"Your weapon load will be depend on your ship, but all will be equipped with a new type of weapon that we recently acquired from the enemy. It is called a *force cannon*. Other weapon systems are the AIM-22 Hydra air-to-air missiles, AGM-74 Scorpion anti-armor missiles and the new AGMS-2 Unicorn laser-guided missile system. And will be equipped with a semi-cloaking system called a chameleon system. This system will shield you from any high frequency EM detector such as radar," the admiral half-grinned. "This was our invention, and Intel doubts they will expect it."

Bruin continued to talk about the different weapons, and about the special systems on the new planes. Although Ford was shown block-diagrams and pictures of individual systems, he began to wonder why no aircraft were actually shown. *How big would this thing be?* If it is supersonic, *would his bomber have variable wing geometry like the old B-1B Lancer?*

"Our satellite imaging shows that the most resistance you'll meet is from an aircraft called a *Dragonfly*." The screen showed a picture of a narrow aircraft with a nose cannon, and four variable jet nacelles. The two rear engines were hugging the sides of the aircraft, and the forward two were at the tips of its thick wings.

Bruin continued as the screen showed various grainy satellite photos of the *Dragonfly* aircraft. "This craft has the ability to hover, and is highly maneuverable. However, you may have an advantage in speed."

"You can expect heavy fire from ground-based turrets when you engage the inner gate, and the power sub station. Their defense will include these *Sentinel* turrets," he continued on as the screen showed pictures of the small dome shaped turrets.

The screen then displayed photographs that looked much like the Washington monument, but slate gray and made of alien metal.

"The *guardian* towers contain a high-powered laser that can incinerate on contact. Your only warning it's about to fire is a high electromagnetic reading just prior to discharge. If you detect that signature, it's your cue to haul ass to somewhere else or you'll be popped like a fly on a bug-light."

The screen went black.

Bruin sighed, "Gentlemen, I can promise you that you will encounter weapons platforms that we have not covered here. My advice to you is to be vigilant, and flexible. Be ready for plans to change... General."

"All of you have been selected based on two factors: Your operation of aircraft, whether in the pilot or navigator role, the other factor deals with your training in land warfare. If you are shot down behind enemy lines, you are not authorized to surrender. No rescue will be possible as long as the shields remain active, so you are to hole up until the they fall and we can come get you. However..." Sterling paused.

"You are not ordered, but highly encouraged to sabotage the enemy in any way possible if shot down. Desert camouflage utilities will be stored in each aircraft as well as small arms and additional survival gear including food rations..."

Ford raised his hand.

"Your question, Lieutenant," Sterling barked.

Ford gestured to the dark screen, "Sir. Why haven't we seen any pictures of the new birds we're going to be flying?"

"Get used to suspense Lieutenant," the general cryptically answered, "you'll have your answers soon."

. . .

Sterling and Bruin walked through the complex on their way to their executive quarters when both men heard a voice. The admiral and general turned and saw the face of a man that seemed very familiar. Although he was not in uniform, they both recognized him.

"Remember me, General?" Gates asked.

"Ah yes. Lieutenant Gates. Our first survivor." Sterling smiled and offered a handshake.

"Nice to see you on your feet, Lieutenant," Admiral Bruin said, noting Gates' recovery.

Gates shook his hand, with a genuine smile. "It's been a while, gentlemen."

"How are your wounds?" Sterling asked.

"I'm fully recovered," Gates said.

"What can we do for you?" Bruin asked.

"Gentlemen, I've been brought here as an advisor to our ground forces," Gates began, "but I'd rather have a more active part in this mission,"

"Well your personal experiences are very valuable," Sterling paused. "No promises, but I might have a job for you on the ground..."

Gates shook his head. "I want to navigate the Revenant, Sir."

"What?" Sterling was taken back by this statement. "How do you know about that?"

"I heard that Brian Cochran is out with appendicitis, at least a week... maybe more. I can take his spot," Gates persisted.

"You can't be the back-seater, you have no experience. You're a damn SEAL!" Sterling said, shaking his head.

"I was a navigator for four years before laterally transferring to the SEAL program," Gates said, his voice raised slightly. "I'm not just any SEAL,"

"No! No way Lieutenant," Sterling said, still shaking his head.

"Sir. I flew in the back of F-35's, the same weapon systems the Revenants are based after," Gates argued.

"But this isn't the F-35, Lieutenant Gates, and this mission isn't dropping bombs from high altitudes on backwater terror camps," Admiral Bruin said sympathetically.

"Besides, you haven't flown in years," Sterling stated.

"The tech boys let me into the simulator. It's all come back to me," Gates persisted further. "I've had over a thousand hours in air and simulator, I'm a natural."

"Cochran was picked from a pool of hundreds of navigators. He was an ace, as navigators go!" Sterling grumbled. His voice was growing louder.

"I can do the job better than anyone else, gentlemen. I've had more time in the simulators than any replacement you can ever find in time," Gates said calmly.

Bruin and Sterling stared at Gates.

"Come on, General, let me be the one to punch the button and knock the shit out the bastards! I've got a score to settle," Gates said hatefully, then regretted it.

"Lieutenant Gates," Sterling shut his eyes very tightly, and spoke calmly, "this mission means everything, possibly the survival of the human race. And I refuse to put this mission in danger, just so a lieutenant can get even."

"I'm sorry, Mr. Gates, but I have to agree. You've done more than any of us would have ever thought possible. Now it's time to sit this one out. I know you understand?" Admiral Bruin said quietly.

Gates was quiet. He couldn't imagine being out of the war.

. . .

Ford sat up in his bunk. It was impossible to sleep; so many things were going through his head. He couldn't stop feeling fear for the aliens. He hadn't imagined he would ever see one in his lifetime outside the fiction of movies and books. Ford lay in his bed for an additional few minutes before accepting that he was getting no sleep this night. He got dressed in shorts and T-shirt, and left his stateroom, which was ten levels below the surface of the New Mexico desert above.

Ford made his way towards the lounge that joined at the center of six the corridors of officer quarters like spokes on a wagon wheel. As Ford walked down the dimly lit corridor he heard voices ahead and was soon within sight of the four other men sitting at a table in the lounge. He instantly recognized the men; they were at the secret briefing.

"Can't sleep, mate?" One of the men sitting at the table asked with an obvious Australian accent.

"No," Ford admitted, as he took a seat, "I've got too much to think about,"

"I know what ya mean," the Australian said, "I can't stop thinkin' about my kids,"

Ford nodded, and then extended his hand. "I'm Dustin Ford." He shook hands.

"James Tobias," the Australian said.

"Eric Drummond," the older man at the table said, reaching across to shake his hand. Ford shook it.

"Carl VanDuinwyk," the man next to Tobias offered his hand, "My friends call me Dutch."

The large, black man on his left followed in suit. "Phil Bishop," he said, shaking hands.

They began to talk. Mostly about themselves; no one seemed to want to talk about the impending mission. However, it was occupying all of their minds.

Ford instantly found them to be an admirable group of men.

Carl VanDuinwyk was his favorite. He was from New York, and was an Air Force fighter pilot. He had been a test pilot for five years and then switched back to fighters. He found that he was an aviation historian as well as an amateur novelist. Like Ford, he was not married and had no children.

Phil Bishop was a large, athletic man in his late thirties. His voice was low and hoarse. He was also an Air Force test pilot and had mostly flown stealth aircraft and some of the newer breed of fighters before he was picked up for this mission. He explained that his mission in life was to be an astronaut for NASA. He had been married and later divorced, and had one daughter.

Then there was the Aussie. His name was James Tobias and he became the life of the conversations. He had grown up in the desolate deserts of Melbourne and had just barely graduated from high school when he joined the Australian army. From that point, he was able to excel so much that he was offered a commission from the ranks as a warrant officer and later a chance to attend flight school. He had five kids and a beautiful wife named Amy.

Eric Drummond was to be the commander of the mission. Like Ford, he was a graduate of the U.S. Naval Academy and had spent a majority of his career getting qualified with every naval aircraft still in service. He was considered by many to be an ace. His demeanor was very calm and confident. Ford sensed that he was a powerful man both in mind, body and ability. He was unmarried and had no children. The Navy was his life.

All of the men in the room had combat experience, but he wondered if it would make any difference. No one had had any combat experience with the enemy they were about to face. And it scared him.

The men continued to talk all through the night. None of them could have slept anyway.

. . .

Admiral Bruin couldn't get any sleep either. He was disturbed by Gates' words. He knew Gates was right. Cochran's replacement would be a top-notch navigator, but these ships were not the same. They were different in ways they didn't yet understand, using technology they didn't discover. The crew selection board selected men based on their previous flying experience and abilities. Admiral Bruin, a SEAL himself, understood the vital importance of selecting a crew that could work together under fire. He would also need someone with experience with the enemy. He couldn't stop thinking that he had made a terrible mistake by turning Gates, a qualified navigator *and* a SEAL down.

"No!" He threw the thought from his mind. He was doing the right thing, but he was still one man short. Not just anyone could be trained to operate these ships in a week without any experience from similar systems. Slowly the indecision crept back to him, and soon he felt as if he was ignoring his better judgment. Bruin rolled over on his side and looked at his alarm clock. It was exactly 0400, and he would have to get up in another hour with a decision.

"Damn," he said aloud. "Gates... if this wasn't a suicide mission, I would be congratulating you."

Sterling was in charge of the ground mission, but Bruin was in charge of VFX-187. It was his decision that Gates would go.

CHAPTER 11 Crash Course

Sanford Lake, New Mexico:
January 2nd, 2034

Wind Walkers... that was the saying written in black before the crossed lightning bolts and arrows with the globe as a background. Ford didn't care much for the new VFX-187 patch he now wore on his flight suit, but at least he was wearing his flight suit again. Crammed in the elevator with Tobias, Bishop and VanDuinwyk, he began to wonder when he'd meet his navigator.

Today, they would finally get specific training in their new aircraft. Yesterday had been spent exhaustively going over details of the new *force cannon* and the new missiles and bombs, as well as a one-day hand-to-hand combat refresher.

The electronic ringing sounded, indicating that the elevator had reached its destination and the doors opened. Drummond was already outside waiting for them.

"All right, fellas, I hope you got your quarters. We got some video games to conquer today." Drummond said smiling.

Ford walked over to the four large generic simulator pods that occupied the room and peered within one of them. He was astonished to see what looked like collective and cyclic sticks... the controls found in helicopters.

"Eric... I know we're flying supersonic aircraft, but I've never heard of a supersonic helicopter," Ford said motioning to the controls inside the pod.

Drummond chuckled, "Trust me Lieutenant, you're not flying a helicopter."

Soon the technicians arrived and the briefing started. The senior man, who wore thick glasses and looked much like Mark Twain began to describe the new controls.

"Your planes will have the capability to maneuver in a full range of directions regardless of speed. In slow flight, you can forget all your training on aerodynamics; there is no Bernoulli, no lift, and no stalls. However, with this added freedom of movement, you will be responsible for keeping control of the aircraft which will be much harder than anything you've ever experienced."

Ford didn't like the sound of slow flight.

"As you gain speed, those aerodynamic properties I just told you to forget will begin to take over, and the plane will fly much like the jets you have been trained to fly."

Sterling and another man in a flight suit approached and stood in front of the artificial cockpits. Ford immediately noticed the VFX-187 patch over his right breast pocket.

"Gentlemen, this is your new bomber navigator, Lieutenant Gates," Sterling announced.

"Lieutenant." Ford shook hands with Gates but did not smile.

"Now let's see if we can beat the computer," Sterling said. Everyone filed into the simulators. Gates looked at Ford with emotionless calculation, but then grinned and extended his hand.

Ford didn't like Gates at all at first as he looked him over. On his flight suit, Gates wore both naval flight officer wings as well as an insignia Ford instantly recognized as the Navy SEAL trident. Sufficiently impressed, Ford finally reached up and grasped Gates' hand.

"Well..." he said. "You must be somebody special."

Gates at first said nothing, and then finally nodded and spoke.

"No. Just lucky."

. . .

"I hope we can learn this stuff faster, gentlemen, because our ships are finished in seven days, shipped here in ten and were flying this mission in fourteen," he said, "We have two weeks to learn this stuff."

The simulator was actually a giant video game, with graphics that looked so real, it had made people vomit and have nightmares. They were currently configured to the Lakota, Nightshade, and Revenant's cockpits. The forth simulator in the room was vacant.

Although the navigators had little trouble operating the new systems, the pilots had to get used to a new way of thinking. They had to get used to an aircraft that could rapidly descend while pointed at the sky, and could fly sideways while keeping its nose facing inward as it flies circles around fixed objects. Even Ford had trouble letting go of the restrictions of *normal* flight that had cemented his piloting skills for the last five years.

They had just finished a fourteen hour-long simulator marathon. Facing an simulated enemy of MiG-127's, they practiced individually, running drills, and flying solo missions. Bishop and Drummond were veteran helicopter pilots and had no problem handling the controls of their aircraft, and soon were flying like aces. Ford, slow to learn the controls at first, dominated in high-speed flight. VanDuinwyk and Tobias were slowly learning where all of the systems were and how they worked. Gates, to Ford's surprise knew everything there was to know about the systems, not knowing that Gates had already spent days training on them before Ford even got there.

In the dog-fighting simulations, Gates and Ford were killed eight times out of twenty engagements with multiple bandits, better than their counterparts in the F-202 and FB-177 but still a dismal performance. Gates became more and more proficient at the use of the tail gun of the B-100 as a result of Ford always finding himself surrounded. Although the simulation accurately simulated the unexpected agility and instability of the Magic Carpet drive, Ford was slow to let it go.

. . .

"So." Ford began, "what came first? SEALs or NFO?" he asked conversationally, gesturing to Gates' patches as he bit into his hamburger. At this late hour, the massive mess hall was mostly deserted except for small pockets of people chatting in hushed tones.

"I was a naval flight officer for about four years and decided to try for the teams." Gates explained, while fumbling with the ketchup packet.

Ford nodded as he chewed, but said nothing.

"How long has it been since you've flown?" Ford asked nonchalantly.

Gates grinned, "Ford, if you have any doubts..."

"No. I don't, we were tearin' it up in there today." Ford said, "I'm just curious..."

Gates finally opened his packet and squeezed ketchup all over his fries. "About what?"

"Well," Ford began, "I've heard you've been here for a couple of months and that you were recently awarded the Purple Heart and the Navy Cross."

"All the rumors are true." Gates said flatly, picking at his fries.

Ford could see his new navigator didn't want to talk to him, and they both ate their meals in silence before turning in for the night.

. . .

Two more grueling days in the simulators ensued. New software had been added and was designed to simulate Operation Locksmith. Instead of MiG-127's, they faced the alien *Dragonfly* fighters, and shared the virtual environment as the simulators were now linked.

VFX-187 would now have to learn to work together from this point forward.

"This is what it'll be like Gentlemen," Bruin said over the radio. "From now until the end of this mission, the only easy day is yesterday!"

The *Wall*, the main line of defense was an absolute nightmare, guided missiles, force shells and enemy aircraft streaked around the screens.

The first attempt to breach the wall, the B-100 Revenant was destroyed in one shot by a rocket fired at supersonic speeds from ahead.

"Juke Ford! Juke! Forget what you've learned... the weakest part of the B-100 is a conventional, ordinary pilot!" Sterling shouted.

"Sir! Why can't we use our damn shields while we are on approach to the Wall?" Ford asked, while they were getting ready to reset the simulator.

"It's because you need to fire your booster engine, and with your shields up, you craft isn't aerodynamic enough to reach the speeds you're going to need to get through the gate." General Sterling answered.

"But Sir. What's the rush? With no shields we're defenseless!" Bishop said with a slight tone of disappointment.

The General paused, and then spoke, "Look. We can't reveal all of the mission details yet. You have to trust us on this one," he finished.

No one responded.

After four disastrous failures, the team managed to knock out the sub-station with the loss of the F-202. Several attempts later they were able to complete the mission with no casualties. And then they did it again, and again, long after they were sick of it.

. . .

Late that night, the crews were allowed to leave on a short period of liberty. All of the men had scattered except for Gates. He remained behind on the base and studied the attributes of weapons he would be carrying. Although most of this material was extremely sensitive and classified, Gates had it on ground level and was studying the schematics under a single dim halogen lamp mounted outside one of the sheet metal Quonset huts that housed an elevator leading to the complex below. The cool dry desert air rushed past him in a gentle but steady gust.

As his eyes broke from the boring data table of the AGM-74 Scorpion missile to see a large desert spider crawling up the leg of his flight suit. Gates smirked and reached down to crush the spider and then stopped suddenly. He instead, reached down and scooped up the spider in his bare hand and stared at it. The spider did not move, and only seemed to stare back at him.

The dark gray and yellow spider, once so alien with its eight black, beady eyes and eight hairy legs, now seemed so familiar. Gates pondered its resemblance to the spideresque aracteroid he had met on the summit that horrible night at the tower. Somehow, the spider was an ally now, as both he and the spider shared the same home. The spider just stared at him. Gates deposited the spider onto the ground and watched in fascination as it crawled away into the darkness to accomplish some objective that only it could know.

"Not a normal thing to see a man spend possibly his last liberty here," a voice echoed from the darkness.

"Who the hell is there?!" Gates said, not recognizing the voice at all.

Commander Drummond, the mission commander stepped into the dim light.

"Oh, it's you. I thought you were some punk Air Force sergeant about to bother me again for sitting out here," Gates said, closing the booklet. Drummond looked at the booklet, and its large orange Top Secret sticker, but said nothing about it.

"Why are you here?" Drummond said, leaning against the wall.

"I could ask you the same question Commander," Gates said coldly.

Drummond chuckled. "Me? Oh hell I've seen the inside of enough bars in my time in. One more won't make a difference."

Gates smiled but said nothing.

"You know I haven't had a chance to meet you Lieutenant," Drummond said, looking down at Gates.

"Yeah. Well that's because I've been avoiding this moment," he said standing up. "You want to know why I am here."

Drummond nodded. "I'm the mission commander, and I can't get a straight answer from Sterling or Bruin and don't think I haven't asked."

"You needed a replacement for Cochran," Gates said.

Commander Drummond smiled. "I didn't just fly Cessnas out of Pensacola, Lieutenant. There were hundreds of people competing for Cochran's position. Why are *you* here?"

Gates paused for a long time. "You ever heard of SEAL team nine?"

"I heard rumors... they were all wiped out," Drummond answered.

Gates pointed to his SEAL trident on his flight suit. “Well... one survived.”

Drummond smirked and nodded.

“So this is revenge for you?” he stated more than asked.

Gates stared at him. “I won’t lie to you Commander. I intend to get quite even and then some with those bastards, I owe it to my men. I owe it to myself.”

“I bet you do Gates. I bet you do,” Drummond said sympathetically, “Welcome to VFX-187 Lieutenant, you’ll get your chance to even the score, I guarantee you that. Just remember... this isn’t your own personal war Mr. Gates,” With that he began to walk away.

“Why are you here?” Gates shouted to Drummond.

“To win wars Mr. Gates, to win wars,” Drummond’s voice said from the darkness.

Gates was once again alone under the dim halogen lamp.

. . .

January 12th, 2034

The completed ships finally arrived. As the men were led into the underground hangar, they watched the ships being unloaded off of three Mack trucks. They were covered with simple blue tarps, not even remotely military looking Among the several other technicians in the hangar, directing the off-loading, was Doctor Richard Tieseler. Sterling walked over to him.

“I must say Richard, I am impressed!” Sterling said shaking his hand.

“Thanks General! I bet you didn’t think I could get these things built so fast,” Tieseler boasted.

"Well..." Sterling chuckled, "I'm not going to answer that."

"Man. These things are built with parts donated by Dodge, General Motors, Ford, Chevy, Allison, General Electric... the list goes on Man. All for the war effort," Tieseler smiled.

Sterling suddenly looked shocked, "You didn't tell anyone what your were building with their parts did you?"

Tieseler laughed, "Hell no Man! They think they were donating parts for humvee trailers and stuff. Boeing did parts of the hull, the engines were built by Lockheed-Martin and General Electric, the weapons built by us, with custom parts from Raytheon and TRW. Hell, these ships are children of the American industry, and none of them know what the finished project was going to be."

"Good. We can't afford to let the Enemy know we're coming," Sterling said.

Ford crawled into the cockpit of his bomber and studied the controls.

Gates stuck his head through the top hatch.

"This thing doesn't even have wings, how can we expect to do any dog fighting in this beer can," Ford complained, climbing into his position, in front of Gates.

"Come on Ford. Have a little faith," Gates said sarcastically.

"I only have one thing to say about this thing, and that is... " Ford was about to say something else demeaning when he noticed a symbol on his cockpit dash board. It was a Ford symbol from Ford motor company, having built the dash.

Ford smiled, "I'll take it."

. . .

Beijing, China
Joint NATO-AC main base of operations

January 15th, 2034

A massive shadow crept towards the city of Beijing... and to those below, the source of the shadow was a spectacular sight. The USS Kentucky seemed to hang in the air as if suspended by some unseen cables being held by God. The massive bullet-shaped sky carrier loitered high above the Chinese sovereign territory below, creating a scene not many imagined to see in their lifetimes. There were no tracers, no flak, and no surface to air missiles streaking towards the massive behemoth airship. The USS Kentucky was an invited guest over Chinese soil as the AC and NATO alliances put aside their political views and focused on their new common enemy.

Ford stood up straight and tall. Gates did so too, with a following salute. As they exited their fat CH-53D Sea Stallion helicopter onto the decks of the USS Kentucky they were greeted like movie stars by the crew on the flight deck.

Although both Ford and Gates had been aboard sister-ships of the same class as the Kentucky in the past, they were still in awe at the vastness of her flight deck. The sky carrier was truly a technical marvel.

Using non-flammable helium gas, each sky carrier displaced 49.5 million cubic feet of atmosphere within 1,038 gas cells, which were basically balloons made of a special rubber material. The cells were attached within a rigid framework of the hull made of titanium and carbon composites. Reserve cells could be inflated by extra helium contained in compressed tanks throughout the ship. The hull was covered in a combination of Kevlar and carbon fiber steel. Two internal hangars carried several wings of aircraft, and between them was a launch corridor known as the *gutter*. The gutter was under the flight deck, and contained two electro-magnetic catapults. Aircraft were literally shot out of the airship.

Near the top of the sky carrier, mounted on the sides of the hull, were two runways used only to recover aircraft and launch helicopters. Between them, two elevators led to the hangar decks and the air traffic control tower was perched at the fantail and overlooked the weather decks. In addition to the sides, front and back of the vessel, the weather deck contained a variety of defensive weapons including potent anti-aircraft laser systems, air-to-air missiles and decoy launchers. It also contained a wide array of sensors and communications antennae.

The ventral side of the sky carrier contained the bridge and four large module bays. The bays allowed the ships to be configurable. They could carry up to three containers that held fifty tanks and armored personnel carriers. They could carry thousands of bombs. Some sky carriers were outfitted with modules containing 22-inch electro-magnetic rail guns that could inexpensively bombard land targets with precision-guided munitions that could not be easily shot down.

Powering the sky carrier were two General Electric G16 lightweight nuclear reactors that in turn powered the integrated power system, which in turn provided electrical power to the airship as well as the sixteen maneuvering thrusters that moved it through the air. To move quickly, the sky carrier is equipped with eight gas-turbine engines mounted externally below the flight decks.

A far cry from the Goodyear blimp, the sky carrier was truly the king of the wild blue yonder. A sky carrier could loiter above anyone it wanted and rain fire upon foes at will. Its superior anti-missile and electronic jamming capabilities made it nearly invulnerable to attacks from the surface. And much like the seagoing naval aircraft carriers that preceded it, it had its own patrolling squadrons ready to intercept any unfriendly aircraft.

The sky carrier was the result of political genius as well as brilliant engineering. General Sterling had recognized that the Navy alone would never be able to foot the bill on either the engineering nor the construction of the gargantuan aircraft, which were roughly ten football fields long. Only with the combined budgets of the Army, Navy and some help from the Marine Corps, the sky carriers were developed under an unprecedented joint-service vision: The Navy maintained control of the ships, and they were also technically army bases as well; they could be used as staging areas for massive troop deployments and rapid invasions of the magnitude not seen since the invasion of Normandy ninety years prior.

Floating only four thousand feet above the surface, the air was unusually warm and pleasant.

"I guess they know," Ford remarked.

Gates nodded, "Here's our five minutes of fame... enjoy it."

VanDuinwyk and Tobias walked out followed by Bishop and Drummond. Tobias, the Australian, smiled upon seeing a deck crewman waving a small Australian flag.

A majority of the men and women aboard the USS Kentucky did not really know where the men were going for security reasons, but everyone knew that these men would be the spearhead of the long anticipated attack on the invaders. The word had gotten around, and soon a majority of the airship's off-duty crew was cheering to the men atop the sky carrier.

In the ready room, the three crews were briefed one last time on the mission. Details that were unknown were finally revealed by none other than General Sterling.

"Gentlemen," Sterling began, "You are it. There is no backup, and there is no retreat. Our uninvited guests have presented us with an opportunity we can't ignore."

The big screen began to show diagrams, and surveillance photographs.

"The actual gate to *The Wall* will be lowered, to allow two metal crushers with full loads of scrap in. We intend to take the shields down just as the gate opened fully. You will have to ignite your boosters just as you come within a half a mile of the gate, you should be able to squeeze through before it closes," Sterling explained.

"Should?" Ford said quietly.

"Intelligence says that this will be the last convoy of metal crushers, so this is our last chance, we can't abort the mission for any reasons." With that Sterling was finished.

. . .

In the sky carrier gutter, all three ships were the slot, their nose gear hooked into to electro-magnetic catapult. They were to be fired in succession, the Nightshade would launch first, followed by the Lakota and finally the Revenant.

"Have they ever actually launched these things with an EM catapult before?" VanDuinwyk asked the other men as they walked towards the launch corridor and their respective aircraft.

Drummond uncharacteristically chuckled, "Hell, I wouldn't be surprised if today was their first day inside a sky carrier," Gates saw it as ironic that the man lightened up the day he embarked on a virtual suicide mission. Before the men boarded their craft, they shook hands with Sterling and each other, and then Admiral Bruin.

Gates climbed into his cockpit and put on his safety harness and attached the lines to his G-suit and radio, Ford did the same. After waiting for only a few seconds, Ford withdrew a cigarette from his pocket and lit it with a Zippo lighter and began to smoke it. Gate thought of saying something, but decided against it, it may be the last cigarette the man smokes, he thought.

"In case you're wondering, I smoke one before and one after every mission. It's superstition," Ford explained, blowing a ring. Gates just nodded indifferently. He for some reason could not stop thinking about the woman with the emerald green eyes he had met when in the bio-decontamination room all those weeks ago. He kept wishing he was with her now instead of in the confines of the B-100 Revenant. Gates reached under his flight suit and retrieved his dog tags, held them in his hand, and began to pray silently.

"If you need a crucifix, I brought three... or four I think." Ford said, looking back.

Gates smiled, replacing his dog tags beneath his flight suit, "We've been through a lot together."

Ford nodded, turned around and began searching the many pockets in his flight suit. Gates imagined he was looking for one of his crucifixes... or another cigarette.

Tobias quietly went over the preflight checklist on the computer display before him.

"How many kids you have?" Drummond asked, suddenly breaking the silence.

Tobias cleared his screen and looked back over his shoulder at Drummond. "Five,"

"Five?" Drummond seemed astonished.

Tobias smiled and nodded, "Yeah, last I checked anyway. How 'bout you?" He asked in his thick Australian accent.

"None, at least, last I checked," Drummond responded, smiling.

VanDuinwyk and Bishop said nothing to each other. They just waited patiently in their cockpits. Any other time the silence would have been soothing, but in the cramped cockpit of the F-202 Lakota it seemed to expand time. Seconds became minutes. It was perhaps the hardest part of the mission...

...to hurry up and wait.

CHAPTER 12 Enemy At The Gates

January 16th, 2034
G-Day

High above the Earth, a visitor loomed. A platform larger than the state of Ohio, it was the single largest artificial satellite to ever orbit the Earth. It was studded with towers, construction cranes, antennae and several small weapons. It had four gigantic reactors buried deep in its innards, reactors that would generate enough power to light up all cities in the world for several hundred years. At this time however, it was only using one reactor. Set at the bottom of the super satellite was a very, very large dish. From it, a golden beam of light, about four hundred meters across, carrying unimaginable gigawatts in the form of raw electromagnetic energy, was projected down to the Earth and upon the top of the enormous tower.

The gigantic, orbital, unmanned power station or Rao Lok as it is called by its creators was not only responsible for powering the facility below, but also had been responsible for its construction. The station had at one point, carried preassembled modules of the tower and the main reactor deep below, as well as much of the building materials used on many of the other structures within the alien base. It also created the mist bubble that shielded it from any observations. Rao Lok meant *Intrepid Voyager* and indeed, it had been a voyager.

Operation Narcissus was one of many intricate parts of the global effort; it was certainly the most original. For the first time in human history, two space shuttles were orbiting the earth together. The Atlantis and Endeavor were currently docked with the A.C. space station Mir II.

Captain Newt Harmon waited for the doors of the cargo bay of the Atlantis to open. A veteran astronaut, he had been up on ten missions and two of them were in the last twenty days. This was to be the last convoy.

Assembled on the top of Mir II was a giant collection of triangular ultra-reflective ceramic plates, essentially forming a giant compound mirror. The mirror was held together by many aluminum cross beams and girders and spanned nearly four hundred yards.

As the shuttle cargo bay opened, Harmon, two other Americans and seven Russians began to unload the last of the triangular plates. With only tethers to move around, the work was difficult and tedious. With over twenty men and women sharing the facilities of the Endeavor, Atlantis, and Mir II, low food, water, and oxygen was always a high threat. But the work had to be done.

Russian cosmonaut Captain Ivan Padalka was in command of the Mir II station, he watched through his gold-tinted helmet visor as the final plate was put into place and bolted from behind. He and Captain Harmon looked at each other and smiled.

Once back inside the Mir II, Harmon radioed back to mission control and said with a very large grin, "Mir Mir is on the wall, Repeat. Mir Mir is on the wall." The cramped area inside Mir II was filled with cheers as the Americans and Russians celebrated the completion of the *Mir Mirror* as it was nicknamed, a full day ahead of schedule.

. . .

Forty-two miles off the coast of China were two other metal monstrosities. Both of them, war veterans. World War II ended on the deck of the USS Missouri when the Japanese signed their surrender in

1945. The other was the largest seagoing battleship in existence, the USS Wisconsin. Both ships were sisters of war. Too expensive to operate, they had both been doomed to an existence as floating museums until a terrorist group, aimed at destroying American morale attempted to destroy the USS Missouri at Pearl Harbor, Hawaii. The attack was thwarted, and all four Iowa class battleships were upgraded, recommissioned and later used to strike down terrorist camps in Malaysia the Philippians and all along the Arabian peninsula. The purpose was to send a message.

Each battleship carried four special and experimental nuclear low-cruise missiles designed specifically for travel over the desert terrain. They were accurately designated BGM-109X *Nomad*. And they would play a crucial role in *Operation Caravan*.

. . .

Captain Padalka took one final look at his space station. The history that it had made and the scientific leaps it had made for Russia and the A.C. and the legacy she had maintained. Tears formed in his eyes, and he accepted that she would now be acting not just for Russia but for the entire world. And the beautiful blaze of glory that ended her predecessor Mir I, would be outdone by her sacrifice here today. He closed the airlock door and boarded the Atlantis.

After both shuttles had begun their re-entry safely, the now unmanned Mir II began its fifteen thousand mile journey to the other side of the planet where its fate lay in wait.

. . .

Aboard the sky carrier USS Kentucky, the three proto-type aircraft sat in the gutter. Ford tried to think that he would somehow come out of this mess with the enemy dead and himself alive, but the fictitious thought kept collapsing under the weight of reality. Ford expected to die in the next hour, and had little problem with it. To die defending the world as you know it, as far as he could tell, was the best way to go.

Gates on the other hand didn't think of anything aside from how painfully tight his flight helmet seemed. Drummond and Tobias were still busy going over the pre-flight checklist over and over again, it seemed to pass the time for them. VanDuinwyk and Bishop both sat silently in the Lakota. Neither of them of them could think of anything left to say. The mission was all that lie ahead, it was as if that was all there was and will be in their life.

The radios crackled " Stand by. Twenty minutes."

. . .

The Mir II slowly came within range of the Rao Lok as it cleared the horizon. The alien super-satellite, not programmed to worry about small, outdated Earth equipment, ignored the incoming craft. As it came within a mile of the golden beam of light below the Rao Lok, its retros fired to slow it down, at the same time, it signaled to mission control that it was at the target.

. . .

The Missouri and Wisconsin floated in the ocean silently, side by side. Their massive hulls barely rocking in the great waves of the pacific. On their decks, on the starboard side of their massive superstructures, the large armored box launcher began to come alive. An aperture in the front of the box launcher swung open to reveal four missiles resting in their tubes. The missiles were completely black except for several white-stenciled markings and a cartoonized camel and Nomad with a white turban decaled on the side. Over a shipboard loud speaker, an alarm blared on the deck of the mighty USS Missouri. An eerie silence endured just before flames spewed from the rear of the box launcher as the first Nomad was released towards China, then another, and another until all four were launched. The Wisconsin began to launch the remaining four, all missiles lined up, one following the next. It truly was a caravan.

The low-cruise missiles would have to make a detour around the enemy compound so they could hit it from the opposite side, at its front gates. The Nomads would be so low to the ground, only fifty feet above in some places, they would escape even the keenest of radar.

. . .

The Mir II station received its final signals. It activated its rear attitude thrusters and rotated into position, with its mirror side facing up towards the Rao Lok. Then it thrusted itself into the beam.

As the edge of the beam hit the mirror, the light was reflected out into space. The sheer force of the high-energy photons of the beam impacting the mirror pushed Mir II downward towards Earth. To compensate, it activated its thrusters. As it reached the center of the beam's path, the entire beam was now obstructed.

. . .

The *Wall* looked threatening. Its defenses out, its weapons slowly sweeping the area in front of it with high intensity scans, to no avail. Its giant gate was lowered, as two metal crushers, full of scrap approached escorted by the usually entourage of smaller support vehicles.

The *nomads* arrived one by one and before the main gate could open fire, the first one plunged into the gate's shield. The blast wave was so bright that the flash could anyone standing within five miles to the point of spontaneous combustion. It totally engulfed and melted both crushers on the spot. Another, then another, then another followed the explosion five minutes later. But the shield was not falling.

. . .

The Rao Lok began firing lasers at Mir, but they just bounced away, reflected off of its mirror. The Mir II in retaliation, rotated its angle and reflected the beam straight back at the Rao Lok. One of its towers exploded as the beam melted nearly straight through it. The beam was suddenly terminated.

Damaged but not mortally, the Rao Lok fired more lasers at Mir II, but again they were ineffective. Being an unmanned station, the Rao Lok's computers were trusted to learn from its mistakes and rationalize solutions. It did this. The Rao Lok swung one of its construction cranes into Mir II, smashing her to bits. It then prepared to reestablish its beam.

. . .

The last Nomad missile plunged into the membranous blue force field, and with a searing flash, the shield fell and did not come back up.

The *gutterball* was a device that housed a series of light signals to communicate to the aircraft pilot when it was time to launch. It went from red to yellow, meaning they were waiting on Gates' ready signal. He snapped a salute to the *shooter*, who was the man who controlled the EM catapult from within a booth overlooking the corridor. Gates watched as the *gutterballs* ahead of him lit up to green and with a thundering roar, the FB-117 and F-202 rocketed out of the gutter.

"This is it!" Gates yelled.

"God Speed Meridian-3," Gates heard over the radio.

The *gutterball* went green seconds before he was violently thrown back into his seat as the B-100 was literally fired out of the gutter. Gates cheeks were pulled back to expose his grinding teeth as the Revenant cleared the sky carrier and headed into the glowing nuclear cloud left by the nomad cruise missiles. As suddenly as it started, the ride was over as the bomber slowed to a cruising speed of three hundred and twenty miles per hour. The computer automatically activated the shields. Although they had covered over five miles already, the metal monstrosity seemed barely closer.

"Be ready to lower shields and ignite boosters only when in range," Drummond ordered.

The enemy, wasting no time, began to raise the great metal gate.

"Two minutes!" Crackled through the headset.

The knot in Ford's stomach seemed to be moving up into his throat. He realized the gate was rising at least twice as fast as expected.

"We won't make it. It's already half up!" Bishop's voice shot through the radio.

"If we light 'em too early, they'll burn out just after we clear, and we'll be shot to pieces," Drummond said.

"It's now or never Eric. We'll never get another shot at this," Ford said, with his finger on the large red ignition button.

Drummond took only three seconds to make his decision. One to evaluate the situation, and two to ask God for forgiveness for sending six men, including himself, to their deaths. "All right. On my mark."

All pilots were sweating except Ford. He wasn't afraid; not of death, and not of failure. VanDuinwyk and Bishop both crossed themselves in silent prayer. Tobias and Drummond had already said their prayers. Gates was only afraid that he would die without taking some of *them* with him.

"Alright mate. Ready to give 'em hell," Tobias said in an Australian accent. Drummond nodded.

"GO! GO! GO!" Drummond repeated, on the third time hitting the large red button.

VanDuinwyk watched the shields around the Nightshade drop before it rocketed away at an impossibly fast speed as its central booster shot out a tremendous column of fire. "Ready or not..." Bishop said into his headset, then pressed the button. The Lakota was catapulted forward.

"...here we come." Gates replied to no one, before Ford punched the button.

Gates half expected the Revenant to fly apart, as the bomber accelerated faster than any wingless, manned, craft ever built by human hands. The main gate came at them at dizzying speeds as his craft reached a steady mach 1.25. Ford was far from terrified, but was beginning to cringe at the prospect of slamming into the wall at a velocity over the speed of sound. The gate was nearly closed.

Little did they know, they had the main gate's full attention.

As FB-117 reached the outer perimeter of the small weapons range all inner defense weapons came to life. At least forty individual small force cannon turrets were concentrating fire on the small Nightshade.

Drummond couldn't see or hear the force shells narrowly missing his vulnerable hull; all his attention was focused on the gap between the top of the gate, and the ceiling of the opening. The gap was narrowing all too fast. The interceptor shot through the defenses and into the one hundred foot gap. The gate was nearly one hundred and fifty feet thick.

Drummond's heart raced as he felt his ship rapidly decelerate. The FB-117 shot out of the gap and into a huge metal cavern inside the main gate, opening into the desert within the compound, his spent booster automatically jettisoned. The tower could clearly be seen.

The F-202 rolled sharp to the left to avoid the hail of force shells raining down on it. Slower than the Nightshade, the Lakota could barely reach mach two with its boosters at full. Bishop cleared the inner defense perimeter, and headed for the tiny gap in the gate. His heart skipped a few beats as he realized it was only sixty feet wide.

"Sentinel dead ahead! It's locked onto us!" Tobias suddenly yelled.

Drummond's face went white as he looked ahead. There in front of him, hanging up side down was a large metal turret, with missile and force-cannon pods.

"What? We're supposed to be clear. Dammit. Give me a lock..."

"They're firing!" Tobias yelled.

Drummond banked sharply to the left, just in time to miss the hail of force shells.

"Jesus! Were sitting ducks," Drummond blurted as he banked right. "Lock all weapons on that thing!"

"Locked on," Tobias reported.

With no warning, Drummond and Tobias were thrown forward, as the Nightshade stopped nearly dead in its tracks. A bluish beam was shining on them from the turret. A tractor beam.

Eric Drummond and James Tobias both knew what was going to happen.

"Fire," Drummond said flatly.

Tobias nodded. "Firing."

"Even the score Gates! Bomb the shit out of them!" Drummond shouted, closing his eyes tightly.

The Nightshade while locked in its tractor beam, launched four scorpions, and two unicorns launched from its internal weapons bay, and began firing force shells at the turret. Seconds later, the FB-117's starboard engine was torn off as several force shells tore through its unshielded hull, the tractor beam was released, sending the doomed aircraft spinning wildly to the dessert floor.

Meridian-2 cleared the gate, just in time to see the FB-117 crash and explode on the sand below, and to see the turret's fate.

As the super-sonic scorpions crashed into the turrets defensive shield its energy was drained barely enough to be disrupted. The final scorpion crashed into it, shattering it completely, leaving it exposed. Although the unicorn scatter-missile was designed to destroy light-armored vehicles spread out on the ground, it was mediocre against fixed armored structures. After attaining a certain distance from their target, they released a payload of bomblets at the turret. The first spread, tore off all weapon pods from the left side. The second spread destroyed the combination shield generator - tractor dish. The turret lost power.

"Bastards!" VanDuinwyk screamed. "Lock scorpions on that turret."

"Locked on," Bishop said emotionless.

"Fire!" VanDuinwyk yelled.

The F-202 banked off to the left, as it fired two missiles at the damaged turret. The turret's right weapons array exploded in a ball of white light as the F-202 rocketed by.

As the B-100 neared the gap, neither of the men on board was breathing, both were watching their lives flash before them as they watched the gap narrow to less then thirty feet. As they came within four hundred yards of the gap, the last of their booster engine's fuel sputtered out in a blast of blue flames, and the booster engine slid out of its cowling and rid the Revenant of its dead weight. The B-100 Revenant began to slow. As they entered the gap, they were down to 110 knots. The gap was narrowing to less then twenty feet.

"Jesus! Were going to be crushed!" Gates yelled as he noticed the top of the gate come up to meet him. Ford inhaled a large gulp of air, and held it in his lungs.

One hundred and fifty feet to go, ten feet of clearance. Gates turned white.

One hundred feet to go, six feet of clearance. Ford knuckles seemed to be carved of ivory as they gripped the cyclic and collective sticks.

Fifty feet to go two feet of clearance. Gates could see the Revenant's shadow on the floor only a few yards below.

Ford was running out of room, he knew that just a slight brush with either the floor or ceiling and the B-100 would ricochet between the two as a fireball. The air currents of the ever-narrowing channel buffeted around both men. Then, as if by a miracle, the ground dropped out from below as they cleared the gate. Gates looked in his rear monitor to see the gate seal behind them. Both Gates and Ford let out a huge sigh of relief. But it was early for celebrations.

The F-202 dodged a volley of spherical, basketball-sized force shells. They were fired from small ground turrets resting on the sand below. Sunlight filled the cockpit as they cleared the main gate and came out into the open space within the gigantic compound. Behind them hanging upside-down was the damaged, but still functional Sentinel class turret. Its exposed wiring threw sparks as it regained power.

Ford grimaced as he endured the volley of force shells from the various small turrets lining the interior of main gate. "We're approaching a non-functional Sentinel Turret," Gates reported.

Ford dove at the ground, then pulled up sharply to dodge a missile that had been launched. It exploded on the metal driveway below. As the B-100 passed beneath the turret, little did they know, it was turning around for one last fight.

The sun was beginning to disappear behind the mountains.

"We're clear!" Ford exclaimed as light from the purplish red sunset poured into the cockpit. Gates smiled only for a second before his control panel lit up. He had no time to report the shot before it crashed into rear of the ship. The Revenant lurched forward hard, sending the it into a dive to the surface. Ford fought to pull her up. "What the hell was that?" Ford yelled.

"It's the sentinel!" Gates yelled as he patched into the tail gun control. Another shot ripped into the unshielded B-100. Gates hit the shields, but nothing happened.

"No!" Was all Gates could say. The engines began to reduce thrust on their own.

Gates locked onto the turret. He depressed the missile trigger, and one unicorn missile flew at the damaged sentinel.

He saw a flash from the turret's force shell cannon. "Brake left!" Gates yelled. Ford hung a hard left, and dodged the shell and before he could comprehend his error, he had juked straight into the path of another incoming shell.

Gates looked helplessly at his monitor. "Oh God..." he mumbled..

The left wall exploded as the force shell tore through the cockpit missing Gates' head by only a foot, punched an exit through the opposite wall and exploded just outside the B-100. Smoke began to fill the cockpit.

The unicorn missile was on course. Its internal tracking system placed the turret just a few hundred feet away. As its released bomblets impacted the already damaged turret, it engulfed it in a brilliant flash of red fire. Internal explosions rocked the turret as it bled sparks and scraps of metal out of its gaping rifts like solar flares from the sun. Without warning the entire turret blew apart, sending shrapnel flying everywhere below. Now a giant fireball, the remainder of the turret fell from its cavity in the underside of the wall and punched a crater into the metal floor below.

"Ford!" Gates yelled. He heard no response. The terminal Revenant began to uncontrollably dive at the ground. "Ford!!" Gates yelled again, barely hearing his own voice over the blast of air blowing through the two holes in the fuselage. The headset built into his helmet hissed constantly.

"We have no engines!" Ford heard Gates say. "We're screwed," Gates knew it was impossible to glide a Revenant, somehow though, he knew he would survive. He had to survive!

The B-100 dove at a forty-five degree angle for the sand below. Trying desperately to pull up, Ford's vision began to blacken as the blood poured from his head.

"Activate the chameleon system Gates!" Ford strained to yell as he watched the sandy floor of the compound rush at him at a sickening speed.

Gates didn't respond, but understood. He reached for the switch, but the G-forces were holding him to his seat. He lunged at the switch, but missed and hit the landing gear override instead, "Come on!" His armed stretched out further. Almost there...

As the B-100 Revenant slammed into the dessert floor at a twenty degree angle, at over two hundred miles an hour, it first bounced ten feet back into the air, then nosed into the sand again, this time burying the landing gear. The Revenant began to slide across the parched, dry surface, its momentum carrying it at nearly ninety miles per hour through sand. Ford who had somehow remained conscious through the crash clutched his flight sticks in desperation as he saw the large sand dune he was heading at under the fading horizon light.

"Shiiiiii!" Was Ford final word before the bomber plowed into the sand dune at over 60 miles an hour. As it came to rest half buried into the sand dune, the Revenant almost seemed to disappear as the last rays of sunlight disappeared over the mountains.

"Jesus! Meridian-3 has just gone down!" VanDuinwyk yelled.

"Hold on!" Bishop yelled as he nosed the F-202 downward to avoid a stream of force shells fired from another ground based turret.

"Turn on the chameleon system!" Bishop yelled back to VanDuinwyk.

With a static hiss, the chameleon system was activated. In the darkness, with no radar contact, the Lakota became as good as invisible.

The landscape completely fell into darkness...

CHAPTER 13 Seeds of Anarchy

As he opened the door to the office, Destarus saw that Kimbett was already there, and wasn't alone. Destarus cautiously walked in and saw that Kimbett was currently being lectured by the commanding officer of the base Admiral Krewtek, who hadn't taken notice to his presence.

"What the hell do you mean? Don't worry? I'm not worried! You should be worried..."

Kimbett gave a sadistic evil grin and pointed one of his six fingers to Destarus. Krewtek spun his head around,

"You! Get in here, and close the door!" The cybernetic cyclopean creature walked into the room and as his commanding officer demanded, he pressed the red button on the wall, and the door silently slid shut.

"You wanted to see me Sir?" Destarus politely asked. "Hmmm... sounded like it Destarus..." Kimbett mumbled out.

"Shut your mouth, Kimbett! Your attitude is what caused this failure! Speak when spoken to..." Krewtek shouted.

Kimbett contorted his face in mock confusion, "But I wasn't talking to *you*!"

Krewtek bared his teeth, "Now you listen to me... we may have the same rank, but this is MY base. I am responsible for what goes on within the shield, and as long as your ship is moored here, you will follow my orders. Am I understood!?"

Kimbett said nothing, keeping only his odd grinning expression.

Krewtek calmed a bit, and began to speak again, "What happened today was absolutely unforgivable," he said pacing.

Kimbett was sitting in Krewtek's chair with his feet on Krewtek's desk. The small yellow irised dotariak was busy gnawing the calluses off of his feet. Unlike Destarus and Krewtek, Kimbett was not of the Trexian race. He was a Thalkaloid, a plant-like organism that held an uncanny resemblance to a human, in fact, except for his green color, his six fingered hands and his carbon life support unit that he wore, he could pass for a tall muscular human.

Unlike Destarus, Kimbett had a nasty temper; a temper only offset by a solid patience and self-control.

Destarus himself was not a normal Trexian; part of defunct cybernetic research program, he was mostly mechanical. His head was encapsulated in an armored helmet, his remaining vital organs encased in a heavily reinforced chassis and are kept alive by a built in life support system. His body still looked relatively Trexian with two arms and two legs and his single Trexian eye peering from behind its transparent visor in his helmet. But his speech was synthesized as he no longer possessed a jaw.

"So, you underestimated their resourcefulness?" Kimbett said flatly, while staring at Krewtek.

"They appear to have adapted our technology to their own uses," Destarus interrupted, "even as we speak the natives are building up a massive fleet outside our main line of defense. They are no doubt waiting for one of their intruding ships to take down our shields somehow."

"They obviously don't comprehend futility," Kimbett mumbled while cleaning his yellow fingernails.

Destarus shook his head, "They have had their first taste of victory against us despite our advantages. I think they will keep coming, until they are destroyed."

Kimbett shrugged.

Krewtek waved his arm, "I have no doubt that they will be hunted down and killed. But I as the commanding officer of this base have to ensure that this never happens again. Now I *ordered* you to move the MegaKore to a defending position behind the main gate. You stalled until it was too late. Remember?"

Kimbett grinned his razor sharp yellow teeth at the commander,

"Yeah, I remember... you also told me there was no way they'd penetrate the gate," his purple irises disappeared as his pupils dilated.

Krewtek gave an uglier grin then Kimbett, all twenty-four of his curved sharp bluish teeth showed. "Beside the point Admiral. I can't afford a loose cannon in my ranks. We are short on personnel, materials and time, which leaves me short on patience for subordinates like you. I've decided to relieve you of command..."

Kimbett's grin vanished, his irises contracted into black dots.

"What?! Watch yourself Krewtek, you have no authority!" Kimbett took his feet off the desk and stood up, his color darkened to a deep green. The dotariak eyeball stopped gnawing and stared at Krewtek.

"I am assigning command of the MegaKore to Captain Destarus," he said pointing at Destarus. "at least he seems to know how to follow orders."

Kimbett was furious, "It's *MY* ship..."

"Wrong Admiral!" Krewtek interrupted, "It's property of the Trexian Empire! *NOT* yours! And when you took this assignment, *YOU* became *MINE*. Don't forget that I'm the senior Admiral here, and you work for me..."

Kimbett regained his grin but his deep color remained. Destarus began to get a real bad feeling about Kimbett's reaction. The two admirals stood a mere two feet from each other.

Kimbett spoke calmly, "All right... boss... what would you have me do?"

"I want you to go down to the garden. I have reports that the plants in sections..." Krewtek searched through a pile of papers on his desk, "...12-7B to 12-9K are rejecting symbiosis. I want you to go down there and see what you can do."

"I'm not a gardener..." Kimbett said with no trace of positivity in his voice.

"I don't care!" Krewtek shouted, his face inches from Kimbett's.

Kimbett stared into Krewtek's eye and was surprised to see no trace of fear. Again, Kimbett smiled.

"You are dismissed!" Krewtek rasped.

Kimbett picked up the dotariak and set it on the desk as he got to his feet. He took a few steps back and said snidely: "Yes Sir!"

Kimbett's color had returned to a lighter green, he saluted Krewtek and walked casually for the door. As he pushed the green button on the panel he muttered something incomprehensible.

"Wait up for me, Kimbett," said Destarus. Kimbett glared at him and walked out of the office, the door closing silently behind him.

"Not a model Admiral, is he?" The Destarus said to Krewtek.

"He's gotten too arrogant," the Trexian commander started, "at first, I liked him. He was strong willed, and a deadly fighter. But his lack of respect has gotten out of hand... now I can't tolerate his insubordination any longer,"

He turned away from Destarus and stared at one of the monitors behind his desk.

"I want you to leave the MegaKore parked in the tower, so if the natives aboard that vessel make to there, they will have the unfortunate turn of luck of meeting you and your battleship. Also, I don't want you to permit Admiral Kimbett access. Do you understand? He is not to get on board at any cost! Is all that clear?"

Destarus nodded, "Yes Sir."

Krewtek slammed his arms down on his desk, "That better be clear! I don't want that arrogant psychopath in control of any deadly weapon for the duration of this mission. Make sure he doesn't get aboard," Krewtek turned to look at the door, "if he even makes it that far..." he muttered.

"Sir?" Destarus looked puzzled, his single blue eye now staring at Krewtek with suspicion. Krewtek became worried, as if surprised that he said that aloud. He turned to face Destarus.

"We both know that Kimbett is not going to stay where he is told. And the distance from the gardens to the tower is long for a Thalkaloid to walk. We understand each other?"

"Of course, Sir. Is that all?" Destarus asked.

"Yes, you may go," Krewtek said, with a long sigh.

Destarus threw both arms in the air in the Trexian salute, and exited the room.

The dotariak raised its paws, mimicking Destarus.

. . .

Destarus was walking down the hallway towards the main hangar.

He heard a creak in the grate behind him, he turned to look to see if Kimbett was following. He saw nothing, when he turned back he found that he was looking directly into Kimbett's cold violet stare.

"Where the hell did you come from?" Destarus asked in a startled tone.

"Does it matter?" Kimbett coldly responded.

"I tell you what Dest, I'll head out for the garden, fix the plants and head back to the MegaKore," he said slowly.

"It's not wise... I'm ordered not to let..." Destarus was cut off.

"I don't care what you were ordered to do!" Kimbett barked. Destarus knew that arguing with Kimbett was never beneficial.

"Remember Destarus, we have a greater purpose here..." Kimbett finished.

"I know we do, but Kimbett... you really need to calm down. We don't need any trouble from Krewtek right now," Destarus said.

"Yeah... When I get back to Trexia, I'll challenge him to the Arena. I bet he'd decline." Kimbett continued on as if Destarus hadn't said a word. Kimbett was gazing off, imagining Krewtek's head held high in the air by himself in front of ninety million soldiers at the Trexian Golgen Arena.

"If I were you I would watch your back. It sounds to me like Krewtek is going to try to get rid of you," Destarus said.

Kimbett smiled, "Get rid of me? No chance, he may be a stupid but not that stupid,"

"I mean it. He sounded like he had plans for you. All I'm telling you is to watch your back," Destarus warned.

Kimbett stopped at a small hatch leading outside and said, "I can take care of myself Captain," and walked out.

Destarus watched him, "Can you...?" he said before continuing down the hallway.

CHAPTER 14 Behind Alien Lines

Ford awoke. Not knowing if he was dead or alive. If he was dead, that would explain why he couldn't see anything, but that wouldn't explain the throbbing pain in his head.

"Where am I?" he thought to himself. "What am I doing here?"

With a cold snap of reality's fingers, Ford instantly recovered from his half dreamy state and knew where he was, knew why he was here, and didn't like either of them at all.

"Gates?" Ford loudly whispered as if not to alert anyone to his consciousness.

"Gates!?" He called again, this time with a concerned voice.

Ford heard a response.

"Ohh," was the response.

"Gates! Are you alive!?" Ford tried to turn around in his seat, but found that his shoulder harness prevented it.

"What the hell?" A voice murmured.

Ford was trying to unbuckle his harnesses, but his lap seemed to be covered with torn metal fragments, broken glass, some sticky warm substance and what smelt like hydraulic fluid.

He found the buckle, twisted the quick-release dial, and it discovered it was jammed.

"Hang in there buddy," said Ford turning his head the best he could.

Suddenly, Ford was blinded by light from behind.

"Are you all right?" the voice said.

"I'll be all right as soon as you get that damn light out of my face!" Ford said with a combination of anger and humor.

Gates poked his head along side Ford's and shined the beam down to Ford's lap.

"Oh my god!" Ford said looking down. His lap was covered in dark crimson.

"Oh, Jesus!" said Gates said with a horrified tone. "It doesn't look bad man," Gates corrected his tone of voice to a reassuring one.

"Not bad!" Ford bellowed. "Just look at my flight suit! I'm going to smell like hydraulic fluid all day!" Ford began to laugh illegitimately.

Gates, realizing the Ford was not injured, began to chuckle too, and felt like punching him a second later.

Now that he could see, Ford finally pulled out the shard of metal that was jamming the buckle, and freed himself.

Gates shined the flashlight on one of the panels on the ceiling and pushed of the buttons on it. Nothing happened.

"We seemed to have lost all power," Gates said plainly.

"See if you can get the aux. up and running, so we can use the internal lights," Offered Ford.

Gates shone the flashlight under his console at the fuse-board in the navigator's compartment where he sat, and he began to search for something. Ford began searching around inside the compartment behind his seat for a medical kit.

"All right, the reactor is still generating power..." Gates said quietly to himself. After a short time of working under his console. A monitor on the navigation console flickered on, and began spitting out system checks, and status reports.

Gates sat back in his seat and looked at the screen.

"What's the story?" Ford asked, bandaging one of the many cuts on his wrists.

"Well, we have 8.2% power from the reactor, but 7.6% of that is being used for the chameleon system." Gates began to do math in his head.

"Which means we only .6% power to play with. And that's not even enough to brew a decently hot pot of coffee with," Gates concluded.

"What is taking the remaining 91.8% of our power away?" Ford began to imagine a list of all the things that could be the cause of this. It was a big list.

"That first shot ruptured our reactor cooling system. The reactor output goes to a trickle if its not cooled." Gates looked unusually calm as he announced this blunt fact.

"What about the aux?" Ford said with a glimpse of hope.

Gates solemnly shook his head. "Gone. The power cell itself was torn out when that last shot penetrated the hull."

"So what you are saying is, essentially... " Ford paused, "is that we're totally screwed!" he said as he passed the medical kit back to Gates, who absent-mindedly set it next to him.

"Not yet," Gates unleashed one of his pearly white smiles, "I don't think they know we are still alive." He lost his smile and gave Ford a serious look.

"Come on man! As soon as dawn roles around, everybody is going to see us," Ford looked at Gates.

"Not gonna happen Buddy," Gates smiled.

"What do you mean? The chameleon system only hides us from radar, and IR detection, but we can still be seen visually" Ford announced.

"That's why we're going to hide this thing as fast as possible," Gates said.

Ford looked thoughtful for a moment and then smiled. "Hide? Hide where? Want me to start digging?"

Gates began to type, "Once we passed main gate, our radar began to record all structures in a hundred mile radius. Not far from here there are several small sheds. They are probably used for storage." Gates said calmly as he brought up the digital chart.

"Sheds huh?" Ford said with a hopeless tone. "We are not going to just hide this thing in some shed! I should have dodged that damn shell!"

"That's in the past," Gates calmly interrupted, "Phil and Dutch will have no way of taking out the sub-station without us, and this bird's not dead yet. We need to start worrying about that now."

"But this ship is a wreck! We can't even get the reactor past 10% power! To say nothing about knocking out a station that is about a thousand miles from here! Oh yeah, did I mention the enemy fighters and anti-aircraft defenses?" Ford raved.

Gates suddenly raised his hand in the air to silence Ford. Ford said nothing.

"Did you hear that?" Ford whispered.

They paused for a while, listening, and both heard the sound, something was tapping against the fuselage. "What the hell is that?" Ford whispered.

Gates didn't answer, but instead was looking wide eyed at the medical kit he had set against the wall. It was moving.

Ford turned his head and looked at Gates, and then down at the medical kit. Ford withdrew his Colt 45, took aim, and nodded at Gates. Gates inhaled slowly and then kicked away the medical kit, to see nothing behind it but the hole where the first force shell had penetrated the hull back at the main gate. Gates exhaled loudly, while Ford lowered his weapon.

Gates turned his head to look at Ford, "It must have been the wind," he said as he turned his head back to see four red eyes glaring at him through the hole.

"Jesus!" He shouted.

A clawed arm suddenly shot through and sliced the seat just as Gates leapt out of it. Then it grabbed the medical kit. Ford raised his gun and was struck in the face by a ten-pound aluminum medical kit.

Ford fell back, the gun flying from his hands into the darkness.

The claw swept back and forth desperately trying to cleave Gates to pieces, but he kept against the opposite wall, and dodged out of the way. In desperation, he grabbed a fire extinguisher that had been attached to the ceiling. The claw then shot straight at Gates' neck. The claw struck the fire extinguisher with loud metal clank. The claw then swept to the left, and then arced to the lower right, at Gates' leg, but he blocked it again. Gates could see all four of its red eyes glaring at him. The claw swept back to the left, and Gates stomped his left foot on its arm at the elbow, immobilizing it. Gates fumbled with the safety pin from the extinguisher seconds before pulling it out and squeezing the handle.

Freezing carbon dioxide gas erupted as a spray of frosty snow from the black horn of the fire extinguisher directly into the Aracteroid's face. Gates heard a screeching sound as the Aracteroid's arm pulled out from beneath his foot, and shot back through the hole.

Ford's head came back up, followed by the rest of him, gun in hand.

"Where is it?" he asked, blood trickled from the gash just below his right eye.

Gates was busy opening the top hatch, since the canopy was under two feet of sand.

"The bastard's wounded, I'm going to finish the job," The hatch swung open and Gates climbed out through it.

Gates felt his weapon twist in his hand and vibrate as he passed through the magnetic field made by the chameleon system and crawled on top of the Revenant. Gates gave the area a quick sweep, but could see no sign of the Aracteroid. He jumped down to the sand, and walked over to the hole where it had been. He couldn't even see footprints in the sand. He cautiously turned around, withdrawing his Beretta out, and began to search for the Aracteroid. Something made a noise, Gates looked up to see the Aracteroid, hanging off of the port engine.

He leapt out of the way as it dropped to the ground, and began to stagger towards him. Two of its claws covered its damaged eyes, and it seemed to have trouble seeing the human. Its only operative eye was blinking rapidly and was oozing a clear substance. Its two other claws were thrashing through the air trying to find him.

With only a second of hesitating, Gates fired two shots at the Aracteroid. Both bullets were imbedded within the tough exoskeleton, as the Aracteroid kept swinging its claws. One of its claws struck one of the B-100's exposed hydraulic lines. Hydraulic fluid sprayed out, covering the Aracteroid as it emptied out of its pressurized cylinders.

Ford, by this time, had climbed out the hatch and was now standing above the Aracteroid with his Colt 45.

"Fire!" Gates yelled.

The Aracteroid violently jerked from side to side as it was pummeled by the rain of bullets from both Gates and Ford.

After a loud barrage of bullets, the Aracteroid staggered out to the sand. Gates and Ford were both out of bullets.

"It's still alive?" Gates said, searching for the extra clip, which he didn't have with him.

Ford jumped down from the Revenant, and withdrew a pack of Marlboro cigarettes from his pocket. He then withdrew a Zippo lighter from the pack, lit it, and threw it at the Aracteroid.

The hydraulic fluid covering the Aracteroid instantly caught on fire, and the Aracteroid began to screech loudly as it fell to the ground and began to burn.

Gates and Ford watched it burn with a morbid sense of curiosity.

“I hope to God that we don’t run into anymore of them things!” Ford said with a big sigh.

Gates broke the trance, “Get this fire out before the damn plane goes up!”

Both men began to throw sand on the smoldering alien until red embers were all that remained.

“We only have one chance to get this thing hidden before the sun comes up in six hours.” Gates said, “and that’s to get it smuggled into one of the small buildings over there,” Gates gestured off in the distance.

Gates walked past Ford, taking the Marlboros from his hand and throwing them to the ground. “Those things will kill you,” he said sarcastically.

“They’ll have to wait in line,” Ford said, while reaching down and picking them up again.

He wished that was funny.

Gates walked to the rear of the B-100, and tried to push it.

“It’s no good, the landing gear is crushed, and it wouldn’t roll on the sand anyway,” Ford pointed out.

Gates stood silently in thought for a moment. And then grinned at Ford.

“I’ve got an idea,” He said.

CHAPTER 15 Undead Or Alive

The Aracteroid walked down the metal hallway. A molluskan walking the other way was pushed aside, as the Aracteroid stormed past. The hall echoed with the clacking sound of its claws on the metal grating below. Its multiple arms swung back and forth with a purpose as it walked.

It reached its destination, the door to Krewtek's office. Before it could reach its claw up to hit the button, the door slid open. The Aracteroid gasped and stepped back.

An eight-foot brownish, armored creature with four arms walked out and looked down at the Aracteroid with its three yellow cat's eyes.

"Where the hell do you think you're going Bakkaraqu?" The giant crab-like creature glared at Bakkaraqu.

Bakkaraqu's fear dematerialized, "That's Captain Bakkaraqu to you. Slave!" Bakkaraqu spit venom at the giant's feet. The giant looked down at the venom on the ground, and then raised one of its gigantic arms as if to pummel the puny Aracteroid to the ground.

"Is that you Bakkaraqu! Get in here!" A voice thundered from inside Krewtek's office. Bakkaraqu casually walked into the office and turned to smile at the giant before its view was cut off by the closing door.

"You're late," Krewtek said impatiently. Sitting behind his great metal desk, with his computer screens flashing random data behind him, Krewtek looked like a Trexian with a lot of power. He was.

Bakkaraqu didn't notice this at all, he approached the desk, stared at Krewtek with his standard disobedient stare, and said crudely: "Your Majesty."

"Knock it off! I didn't send for you so you could mock me. I actually have a job for you," Krewtek began typing on his computer console.

"A job? What kind of a job?" Bakkaraqu had not expected his visit to start like this.

Krewtek smiled deviously, "It's your kind of work. Trust me."

Bakkaraqu knew where this was leading, it's obvious that Krewtek wanted someone killed. But who?

"I'm listening," Bakkaraqu waited.

"Let us be frank. I'm aware of your work on Captain Gormo. It was a perfect accident. I want you to perform another accident on an old friend of yours."

"Who?" Bakkaraqu's eyelids partially closed over his pupils, giving him a deathly appearance.

Krewtek began typing again on his console. Within seconds, the monitors behind him flashed and then changed to show various scenes in what looked like a jungle. Lush plant life was everywhere. Blooming flowers, and fruits studded the bushes and trees.

"What the hell is this crap?" Bakkaraqu shrugged.

"Shut up and watch," Krewtek said as the view panned over to the right. Although it was dark, the full moon in the night sky barely illuminated a figure. Bakkaraqu hissed. For on the ground, surrounded by vegetation, lay Admiral Kimbett. With his bare six toed feet propped against a tree, and his hands beneath his head. Nearly naked except for his gray shorts he looked very comfortable.

"You want me to kill Kimbett?!" Bakkaraqu at first showed his enthusiasm, but then wisely held it back. "What help will I have?"

"What ever help you need, I had a tracking device planted in his clothes, you will be given a handheld locator," Krewtek explained.

"But...?" Bakkaraqu paused methodically, waiting for Krewtek to deliver the catch.

"But, it will have to look like an accident. And I won't be able to watch you, or help you in any way. You'll have to hunt him down with the tracking device alone. You'll be able to talk to me on a coded channel only." Krewtek stared at Bakkaraqu.

"And what do I get out of it?" Bakkaraqu lashed at Krewtek.

Krewtek looked at Bakkaraqu in mock confusion. "What? Is killing Kimbett not enough for you?"

Bakkaraqu spoke, "It isn't. I have some conditions of my own, you see..."

"There will be no conditions. You take the job or you do not take the job. Those are your options," Krewtek interrupted.

"I can't accept a job without payment. And my price will be a promotion to Commander again." Bakkaraqu knew that this was steep, but had to gamble.

"Never. Your lucky to have maintained Lieutenant with your dishonor in Spearax." Krewtek stated.

"Then I guess I'm out then," Bakkaraqu said coldly, trying to use what edge he had left.

Krewtek looked at Bakkaraqu the way that a cat looks at a struggling mouse trapped under its paw. "Fine. Your not my only option. It's too bad, you realize that with your knowledge of this attempt, I cannot allow..." Bakkaraqu suddenly felt the walls closing in on him.

"Wait. If you try to get rid of me, I'll make sure you'll go down with me," He said coldly.

"Sure you will. A dishonored lowlife Aracteroid Lieutenant making outrageous accusations against a respected Trexian Admiral. It will be your word against mine!" Krewtek said with a chuckle.

Bakkaraqu knew he was beat. An expert in bargaining and persuasion, Bakkaraqu had swindled his way through his career, but clearly lost this match. Krewtek clearly had all the cards.

"Now, I ask again, do you want to kill the one responsible for killing your family and defacing your name, or do you want to *die*. It's your choice." As Krewtek finished this sentence, his Molluskan bodyguard put its hand on its *hellion* multi-barreled sidearm.

Bakkaraqu briefly pondered the thought of making one more small compromise, but then thought against it. It wasn't in Krewtek's nature to negotiate.

"Looks like I'm working for you weather I like it or not," Bakkaraqu said with a surrendering tone.

Krewtek leaned over his desk, with a big grin, and put his hand on Bakkaraqu's shaved head. "I knew you would see it my way." After this he sat back in his chair.

For the second time in his life, Bakkaraqu felt powerless. The first time was it the Trexian Spearax Arena, when Kimbett nearly killed him, and to survive, he had to plead for mercy. The second was now, only this time it was Krewtek who he had to plead to.

"Now, you talked about a tracking device? And any help that I want," Bakkaraqu said with his usual coldness.

"The tracking device is hidden in the Trexian patch on his uniform, as long as he doesn't take it off, you can track him anywhere within this base. And as for help, I'll supply you with a squad of Molluskan, and twenty or so yellow Dotariak," Krewtek explained.

"No Dot. I don't like those little walking eyeballs, they give me the creeps," Bakkaraqu objected.

"The yellow Dotariak colony is loyal only to me. They'll help..."

"I don't care! I don't like them all right," Bakkaraqu spat out.

Krewtek shrugged. "Very well. No Dotariak." The yellow eyeball on Krewtek's desk stared hatefully at Bakkaraqu.

"All right. You want him dead. You have a plan or what?" Bakkaraqu asked.

Krewtek pushed a button on his desk. Seconds later another Aracteroid walked in with a bundle of rolled up papers under one of it's arms.

"Lieutenant Grakconn, meet Lieutenant Bakkaraqu," Krewtek said with a smile.

Grakconn nodded at Bakkaraqu and was mildly surprised when the fellow Aracteroid didn't nod back. Instead he stared back at Grakconn.

"Now put the charts down and leave us," Krewtek ordered. Grakconn saluted and walked out. As soon as the door shut, Bakkaraqu busted out laughing.

"What a fool," He chuckled.

"I wish we had more like him, " Krewtek said, "respectful, subordinate and polite. Unlike you."

Bakkaraqu smiled, and looked at the view screens behind Krewtek. There, peacefully, lay Kimbett. Every now and then, he would twitch a little. His chest raised and lowered as his lungs inhaled and exhaled the carbon rich atmosphere. It was all too perfect.

"You're going to die," he thought.

Krewtek grinned, he knew that he had chosen the right character for the job.

As Bakkaraqu stared at the murderer of his father, and basis of his expulsion from the Aracteroid aristocracy, he became instantly enthusiastic about his new job.

For two hours he and Krewtek would discuss the details of the assassination of Admiral Kimbett.

The dream would become reality to Bakkaraqu,

Death would find Kimbett.

CHAPTER 16 Highway Robbery

Ford furiously swept sand away from the wrecked landing gear, the light shining up and down as the miniature flashlight clenched in his teeth bobbed as he dug. Still not knowing entirely what his navigator had in mind, Ford swore as he dug. He began to wonder what the hell Gates meant to do. All he had said before disappearing was that the crumpled landing gear needed to be dug out. Ford asked no questions.

Gates suddenly bounded over the sand dune. He was no longer in his flight suit, but was now instead in his desert camouflage utilities. In the darkness, it was hard to see him.

"Ford?" He whispered.

"Yeah, what's up?" Ford got up dusting himself off.

"The closest shed is deserted. We can hide the ship in there. I also saw a large structure about eight miles northeast."

"You mean the Molluskan Barracks," Ford corrected.

Gates nodded, "So, get ready, we're going in five minutes," Gates said crouching down next to Ford, assembling a pack of supplies.

Ford was just stood there. "Going? Why the hell would you want to go the Molluskan Barracks?"

"Because, in a little under six hours, the sun will come up, and we'll been spotted by the first thing that flies over us. Then we will have no chance," Gates said while throwing Ford his pack. "I also suggest that you get out of your flight suit, and into these desert cammies the fine engineers of this ship decided to pack for us."

"Wait. What's at the Molluskan Barracks besides Molluskan," Ford said as he began to walk with Gates away from the Revenant.

"I'm looking for something to tow this ship with... or maybe some kind of sled." Gates asked.

"First off, you don't know how to drive their trucks, second off..." Ford began.

"Do you want to just wait here?" Gates interrupted, while scowling at Ford.

There was a pause.

"So you're saying that we need to rig something?" Ford asked, momentarily disappearing into the cockpit of the Revenant, the canopy of which was now excavated and open.

"Yes. And soon." We don't have much time.

Ford re-appeared with his camouflage uniform, "The gear was badly damaged," Ford said while changing.

"I'm thinking of making some kind of wagon. As long as the landing array is still there, we either have to shear it off or use it as part of our wagon," Gates said.

Gates pulled out a small box with two stubby antennae sticking out of it, Ford recognized it as a Navajo tracking device used by the Navy SEALs. The tracker began to beep quietly as Gates pointed it in the northeastern direction. "A whole lot of heat is being generated in this direction. That's the way," he said pointing.

They had walked about one hundred yards away from the B-100 when Gates heard a familiar sound. Turbine engines.

"Duck!" he said as he saw the spotlight come at them. The whine of the turbine engines hurt Ford's ears as he watched the circle of illuminated sand miss his leg by about two feet. Both Ford and Gates watched helplessly as the aerial patrol craft swept the sand with a spotlight in a zigzag pattern. Gates held his breath as its right sweep passed two yards in front of the Revenant. Ford held his breath as its left sweep passed a mere three feet behind the bomber.

Gates prayed that the pilot would not notice the trench left by the crashed B-100.

"Jesus. That was close," Ford said.

"What an understatement," Replied Gates.

. . .

The Aracteroid was getting bored. He hadn't seen anything out of the ordinary the entire two hours he had been patrolling the desert except for an unusual trench. He scratched his head with a dull gray claw while his three remaining arms held the controls to his craft. his search was almost over, and he was getting anxious to land. He was barely able to catch a glimpse of something small and metallic in the trench below, but decided that it wasn't worth investigating as the area below was the site of several construction sheds and debris. Besides, he knew he wouldn't get any special rewards for finding a wrecked human ship with two dead humans in it. Soon he would land and report that he found nothing, then some other unfortunate Aracteroid would have to search. *Such is life* he thought to himself, and continued his search.

. . .

Ford was the first to reach the crest. His jaw dropped at the striking sight: the building looked as if M.C. Escher had designed it; being both a military installation and an optical illusion. The building was about two hundred feet tall, with two towers that seemed to grow from the walls rather than the roof. Domes and spires studded the top, and large missile racks and gun turrets could be seen. In the front of the building was a large, well lit, courtyard with four obvious landing pads, resting on one of the pads was one of the flying patrol vehicles. Molluskans in and out of armor were scurrying around like ants on an anthill, also walking around was very large Molluskan in armor, and it was carrying a very large gun. Gates and Ford both recognized it as the creature they had seen in the films.

Set in the front of the building, facing the courtyard, was a very large open hangar door, with eight large multi-barreled gun ports guarding it. Inside of the hangar, Ford could make out two more flying vehicles, one of the *Troop Transport* vehicles, and at least one hundred Molluskan troopers, and about forty Aracteroids. The whole building seemed to glow with a radiance of its own.

Gates reached the crest seconds later. Unlike Ford, Gates looked at the sight with disgust.

"Damn Molluskan..." He said under his breath.

"Now how the hell do we even get close to that transport without being spotted and turned to fertilizer?" Ford said sarcastically.

Gates said nothing. He instead pointed to a smaller building that was obstructed from Ford's point of view by a sand dune. Ford moved over towards Gates to have a look. Gates squinted his eyes.

"Damn, what I wouldn't do for a pair of ordinary binoculars," Gates said.

"It looks like a repair facility, there are two Brawlers parked inside and it looks like at least five *Troop Transports*, and I only see about five Molluskan." Ford looked over at Gates who just looked at Ford in wonder.

"And in 2nd grade they said I needed glasses," Ford said with big smile.

Gates just shook his head.

The air was again filled with the whine of turbine engines. Both Gates and Ford were already lying flat against the sand. This time the craft flew directly over them. Sand whipped around Ford's head and body, he felt the heat as the exhaust from the jet engines poured down from above. When the noise died down Ford found that he was buried under an inch of sand. He got up to see Gates covered in sand like he was. Gates coughed quietly to clear the sand out of his throat.

"Lucky for us, his spotlight was off," Ford said, while trying to blow sand out of his nose.

The flying vehicle landed one of the pads in front of the Molluskan Barracks. Gates and Ford watched the canopy open and an Aracteroid scrambled out. Not more than thirty seconds after the vehicle had landed, another Aracteroid scrambled into the cockpit of the other flying craft and started it up. Gates and Ford both shook their heads in annoyance as the flying craft lifted off and came in their direction.

"Not again," Gates said with a look of disbelief.

Less than twenty seconds later, both Ford and Gates were covered in sand again.

"Let's go," Gates said while brushing sand out of his hair.

Ford didn't need any persuasion. He and Gates crawled down the slope. When they reached the bottom, they found a small forklift like vehicle to hide behind.

Now, closer to the repair facility, Gates could see four repaired Troop Transports, and one was on what looked like a hydraulic lift, and it was being repainted. Two Brawlers sat in the corners, in various stages of repair, one was on jack stands. A Molluskan trooper was patiently waiting for two Molluskan repairmen to fix his oversized *decimator* multi-barreled gun. Two Molluskan mechanics were working on one of the Brawlers. When one of them stood up, Gates expected to see a little nametag on it that said Jim or Gus, like all the grease stained car mechanics back home. Instead there was only the typical Trexian triangular symbol. *How creative.*

"It looks like we'll have to grab one of the repaired ones," Ford said while nodding at Gates.

"I don't think we have a good chance of surviving until the big guy there goes for a walk," Gates said dryly, pointing to the Molluskan soldier.

Suddenly several green lights began to flash, as a buzzer went off.

"Shit! Get down!" Gates said while dropping his head behind the forklift vehicle. Ford was down before Gates was.

"What's the hell is going on?" Gates said. Ford climbed all the way to the sand and looked, from under the forklift, at the repair facility. The interior was now bustling with at least a hundred troopers of various colored armor and weaponry. The mechanics had disappeared in the confusion.

"It looks like about a hundred Molluskan are loading into the Troop Transports, and they're leaving! Dammit!" Ford beat his hand against the sand. "They are probable scrambling because that damn Dragonfly found our bird."

Gates got down next to Ford to have a look. "I doubt it." Gates really didn't.

One by one the transports left the hangar. The last one kicking a wave of sand into the air, covering the forklift, Gates, and Ford, yet again, with a blanket of sand.

"When this is over I am going anywhere but the beach," Gates said knocking sand out of his ear.

The hangar was now deserted all except for the two inoperable Brawlers. There was no useable equipment visible to Gates or Ford.

"Dammit! Now what?" Ford looked at Gates. Gates was about to speak when they both heard the sound of a high revved engine.

"Look out!" Gates yelled as something screamed by and side swiped the forklift nearly knocking it over and crushing the both of the men. They both watched the vehicle jet forward into the hangar and brake too late to avoid hitting on of the Brawlers, knocking it off its blocks, and sending it to the floor with a crunching sound. The vehicle's engine was shut off.

MT (Molluskan Trooper) One struggled with its safety harness while telling MT-Two to wait until he gets back. MT-Two nodded idiotically. MT-One finally released the harness and told MT-Two that he would be back very soon. MT-Two nodded idiotically again. With a grunt, MT-One opened the forward right door and waddled out. MT-Two was still nodding, unintelligently.

"If I didn't know better, I'd swear he has to take a dump, *real* bad," Ford smiled, sand sticking to his teeth. The Molluskan disappeared through a doorway inside the hangar. Gates looked at the smoking tires of the six-wheeled vehicle that rested in front of him.

"I think we found our victim," Gates said to Ford pointing at the wheels, which were identical to the ones on the Molluskan Transports. Gates and Ford stealthily sprinted out to the hangar, and crawled behind the vehicle.

MT-Two really had no idea what his buddy was doing, or why he was here. He faintly remembered that when he forgets what to do, he should consult his keypad. After fiddling around in his hip-pouch, he found his keypad. It was a flat silver rectangle, with a big blue square button set in the center. Several keys lined the area below, but MT-Two had no idea what they did. In fact, he couldn't even remember how to work the keypad. After intense deliberation, he remembered.

Without real thought, the Molluskan pushed the blue button, and a computerized voice rang out in Molluskan. It said: "ORDERS AS FOLLOWS: --- LISTEN TO MT-One --- IF SEE ENEMY, SHOOT ENEMY --- IF NOT SEE ENEMY, DO NOT SHOOT --- END ORDERS," After hearing this, MT-Two quickly decided to put his keypad on the edge of the dash board. It immediately slid off and landed at his feet.

"All right, you go see if there is anyone else in there," Ford urged Gates.

"Screw you buddy. I'm not crazy or stupid. You do it," Gates shot back at Ford.

"Come on. Be a man." Ford smiled at Gates again.

Cursing Gates got to his feet and looked through the right front window to see nothing but an empty interior. "Empty," He said to himself, as he crawled back to the rear of the vehicle. Through the very window Gates had peered through, there was now MT-Two with his keypad in hand. He wondered what that noise he heard while he was getting his keypad was, but then quickly forgot about it.

"It's empty." Gates slapped Ford in the shoulder. "So how do we open this thing? There are no handles."

"I have no idea." Ford replied.

Gates closed his eyes, "Shit."

"I got it. We'll wait for that thing to come back, wait for it to open the door and kick its ass." Ford recommended.

Gates shook his head, "Yeah... I've got a nine-mill with seven bullets... did you bring your rocket launcher? We can't get through that bastard's armor Ford."

Ford rubbed his hand along the door.

"I've got it," Gates said, "we need its tires."

"And do what with them, MacGyver?" Ford asked.

"Just work with me here... now we got to get this thing off the ground..." Gates said, looking around.

"Alright Gates, I'm no expert, but I think we should do it like they did it." Ford pointed at the fallen Brawler, and at the two jacks lying in front of it. Gates smiled. He quietly crawled over to the Brawler and grabbed one of the jacks. Ford looked at the jack curiously. It was a green cylinder, with another retractable silver cylinder protruding from it. There were two arrow shaped buttons, obviously, one to go up, and the other to go down. Gates pressed the one to go down. With an audible hiss, the silver cylinder crept back into the green cylinder, as the jack collapsed.

"So simple, even us dumb Humans can use it," Gates joked as he leaned over to examine one the rear tires.

Ford put the jack under the right side of the rear axle, and pushed the button to go up.

MT-Two noticed something. The entire hangar seemed to be leaning to the left side. He happened to know that this was physically impossible. Therefore it wasn't really happening. MT-Two deposited it's keypad on the dash board again.

Gates reached over to grab a long metal L shaped bar that much resembled a tire iron, with a large Phillips-head screwdriver tip at one end. Gates put that end in the center hole of the hub, and started pushing the bar down.

"Go higher. Take some of the pressure off the tire," Gates ordered Ford. Ford pushed the up arrow again.

MT-Two noticed that the room was turning diagonal now. His keypad slid off the dash and landed between his feet. Just as MT-Two leaned down to pick it up, Gates stood up to get better leverage at the tire iron.

His muscles bulged as the locking bolt in the wheel screeched in protest. "Come on you sun of a..." The bolt crackled and came loose. The tire iron slipped from Gates hands and landed on the ground making a loud clatter. Gates knelt to the ground to pick it up as MT-Two popped his head up in confusion. It looked around, and through the back windows, but it couldn't see anything. It quickly forgot about the clatter.

MT-Two waited for a couple minutes. And suddenly, it felt as if it was falling, the whole vehicle jerked as if a rocket had hit it. He heard a terrible crash. MT-Two was thrown back into his seat, as the rear of the vehicle sank to the right. He was shaken up pretty badly but not hurt. He franticly looked around, but couldn't see anything! He was about to grab his *viper*-class medium assault gun, open the door, and shoot everything in sight, but then, miraculously, he remembered his orders: "IF NOT SEE ENEMY, DO NOT SHOOT ANYTHING!" He decided to stay put.

"I said let it down easily!" Gates scolded Ford. The vehicle now was leaning considerable to the right in the absence of two of it's rear right wheels. Ford was leaning on one of the two tires they had already taken off the right side.

"Sorry, I didn't know that damn thing would collapse so fast!" Ford said, deflecting the blame. He reached down the grab the jack.

"I'd be surprised if the entire facility didn't hear that," Gates said shaking his head in what Ford correctly guessed to be annoyance. Ford put the jack directly in the center of the rear axle and pushed the up arrow.

MT-Two began to think that maybe he was getting tired, as he now felt as if he was being pushed forward. The whole repair facility seemed to be tilting upward. MT-Two grunted and made Molluskan noises, then began to violently beat it's arms in protest. Eventually it gave up.

After removing the fourth wheel Gates reached down to push the down arrow.

"Don't bother, all that thing's weight is resting on that jack. It will collapse and make a lot more noise this time," Ford warned Gates.

"Well, we might need this thing for the B-100," Gates said.

"Just take the other one," Ford replied, pointing at the second jack lying next to the brawler. Ford tied his belt around the jack and slung it over his shoulder.

"Are those two poles over there heavy?" Gates asked, pointing to two silvery poles leaning up against the wall. Ford raced over and grabbed one.

"No. It's that light weight metal they've got," He said, while picking up the pole with one arm. Gates grabbed the other one and they left with two tires each.

Both Gates and Ford were rolling two wheels each. They began the difficult journey to the top of the crest, with their captured wheels.

. . .

MT-One walked back in the hangar, rubbing its abdominal region. As it climbed back into the vehicle, it failed to notice the incline. MT-One secured itself in its seat and looked over at MT-Two, who was staring dumbly, through the windshield, at the wall. MT-One asked MT-Two if it was ready. MT-Two just nodded idiotically.

Although MT-Two had something to tell MT-One something important, it couldn't remember what that was.

MT-One pushed his thumb against the ignition plate. The engine suddenly revved to life. MT-One didn't bother to look at the status screen that would have showed him that he was missing four rear tires. As MT-One pushed the accelerator lever forwards, the vehicle suddenly lurched back and the rear end dropped four feet and slammed against the ground, throwing both Molluskan into each other. The engine shut itself off.

MT-One looked over at MT-Two, who was continuing to stare blankly, through the windshield, at the ceiling. MT-One asked MT-Two if there is anything that he would like to share. MT-Two nodded idiotically.

. . .

Lieutenant Grakconn walked down the hallway. As he turned the corner he saw Captain Bakkaraqu walking down the hallway towards him. "Lieutenant." Grakconn greeted Bakkaraqu with a polite nod. Bakkaraqu hissed at Grakconn in return. Grakconn stopped and glared at Bakkaraqu in response to his threat.

"Don't push your luck," Bakkaraqu said while walking around Grakconn. Bakkaraqu continued to walk down the hallway, scraping his claws on the metal walls and laughing.

Grakconn's fangs dripped venom. "I want to be there when you run out of yours," he hissed to himself. He continued down the hall towards Admiral Krewtek's office.

Krewtek's door slid open, and Lieutenant Grakconn walked in.

"Ahh, Lieutenant. I've been expecting you," Krewtek said, motioning Grakconn to come inside.

When Grakconn reached the front of Krewtek's metal desk, he saluted.

"At ease," Krewtek said while opening a small canister of something that resembled tofu. Grakconn relaxed.

"Sir, may I ask what Lieutenant Bakkaraqu was in here for?" Grakconn asked politely.

"No." Krewtek said cheerfully. That ended that.

"Now, what's your report," Krewtek grinned fiendishly.

"Well Admiral, the human forces have retreated back outside of weapons range of the main gate." Grakconn began flipping through pages of a clipboard with his claws.

"Our losses?" Krewtek took a bite out of a ration biscuit.

"We lost around two hundred Molluskan, four Troop Transports, Eleven Brawlers, and thirty Aracteroid," Grakconn read off, "Most were vaporized by their nuclear weapons as their metal crushers waited outside of our gates."

Krewtek buried his face in his hands. "And their losses?"

"We destroyed two of their ships... apparently made from our captured metal crusher," Grakconn shook his head, "It was a cheap shot Sir, they can't pull that stunt again."

"No, you fool. They can replenish their losses, we cannot," Krewtek said. His head still buried in his hands.

A long silence endured.

Finally Krewtek looked up, "What else do you have?"

"Also, some Molluskan decided to play a real nasty trick on two of my MT's. But this joke wasn't funny," Grakconn said.

"Joke? Molluskan don't joke. They're too stupid to know how to play tricks," Krewtek said with a curious look.

"Well Sir, how shall I explain this in my official report? They park the vehicle in a repair hangar, one of them leaves to relieve himself, and while he's gone, the four rear tires are removed from the back of his vehicle. He gets back in, and the rear end falls off the jack that they left to hold it up," Grakconn chuckled slightly.

"I don't buy it..." Krewtek mumbled, lost in thought. "What about the invaders' wreckages?" He asked with a noticeable tone of anger.

"Ah yes Sir," Grakconn shuffled through his clipboard, oblivious to Krewtek's anger.

"We found the first wreckage, completely obliterated. What remained of two humans was inside," Grakconn said cheerfully.

"And the second wreckage?" Krewtek asked. The grip on his canister tightening.

Grakconn continued casually. "We have turned up nothing as of yet, sir, but patrols..."

Krewtek suddenly threw his canister at the Grakconn, missing him by inches, but spraying him with the tofu like stuff. Krewtek grabbed Grakconn by the throat and pulled his head just inches in front of his own. Grakconn found himself staring into Krewtek's cyclopean eye. The black slit in his yellow iris began to dilate. Grakconn began to shake violently.

"You have had four hours to find them. *ALL of them!*" Krewtek yelled.

"We searched the area twice! My Aracteroid didn't even find any debris!" Grakconn desperately trying to explain.

"Excuses don't find the humans!" Krewtek thundered as he threw Grakconn across the room, and into the door.

"If there are any survivors, and they interrupt my plans..." Krewtek projected a very evil look at his lieutenant. "...I'll kill you Grakconn... *You.*"

Grakconn got back on his feet still covered in Krewtek's tofu.

"I'll find the humans Sir!" He blurted out.

"Good. I like your attitude! Now get out there and do it!" Krewtek sat back in his seat.

Grakconn opened Krewtek's door.

"Oh, and Grakconn..." Krewtek waited for him to turn around, then pointed at the tofu covering the Aracteroid, "...if you are ever filthy in my presence again, I will have your eyes pulled out."

With that, the door shut and Grakconn was now standing alone in the hallway. His heart was pounding, and he was breathing heavily. *I cannot take any more of this* he thought to himself . Grakconn knew he would have to endure...

Failure was not an option.

CHAPTER 17 Scorched Earth

The sky was black with the exception of the moon, which shone down upon the installation like a spotlight. Had any of the beings below been looking up, they would have briefly seen the F-202 silhouetted before it.

Bishop could see a large structure below him. He recognized it instantly as the Molluskan Barracks.

VanDuinwyk sighed loudly. "No sign of any enemy activity. We're in the clear."

"Any sign of Meridian-3?" Bishop asked.

"No. I saw them go down," VanDuinwyk said gloomily.

Bishop felt his eyes water slightly, "Did you see an explosion?"

"No. But even if they did survive, they're as good as dead down there," VanDuinwyk said.

Bishop looked down at the Molluskan Barracks below, "Well, this world lost four good men today..."

"Bishop," VanDuinwyk cut him off, "You realize that we can't complete our mission without Meridian-3... without the bomber."

Bishop was quiet for a minute.

"You're right Dutch," he finally said, "So maybe we should find a new mission,"

"Are you thinking what I'm thinking?" VanDuinwyk asked.

"Yes I am," Bishop said smiling, "I'm scanning for the largest unarmed structure in the area."

VanDuinwyk brought up aerial map of the facility. "Five degrees due east, there is a power plant, four radar outposts and an airbase," Dutch said.

"Now we have a target," Bishop said coldly.

"All weapons systems fully charged. Shields operating at ninety-one percent. Locked on course," VanDuinwyk reported.

"We're comin', and we're bringin' hell with us," Bishop muttered vengefully.

The power plant was actually a temporary power station powering the central construction plant, responsible for building most of the structures within the compound. Over a thousand Molluskan and about six hundred Aracteroid occupied it. The four radar stations surrounded the vital station, but were blind to the chameleon system. Next to the power plant was a small air base, with only two landing pads and four hangars.

With no warning, a lone human ship plunged from the darkness in the black sky and swooped down over the power plant. Many Molluskan looked up and pointed, but most were just standing still, confused. Most of the Aracteroid dropped to the ground, some shouted a single word: "Down!"

The ground shook as a scorpion missile impacted the side of one of the four great generator towers in the station. Sparks began to erupt from the gaping hole. Severe internal explosions then rocked the station.

The alarms began to go off all over the air base. Two Aracteroids boarded both of their Dragonflies on the launch pads. The phantom Lakota strafed the airbase, its twenty-millimeter nose cannon, shooting the first Dragonfly to pieces, causing it to explode on the launch pad. The F-202 Lakota then continued its strafe over the second hangar, launching a unicorn scatter-missile through its thin roof which exploded inside, destroying all vehicles and equipment inside, and like a chain reaction, the two other hangars behind it also caught fire. The second Dragonfly lifted off the launch pad for only thirty seconds before being cut down by a hail of twenty-millimeter force shells. The ravaged Dragonfly fell back to its launch pad, and exploded. The last hangar was riddled with force shells as the Lakota passed over it, guns-a-blazing.

The hangar exploded into flames as the highly volatile ester-based fuel stored inside caught fire.

"Look at those little bastards run," Bishop said, picking off the individual Molluskan on the ground.

"Let's finish the job," VanDuinwyk said.

The fires inside the power plant were coming under control slowly. The radar stations were still unable to detect the closing F-202 Lakota because of its chameleon system. As the F-202 leveled out directly in front of the station and launched a single scorpion missile. The missile impacted the side of the station, and mortally wounded, the station was engulfed in a blazing inferno. All of the radar stations went totally dead, as their power was cut. Finally, an unseen human vessel destroyed all four of the powerless radar stations. The fighter made one final sweep over the airbase, destroying the remainder of ground equipment near the hangars.

With that, the Lakota flew off into the darkness from which it had come.

CHAPTER 18 Scavengers

January 17th, 2034

The sky was a murky gray color, and brightening fast.

"Come on, come on, come on!" Ford yelled at Gates as they muscled the last wheel onto the pole which they had running through the smashed landing gear struts in the rear of the Revenant. Ford held the heavy wheel in place while Gates tried to screw in the locking bolt down onto the pole.

"Think this will work?" Ford said as Gates wrestled with the tire. Gates only frowned in response.

"No... this won't work. These wheels will slide right off when we start rolling," Gates shook his head.

"Jesus! It's gonna be dawn in five minutes!" Ford raved.

"If you think of another idea, now is the time!" Gates yelled, his mind racing into a dead end as he searched for a solution. "Damn, all we need to do is bend the ends of these poles to keep the wheels from sliding off."

Ford lowered the jack, and the fuselage of the Revenant groaned as the back end put its weight on the pole and two tires.

"What are you doing?" Gates asked him.

"Here's our hammer," Ford said raising the jack above his head.

Ford began to beat the protruding ends of the pole and after several hits, the pole finally bent. Ford ran around the back of the Revenant and started on other the rear wheel.

"Shit! The sun is coming up!" Gates shouted to Ford.

Ford looked back at him, beads of sweat dribbling down his forehead. "I'm doing this as fast as I can."

"Give it to me, I got it." Gates said, taking the heavy jack from Ford and beginning to furiously beat down the end of the pole protruding from the front left tire.

The orb of the sun was mere seconds from peering over the flat horizon just as Gates finished distorting the tip the makeshift axle.

"Its done!" Gates shouted to Ford, who was already boarding the craft.

Taking the jack with him, Gates labored to crawl up the side of the Revenant and in through the top hatch. After throwing the jack into the cockpit, he quickly followed and shut the hatch behind him.

"We are screwed unless we can get there in the next sixty seconds," Gates informed.

Ford didn't remark. He was too busy trying to start the engines.

"We may not have enough thrust to push us out of this trench, and the front right landing strut is bent all to hell, expect heavy pull to the right," Gates reported.

"We're lucky if we can get out of this trench," Ford said as he added throttle and heard the engines ignite.

"Just go!" Gates shouted over the roar of the starting engines.

Sand was blown out of the engines as the Revenant plowed out of its ruts, and crawled out of the pit where it had crashed. With no suspension, the ride was sickening as the bomber sloppily bounced over the dunes. The sound of the tires grinding against the bent poles serving as axles would have been disconcerting if the engine noise hadn't drowned them out. In any case, there was nothing either man could do about it.

"Can't we go any faster?" Gates asked, watching the sun peak up from below the horizon.

"This is as much thrust as I can get with what power we have," Ford shouted back. "Besides, we'll be lucky if the wheels don't fall off right now,"

Light streamed over the horizon. As beams of light pierced the darkness beyond the main gate, the shadow formed stretched over three miles, seemingly pointing an accusing finger at the fleeing human aircraft. The B-100 careened on two wheels over a rock, and then disappeared into a pit of sand. Seconds later, it lazily pushed itself out of the pit and headed off towards the sheds.

"The sun is up! Shit! Move dammit!" Gates kicked his navigation console.

"Almost there!" Ford attempted to lie. In fact, they had only covered half the distance. The ground began to vibrate.

"What the hell is that?" Gates said bewildered. Loud thuds could be heard, they seemed to be coming from beneath the ground itself. They came once every thirty seconds. Then they became louder and more rapid.

"Who cares?" Ford said. In front of the bomber, sand was blowing everywhere. "It looks like me might have a sand storm!" he added. The sun was now over the horizon, but the bomber was bathed in dust. The thunderous underground pulses were coming only five seconds after each other. Sand spattered the B-100 like spray of an ocean against a cliff wall. Visibility was near zero.

"It's a miracle! A sand storm! Hallelujah!" Ford cheered happily.

Gates, on the other hand, didn't know how to take the omen, although it hid them from air patrols. It also hid the sheds from them.

"Do you know how close we are to the sheds?" Gates asked. Just then Ford saw a metal wall closing at him dizzily. He threw back the throttle and reversed thrust to the engines, stopping within two inches of it.

"Yep. It's directly in front of us," Ford smiled.

Gates reached his hand into the hole and found the lever. After pulling on it, the large sliding metal door slid open half way. The wind nearly took Ford off his feet, and sand stung his face as he opened the top hatch to the Revenant. He poked his head out and yelled something to Gates, then he heard it too. Turbine engines again.

A spotlight came down from the brown sand filled sky, but only trickles of light actually reached the ground. The beam swept back and forth until it rested on the shed, mere feet from Gates. It began to sweep left in his direction, but luckily stopped at the Trexian triangle symbol painted on the metal door to the shed. The beam swept back once more then trailed off into the distance, with it, disappeared the dreaded turbine whine.

Gates pulled the door open completely and Ford cautiously drove the crippled bomber into the shed, Gates quickly closed the door.

The Trexian were the gods of cheap construction. The walls were hung from the ceiling on metal studs, the ceiling itself was bolted on a steel skeleton that was supported by a single crossbeam. Eight bolts alone held the ceiling together. Although light panels hung sloppily from the ceiling, they had no power to them. The entire interior of the shed was illuminated by the eerie green glow of Gates' emergency chemical lamp. The shed was barren except for several bags of what looked like compost, two steel drums full of a non flammable blue liquid, A drum full of water, and two counter tops with several metal instruments on them that were probably used in the shed's construction. There was no sign of any recent visit by anything but Gates and Ford.

The door slid open, and sand poured in; in walked Ford. He dragged with him a 3x3 foot plate of steel.

"Look what I found in the last shed over there!" he said excitedly as he closed the door. "We can use it to patch the holes!"

Gates looked up. "Excellent. I was about to make myself some chicken soup, want some?" he said holding up a sealed MRE (Meal Ready to Eat).

"Sure. How long will it take before the computer will work?" Ford asked, catching an MRE thrown by Gates.

"The chameleon system is shut off and all remaining power is charging the batteries, I'd say..." Gates did the math in his head, "Six or seven minutes."

Gates and Ford barely spoke while they ate. Neither of them wanted to think about what was happening. Gates finally broke the spell: "Holy shit... I can't believe we are still alive."

Ford nodded but remained silent.

Gates raised his heated packet of chicken soup, "A toast! To the human spirit. May we survive to tell our grand kids about this," Ford raised his still cold packet.

The thunderous pulses abruptly stopped and the winds slowed.

"It stopped," Gates said.

After scarfing the rest of his soup, he threw the empty packet into the corner of the shed, walked over to the left counter, and looked at the wall. After pushing on it, it gave way, revealing a window. The room was basked in dusty brownish light.

"Close that thing, man. There's enough dust in here already," Ford complained, shielding his packet of soup with his palm.

"I though you liked dust, Dusty," Gates said as he put his hand out the window, "the wind stopped too."

The computer in the Revenant beeped several times. Gates closed the window, walked over and jumped into the cockpit.

Ford ran over, "Run a diagnostic..."

"Yes, yes," Gates said irritably. "what I wouldn't do for a shower right about now." The computer laboriously activated several other systems before giving control to Gates. He began the diagnostic systems check. More waiting...

. . .

Grakconn uneasily walked into Krewtek's office again.

"Hello Grakconn. It's nice to see you clean for a change," Krewtek insulted. Instead of sitting at his desk, he was standing, looking at the chart of the facility of the left wall.

"Thank you Sir," Grakconn said without an ounce of his usual cheer.

Krewtek turned and looked at Grakconn despisingly, "Why isn't our reactor running Grakconn."

"We tried starting it. But it overheated faster then we anticipated," Grakconn reported, "We'll have to try again. Sir."

"So try again!" Krewtek yelled.

"We are out of coolant Sir," Grakconn stated flatly.

"Do you know how long the Rao Lok can power this station before it runs out of power itself?!" Krewtek asked vindictively.

Grakconn started, "Yes Sir, 27.5 hours until..."

"The shields drop! And we all have to abandon this station!" Krewtek finished his sentence.

Grakconn stuttered for a moment and quickly calmed himself.

Krewtek "How long until you can recondense enough coolant to try again?" Krewtek said turning back towards the chart.

"Just under twenty four hours Sir." Grakconn said nervously.

"Hmm... that gives us just one more chance..." Krewtek turned again and began walking to his desk, "you'd better not screw this up Grakconn."

"Yes Sir," Grakconn whispered.

Krewtek sat down again. "You know Grakconn, I don't think you realize how much you have disappointed me recently. I wanted the human wreckage found, and you failed me. I gave you more time and you failed me anyway."

"Sir. A little more time, I can double the..."

"I will not allow you to waist anymore fuel, time or energy on this simple matter. I will employ my own scouts to find the wreckage."

"Sir. I don't think the craft is out in the desert, I believe they might be hiding..."

"We'll find out soon enough. If I were you, I'd pray I don't find them lying out in the open," Krewtek snapped, "Now get out of my sight."

Grakconn saluted and left the office.

The small Dot on Krewtek's desk stared at him intensely.

"What? You hungry again?" Krewtek asked, petting his only friend.

. . .

The inner gate was nothing like its counterpart, *The Wall*, but was only an unarmed wall protecting the innermost structures, mainly, the tower and its sub-station. The opening at the base wasn't sealed by a force field, rather large mechanical gates sealed the two openings.

Set at the bottom of the metal wall, just where the ground met with the metal, a door was cut out. Not a large door; it was about the size of a credit card. The small door quietly swung inward, and a green irised Dotariak casually stepped out and looked around. After a gazing at its surroundings, it reached inside the doorway and retrieved a telescope and what looked like a water pouch that was bigger than itself. It slung the water pouch and telescope over its shoulders and head out into the desert. Its mission: To locate second human wreckage.

Several other dotariak exited the opening and went their own way.

. . .

"One Trexian power cell, two liters of standard Trexian reactor coolant, and 4.2 kilograms of compressed CO^2. And a shit load of luck." As Gates read off the list, Ford wrote it down on a piece of paper he peeled off the interior of the medical kit.

"Where the hell are we going to find 4.2 kilograms of compressed carbon dioxide?" Ford asked mockingly.

"I don't know. But were going to need it if we want to use our weapons," Gates said.

"What about the fire extinguisher?" Gates suddenly thought.

"Nope," Ford said while wrestling with the window. "We used it all up, so I left back at the crash site." Gates pulled on the window, and it opened with a screech. Light bathed the interior of the shed. "Looks like the storm completely cleared up."

Gates got up and walked over to opposite window and forced it open. Now the shed was well lit. "It looks like our tracks were totally obliterated too," Gates said with a jovial tone, "Well, all we have to do is find all the stuff and fix this bird," he finished as he walked to the hole torn in the Revenant. Inside he could see the compartment where the power cell had once been, and a crumpled mass of metal still connected to its power cable. Gates wrenched it free and studied it under the light from the windows, it was the ruined coolant pump.

"And we'll need a new coolant pump," Gates added.

"So where are we supposed to get any of this stuff. Sneak into the compound and steal it?" Ford's face dropped as Gates nodded.

"Yes. That's exactly what we're going to do. But we have to move quick. If Meridian-2 is still airborne, they're going to need our help. Our Atlas bomb is undamaged, and we can still do this. We'll leave as soon as you're ready," With that Gates dropped the crushed coolant pump in Ford's hands and picked up his empty satchel. Ford was about to say something in protest, but realized that Gates was right, time was absolutely critical.

Wasting no time, Ford began to put his boots back on.

It was time to go back to work.

CHAPTER 19 Hell's Mississippi

The day was beautiful. The fiery sun burned overhead behind a thin layer of cirrus clouds. The shield above looked like the aurora borealis. Over the sand dunes two humans were running. Every now and then, the humans would stop and drop to the sand as an aerial patrol craft would fly over.

"Thank God for these desert camouflage... he didn't see us," Ford said looking back.

"I wonder why they are not using infrared?" Ford asked.

"Too much interference from hot sand," Gates explained.

They continued through the dunes for nearly an hour, digging themselves into the sand at the slight sound of engines of the patrol craft.

All at once, a new sound was heard. Ford was the first one to hear it, followed by Gates. "That sounds like running water," Gates said. Ford crawled to the crest of the dune and looked down at the sight. Gates arrived next, he also stared in awe. In front of the men was a huge rift in the surface of the Earth. A crevice about one two hundred yards in width, through the bottom of this crevice, water ran by at dizzying speeds. Gates and Ford took the opportunity to survey the area, they were at the highest point in the wasteland.

"Down there somewhere is the reactor's water intake," Gates said pointing down river. "And over there, the steam from the reactor is condensed back into liquid, cooled, and it flows around the compound and back this way."

"There's no way that reactor could consume this much water at the rate it is flowing and be able to condense it fast enough," Ford said puzzled.

"I agree, maybe they are adding water to it. Who cares," Gates said indifferently. "what we should be worrying about is how to cross it."

"If I'm not mistaken, that right there is a bridge," Ford said, squinting his eyes. Gates glanced over, and indeed saw two bridges. One large, thick, sturdy one, and one seemed to be a bunch of pipes, flimsily bound together.

Gates and Ford quickly crawled up river along the crest of the hill. They stopped when they met up with a road that connected with the bridge that led out into the desert.

"This road probably leads to the Molluskan Barracks," Ford poked his head over the crest, "Shit!" he said, "Shit! Shit! Shit!"

"What?" Gates asked as he raised his head over the crest, "Molluskan!"

Both Gates and Ford said it at the same time: "Dammit."

"It looks like six of them. Big force cannons..." Ford said as he stared intensely.

"I don't think we can get across..." Ford suddenly stopped, "wait... let's just cross the other bridge. Ford pointed to the other bridge-like structure.

Gates strained his eyes at what Ford had mistakenly called a bridge, it was actually a two foot wide collection pipes that ran from the cliff wall to two small support towers that were sticking up from the water below, and from there continued to the opposite side.

Gates laughed, "That's not a bridge. That's a death trap."

"Would you rather walk to the reactor intake and cross there?" Ford said sarcastically.

"That has to be over five hundred miles from here!" Gates quietly exclaimed.

"I know. So either we cross here or we start walkin' now," Ford said sternly.

"All right. But if you fall... I'm not jumping in to rescue your ass," Gates said shaking his head in horrified humor.

"That's why your going first," Ford stated.

None of the six Molluskan noticed the humans crawling out to the small bridge, they were two busy trying to look like they were looking for intruders. As Gates put his weight on the warm metal pipes, they creaked and groaned. He wasn't sure if these pipes could hold his weight, but with time running out, he closed his eyes and began the long crawl across the rushing water eighty feet below. Ford crawled out only two feet behind him.

Looking down, Gates saw the water rushing by at what he judged to be sixty miles an hour. He stared at it for so long, it began to seem as if the water was still, and the bridge itself was rushing by at sixty miles an hour, making his dizzy. He shook his head, and tried not to look down again.

Gates tried to think of his family, but that made things worse, finally, he decided to grit his teeth and think about what he was doing. He swore he could hear Ford humming to himself. Both men passed the first support tower. The Molluskan seemed to be staring at the road, they never once looked their way, but if they had, they probably wouldn't have noticed them anyway. *Who would ever expect an intelligent being to try this...*

Ford nearly slipped off of the pipe at one point, but silently pulled himself back up, and gave a thumbs up. Ford was no coward. Both men then reached the second support tower breathing heavily.

"Almost there!" Gates said between deep breaths. Ford said nothing but nodded instead.

The two men rested for only two or three minutes and they were crossing the final section of pipe. As Gates saw the opposite cliff approach, he felt more and more in need to get off the bridge. Twenty more feet. Ten more feet. Five more feet. Within an arms reach.

As Gates reached solid ground, he felt like kissing it, but he had had enough mouthfuls of sand. Ford landed a minute later. Neither stopped to rest, both Ford and Gates noticed the small dark shed next to the larger building. They also noticed the Molluskan troopers stalking around on the roof of the building.

"I don't see any Aracteroid. We're clear," Gates said before sprinting to the shed without thinking. Ford grunted, and he found himself running right behind Gates. Both dove into the shed at nearly the same time.

"Next time warn me before you do that!" Ford choked out.

Gates quickly surveyed the room, "Now let's have a look around here..." Gates eyes fell upon a pile of metal components.

. . .

Grakconn walked into the MegaKore's lounge. Nobody seemed to be watching. Confident that he was unobserved, he sat down at the small table with Captain Destarus.

"Glad you could make it Grakconn. No one else of your kind has the abdomen to be seen with me." Destarus greeted the Aracteroid.

"I'm taking a big risk here Destarus." Grakconn's eyes darted around nervously.

"So? I'm taking a bigger one. Now what's the word on Kimbett," Destarus said harshly.

"I don't know, I only saw him on Krewtek's view screen. Bakkaraqu was there too," Grakconn said quietly.

"Bakkaraqu..." Destarus said, disgusted. "I hate that little bastard."

"Most do," Grakconn relaxed a little, "I also have a rumor for you."

"Tell me," Destarus said.

Grakconn leaned over the table, closer to Destarus. "I hear that Captain Non Risolm is coming aboard the Battekery. And when he gets here, he's going to take command of the MegaKore."

Destarus' round pupil dilated, "That would be Krewtek's biggest mistake."

"Yeah, well he's on his way. And with Kimbett gone, there will be no one left to fill the position." Grakconn thought about what he was saying.

"Well, little has changed. I can't help Kimbett until he reaches the MegaKore. Now I'll have to keep Non Risolm from killing him before I can let him on board." Destarus closed his eye.

"What are you going to do?" Grakconn asked.

"There's nothing I can do. Kimbett is on his own," Destarus said flatly. "We'll have to work hard enough just to fend for ourselves."

"I can't stay here any longer." Grakconn got up.

"Thanks Grakconn." Destarus looked admiringly at the brave Aracteroid. Grakconn nodded politely, and scurried out.

Destarus beat the table with his fist. As he did this, another older Aracteroid walked over to Destarus.

"May I join you Captain?" It said. The aracteroid had a head of snow-white hair and looked like it had been in many battles; It was missing a leg, half an arm, and a fang. Its face was the worst; rippled with pits and scars. One eye was damaged and inoperative, one had a leather patch bolted over it, one was slightly scarred and had a monocle covering it, and the last one was peered at Destarus with a vast intelligence. The Aracteroid's abdominal symbol was the four pointed star, a holy marking.

"Hello Kailecko. Sit down please." Destarus motioned him to sit.

"So how is the life of a Captain today?" Kailecko said while sitting.

"We need to talk about the future," Destarus said simply. "And the different roads we can take..."

. . .

"The coolant pump the Revenant uses is the same one they use in their big force cannons," Gates explained as he rummaged through the pile of parts while Ford stood guard. Gates finally found something, a metal ball with two metal tubes and one plastic cord protruding from it. "Looks like the right sized standard Trexian coolant pump, Ford," Gates said enthusiastically, before putting it in his satchel.

"Good! Now maybe we can get the fuck outta' here already," Ford hissed.

"Not yet, I need to find some hoses," Gates said, still searching. "Here! Got some."

"Down!" Ford yelled spontaneously. And both him and Gates hit the dirt. Just then a trio of molluskan walked by making obscene noises to themselves, none of them noticed the two cowering humans hiding in their storage shed.

"That was close. Here, take these hoses, I'm already carrying a thirty pound coolant pump," Gates said handing them to Ford, who put them in his satchel.

"Why don't you just leave it here? Pick it up on your way back," Ford asked.

"Nah. Something tells me that on my way back, I'll be in a rush," Gates smiled, "here take the tracking device, it's set to search for X-rays... Trexian power cells radiate X-rays. When you find it, take it back to the Revenant. I'm going after some coolant and hopefully, some CO^2." Ford nodded.

Gates put out his hand and Ford grasped it and shook hard. "Good luck," Gates said.

"To us all," Ford replied.

With that, the men went their separate ways. Ford sprinted into the building next to the shed, and turned on his tracker. The readout read that he was only 103.2 meters from the closest power cell, which was northeast of his current position. He looked northeast only to see a ventilator shaft embedded in side of the adjacent building. “Oh great!” he mumbled before quietly pulling off the grate.

. . .

Diving behind metal crates and the few boulders scattered about, Gates made his way towards a very large geodesic dome. Intelligence reports had predicted that a vast garden lay inside. It was only a few miles away, and well within walking distance. After a short sprint to a kind of water tower, Gates stopped to catch his breath and look around. For the first time since he had been in the alien compound he noticed vegetation. Strange plants of unknown species grew from the otherwise lifeless sand on either side of his position.

As he bolted from the water tower to a rock, and from the rock to some alien bushes, he began to notice he was more and more alone. After only about a mile from the bridge, he was walking down a completely deserted gravel path to the garden domes. He hoped to find a way underground, and possibly find some carbon and coolant there... but it was a long shot.

One way or another, he was going to accomplish the mission.

CHAPTER 20 Greenhouse Effect

Gates slowly crept through the dark passageway leading into the dome. Upon reaching the inside he was stunned at the sight before him. He was standing in a narrow transparent corridor that led to the center of the dome where an enormous tower sprang from the ground like a stalk of corn. Through the transparent walls of the corridor, Gates saw that the interior of the dome was choked with alien plant-life, the canopy rising one hundred feet above him and the corridor he walked through. The corridor was dark, as little sunlight percolated through the dense foliage above. Gates walked very slowly towards the tower and as he neared the center of the dome, looked up in awe as he realized how high the tower actually was, and he could see a small rectangular structure perched on it. In front of him, the glass walls met up with dark gray walls of the tower, and a door stood in front of him. Strangely enough, it was already open. Inside, he found a stair well, and it only went up. After a moment of indecision, he began climbing.

After what seemed like over a hundred feet, the stairs stopped at a metal ladder, set into the wall next to it was a door. The door looked like it could withstand a heavy beating before opening, and he could see no handles, latches, buttons, or levers. The only characteristics the door had were the tiny slot just on the border, where it looked like a keycard of some type would go and a zigzagged symbol of descending stairs. Gates now faced a dilemma: Go back the way he came or look for another way into the substructure of the garden.

"Well, I'm already here. Let's have a look..." he said under his breath as he turned to the ladder. It led to a trapdoor fifteen feet up. He didn't like the idea of climbing up and opening a trapdoor, when fifty Molluskan soldiers and technicians could be up there up there waiting. But he felt it was a small risk compared to the risks he had been taking all day.

When Gates opened the trapdoor, he was nearly blinded by the sunlight. Fresh air rushed up to greet him. As he cautiously clambered out of the trapdoor, onto the large platform, he looked around.

He was alone on a large metal platform that covered the top of the circular building, the huge tower that protruded from it took up most of the platform. Directly to his left was a mechanical lift, but like the door below, it required a keycard that Gates didn't have. He could see a staircase winding around the tower above, but could see no way to scale the fifty feet of tower that lay between him and the bottom stairs. Walking around aimlessly, Gates eyes looked for something that he could use to get to the staircase. The platform was littered by several pieces of metallic junk, metal plates, and a long cable.

Gates began to formulate an idea: He grabbed the cable and tied it around a jagged piece of metal. In seconds, Gates had built himself a crude grappling hook. He began to swing the grappling hook around and around over his head. After a few swings he let it go, and sent the metal scrap sailing through the air until it fell on the steps high above him. Gates pulled on the cable, it didn't budge. The thought of climbing the cable with the 30 pound coolant pump in his satchel was enough to convince him that he should put it down somewhere, then make the climb. After removing his satchel, and placing it next to the trap door, and readied himself.

Gates had never climbed a cable before, and it was considerably harder than he had anticipated, being as how there was no traction what so ever. Little by little, he made his way to the steps above. Gates finally reached the staircase, exhausted, and he laid down to rest for a moment to regain his breath. He looked up at the tower while picking a metal sliver out of his index finger. *Damn there better be something up here that is worth it.*

. . .

The eyeball continued to drag its rubber water bag over the dune. Upon reaching the top, it raised its telescope and observed the surrounding sand. As the sun beat down through the force field, it was burning the sensitive skin of the dotariak. Although aware of its skin blistering, the dotariak wasn't concerned with its own meager life, and continued its mission.

It conducted a short survey of the sand around it, and noticed a large trench nearly fifty feet away. After a tedious journey, the eyeball reached the trench that had nearly been obliterated by the sand storms from the reactor. The eyeball dropped its water bag and telescope down on the ground, and climbed down into the trench and began to look around for any evidence of a human ship. Suddenly the eyeball fell forward and rolled in the sand, having tripped on something.

It picked itself off of the burning sand, its emerald green eye glaring at the small metal fragment sticking up out of the sand. It trotted over and began to unbury the fragment. It stopped when it uncovered several symbols it recognized. On the fragment were the words: *CAUTION: CONTENTS UNDER PRESSURE. DO NOT PUNCTURE OR INCINERATE*, *Hydraulic Fluid Here*, and *Made in the U.S.A.*

The eyeball's green iris narrowed, it knew it was close.

. . .

Gates got to his feet and began climbing the stairs. Damn, there were a lot of stairs. As Gates ascended up the stairs he began to get the impression that something was watching him from above. He stopped and looked up, but could see no cameras or any equipment aside from the platform above. He could only see twelve more flights of stairs remaining and continued his trek up the stairs again.

On the last flight of stairs, Gates paused for a moment while looking up at the opening into the platform, and then darted through.

CHAPTER 21 The Shaft

Ford nervously crawled through the cold windy shaft. The smooth metallic walls reminded him somehow of a slab in a mortuary. As he crawled on he kept looking back to make sure that nothing was following behind him. To his relief all there was the closed metal grating covering the opening to the airshaft from the outside.

Ford withdrew the Navajo tracking device from his satchel and activated it. The green LCD screen lit up, and revealed all system settings. Ford set the device to pick up X-rays.

The small LCD display flickered and then showed a circular grid with a bright green arrow pointing in a southeastern direction. On the lower left hand corner, a readout read 'XR - 425.4m'.

He exhaled a loud sigh of disappointment. 425 meters is a long way to crawl. Ford replaced his tracking device and began his long trek down the cold dark metallic shaft. Every twenty or so feet, there would be a junction or vent. When there were vents into other rooms, Ford could sometimes see Molluskan through them, endlessly chattering either to themselves or each other.

After ten long minutes of crawling Ford noticed a change. The air was breezing past him faster than before. He stopped to check his tracking device, it read 'XR - 303.9m'. Ford began to quicken his pace through the shaft. The cold breeze became a chilling wind, and he noticed that the shaft was now slanted slightly downward. His fingers began to numb and he began to shiver violently from the chilled air. After another ten minutes, Ford came across a large intersection of winding shafts that all combined into a rounded tunnel four feet in diameter. Ford crouched on one knee and peered tried to peer into some of the other shafts when his knee slipped forward, sending him into the intersection, with his feet dangling in the open circular tunnel as he held onto the smooth cold lip of the shaft. He held onto the walls for a moment before his numb hands slipped off of the slip and he slowly slid into the circular tunnel where he was caught by the tremendous wind currents.

His eyes burned, and all he could see was blackness. The wind was blowing at gale force, driving him down the tunnel, which was slanted downward at a 45-degree angle. Ford could make out a bluish glow beneath him, and looked down to see the tunnel was now rectangular again but much wider than before.

Ford's heart jumped, as he became aware of what the blue glow was; With as much strength as he could muster, Ford pushed his arms and legs against the metallic walls. His skin burned, and his knees squeaked against the walls as he slowed his decent into the glowing section of the shaft. He pushed harder and harder, and finally squeaked to a halt a mere five feet from the bluish pulsating force field.

The shaft throbbed with a sickly blue glow as the force field pulsed twice a second. The freezing air blew past him with such intensity, it pulled his cheeks away from his mouth, and was freeze burning his tongue.

Ford looked down at the force field and his mind began to try and figure out what to do while his body tried to figure out how the hell it was going to hold him here long enough to do it.

The force field was rectangular, and completely obstructed the shaft. Every half second, it would pulse out, the center bulging four inches past its corners, and then it would swing back in, sucking the air with it. Ford correctly guessed that this one-way force field was a Trexian equivalent to a ventilator turbine. And he had no desire to find out what effects it would have on his body either.

However, Ford couldn't push out forever, and before his mind could come up with a solution, his body began to give up. Ford's feet began to slowly slide towards the field. His limbs ached, and his frozen face burned, but he still managed to phrase the situation: "Oh, shit!" The tip of his boot touched the outward pulsing field.

Ripping pain shot through Ford's foot, and then both shins, then his thighs, and then his waist, chest and arms, and then his neck and before the pain from the top of Ford's head reached his brain he was already far beyond the force field. He had been catapulted into the cold darkness below. Bouncing off the walls at dizzying speeds and in unknown directions, Ford mercifully blacked out.

. . .

His eyes were sealed shut with dried mucus. Ford feebly picked the crust and painfully forced open his eyes. He felt as if a man with a sledgehammer was trying to pound his way out of his head. His clothes were wet with his own vomit, and could barely determine if he was lying on the floor of the shaft or hanging from the ceiling. Every inch of his body was on fire. His knees were bruised badly, and his elbows were rubbed raw. He had bruises all over his body and dried blood covered his hair over a nasty wound where he had slammed head first into the base of the shaft.

As Ford tried to get up, he collapsed as the shaft began to spin wildly. He began to vomit again, and again, until there was nothing left in him to throw up. He wiped the bile from his chin and tried to get up again. This time he was able to lean up against the wall.

The shaft was now a level 90 degrees, and well lit by several vents along the southern wall. The wind had died down considerably and the air was warm and dry. Checking his pockets and holster, Ford realized he carried nothing, not even his Colt 45. Ford went through a series of violent convulsions again and then relaxed. His entire system had been disrupted by the force field. Wiping more bile from his mouth, Ford crawled further along the shaft and luckily found his satchel and quickly retrieved his tracking device.

When he activated it, the LCD arrow pointed directly southeast. Ford managed a smile as he noticed the distance, 'XR - 32.2m' or 32.2 meters. Ford replaced his device and continued down the shaft. His stiff arms and legs shook as he moved as if he was a puppet, controlled by a poorly skilled master.

After passing three vents, he stopped to try his tracking device again. It read only 21.5 meters. Ford looked through the vent, at the room beyond. It was a large circular room, with several rolling carts parked side by side against the wall opposite the door, they were filled with hammers, axes, and several other mining devices. One of the overhead light panels was flickering. Ford contemplated kicking out the vent and grabbing an axe. Before he could form a plan, he heard a noise.

Ford strained his eyes to see. In the room, low, where the floor met the ground, a tiny metal door slid open. Ford was mesmerized, *What the hell?* he thought to himself. From the doorway, a small bipedal eyeball with two antennae and arms strutted out. Ford was without words. He watched the eyeball with fascination.

It strode across the floor, to the other side of the room until it reached another small door. After pressing a couple buttons, the door opened and the eyeball retrieved what looked like a tiny blow torch, and a bulky instrument that Ford did not recognize. After closing the door to the closet, the eyeball walked directly under the flickering panel and gazed up. Its blue iris contracted as it studied the panel. After a second, it pointed the bulky instrument upwards and fired a flat, black, disk at the ceiling. The disk clicked upon hitting the ceiling and stayed in place, attached to the disk was a towline. The eyeball pulled a lever on the instrument, and with a mechanical hum, it began to retract the line, pulling the eyeball off the ground, towards the flickering panel. Once it was at the ceiling, next to the panel, it opened a small hatchway next to the panel, and climbed up out of sight.

Ford continued to watch. After four minutes the light stopped flickering, and the eyeball reappeared from the hatchway, and descended back to the ground, like a spider dropping from a line of silk. Upon reaching the ground, the plate detached from the ceiling and retracted back into the bulky instrument, and then the eyeball replaced its tools and returned to the door from which it came.

Ford shook his head and chuckled a couple times in sort of a disbelief at what he had just seen. *Now I really have seen it all.* He continued down the shaft until he came to a dead end with only a single vent to the right. Beyond the vent, Ford could hear several Molluskan voices. He looked at his tracking device, it pointed directly east of his position, 18.4 meters away. It was through the vent, or not at all.

Ford peered cautiously through the vent, and could see eleven Molluskan getting dressed in what looked like bib overalls. The room was virtually barren except for two carts filled with clothing. One open doorway lead out of the room, and it was in the direction of the power cell. The Molluskan were chattering happily, but behind the Molluskan noises, Ford could make out a slight thud. He then heard it again, only louder, and then again. The molluskan quieted down. *Footsteps?* Ford thought. Then came fourth a tremendous roar from through the doorway. The molluskan began to panic. The roar came again, it seemed to form syllables that sounded like the molluskan language, only much louder. The molluskan worked to put on their overalls in a wild frenzy. As if their life depended on it. In less than a minute they had all filed out.

Ford heard the deep thuds grow fainter. He had no idea what the hell that was but it was big. He thought against kicking out the vent's grate and dropping into the room, but he knew it was the only way. Mustering all his courage, Ford kicked out the vent, and the grate fell to the ground, making a quieter racket than he had expected. He jumped out and replaced the grating. Ford's hands were shaking. He stealthily headed out the door.

Ford walked into a large hangar, and found that it was occupied with at least twenty Molluskan, all wearing overalls. He ran from the doorway and hid behind a couple of metal crates. Nothing saw him. For about a minute, Ford considered his options, and then decided to run from the crates to the side of a large tracked vehicle that looked like a tractor with a forklift scoop mounted in front. Ford again heard the thud, followed by another... and another. They grew louder as something massive approached. Ford heard the molluskan quiet down, he knew that it was in the hangar now. With intense bravery, and a touch of ignorance, Ford peeked over the hood of the tractor and saw it. His heart jumped, and he found himself once again crouched and out of sight. It was real, *real big!*

Ford again checked himself for weapons, and quickly searched his surroundings, but he had nothing. Nothing but his wits could defend him now.

David had lost his sling...
...and Goliath brought his friends.

CHAPTER 22 Boratus

Ford didn't dare to even glance at its face. Driven by curiosity only, he was only able to make out simple details: It was big, real big; It was a dark orangish brown; It had more than two arms and stood about seven feet tall... maybe closer to eight Ford sat stunned as it thundered into the center of the room. It walked slowly, but it thundered none the less. With each footstep, he felt his heart jump into his ribcage. The giant mumbled a couple syllables very loudly. It suddenly had everyone's full attention, for Ford could no longer hear any other sound. He peeked up over the hood of the vehicle where he was hiding.

He now saw the back of the giant in detail. Its body was made up of several overlapping plates, as well as spaced plates. Between the spaced plates, red skin could be seen glistening. The creature definitely had four arms. Not with hands at the ends, but with claws, which looked much like lobster claws.

Ford watched a large Molluskan walk up to the giant and hand it a metal slate. The large Molluskan carried a huge twin cylinder gatling gun, which Ford vaguely recognized from one of the videos he had seen during their briefing. He watched it walk out of the room.

Ford heard several noises behind him now, he swung around.

Behind him was a team of Molluskan, operating heavy loading equipment, moving the very crates he had been hiding behind before he luckily moved to the vehicle where he was now. He also was lucky none of them looked too closely in his direction, for he would surely have been seen cowering against one of their construction vehicles. They didn't look in his direction.

What the hell have you gotten yourself into Dusty? Ford thought as he felt fear like he had never felt before, but it didn't stop him. He inched his way around the vehicle and crawled along the ground until he reached the opposite wall and stealthily crept through the doorway. He still hadn't been seen.

Ford found himself in a small room basked in blue light. Lining one wall was a row of what looked like Xerox machines. His tracking device's directional indicator was wavering at all of them, and the X-ray power readings had jumped into the six-digit range, he had found the power cells.

Loud yelling could be heard from the hanger, the large thing sounded on the verge of exploding into a violent frenzy. Ford peeked around the corner to see it picking up one of the crates the Molluskan had to use a forklift on! He pulled his head back around the corner and rested it against the wall. *What the hell am I waiting for*, Ford thought, squeezing his eyes shut.

Not wasting any more time trying to figure out how to properly open the containers, Ford began to pry one open. It seemed to be locked, but soon gave way with a loud snap. As the lid lifted open, cold water vapor poured out with a gentle hiss, a light inside instantly came on, illuminating six power cells. Ford reached for one and tried to pull it out, it proved to be very cold, extremely heavy and took both arms. After successfully retrieving the power cell, he put it in his satchel with the rubber hoses Gates had given him earlier.

Ford's heart jumped when he heard Molluskan chattering behind him, he instantly dove behind one of the containers. A lone Molluskan walked in, and eyed the open container. Ford expected it to sound the alarm and call in its buddies, instead it simply grabbed one of the cells, replaced it with a used one, and closed the lid. Ford sighed in great relief as the yellowish creature exited the room, content with its power cell.

Ford jumped up onto one of the containers, pried off the ventilator grate in the ceiling, and hoisted himself up. As he crawled through the shaft again, Ford's stomach churned at the thought of going through another membranous force field, he wondered if it would cause his power cell to explode. He crawled for a good distance before slowing cautiously as he heard Molluskan noises, coming through an opening ahead. As he crept towards the grated opening, he felt the metal supporting him groan softly. Apparently, with the added weight of the power cell, he was too heavy, but there was no turning back now. When he reached the vent Ford saw a long rectangular room below, one wall was lined with shelves full of various weapons and armor. In front of the shelves were two Molluskan, one was covered in silvery trooper amour, and the other wore all but a helmet. They seemed to be talking. *Probably the same two idiots we stole the tires from,* Ford mused. He began to crawl onward, but the metal groaned again. Both Molluskan looked up. Ford stopped and remained perfectly still. After a small pause, the Molluskan both began talking again. Ford decided he would wait until they left before he would continue.

Ford waited almost a minute before the fully armored Molluskan left. *One down,* Ford thought. The remaining Molluskan was mindlessly searching the shelves for something. Ford felt lucky... how wrong he was.

Ford closed his eyes in disbelief when he heard the first snap. The metal below him began to sag, he heard rivets popping, metal bending and the sound of plastic splintering. "Shit," he uttered before crashing through the sheet metal and landing on the shelf.

The unfortunate Molluskan had only a fraction of a second to look up and see the bulging eyes of a human as Ford brought the entire shelf down on the Molluskan. As it fell to its back and screamed, arms flung before it, nearly three hundred pounds of armor and weapons rained on top of it. The shelf came to rest atop the pile of metal, and buried Molluskan. Ford was thrown off and hit the ground hard. He rolled several times until he rested against the opposite wall. Shaken, bruised, but still scared as hell, he dashed for the closed door. As he got close to it, he heard several footsteps. Ford backed against the wall as the door swung open and nearly hit him. Luckily, it was hinged on his side, so he was now partially concealed behind the opened door.

Four Molluskan, in and out of armor, ran in. Ford watched as they began searching through the pile. When they found their comrade, they pulled him out. Rather than hitting the alarm button and searching the rest of the room, they began laughing. Ford watched in awe of their stupidity as they stood the unfortunate Molluskan up and slapped it until it woke up. When it did, it was escorted out of the room. None of the Molluskan even bothered to look up at the giant hole in the ceiling above.

Ford felt that he was off the hook as the remaining two Molluskan began to leave. Waiting for his heart rate to diminish, he felt something, a soft distant rumble. Then it became a sound, thundering boom after thundering boom. He heard a familiar voice, the voice of the giant. All five of the Molluskan ran back into the room, and five lengthy seconds later something else was there with them.

Ford heard the unearthly voice as it seemed to scold the Molluskan. He knew that it was a mere two feet from him and only a metal door separated him from it. Although Ford was terrified, he was also deep into planning his escape. At the other end of the hallway was a door, it looked like an exit to God-knows-where. Ford looked around the door, only to again see the giant. Its back was to him, and the creature was currently yelling at one of the Molluskan, the others were nowhere to be seen. After a lengthy conversation, the giant creature threw the Molluskan through the doorway and was about to step out when it stopped.

Ford's heart nearly stopped with it. The creature looked up and noticed the hole. Ford began to break into a cold sweat for the very first time. The giant slowly turned its head and scanned the room. Ford disappeared behind the door, too frightened to peek around. Beads of sweat dripped from his brow and plopped onto his arm. Ford was keenly aware that he smelled like vomit, blood and most of all, fear. He was amazed to hear the creature stomp away.

Ford waited for thirty seconds, and heard nothing. He looked through the crack between the wall and the door at the hinges. Nothing but a hallway beyond the door. Then his vision went black. Ford instinctively blinked but when his eye opened again, he was staring through the crack at a yellow eye. Ford let out an audible scream and threw himself back as the vertical iris contracted.

Splinters of metal and plastic sprayed at Ford as the door was kicked open so hard, it swung through the wall where he had been leaning a second earlier. Simultaneously, he heard a roar that could blow a brick house down. Ford landed on his back and rolled to his feet. He was now looking face to face at Boratus. The three yellow eyes set deep in its armored head weren't friendly. There was no pause, the giant was already running straight at Ford when he began to run backwards. As the creature's feet pounded into the ground, the ground shook. And it was gaining momentum. Ford found himself jumping backwards over the pile of fallen weapons. He picked up a small gatling gun and pointed it at his predator; Ford nearly lost his thumb when the creature's claw swatted his weapon to pieces. Boratus closed on the small human, and Ford's instinct to run had to be overridden for he knew he wouldn't have made it to the other door. He instead ran backwards against the shelf with his hand reaching for the top until he felt a pole at the corner. Ford jumped into the air and put all of his weight on the corner of the filled shelf, bringing it down and spilling its contents onto the ground between him and the giant. The giant tripped and fell three feet from Ford, its outstretched arm just close enough to reach the human.

Ford suddenly felt lighter as he stumbled backwards. He noticed his satchel on the ground in front of him. Boratus's claw had grazed his chest, slicing through his camouflage uniform, satchel strap, brown T-shirt and several layers of skin. The giant began to get to its feet as Ford reached to grab his Navajo tracking device and hurled it at the giant's head. The small plastic box shattered upon impact but causing no affect.

Ford was on his feet already when he snapped up the satchel from the floor and sprinted as fast as he could to the door at the other end of the room. He didn't look back as he heard the thundering steps and heavy breathing just behind him. Ford reached the door, he threw himself at the red button. The door was open just enough for him to squeeze through before he bolted through, turned around, and punched the green button to close the door. Through the diminishing crack between the wall and door, he saw the giant coming straight at him. Just as he heard the door's internal lock click, Ford slid the massive locking bolt across the door. As he did this, he was thrown back as the door bulged out of its frame and lurched at him.

Recovering from the blow, Ford got up and looked around in terror. Lining the walls were uniforms. But there were no other doors.

"I've run myself into a fucking closet!? " Ford shouted as he kicked the wall. The center of the door bubbled out as something pounded into it from behind. Ford heard a thunderous roar from behind the disintegrating door. He looked around frantically for a way out. All he could see were uniforms. The small light panel in the ceiling did little to illuminate the closet and Ford felt as if he was in a tomb. The door began to come apart as the frame bent and groaned with each punch, and each powerful kick from the other side. Ford looked up and realized his salvation as his eyes fell upon another ventilator set high on the wall directly across from the weakening door.

Metal shards erupted from the door and sprayed into the closet. With a final metallic tearing sound, a red claw shot through the center of the door. It searched blindly until it found the locking bolt.

Ford had torn away the grating and was scrambling up when the claw wrenched the locking bolt off the door and threw it at the floor before pulling back through the hole. Ford boosted his upper body through the hole. A tremendous roar filled the tiny closet, as Ford pulled himself into the shaft yet again. The door was meant to slide into the wall, but instead it was kicked in, Boratus exploded into the closet.

With the straps of his satchel knotted and slung over his shoulder, Ford frantically pawed his way through the narrow shaft, ignoring the metallic groans of protest. He looked back to see three yellow eyes glaring at him through the opening, he was almost deafened by the roar that followed. A claw shot through and tore into the metal wall inches from his foot. Ford continued to crawl as fast as he could while Boratus disappeared from the opening.

Ford crawled down the straight tunnel a couple of feet. He came across another grating in the flooring of the shaft, as he made his way over it, he down to see another room below. It appeared to be a boiler room of some type, basked in red light, the room was mostly filled with a maze of black and silver pipes. Several pipes led into the walls bordering the room.

Steam rose from valve assemblies studding the arrays of pipe work. He heard a loud roar, followed by several heavy footsteps growing louder and louder.

Ford jumped up, smacking his head into the ceiling of the shaft as he heard a thundering racket of metal bending and snapping. Ford looked through the grate and gasped in absolute horror. Boratus had broken through the wall separating the closet from the boiler room. Ford began to hear the familiar sounds of rivets popping out and metal giving out. Without reservation, he began to bear crawl through the shaft as fast as humanly possible.

Boratus immediately looked at the exposed sheet metal shaft attached to the ceiling by several fixed U-shaped bolts. He followed down a couple feet until he was under a section that was sagging and thrust his claw deep into the area just before the grating.

Ford heard metal punctured and he turned his head back to see a red claw stabbing through the flooring where he had just been twenty seconds ago. This was followed by a roar.

A water heater that was blocking Boratus's way was kicked apart as Boratus destroyed everything in his path to reach Ford. After jumping through a wall of pipe work, Boratus threw his claw up into the shaft.

This time, the claw was only a foot away from him, it was gaining. Ford looked ahead, a vertical fork in the shaft could be seen. Ford screamed and tapped an energy resource he didn't know he had as he bear-crawled through the shaft.

A large cylinder of pipe work stood between Boratus and the human. After a swing from both right arms, they stood no more. Scalding hot water spewed all over the ground and Boratus, but he didn't care, he wanted the human!

Boratus was a typical Maquiasan, put simply: it was fun to kill. A violent natured race, the Maquiasan had historically enjoyed hunting and killing prey. Ford was Boratus's prey. It was unacceptable for the prey to escape.

The red claw shot up from the floor of the shaft just to the side of Ford's boot. When the claw withdrew, red steam from the water heaters poured up from the hole left and red light filled the interior of the shaft. Ford felt as if Satan was trying to pull him into hell. He was only five feet from the fork. After hearing a crash below, another red claw shot up between his legs. Ford screamed and scrambled away before it could crush him.

The next stab would kill him.

Boratus withdrew his claw and punched the rack of water purifiers into metal shrapnel and finally stopped before the wall at the end of the room. He took several steps back and charged the wall.

Ford was at the fork, luckily for him, it went straight up. Suddenly, the ground shook as Ford heard, by far, the loudest crash yet. He nearly had a heart attack when the flooring collapsed behind him and the head of his predator rose into the shaft. Ford stared at it. It stared right back at Ford and growled. Ford, with all fear turned to rage kicked it in the head. He expected it to fall back, on the contrary, the creature was unaffected. It instead let out a deafening howl and began thrashing at the walls around Ford.

Ford pulled himself up into the vertical shaft. He heard the metal behind him screech and rip as he climbed. Just as his foot left the flooring of the horizontal shaft, the entire horizontal shaft fell away. Ford didn't look back as he heard the creature bellow below him. As he reached the horizontal forks at the top, he looked down at Boratus.

"Fuck you!" Ford yelled and spit at the creature below before disappearing into the ducts. Boratus stared up at the vacant shaft, almost as if in a trance. The hiss of water boiling and the giant's heavy breather were all could be heard. Boratus threw back his head and let out a roar louder than any other creature ever to walk the Earth, and then fell silent.

Boratus was embarrassed and disappointed. He seemed to weep a bit at the idea that a human had escaped him. He then chuckled to himself in genuine laughter...

...Indeed he had finally found himself a worthy prey: *Humans*.

CHAPTER 23 The Weed

Gates slowly raised his head from the stairwell below and cautiously peered inside the dark room. The enclosed platform was more of a rectangular tube than a room. Both ends were open to the outside, and a fresh breeze was continuously wafting through. Some moss grew on the walls, and two thick vines hung over one of the openings and were swaying in the breeze. Keeping alert, he climbed through the hatchway onto the platform. A bank of computers hummed against the wall, and several control panels lined the walls. Most of the equipment had droplets of condensed water forming on their surfaces, occasionally dripping to the floor and giving off the only other sound on the platform aside from the whispering breeze. The silence was deafening, and the hair stood up on the back of Gates' neck.

Although he was alone, Gates felt a presence; he could feel something was listening to his every move. As he walked closer to one of the edges, he heard a noise. Gates swung around with his Beretta out. The two vines that were hanging over the opening at the other end were moving irregularly. With a sudden sense of sick realization, Gates realized that they were legs, green with six-towed feet attached. With a graceful leap, the two legs landed on the metallic platform with a loud hammering noise. Gates was terrified at what he saw before him. The feet were attached to a green humanoid figure. It turned around and stared at Gates with a set of dark eyes that seemed to burn into Gates.

The creature began to speak in a deep voice. It said things that were incomprehensible to Gates at first. He recognized some of it as Russian, Italian, Japanese, Chinese and many more.

"What the fuck are you?" Gates finally uttered when the shock began to wear off.

"Ahh, Yankee English! I should have known," It said with a perfect American accent.

Gates nearly staggered backwards at hearing this. The creature smiled with a mouth full of razor sharp yellow teeth.

It was at least six foot tall, with arms and legs just like a human, except for that it had six fingers and toes. It also had large pores on its shoulders, and in between its knuckles. It was wearing some kind of mechanical apparatus from its shoulder that stretched across its chest and rested on his opposite hip. It was a black leathery belt with twenty-four silver cylinders hooked into it. Gates didn't know what it was. The only clothes it wore were gray shorts with pockets and the *Eye of Kroyce* badge.

"Who are you?" Gates boldly asked, his Beretta shaking slightly.

The creature grinned, "I am Admiral Kimbett,"

"Now, human tell me, who are you," Kimbett added.

Gates said nothing.

"How did you get in here anyway? Did they finally shoot your ship down like the other two?" Kimbett stared at Gates with a look of wonder.

Gates remained silent. Then Kimbett smiled deviously. "I see, your from one of the crashed ships. The big one... the bomber."

Gates shook slightly at realizing the intelligence of this being. However, he had an advantage; the enemy didn't know he and Ford were alive. And he now knew that Meridian-2 was still in the air. This would have been a joyous moment, except for the fact that he was now talking to some green thing that calls itself Kimbett.

"Well human, it looks like your extraordinary luck has finally run out," the admiral stated.

Gates smiled, "I don't know what the hell your supposed to be but you look like a fuckin' weed to me."

Grinning, Kimbett nodded slowly. Gates stomach began to turn.

"So tell me human, what do you think of the Trexian?" He stared at Gates once again.

Gates' Beretta trembled slightly. "The what?"

"Trexian! The idiots you've been fighting!" Kimbett yelled.

Gates nodded, "The yellow morons..."

"No! Not the Armacksis," Kimbett corrected, "not your *Molluskan*,"

Gates wondered how this alien could possibly know that they called the yellow stupid creatures *Molluskan*.

"And not the *Aracteroid* either... I'm talking about the masters... the Trexian. You mean you don't even know who your at war with? Pathetic..." Kimbett cleaned his long yellow fingernails.

"To answer your question..." Gates started, "we're going to bring this whole place into the sand."

Kimbett chuckled slightly while smiling that evil grin of his. "Then what?"

Gates gave a puzzled look. "What do you mean then what?!"

"I mean what are you going to do when they actually send an invasion force in? " Kimbett laughed.

Gate's eyes widened, but he said nothing.

"See, you think *this* is an invasion force," Kimbett shook his head, "This is a construction fleet. Human... an inadequately supplied construction fleet at that."

Gates continued to hold the weapon on the alien, but refused to show how unsettled he was at the news. The idea that the human race was facing an interstellar construction firm was unacceptable to him, although it seemed to explain many enigmas.

"I have an idea!" Kimbett suddenly gestured with his hands, sending a jolt through Gates and causing his tiring arm to shudder.

"Why don't we play a little Q and A. You first..." Kimbett said pointing at him.

Gates lowered his Beretta, but kept it close.

"What do you want with Earth?" Gates asked immediately.

Kimbett chuckled, "They don't want war with you," he started, "they have more war than they can handle right now. But they need your real estate because they believe if they can plant a star base here, they can turn the tides of the war. My turn..."

"Who are they fighting?" Gates demanded.

"I said it was my turn," Kimbett glared.

Gates was silent.

"I'm sure you've killed a lot of your own kind... about how many puncture wounds can a human sustain before dying?" Kimbett asked nonchalantly.

Gates shivered in disgust, "What?"

"Alright, an easier question," Kimbett replied, "If you had one bullet in that gun of yours, which organ would you use it on? The brain? Heart?"

Gates scowled, "The heart... probably, you sick bastard, my turn."

"Why not the head?" Kimbett asked.

"I said it was my turn." Gates replied, evoking a grin from Kimbett.

"How can we stop them? The Trexian?" Gates asked, as beads of sweat began to roll down his forehead for the first time since his odd conversation began.

Disturbingly, Kimbett laughed out loud, "You have no chance... well, I suppose your friends who continue to raze some of the buildings around here may have some fraction of a chance. But you... you had a chance until I saw you sneaking up the stairs." Kimbett's eyes seemed to glow with a violet hue.

Gates gulped, as any possibility of a peaceful conclusion to this conversation vaporized.

Kimbett folded his arms, "This conversation is beginning to bore me, one more round,"

"Why did you come here? To Shanghai, to Grantex. This isn't your country. You're American..." Kimbett asked.

Gates gulped again, "This land is not mine, and its not yours either. You can't just take what you want."

Kimbett cracked his knuckles, "You may live in a dreamland here on Earth, human. But outside this system, that is *exactly* how things work. We're just pawns."

"You?" Gates asked.

"All of us!" Kimbett shouted, "And that counts as your third question."

"Where do the Trexian come from?" Gates asked, ignoring him.

Kimbett just smiled, "My question,"

"Where?!" Gates demanded.

"The sky." Kimbett said sarcastically, "So, what is the climate like in your America, that's my last one."

"Where do their enemies come from? Would they help us?" Gates asked, ignoring him again.

Kimbett sighed. "Ok..." he said resentfully, "Well let's just say there are forces out there much worse than the Trexian. There is evil that you could have never known lurking in that sky you look upon at night. They're not your friends... they are no ones friends. Death is out there, and is on its way here."

There was a five second pause.

"But you need not worry about them... you have more prominent issues." Kimbett said, while depressing a gray button on the black strap across his chest. With a loud hiss, all twenty-four silver cylinders detached themselves from implants imbedded in his chest and abdominal region.

Gates raised his Beretta again, "Why do you fight for them?"

Kimbett glared at Gates. "I am the last of my race human." Kimbett's eyes burning with rage, "My species paid the same price yours will if you somehow succeed in driving them out. You'd be better off leaving them alone... if you're lucky, humans will continue on as a subordinate race like the Armacksis."

Kimbett removed his life support system and dropped it to the floor with a loud clatter.

Gates grit his teeth, "But why. Why not fight along our side?"

Kimbett laughed, "Not that this will help you, but I don't plan to be a slave forever human. It's a shame your race is so weak, or I'd accept your offer."

Gates now realized, Kimbett's eyes were rapidly dilating.

"Time's up..." Kimbett lost all expression, "you know what comes next..."

Gates readied his weapon.

"You fear me don't you human," Kimbett's eyes suddenly dilated completely revealing only massive black pupils, his violet irises could no longer be seen, and his skin had turned deep green.

Gates didn't answer. But the answer was yes.

"When you fear, you will pray to God for salvation. Who is to say I am not God." Kimbett bared all his teeth at Gates as he said this.

There was a silence lasting for only a second. In that second Gates realized that Kimbett was no longer a sentient, intelligent being, he was a wild animal ready to pounce.

Kimbett's smile disappeared for the last time.

CHAPTER 24 Herbicide

With tremendous speed, Kimbett threw his left arm up and arced it down. A bolt of fear struck Gates and he instinctively dropped and rolled out of the way just as several hundred tiny thorns pierced the metallic wall just behind where he had been standing. Gates came up on one knee and aimed his weapon at the green blur coming straight at him. Kimbett had broken into a sprint, thirty-five feet, thirty feet, twenty-five feet and closing, Gates squeezed the trigger.

A small yellow oozing hole opened up just above where his heart should have been. Ten feet... Gates shot four more times into Kimbett at near point blank range. Holes opened up all over Kimbett's chest and abdominal region, but his speed unaffected.

Kimbett reached for Gates. Something swatted the gun out of Gates hands. Gates was barely able to see a tentacle retract into Kimbett's left palm. It was too fast too make out any great detail, but it seemed to be brown, and covered with thorns. Then five feet away Kimbett reached for gates with his right hand. He stood up and prepared for hand-to-hand combat.

Gates had barely been able to see Kimbett project a tentacle from the duct on his right palm before it was violently wrapping around his neck. Gates tried to pry then tentacle off but it just wrapped around tighter, he could feel tiny thorns digging in. Kimbett had stopped running upon capturing his prey and was now standing only four feet away, he began to retract the tentacle, pulling Gates towards him. Gates was laying like a rag doll, with both hand pawing at the tentacle and his feet stuttering on the ground feebly trying to slow his progress towards Kimbett, but to no avail. Kimbett retracted his tentacle all the way up to Gates' neck and now had his right hand griped at Gates' throat. He pulled Gates' face towards his own.

Gates and Kimbett now were looking face-to-face, their visages mere inches apart. Gates felt Kimbett's warm breath as he stared, wild-eyed into Kimbett's eyes, which seemed to be windows into hell itself. Kimbett's razor toothed jaw was clamped shut, but his lips were open exposing sixteen razor sharp yellow teeth. Gates was beginning to asphyxiate.

"You expect to win this war? You can't even begin to compete with what's waiting." Kimbett was about to say something else when Gates suddenly spit in his face. "Kiss my ass, you fuckin' weed!" Gates rasped.

Gates unexpectedly head butted Kimbett in the face. Kimbett's blank expression turned into that of severe rage as yellow liquid dribbled from his nose. Kimbett grasped Gates by the throat by both hands and picked up off the floor. Kimbett began to roar as he slammed Gates up against the left wall, and then slammed him up against the right, and then the left again. Kimbett walked over to the edge of the platform and grabbed Gates' hip and lifted him over his head. Gates looked down to see over one thousand feet to the foliage below. *Holy shit!*

Gates brought up his knee and crashed it into Kimbett's face, Kimbett fell backwards with Gates still over his head. Upon landing Gates rolled away from Kimbett but was suddenly jerked back by the tentacle that was still harnessed around his neck. Without thinking, Gates grabbed the tentacle, put it in his mouth and bit down as hard as he could. He felt the tiny thorns pierce his gums and hands as Kimbett let out terrible scream of pain. Gates hurled himself back as Kimbett released the tentacle.

The human scrambled to his feet and got into an Aikido stance. Kimbett was just rising from the ground when Gates surprised him with a flying jump kick, planting his boot square into Kimbett's chest, sending both to the ground. Gates felt like he had hit a tree, but knew it would have broken a few ribs in a human.

Before Gates could get back to his feet, Kimbett picked him up by his arm and kneed him in the chest, then punched him in the stomach. Gates thought for a second and then took two fingers and plunged them into one of the gunshot wounds in Kimbett's chest. Screaming, Kimbett grabbed Gates by the hair and drew back his fist. The human tried to duck but Kimbett's grip was too strong. Kimbett's fist smashed into his jaw and nearly knocked him unconscious.

Gates was seeing stars; he saw the floor then the ceiling, then the floor again, then finally the ceiling, before he snapped out of it. Kimbett's hit had sent him rolling to the other side of the platform. The human was running on adrenaline alone as he looked up to see Kimbett's left palm open up to expose another tentacle. It sought his throat yet again.

Gates reached out his forearm to block his neck, and the tentacle wrapped itself around his forearm. He was dragged to his knees as Kimbett was retracting the tentacle, "Come here!" Kimbett's foot came into his stomach. Gates went to bite the tentacle and was rewarded with a kick to the face, spraying crimson onto the wall.

With a fury of movements, Gates reached into his boot, withdrew a large ka-bar fighting knife, and with a cleaving motion sliced off one third of the exposed tentacle. The remainder around his arm squeezed and went limp, falling to the ground twitching while Kimbett screamed in pain and anger, as Gates scampered back.

"Now you die! " Kimbett leapt at Gates, landing on top of him and pounded him with his fists. The knife flew from Gates' hand and went spinning across the platform to the other side. Gates kicked and kneed Kimbett until the admiral rolled off. Gates reached back to feel something: it was Kimbett's life support.

He swung it down over Kimbett's head, causing Kimbett to spring to his feet, holding his head.

Gates didn't waste any time; he swung the twenty-pound chain of cylinders around and hit Kimbett in the side sending him into the wall. Kimbett was backing up, when he raised his arm is if to throw more thorns, when Gates brought the life support up into Kimbett's abdomen, and then brought it down into Kimbett's head again, sending a mist of sweat and alien blood into the air as the admiral fell to the metal floor.

Gates wound up to hit him again, but this time Kimbett caught it. Releasing the chain of cylinders, Gates threw himself into Kimbett and savagely battered the alien as he got to his feet. They were both standing at the edge of the platform thousand twenty-three feet above ground.

Gates was again seized by the throat by Kimbett, and thrown down to the ground by Kimbett. As he frantically looked around, Gates saw his Beretta, but as he went for it, Kimbett's foot slammed down upon his hand. Gates didn't feel the pain, but knew from the crackling feeling that his hand was broken.

It seemed like eternity before anything happened.

"Well human, I have to say I was wrong about you," Kimbett said while breathing hard.

"You're not weak. If only I had known... this might have been the time." Kimbett began to regain his lighter green color, and his irises contracted again, showing violet with black pupils.

"Please accept my apologies." Kimbett said, kicking the Beretta away from Gates' smashed hand.

Gates was violently flipped over, and found a foot planted in his chest, pinning him to the floor. Kimbett reached his arm up, made a fist, and four yellowish spines grew from the pores in between the knuckles. Gates could feel that his life was about to end, but for an instant his right hand brushed against something. *The knife!*

Gates grabbed the blade and thrust into Kimbett's abdomen with all the power he didn't realize he had. The fist flew at Gates, and miraculously missed his head and smashed into the metal floor as the knife was buried up the hilt. Kimbett, shocked, stood up. As he did, Gates grasped the leg that pinned him to the floor and twisted it, and with both feet, kicked Kimbett off balance. Kimbett took a step back and was too late to realize that he was over the edge of the platform. Without a sound, he disappeared over the side.

Gates heard the sound of a bullwhip followed by a metal *thunk*. Gates crawled to the ledge and looked over the end. Below the platform, a single tentacle from his right hand suspended Admiral Kimbett. Kimbett was dangling there for a second before reaching his left hand over and with some effort, wrenching the knife out of his abdomen. He looked at it in disgust and threw it away, and Gates watched as his knife descended until it couldn't be seen.

Kimbett shot up the remaining two thirds of his left tentacle and tried to grip the bar, which his other tentacle had found. Missing the claw at the end, it was unable to grip the smooth bar. Retracting the damaged tentacle, the admiral began to pull himself up with his left hand, retract a little, and pull up again... gaining inches at a time. Gates realized that his the muscles that retracted his tentacles weren't enough to pull him up alone. Gates raised his boot and stomped on the tentacle on the bar, prompting a glare from Kimbett below. Gates stomped on it again, this time Kimbett snarled at him, but kept inching his way up.

Kimbett was mumbling something to either himself or to Gates in another language.

For the first time Gates realized how much he had damaged Kimbett. The alien admiral's chest wounds were bleeding profusely, his knife wound was spilling orange fluid all over his lower half. He had yellow blood all over his mouth, and blood was oozing from his ears and nose. Gates, dizzy and depleted, disappeared from the ledge to search for something to throw at Kimbett.

Kimbett was hurting very badly; his right tentacle was getting very tired, but he only had two more feet to go before he could grab onto the ledge with his hands and pull himself up.

Just then the human reappeared and Kimbett saw something he hadn't counted on seeing: Gates grinning... gun in hand.

Kimbett was stunned.

"Impossible," he flatly said.

Gates slowly pointed the gun at Kimbett's head.

"Human." Gates calmly said, "You fucking weed! Human!"

Gates fired. One shot hit Kimbett above the left eye, another where the trachea would be on a human, the third and last bullet pierced the tentacle and sent Kimbett on a one way trip to the ground over a thousand feet below.

Gates continued to pull the trigger of the empty weapon repeatedly before collapsing onto his back exhausted.

Kimbett retracted what was left of his right tentacle. He felt the wind pick up more and more as he gained velocity. He was already falling for over five seconds as he watched the foliage come closer and closer.

"This is..." His only functional eye opening wider.

"Ahh this is gonna' *HURT!*" he yelled just before his ripped through the foliage and smashed into the soil below sending water and soil erupting into the air as if a bomb had exploded beneath the surface. Kimbett was down.

Gates tried to get up but realized it wasn't going to happen, he was too tired. Kimbett had torn up Gates pretty badly: His left forearm was ripped up, his gums and the roof of his mouth were bleeding, his lips were cut, two molars were knocked out of his jaw, and the interior of his left cheek was bleeding freely. Not to mention that his hand was swelling from Kimbett stomping on it, and he believed it was broken. His neck was also a mess and had thousands of bloody cuts. Gates grabbed for his dog tags and wasn't too surprised to find they were missing.

As the room spun, Gates closed his eyes and slipped into oblivion.

CHAPTER 25 Mission Attrition

Bishop increased speed to near three hundred knots, and pitched the nose down, in a very steep dive.

"Steady..." Dutch said loudly, his voice raised over the sound of the air rushing by the fuselage as the F-202 Lakota dove at the ground.

"Steady..." Dutch watched as the Garden Barracks came into view. Although its radar could not detect the closing human aircraft, and infrared was seriously degraded within the shielded compound, VanDuinwyk recognized that the heavily armed Garden Barracks could still put up a good fight if it had spotted them visually. So he decided they dive at it in a near vertical bomb-run.

The Garden Barracks was similar to the Molluskan Barracks, only it was about half the size. In the technical specs VanDuinwyk had read on it before this mission, it showed the Garden Barracks to be an unarmed, poorly armored building, but in would seem the enemy had done some remodeling since then. The building was now studded with multi-barreled force cannons and missile arrays. Molluskan and Aracteroid swarmed all over the six silver launch pads lined up in front of it. One of the launch pads currently had an extremely large aircraft parked on it. Weapons studded the sides of its fuselage and on top there was a double-barreled turret.

"Drop now... Now... Now," VanDuinwyk ordered.

A mere thousand feet above the Garden Barracks, the F-202 fired its last scorpion missile at the roof of the Barracks, before pulling up and banking sharply to the left. The missile closed on the structure with dizzying speed. A point defense chemical-laser mounted on the roof shot wildly at the super-sonic missile, but missed every time before the scorpion plunged through the heavily armored roof of the Barracks.

Most of the windows on in the barracks exploded outward as the missile exploded inside. A fire began to consume the floor it exploded on. The Garden Barracks seemed to sink into the ground for a second, before disappearing in a cloud of black smoke. The force cannons went wild, shooting randomly at the sky, hoping to hit what they couldn't see.

By this time, Bishop and VanDuinwyk had already leveled off, and were now flying directly over the structure.

"How many Unicorns do we have left?" VanDuinwyk asked.

"Three," Bishop said, looking at his weapons readout.

"Let's drop one on that launch pad with that big jet thing parked on it," VanDuinwyk suggested.

"Copy that," Bishop smiled.

The engines of the Savaad-class bomber were powering up slowly. The captain had only a four second warning of a bomb drop, and the shield needed five seconds to energize. The Unicorn's nose cone split apart to reveal twelve highly explosive bomblets, which rocketed away from the central bomb, which retained a sizable warhead of its own. This spread out the field of destruction considerably. A deluge of high-powered explosives, first pulverizing the wing, then the cockpit, and finally the entire ship, rained on the helpless Savaad bomber. As the fuel tanks detonated, the Savaad exploded, sending a column of fire high into the sky. The explosion triggered off a series of explosions along the string of launch pads. The explosions jumped from vehicle to vehicle, until all but two Dragonflies were destroyed.

The F-202 swooped down over the crippled barracks and fired a another hydra into one of the hangar bays. Explosions rocked the building over and over, until it crumbled upon itself and then began to burn.

"Bishop!" VanDuinwyk said aloud, "We have two Dragonflies going airborne."

Bishop dove the Lakota through the column of black smoke and began to fire the twenty-millimeter force cannon at the two Dragonflies lifting from their pads. One of them was hit in its engine and slammed back into the pad, the pilot managed to scramble out unharmed. But the second's canopy shattered as the force shells ripped through the cockpit, killing the pilot. The vehicle collapsed back onto the pad, smashing the it beyond repair.

The Lakota pulled up into the sky again, and headed off in the direction of the inner gate.

"Scratch another one Bishop," VanDuinwyk laughed.

"Oh yeah! How many buildings have we destroyed now? Eighteen?" Bishop smiled. "An even Twenty," VanDuinwyk corrected.

"How are we on fuel my friend?" Bishop asked.

VanDuinwyk stopped smiling. "We have about fourteen four hours left if we conserve."

Bishop's mind was wrestling with a forbidden thought, "We'll have to find a place to land this sucker," He finally said.

"That's not a good idea. If we were to get captured, the enemy would have a working model of our chameleon system as well as us to torture and interrogate," VanDuinwyk cautioned.

"I know, but we need sleep. I'm so damn tired right now I'm not going to be much good in another dog fight," Bishop said.

"Yes... me too, and I'm hungry..." VanDuinwyk grumbled, "But what happens in the next twenty-four hours may determine whether or not the human race inherits the Earth."

Bishop nodded. Then a long pause ensued.

"How about weapons?" Bishop asked, his voice restored to confidence.

"We have eight Hydras left, and two Unicorns," VanDuinwyk said.

"I think it's time to pay the mission's primary target a visit, what do you think Dutch?" Bishop said with an unusual cheerfulness.

"You mean before we get shot out of the sky?" VanDuinwyk said.

"If need be, I intend to fall out of the sky, and into the damned station! If that's what we have to do," Bishop said gritting his teeth.

"Setting a course," VanDuinwyk said, "we've got a long way to fly."

"Let's do it," Bishop said as the F-202 Lakota rocketed off towards the inner gate, en route to the power sub-station.

. . .

The afternoon sun glared high overhead.

Grackconn stood on one of the two massive landing pads in front of the Molluskan Barracks. As he stood there waiting, a massive shadow fell across him, as the massive metal crusher drove past him on its way to the hangar. As it approached, its magnetic crane withdrew a metal platform from its crusher pit and set it down in front of the hangar bay doors, which were now opening. On the platform was a twisted and charred heap of metal, with several metal bins containing scrap.

The metal crusher lowered its rear ramp and a very large Molluskan, carrying a dual-cylinder gatling-weapon emerged with a working party of Molluskan whom he instructed to move the platform into the hangar. They energetically ran off to do their mindless task as the large Molluskan approached Grackconn.

"This is it, Ensign Xo?" Grackconn shouted in his language over the thundering sounds of the metal crusher's engines.

Xo nodded, "This is all we found, a lot of it was blown into the air upon impact, and later buried by the sand storm though." The Molluskan answered in the language of the Aracteroid.

Grackconn nodded in comprehension.

"Any word on the second wreckage yet, Sir?" Xo asked.

Grackconn grimaced, "No, not yet... I don't know where the hell it went."

Xo shrugged. "It'll turn up, probably buried. Hopefully, the little humans on board ended up dead like these ones," he said, pointing to the platform that was currently being pushed and pulled into the hangar.

Unlike the average Molluskan, Ensign Xo was remarkably intelligent.

. . .

Krewtek looked up from his desk as his Molluskan bodyguard entered with his lunch on a rectangular plastic tray.

"Hurry up, I'm hungry!" Krewtek said without looking up again.

The Molluskan deposited the tray on his desk in front of him and exited the office. The tray was full of colorful Trexian fruits as well as five large green strips of meat from some alien animal. The yellow Dotariak eyed the food hungrily, and took a few steps towards Krewtek's lunch.

"No!" Krewtek said shooing it away. The eyeball threw its paws up, balled into fists. "I don't care how hungry you are, its mine!" He said picking up a sharpened three-pronged fork.

Just then, the intercom beeped several times. Krewtek threw down his fork with a metallic clatter.

"Now what!" He yelled pressing the intercom button.

Xo appeared on his screen.

"Sir, we have the human wreckage here if you want to come down a have a look," he said, with the sound of machinery in the background.

"I'll be there Ensign..." Krewtek said, disconnecting before Xo could respond.

He got up and walked towards the door. Before leaving he looked back at the yellow Dotariak. "Be good," He said before opening the door, turning off the lights and walking out.

. . .

"Looks like a shield generator to me," Grackconn said, holding up a large toroidal coil. "I think this is actually better craftsmanship than our own," he said studying the intricate wiring and circuitry integrated into the large ring.

Xo was standing in front of a twisted piece of metal that was once the FB-117 Nightshade. It was nearly completely destroyed, with most of the machinery inside utterly pulverized. Only some individual components survived. Including the twenty-millimeter force cannon, which was at one time the very same weapon used by Molluskan, but adapted by the humans.

"They knew they couldn't replicate our technology in time for an attack, so they actually incorporated it directly into their new design," Xo said, studying the force cannon that had been salvaged, "...ingenious,"

"I give them credit for creativity," Grackconn said as he deposited the shield generator on the metallic floor of the hangar building, "But what a waste..."

A door opened up, and four creatures walked in. Krewtek, and three of his Molluskan escorts. He didn't look happy.

"So this is what we're up against eh?" He said to Xo as he walked to the pile of debris.

Xo nodded, "Yes Sir. This ship, or rather what is left of it, is probably the same design of the ship that is still airborne."

"What can you tell me about it?" Krewtek asked, picking up a metal ring from one of the many baskets containing assorted metal fragments.

Xo began, "Well Sir, it's destroyed beyond recognition..."

Krewtek rolled his eye, "Skip the obvious Xo, and tell me what I don't want to hear,"

Xo nodded, "Sir this thing is mostly our own technology. The airframe, force cannon the power-cell... all of this they got from our metal crusher. In other cases, our technology was copied, like with their shield generator and engines."

"All right... what about this cloaking device the airborne ship seems to have?" Krewtek asked.

"Probably here Sir," Grackconn said, holding up a bucket of scrap.

"I didn't ask for sarcasm Grackconn!" Krewtek shouted.

Xo interrupted, "Sir, this ship is smashed to the point that I doubt its designers could recognize it. It's hard enough recognizing the components that we designed, let alone new stuff."

Krewtek was silent for a moment as he examined what was once a console mounted within the cockpit, it lay in a basket with much of the smaller bits of debris. As he picked it up, a very uneasy feeling washed over him. He stared at the smashed buttons and switches, the reddish brown stains covering half of the panel. He studied the human blood intensely as an uncomfortable pause endured.

"These humans are not as stupid as we lead to believe..." he said quietly.

Krewtek dropped the panel in the basket with a loud metallic clatter that echoed within the hangar, and gave a very heavy sigh, "Very well. Keep me posted and let me know when you find anything," he said finally.

Xo and Grackconn nodded in compliance.

. . .

Krewtek entered his dark office and fumbled for the switch to activate the overhead lights. He found the switch and flipped it. With an electrical buzzing sound the lights flickered on. Krewtek instantly noticed something on his desk, something that was wrong.

On his desk, was his lunch tray. It was immaculately clean, every trace of food was gone. Next to his barren lunch trey was a horribly disfigured eyeball. Its iris clouded and dried, its body no longer spherical, but now gumdrop shaped. Its antennae, arms and legs had fallen off and lay on the desk next to it. Its entire body was attached to the desk by a kind of mucous that covered all of its bloated form.

Krewtek shook his head and walked inside.

"I told you not to do this in my office anymore!" He shouted.

The eyeball's body split open, and from inside, covered in mucous, four smaller Dotariak emerged, their yellow irises contracting as they came into the light for the first time. All of them gestured at Krewtek simultaneously and in perfect synchronization.

Krewtek smiled, "Just clean up your mess, and I'll let it go for now."

The four eyeballs nodded synchronously.

CHAPTER 26 Down, But Not Out

Gates briefly dreamed of the beautiful woman with the green eyes. She was healing him, his many wounds hurt, but he felt the pain was worth it if it kept her there with him.

An explosion shook the ground, and reverberated through the garden dome with a distant thunderous roar. Gates opened his eyes and watched through the many transparent triangular plates of the dome as a great pillar of smoke rose from the horizon. The ground shook again, and he realized that something near the dome was under attack.

"Go get 'em fellas..." Gates rasped.

He slowly got to his feet, and re-examined himself for wounds. Besides the scratches in his neck and on his forearm, the constant aching of his lower jaw, the intense migraine headache intense bruising all over his body and broken hand, he couldn't find anything else wrong with himself.

He searched around for the extra clip to his Beretta, it apparently had fallen out during his battle with Kimbett. But to no avail, it was not to be found anywhere on the platform. "Must have fallen off..." he murmured. He knew that without any bullets the gun is useless, never the less he kept it. Gates began searching again. "I gotta' find it!" he said under his breath.

The tower was hardly ever serviced, most of its systems were self-repairing. It would be unusual for any armed patrol to bother traveling all the way up the stairs to the platform, but today was an exception, in the depths of the geodesic dome, a squad of six Molluskan troopers trod through into the large transparent tunnel leading to the base of the tower, trailing behind was an Aracteroid.

Gates, during his search, had run into something. A black belt of nylon-like material, four inches wide, about quarter-inch thick and endowed twenty-four small silver cylinders, with a small patch of electronic equipment on one side. Gates still didn't know what it was, but studied it for a moment and realized it must have been some kind of life support system.

"Well... you're a weed... plants like CO^2..." Gates said with a smirk, "thanks Weed." Gates then noticed a small compartment below the patch of electronic equipment with a button pressed into it. Gates pushed the button with the thought of throwing the belt over the side if it looked like it was about to explode. Instead the small compartment spat out a plastic card, covered with symbols much like the symbols he had seen during the briefs. Gates plucked the card out of the compartment and gave that smirk again. "Access card..." he said as he walked over to the edge where Kimbett had fallen, looked down, and spit a large mucus-laced glob of saliva down at the green depths below.

"Thanks again, weed," Gates muttered.

With that, Gates slung the carbon support over his shoulder, put the card in his pocket and staggered back down the stairs, ultimately to the door at the base of the tower that he didn't have access to before. Gates chuckled, wincing through the pain in his chest.

The glob of saliva fell to the ground, its course altered by the wind currents.

At the base of the tower, there was a great hole in the foliage, below that was an even bigger crater in the muddy soil. The crater was filled with dark murky water, with streaks of yellow and red liquid. Every couple of seconds, a bubble could be seen rising to the surface.

The glob of saliva splashed in it.

Almost too small to be seen, a tiny blade of grass poked up from the muddy soil and reached for the beam yellow of sunlight reaching through the hole in the foliage above. The tiny grass blade began to thicken and lengthen until it no longer looked like a grass blade, now it was a vine. Still stretching for the light, the vine began to branch into many smaller vines that began probing for any source of sunlight. The highest vine penetrated the beam of sunlight and within seconds, it had sprouted small biological solar cells, or leaves. The rest of the vines now were bathing in the sunlight, twisting and turning as if in total ecstasy before sprouting tiny leaves.

With a large splash, a chunk of greenish brown flesh exploded out of the mud and landed in the light that was spilling onto the ground next to the hole. A long tendril of pulsating tissue that led back into the murky water tethered the flesh. With another splash, a larger, slug-like, pile of tissue emerged from the water and slithered towards the light. The tissue was leaving a combination on transparent yellow fluid and opaque crimson fluid in its trail. On the lump just below the tendril, an orifice opened and expelled a great deal of water and mud, and then inhaled the carbon rich atmosphere in one huge breath. Inside the orifice, a single pointed yellow tooth could be seen. Just above the mouth another orifice opened and revealed an undamaged violet eye. The eye swiveled around until it saw the ground basked in yellow sunlight just ahead, the iris narrowed.

As the lump of flesh entered the light, it began to cover itself in scores of leaves. The giant tendril of tissue that had been in the sun began to take on the shape of an arm, the blob of pulsating tissue at the end split open and revealed a six-fingered hand. The bone fragments in its wrist began to realign. Its face was inflating with blood and tissue, its crushed skull was being rebuilt on the cellular level. Its left arm dropped off all of its leaves before it plunged into the muddy ground and began to rapidly grow roots to absorb minerals from the soil. The lump of tissue stayed there for fifteen minutes, growing and repairing. When it developed feet, it stood up, opened its mouth and vomited yellow and red fluid all over the ground.

Once again it vomited, this time it vomited a large gray, blood soaked piece of cloth-like material. Its chest was being reformed. Ribs re-aligning. Twenty-four pieces of crushed metal studded its chest from left shoulder to right hip. It stood in the light, absorbing energy and nutrients from the soil through its feet. It threw back his head and gave a scream that could only be spawned by two entities in the natural and super-natural plains of existence, Satan himself and Admiral Kimbett.

. . .

Far from Kimbett, entering the base of the tower, was a squad of six Molluskan troopers, assigned to Lieutenant Bakkaraqu. Bakkaraqu raised a small metal device and stared intensely at it. It was a tracking device.

"Move!" Bakkaraqu scornfully commanded his troopers in fluent Molluskan. The Molluskan grunted there own Molluskan sounds and proceeded up the staircase towards the platform many stories above. Bakkaraqu was drooling venom from his fangs in anticipation, he couldn't believe his luck. Krewtek had been on his side all along, the unexplained pardon after his incident at the Spearax arena, the strange assignment to Earth, and finally the assignment to assassinate Admiral Kimbett! *Praise Krewtek!*

Kimbett was now in the final stages of regeneration. His body was now building up the required amount of blood to go into combat with the human again.

All except for the deep scares on his face, chest and back, the crumpled life support implants in his chest, his missing life support, and the absence of any clothes, he was in great shape. Kimbett reached down and picked up the blood soaked rag that was once his loincloth. He twisted it until almost all the blood was out of it and then put it back on. His right tentacle was still in the sunlight, he retracted it. Kimbett began his journey back to the tower to pick up his life support system.

Bakkaraqu was at the last flight of stairs, a ladder lead the way to the platform at the base of the tower. Bakkaraqu activated his tracking device again and got a fix on Kimbett's position. "Got you..." he thought out loud. The Molluskan troopers just grunted incomprehensibly.

Bakkaraqu was never an admirer of Molluskan, where as the Trexian saw them as the ultimate soldier, "They don't ask questions, they don't defect, they don't feel fear, they don't feel pain, and they don't complain," he was once told by a Trexian officer. However the Trexian only saw half the picture. *They are too stupid to ask questions, they are too stupid to defect, they are way to stupid to feel fear, and if they did feel pain they are to stupid to yell.* Bakkaraqu thought to himself. Using his security access card, he activated the lift that elevated him and his squad of Molluskan to the stairs leading to the top of the tower.

Bakkaraqu checked his tracking device again, and it indicated Kimbett was straight up, and they laboriously made their trek up the stairs to the top of the tower.

With a sudden explosion, the hatch way to the platform flew open and Molluskan filed up the stairs and filed onto the platform where they shot every thing on the east side of the platform, moving or not.

The computer screens and control panels shattered into pieces and the walls buckled as the eastern ceiling sank. Bakkaraqu shot up through the hatchway and fired his small customized tri-barreled sidearm at any shadow on the eastern side. The computer equipment disintegrated into a smoldering heap of scrap.

"Hold your fire!" yelled Bakkaraqu. The Molluskan instantly complied. Bakkaraqu activated his tracking device again and scanned the area. The tracking device stated that Kimbett was 2.4 degrees to the left and 12.4 feet away. Bakkaraqu pointed his weapon there and fired several times piercing the floor. The Molluskan began firing again, tearing away at the flooring. The shredded computer banks leaned over and fell through a large hole floor. A Molluskan fired a *venom* rocket from the side of its force cannon at the floor, but it flew through the hole and struck one of two main support beams holding up the platform, and blew it apart.

"I said hold you're fire! " Bakkaraqu screeched in a panic. The Molluskan stopped firing. Bakkaraqu looked over the area, and failed to see an arm, a leg, or even a thorn from Kimbett. He did however see a lot of yellow and red blood. The entire platform began to tilt to the eastern side. Bakkaraqu looked at the tracking device once more, and then finally noticed it. On the lip of the big hole in the floor was a Trexian insignia, the same one with the tracking bug wired into it. Bakkaraqu crawled out to it and picked it up careful not to shift the platforms weight and send all seven of them plummeting to their death. Bakkaraqu examined the insignia, turned it over and saw the tiny black transmitter no bigger than head of a nail. Bakkaraqu dropped the insignia on the steel surface of the platform and then violently threw the tracking device into the wall, shattering it.

"We've been made a fool of!" he screeched. "Kimbett! Damn you!" he shrieked as loud as an

Aracteroid can, pushing all four of his lungs to their limit.

Back on the surface, below the tower, Kimbett had watched an amazing thing, the platform had been attacked, damaged and then finally fell over to the opposite side from where he was standing and exploded. Seconds before he had heard some Aracteroid screeching and then his name.

"My life support!" Kimbett exclaimed. Although he could survive without his carbon life support indefinitely, Kimbett realized that his access card was in the life support system, and without that, he would be locked out of everything.

"Shit!" Kimbett said under his breath. He began to wonder what the hell had happened. Maybe the human had tried accessing the computer in the tower and a patrol went up there and blew him up. Maybe the Aracteroid screech and his name were all in his imagination, and the dumb human blew himself up. Before Kimbett could think of another possibility, he noticed several figures marching down the stairs, and one in the rear. The one in the rear was multi-legged, and had a shaved head.

"Bakkaraqu." Kimbett's eyes narrowed again, "Lieutenant Bakkaraqu... the disgraced," He began to understand what was now going on. Destarus was right, Krewtek never intended to give Kimbett the MegaKore battleship, he intended to bring Kimbett to Earth so could be cornered and assassinated, and Bakkaraqu could get his revenge.

Kimbett gave his trademark grin and sprinted stealthily towards the base of the tower.

"Sorry sir, we found evidence of Admiral Kimbett at the platform, but he already..." Bakkaraqu attempted to explain to Krewtek.

"Why don't you use the tracking device?!" Krewtek shouted. Although his voice was over a communicator Krewtek was so loud that Bakkaraqu held the device away from his audio membranes on the sides of his head.

"Kimbett must have torn it off, we found it on the tower..." Bakkaraqu tried to say.

"Well, get a sensor team up there and track him down!" Bellowed Krewtek. Through the little screen set in the center of the communicator, he could see Krewtek's enraged Trexian face, his cyclopean eye staring directly into all four of Bakkaraqu's eyes.

Bakkaraqu tried to explain: "We already tried to pick up a trial on the staircase below the platform, we couldn't find..."

"Shut up you blustering fool! I want you to search the entire dome of the Garden, from the platform, work you're way down to the surface. I'm sealing off the area. No one can enter or exit until you find Kimbett."

Krewtek's eyes narrowed, "If he has escaped us, I will personally carve your eyes out. And send them as gifts to Rokoak back on Trexia, you know how much he loved your eyes."

"Don't worry sir, I'll get him." Bakkaraqu attempted to hide his fear.

"Oh, and one other thing." Krewtek suddenly looked curious, "what evidence of Kimbett did you find."

Bakkaraqu searched his mind, fumbling for the correct answer.

"Just a whole lot of fluid that resembled Thalkaloid blood, and we found several tiny thorns stuck into one of the walls. And we also found some other drops of liquid, dark crimson liquid."

Krewtek thought about it for a second. "Kimbett was fighting with a human?" he quietly said aloud. "Get a samples of your evidence and send them to Doctor Kailecko."

Bakkaraqu's eyes darted away from the screen. "I'm afraid that's impossible sir. The Molluskan destroyed the platform."

Bakkaraqu had expected Krewtek to explode in a destructive frenzy, but instead he simply smiled, in fact, Bakkaraqu heard a light chuckle. This reaction made Bakkaraqu welcome death.

"Do you know how expensive the oxygen retrieval system on that platform was? It can't be replaced!" Krewtek suddenly acted out the frenzy Bakkaraqu had expected, he began throwing everything on his desk onto the ground. He even threw the newborn four-inch tall dotariak that usually camped out on his desk, in the waste disposal port set in the wall. But it was quickly pulled out by its brethren that quickly arrived on the scene, before it was vaporized.

"You find Kimbett! Or I will tear off all your limbs, and let the retarded Molluskan play *Bounce* with your decapitated head! Do you understand Lieutenant!?" Krewtek was breathing hard as he reached over and shut off the communicator before Bakkaraqu could answer.

"Yes Sir..." Bakkaraqu said trembling. He was watching his whole life and career dissolve in a pool of blame and failure.

With the Molluskan troopers leading the way, the squad moved down the winding stair case to the metallic base of the tower, and down the lift. As the Molluskan got to the platform at the bottom of the lift they began to scan the area for Kimbett. Bakkaraqu continued down the stairs leading into the tower's base, and stopped just six steps short from the shiny steel flooring at the base of the tower..

"Kimbett, you may have escaped me for now, but I'll find you dammit!" Bakkaraqu began to stomp his four feet on the stair and beat his claws on the rail.

"I'll get you soon enough, Kimbett. It's only a matter of time," Bakkaraqu spat acidic venom on the ground.

"As you wish, Bakkaraqu," A voice said from somewhere.

Bakkaraqu's heart nearly jumped out of his abdomen. For the first time since he entered the Garden, he felt another presence besides his Molluskan. The presence was only constructed from the most evil of emotions. Bakkaraqu knew that in the next couple of seconds, he would be dead.

Before Bakkaraqu could move, his left rear leg was jerked out from under him. And he collapsed onto the stairs before him. His right forward leg was grabbed and then pulled between the stairs. Bakkaraqu looked back and saw only a crooked yellow tooth grin and a set of violet eyes glaring at him through the gap in between the stairs where his limbs were being pulled into.

"Help me!" Bakkaraqu instinctively yelled in Aracteroid as hell clutched the railing. The Molluskan troopers didn't need the call for help to be spoken in Molluskan to see that their commander was being attacked.

Bakkaraqu frantically kicked his two free legs in a desperate attempt to stop himself from being pulled into the gap between the stairs. In one instant Bakkaraqu remembered his tri-barreled side arm, and reached for it with his lower left arm and to his relief, it was still there.

Bakkaraqu never had the chance to fire it though; his lower right arm was grabbed at the elbow by a thorn covered green tentacle, and then pulled under. Under the staircase he could feel his weapon being pried away from his claws. But Bakkaraqu valiantly clutched his weapon. With an intense crunching sound, Bakkaraqu's lower right arm was severed, and his tri-barrel taken anyway. With his two legs pushing against the stairs above and below the gap, and three arms grasping the rail, Bakkaraqu desperately resisted being pulled down between the stairs and under the staircase, the fact that he wouldn't fit between the stairs was also a contributing factor to his resistance.

The Molluskan troopers took about three seconds to decide what to do. One of them, opened fire on the stairway just to the left of Bakkaraqu, missing him by less that a foot. Another one went along the side of the staircase and opened fire on the wall separating the chamber below the staircase from the outside. And another one headed past the other two and attempted to open the door leading to the chamber under the staircase, but alas, Krewtek had terminated access to any room within the Garden dome.

Bakkaraqu felt a shell sever his rear left leg, his front left leg was then grabbed from the stairs and pulled under. Bakkaraqu was certain the shells were hitting Kimbett but he wasn't letting him go.

Molluskan trooper Three was never the type to make decisions, when it saw Five begin firing at the staircase, it immediately figured there was something bad under there. So with a feeling of duty, walked over along the side of the staircase and fired into it with his GOR-6 Multi-Barrel Heavy Assault Gun, or *decimator* as named by the humans.

Only seconds after Three began firing, it suddenly lowered its weapon, clutched its shattered eye-lens in its helmet, made gurgling sounds, and then fell backwards, dead.

Five saw it's comrade go down, and realized that the bad thing under the stairs must be armed. But before it could communicate this remarkable discovery of the obvious, its thin armored eyepiece, its weak spot, exploded inward as the tri-barrel's force shell shattered into multiple fragments, and tore into Five's head, partially blinding but not killing it.

By this time the last three troopers scrambled up from the surface onto the tower base after hearing the firing, and not seeing any of their buddies firing at any body, they defaulted to do exactly what the only active Molluskan on the scene was doing, struggling with the door to the chamber under the staircase, where the enemy was.

Bakkaraqu was still desperately clawing to get away, he could feel something try to wrap itself around the junction between his abdomen and his thorax, but it couldn't get a grip. With great force, Bakkaraqu felt his front left leg torn from its socket. He screamed as his last free leg pulled from its position, pushing against the staircase, and pulled down into the gap between the stairs. Bakkaraqu was no longer trying to push away from the gap, without any free legs, this was impossible. He was now trying just to hang on to the rail with his remaining three arms. He was being taken apart a piece at a time.

"Help!" Bakkaraqu pleaded. One of the Molluskan trying to force the door open sprung around the corner and let out a series of unrecognizable astonished Molluskan sounds, as if it had just noticed its mutilated commander. Bakkaraqu felt his own abdomen touch the stair below the gap. Before he could really begin to panic, he felt the tentacle wrap around the junction between his abdomen and thorax again, but this time it had its grip; its thorns digging into his tough exoskeleton. The Molluskan ran around the rail and tripped on the twitching blind Molluskan on the ground and falling just short of Bakkaraqu, but miraculously grabbing his arm.

Bakkaraqu felt his stomach crush, he felt his kidney-like organ compress and he felt his heart beat irregularly as the pressure increased, the exoskeletal coat over his abdomen split open, and finally, his deformed abdomen popped through the stairs.

"Help! You stupid, worthless, brainless, ugly piece of shit! " Bakkaraqu shouted through riveting bolts of pain. But the Molluskan was doing all it could do.

The door was slowly sliding open, three Molluskan strained against the hydraulic motor holding the door. None of them realized all they had to do was shoot it and the door would have opened on its own.

Bakkaraqu was beginning to go into shock, he had long since lost the strength to hold onto the railing and the only thing holding him back was a Molluskan.

"Don't let me... me go.. Don't let me... Die!" Bakkaraqu managed, as yellow foam dribbled out of his mouth.

The Molluskan held on with everything it had. Suddenly Bakkaraqu let out a scream of severe agony. The Molluskan flew back still clutching Bakkaraqu's arm, and the mutilated Bakkaraqu flew under the gap, smacking the upper stair with the back of his shaved head before disappearing into the void between the stairs. The Molluskan sat on the metal floor, confused, as it looked at the twitching disembodied arm still in its grasp.

Bakkaraqu opened his eyes to see the smiling, and horribly disfigured face of his long time enemy, Kimbett.

"I would have let you live, but you couldn't let your failure go, could you?" Kimbett was talking at a loud tone so Bakkaraqu could hear him over the pounding on the door by the Molluskan trying to get in.

"Please don't kill me Kimbett, I was under orders," Bakkaraqu whispered.

"Please... Don't... Kill... Me... Kimbett..." Kimbett echoed, mocking Bakkaraqu. "Sorry Captain Bakkaraqu, they stopped me from executing you in the Spearax arena, but you're daddy isn't here now."

" Kimbett... I'll see you in *Hell!*" Bakkaraqu said with an angry grin and then spit yellow foam in Kimbett's face.

"You first," Kimbett's irises fully dilated and his skin turned deep green.

The door was almost open enough to get in, when the Molluskan heard a scream, a scream never heard before, a scream of ultimate agony and suffering. Although the scream only lasted a couple seconds, seemed to have been spawned by many years of torture.

A Molluskan still clutching Bakkaraqu's arm, ran over to the door and helped pry it open. With a loud bursting sound, the hydraulic cylinder to the door exploded, spraying hydraulic fluid all over the interior of the room, and the sliding door was pushed aside. One of the Molluskan walked in and turned on the lights. Its brain did not understand the images its eyes were sending it.

One side of the room was its commander, but it would look over there and there also was its commander. It finally realized its boss was torn apart by the unseen enemy. By the green thing they had shown it pictures of and told it to kill, probably. There was no sign of this enemy now though, all except for Bakkaraqu, the room was virtually empty, except for some canisters of plant food.

The other three Molluskan filed in and saw the disgusting scene around them, but lacked the ability to be disgusted.

Bakkaraqu was quite dead, all his major organs were neatly arranged as if on display, and all limbs except for the one that the Molluskan still held, were piled next to the organs. The rest of the body sections were arranged in a ring around Bakkaraqu's head. All four of Bakkaraqu's eyes were open, and his face only betrayed a look of terror. The Molluskan were too stupid to realize what this was, they had never heard the legend. This was the sign of Kimbett. Kimbett had held all his opponent's heads high in the air, back in the Spearax Arena on Trexia. All except for

Lieutenant Bakkaraqu, saved by God himself, Kroyce let him live in shame, at the behest of Bakkaraqu's father, who himself was murdered by Kimbett one day later. Bakkaraqu's father was the highest-ranking Aracteroid in the Aracteroid consulate. He tortured and executed Aracteroid revolutionaries was a traitor to his own people...

Unseen on the wall, written in Bakkaraqu's foamy yellow blood, were four characters written it Trexian. Translated to English they meant *It begins.*

The Molluskan didn't see Kimbett with the *decimator* gun he had taken from the blind Molluskan. It wouldn't have mattered.

They turned just in time to see him squeeze the grip and add their blood to the wall.

CHAPTER 27 An Eye For An Eye

Pipes and cables lined the ceiling and floor. The air was uncomfortably humid, and the entire underground complex seemed to be a steam bath. Gates felt as if he had been walking for miles, when in reality, he was only four hundred yards from the ladder that lead him down here from the tower. *Where the hell was he going?*

As he walked, his footsteps came unevenly, his lungs ached, his satchel seemed to be heavier every step, and the bandoleer of carbon cylinders was bearing down heavily on him. Gates felt as if he was going to collapse any second, but knew there was no time for rest. He needed coolant for the B-100's reactor, and he needed it now.

Finally, he saw a rusted and moss covered door. Gates couldn't open it, and as he tried, the white slimy moss stuck to his hands. The door appeared to have not been opened since it was installed. Gates wiped his hands on his pants, and went onward.

The journey led him another four hundred yards, he passed up several sealed doors. Finally, the hallway ended with a well-lit, metal door. Gates hit the blue glowing button, and it silently slid open.

Gates trembled as he walked into the shimmering white room. The door closed with a soft hiss behind him. As he walked in, the temperature was much dryer and cooler, and caused him to shiver slightly. With a sense of fear and curiosity, he explored the room and noted all entrances and exits. After looking around, he began to think that maybe the room was a laboratory of some sort.

On the left side of the room was a large countertop with several instruments, and a pile of gray, black, and brown leathery objects. On the right were eight vertical tubes nearly three feet across, with small windows set in them, upon which was undecipherable

Trexian block writing. At the end of the room was another door. Smudges and stains marked its buttons and Gates knew it was obviously used often.

As he walked closer to the countertop, Gates noticed that one of the instruments was actually an old disassembled DVD player, still widely used by Chinese families. The words G.E. were clearly written on its black plastic cover. Gates went on to find a jar full of Chinese and American coins. Upon closer inspection, the leathery objects were actually wallets, all empty. The next pile had car keys. A knot moved into his stomach when he saw a pile of family pictures, driver's licenses and credit cards. Gates knew that these people were probably dead. Gates scanned the counter top again and noticed a small pile of silver metal plates. Dog tags.

Gates walked over to the counter top and began flipping through them. To his surprise, he knew some of these men, they were his team. The names were Benning Horris J., Cunningham , Marcus M., Miller, Thomas J...

Gates grabbed all of them and put and held them in his hands. Tears or rage flowed from Gates for the first time as he realized he was looking at all that was left of his brothers, there had been no survivors.

"This won't end here..." Gates said, his voice full of rage and grief. He took the tags with him, putting them each in a different pocket to avoid excess noise. Before leaving, Gates examined the metal tubes, but all were empty. Opening the opposite door, Gates cautiously crept inside.

Gates was surprised to find an Aracteroid slumped in its chair. It was an old Aracteroid, with a head of white hair. Scarred and wrinkled, it wore a patch and monocle on its face. Lucky for Gates it was asleep and generating an odd sound that could have been snoring. Lying on the counter next to it was a rather beautifully carved wooden staff with a silver ball on top. Gates continued into the room until the door slid shut behind him.

This room was full of laboratory equipment, and stacked high to the ceiling were crates and boxes. There was a spiral staircase leading up and a dark doorway to the right. Gates briefly looked around before heading left. As he fumbled for a light switch of some kind he wondered if he was looking in the right place for coolant. His fingers fell upon a red square button, and with a muffled click, the lights came on.

Gates immediately noticed a box of impossibly small tools lying in the corner next to two very small doors, set low on the wall. Gates didn't know what they were for.

Surround Gates were shelves upon shelves of metal pressurized cylinders containing nearly everything from glass cleaners to compressed helium. "Jackpot!" Gates said to himself. "But which one is the coolant?"

. . .

The sunburnt eyeball ambled through the desert, following the half buried trench before it abruptly ended with a pit. The eyeball immediately jumped into the pit and dug around, all it found was broken glass, metal fragments and short, yellow, metal tubes that tasted like fire. With a feeling of frustration, the eyeball bounded out of the hole and looked for tracks. But there were none to been seen; all probably blown away when they tried to start the reactor. Then its yellow eye picked up an object, a yellow object. It looked like a yellow spike or something sticking up from the sand. The eyeball raced over to the object, dropping its water pouch and telescope. Upon reaching the strange thing, it began to dig and suddenly jumped backwards in astonishment. It had uncovered a foggy red eye in the sand.

Curiously, the eyeball walked back. It began to uncover the charred body of an Aracteroid. It was confused. As it uncovered more and more, it was blinded as a reflective object was uncovered. Shielding its eye from the glare, it pulled the metal object out of the sand and studied it. It was a small metal rectangular box, on one side were the human words *Dusty Ford* written in cursive, below that was a blue 1952 Ford step-side truck, on the other side was a pink smudge of hydraulic fluid, with a human finger print.

Although the eyeball was again without a clue as to the whereabouts of the humans, it never the less was happy. It liked its new prize, and decided to tuck the lighter into a pocket in its water pouch, and take it with it.

Again it set out into the desert.

. . .

Gates pulled out the coolant pump. There were two Trexian symbols on it. One that looked like a backwards 'K' and one that looked like a happy face with no eyes. Gates began searching the shelves for cylinders with similar markings. In the end, he had two cylinders with the same markings. Gates grabbed a third in case two cylinders wasn't two liters worth. Gates quickly stowed them in his bulging satchel after his pump. He was done here.

A small hiss could be heard. Gates looked down in confusion as one of the small doors had opened. He only watched, stunned, as a small red irised eyeball marched out with a tiny screwdriver in its hand. It noticed him instantly, and in a second, it was charging Gate's ankle with the tiny screwdriver raised as a knife. Gates kicked it apart. Then another eyeball came out, then another and another.

One of them jumped on Gates' leg and began biting, he pulled it off and crushed it in his bare hand. They began chewing through his camouflage pants into his vulnerable flesh as he began to shake his legs and jump up and down in a frenzy as if he were covered in ants. One of the eyeballs climbed up to his ear and bit. He tore it off and hurled it at the wall. Gates began to dance on the scores that poured out onto the floor from the two doors. Red irises, purple irises, blue irises, green irises, brown irises. All types and colors were flooding out of the doors. Small screams and hisses were coming from the crowd. He jumped up high and despite his swollen hand, caught of the bars in the ceiling and pulled himself up. With the sixty pounds of cargo he was carrying, in his satchel and on his shoulder, he knew he couldn't stay there for long. Tiny tools harmlessly pelted Gates' boots and metal scraps. The yellow irised eyeballs were trying to form a totem pole to reach his foot, while the red ones were scaling the shelves. Gates in a panic grabbed the crates that were stacked against the left wall and pulled them down with him.

The room echoed with the thunderous crash as the metal and plastic crates struck the ground and crushed hundreds of eyeballs. The Aracteroid woke up to see a bloody human running out from the storage room. A Molluskan jumped in his path and Gates began to fight with it. The Aracteroid grabbed his staff and came at the human. Gates ducked just as the Aracteroid swung, the staff missing his head by half an inch and hitting the Molluskan in the face instead, sending it to the ground.

Gates made a run for the door, he waited half a second for it to open before running through as the Aracteroid threw its staff like a spear, missing him and tearing into the crates just to his left. Before Gates closed the door he saw a larger, gatling-weapon toting, Molluskan trooper enter the room. As the door hissed shut, the metal bulged out in large dents as the force shells impacted the other side of it. Gates continued to run to the exit. The Molluskan tried to open the door, but the dents it had punched in it, prevented it from sliding open.

As Gates ran down the humid black hallway, he noticed it was far wetter than before, and it seemed even hotter. He stopped dead in his tracks as he noticed one of the sealed doors was now open. But in its path was a creature unlike anything any human had seen before. It was a white creature that was partially covered by a shadow. Its shoulders had pores on them like Kimbett's and it had six fingers like Kimbett, but it had no carbon life support and it didn't look like a plant to Gates. It wasn't.

In a blink of an eye, the creature literally melted into the grated floor.

Gates frantically looked around and upon turning around he was grabbed by the throat by the white creature and lifted into the air. The creature's skin was warm and slimy, and Gates stared into its two white-irised humanoid eyes as they stared right back into his. The creature looked the human over thoroughly, and Gates was too terrified to resist.

The Molluskan began to pry open the white door, and the creature dropped Gates and stared at them. It turned again to look at Gates, and after gesturing to the doorway it had come from, it liquefied and splashed into the floor and disappeared beneath the grating. Gates was confused, but not in a position to argue as he sprinted into the once sealed room and found a ladder leading up. He began to climb as fast as he could.

A Molluskan immediately followed. Gates recognized it as the one that was struck by the Aracteroid's staff by the huge dent in its chest plate. Lucky for Gates it was an unarmed worker. As Gates climbed he heard more Molluskan below him, and they were gaining. Shots were fired but none below could shoot around the unarmed Molluskan directly below Gates. He really had no idea where he was going, maybe that white thing was trying to help him, or maybe it's only toying with him. All that Gates knew is that he must climb.

Gates' leg was suddenly jerked off the rung of the ladder. Pain shot through his broken hand as he held on with his hands as best he could. Looking down, he kicked the Molluskan square in the face. Its hand flew off Gates' leg as it nearly fell down, and Gates continued to climber shortly before again being pulled off the ladder by the Molluskan. Gates, with intense anger building up, jumped off the ladder and bounced both feet of the Molluskan's head, sending it down into the others, knocking them off the ladder and fifty feet to the solid metal floor of the room below. Gates reached a trapdoor and with great effort, heaved it open. He heard alien alarms sounding, and found himself outside in the daylight and fresh air. Scanning the area, he saw that he was less than half a mile to the garden dome, and woefully without cover. Far off in the distance, he could see two Dragonfly aircraft closing in, possibly on his position. He quickly closed the trapdoor behind him and sprinted to the nearest cover, and from there sprinted again to a small building where he hid under a tractor parked next to it. He was alone. But the alarms kept sounding.

He waited for six hours. It was like being stuck in the waiting room of hell with an appointment to see the Devil. Molluskan ran by and Aracteroid searched. What scared Gates were the eyeballs, for he knew they would sniff him out like a dog. Luckily, he saw none, or at least they didn't see him. The alarms stopped. Gates would wait until sunset to make his attempt across the bridge.

It came in another three hours. Because after all...

...The Devil was a busy man.

CHAPTER 28 Fatal Error

A low mist was forming over the flora of the garden dome as the unregulated temperature of the dome began to drop. Off in the distance, the burning remains of the regulator tower could be seen. All was quiet. Kimbett emerged from the chamber under the staircase with an uneven smile. He was covered in Aracteroid and Molluskan blood. In his grasp was a *decimator* heavy assault cannon.

"So. The game is on? You are not going to like how I play Krewtek," he said to himself before running off into the foliage.

. . .

One of the now full-grown yellow irised eyeballs began jumping up and down as it realized it had back its master into a corner. The other three were nowhere to be seen.

"No, no, no. You can't put your Marauder here without me doing this..." Krewtek said as he moved a small miniature Molluskan figure across a triangular board until it was in front of the eyeball's miniature tank.

The eyeball stomped its foot in frustration. Krewtek and the eyeball were alone in his office playing an alien game simply called *Battle*. Battle was uncannily similar to Chess, only the goal was to destroy the *Heartland* of the enemy. The *hearland* piece was positioned before the start of the match, and could not be moved. It represented the civilians in war. Although the dotariak had beaten its master in Battle before, he seemed to have gotten wiser.

Krewtek threw two eight sided dice and laughed.

"Ha! Sixteen! More than enough!" Krewtek boasted, flicking the small tracked vehicle off of the board.

The eyeball studied its options for only a brief moment before it stopped and seemed to stare off into space.

"Hurry up..." Krewtek, said impatiently, before the eyeball raised its tiny, clawed hand to quiet Krewtek. It was listening.

"What is it?" Krewtek said as the eyeball began to frantically jump up and down.

The beeping sound of Krewtek's intercom went off. Krewtek rolled his eye and hit the button.

"Yeah!" he said into the small panel in his desk as his screen flickered until it revealed a large brownish armored creature's head.

A low thundering voice came back over the radio. "This is Boratus. I've seen one here..." it paused, "...and it escaped."

"What are you talking about Boratus? You saw what?" Krewtek had an ugly feeling in his guts. He felt an almost sickening feeling. The yellow eyeball looked at him as if it knew too. It did. "A lone human," Boratus said flatly.

"And it got away," Krewtek finished morosely.

"Yes. And I have no idea where it came from either!" Boratus said with a tone of severe shame.

Krewtek shook his head. "What damage was done?"

"Major damage to a water purifying plant in section 28, but it isn't vital. We could repair it in time..."

"Wait," Krewtek interrupted, "is that all it did was destroy a water purifier?"

"No, actually it also stole a type C power cell," Boratus finished.

"Strange..." Krewtek said, thinking.

Boratus broke the silence, "I'll hunt them down for..."

"No. Save your anger Boratus," Krewtek thought for a while, "Stand your station fast, and report to me if you see any further human activity."

"Yes Sir." Boratus nodded and disconnected.

Krewtek stared at the eyeball. "What do you know? Tell me, have your buddies seen something?" The eyeball nodded.

Krewtek began to think about how a human could have gotten into the facility. 'It must be from the lone ship flying around' he thought.

On his desk, the intercom beeped again.

. . .

Kimbett ran full speed at the irrigation ditch until he was a mere foot away when he leapt from the ground and sailed over it, landing without slowing down, he continued to run through the foliage at Olympic speed. As he ran he thought of Destarus, and how he was right. *I should have listened to you Captain Destarus. I never should have left the MegaKore.*

Kimbett had run for over a mile through jungle terrain in under six minutes. He stopped and looked around for the nearest tree. After spotting a thick fleshy green tree with reddish leaves, he scaled it all the way to the top to get a look at his surroundings. To the west, he saw the tower. Just north of him was one of four doors leading out of the garden. Kimbett jumped to the ground and ran in the direction of the northern door.

"It was a setup from the beginning..." he muttered, "You knew I wouldn't come all the way out here unless you offered me a command... but why now?" Kimbett tried to imagine Krewtek's timing for his assassination.

Kimbett had to accept the possibility that Krewtek was playing him just as he was playing Krewtek. *You sly bastard.*

. . .

"It was only one. And I saw it running from a storage closet," Said the elderly Aracteroid over Krewtek's intercom.

"Did you find any explosive?" Krewtek asked.

"We didn't find any sir," Kailecko answered.

"Was there anything missing?"

"I don't know yet. It knocked over all the shelves. Inventory would take at least..."

"Forget the inventory Kailecko. Why don't you return to the MegaKore and await further orders."

"Why the MegaKore Sir? I still have to help treat our wounded here," Kailecko asked confused.

"Don't worry, we'll take over. Now get back to your ship," Krewtek said irritably, "That is an order."

Kailecko saluted before disconnecting. After he did this, Krewtek slammed his hands on his desk so hard that the eyeball was shaken off its feet.

"Go. Go to the MegaKore! Get away from this place!" he droned.

"I can't have you or Boratus snooping around now!" he muttered, "If they discover Bakkaraqu..."

Krewtek knew that until Bakkaraqu had killed Kimbett, he would have to keep security paralyzed. The humans couldn't have been discovered at a worse time.

As he made a fist, Krewtek cursed, "Where the hell did you come from, human?"

A breach in the force field? Impossible. *A tunnel under the wall?* Unlikely. They had to be from the crashed ship that Grakconn had failed to locate.

Krewtek managed to pull a smile from the situation: He knew at least Kimbett was dead by now.

. . .

Kimbett was very alive at this point in time. In front of him was a giant metal cargo door. He reached out a broken, twisted finger and pushed the open button, but the door didn't budge. He hit the button again, but it continued to remain closed. Kimbett reached back to get his security card, but then he remembered he had left it in his life support unit in the burning wreckage of the platform. Cursing he walked over to a small keypad and punched in his override code. But the doors still didn't budge.

"Dammit!" Kimbett bared his shattered teeth at the keypad before punching it apart with his bare fist. "Looks like I'll have to find another way out off here," he said before walking back into the foliage along the metal wall.

As Kimbett walked, he looked around. Around him were several small bushes, baring fruits and a couple fern like plants.

"Too small," he said to himself. He continued to walk for a good five minutes, keeping close to the wall. Kimbett finally stopped and smiled another uneven smile. "Now *you* are perfect," Kimbett said while approaching a very large tree. The tree was nearly completely green, with fleshy wet bark, and a mop of green furry vines towering fifty feet above.

Kimbett walked up to the base of the tree.

. . .

Krewtek's door opened once again. Krewtek nodded for Ensign Xo to enter, and the husky Molluskan walked in, with his GTR-22 *Pulverizer* twin cylinder gatling-weapon under his right shoulder.

"Hello Ensign," Krewtek said morosely. "all right, here's the deal: We have one, or possibly two humans in this compound sabotaging things, I'd really appreciate it if you'd do your job, and *KILL THEM!*" Krewtek shouted.

Xo swallowed and spoke up, "I already have measures underway to locate them Sir. I just need more time."

"Time?" Krewtek walked around his desk and up to Xo, "Time is what we *don't* have Xo!" He said pointing his finger in Xo's face.

Xo, said nothing, but his black Molluskan eyes hid his disgust for Krewtek. The door opened suddenly as Grackconn walked in with his clipboard.

"Sir." Grackconn removed a sheet of paper from his clipboard. "I don't think they are sabotaging," he said handing Krewtek a report of missing components. And a report on the search for the second human wreckage, which they never found.

Krewtek studied the report.

"Four wheels, Type B coolant, reactor pump." Krewtek's eye widened, "...Type C power cell..."

Krewtek opened his eye all the way in shock. He slammed his hands on the desk, then knocked all the game piece on to the floor.

"Of course!" Krewtek's eye raced back and fourth as he thought. There was an eerie silence as Krewtek stared at the chart of the compound, he focused on the river that separated the desert, where the second human ship crashed, and the rest of the compound, where the humans kept showing up."

"Xo! I want you to take your troops and set up patrols following the river," Krewtek commanded.

"May I ask why, Sir?" Xo asked simply.

"Don't you see? Grackconn is correct! They are not trying to sabotage! They are trying to repair their ship!" Krewtek suddenly put it all together.

"What ship?" Xo asked.

"These humans aren't from the outside! They are from the second human ship, and they must have hid it, and are trying to get it airborne again," Krewtek raved.

"Xo's green black eyes remained emotionless, but his tentacles flicked with astonishment. I'll get right on it Sir!" he saluted and left the office. Grackconn followed.

Krewtek beat his hands on his desk several times. He looked at his chronometer and sighed.

"Bakkaraqu! Where the hell are you," he irritably whispered while punching in the sequence to Bakkaraqu's communicator. But Bakkaraqu didn't respond.

Where were the humans?

Where was Bakkaraqu?

Krewtek's stomach churned.

Where was Kimbett?

. . .

Kimbett pointed his index finger at the tree, and a small green vine grew from under his fingernail and touched the side of the tree and burrowed itself into the bark. Kimbett concentrated. Inside the tree, things were changing. Hormones and other chemicals were flowing from Kimbett into the tree.

The tree began to lean away from the wall as the left side bulged with massive cellular growth and filled with fluid. The tree groaned and tiny splintering noises could be heard as Kimbett continued to manipulate it. Slowly it stopped leaning.

Kimbett began to inject different chemical and hormonal instructions to the tree now. At the top, a large rock-solid growth began to form as the tree cells began to grow at an accelerated rate. Groans of protest riddled the tree as the weight of the giant ball on top of it, pushed it towards the ground as its elastic frame struggled to hold its shape. Kimbett stopped transmitting signals to the tree, and took a deep breath.

The tree vibrated slightly, like a muscle when straining to hold something too heavy for it. With a grin, Kimbett jerked his hand back, ripping the small vine from the tree.

With a deafening pop. The large abscess on the left side of the tree exploded, spraying the wall with water and tree sap. Then, like a catapult, the tree, with nothing to hold it back, swung hard to the left, with the one-ton ball on it.

As the tree met the steel wall, the ground shook so hard that Kimbett was literally thrown from his feet. He heard glass break as four triangular panels from the geodesic ceiling broke free and fell to the ground, shattering into thousands of tiny glass fragments that rained on Kimbett.

Seconds later, there was silence.

Kimbett got to his feet and looked around.

"Damn I do good work," He said happily while looking at the twenty-foot rift the tree had torn through the wall.

"I'm comin' Krewtek you bastard!" Kimbett said before hopping through the opening.

. . .

The stars stretched off to infinity behind the Earth. From orbit it looked like a blue green pearl in a black sea with sand as the stars. The Rao Lok hovered over Grantex menacingly, its colossal transmission dish sending terawatts of raw light to its base below. Slowly, the beam of energy narrowed and disappeared completely. The Rao Lok stopped transmitting power.

The night was beautiful.

On the Chinese horizon, a yellow-red sunset marked the end of the day. Its magnificent yellow beams caused the surrounding clouds to light up as if on fire. The yellow gradually turned to orange as the sun dropped behind the horizon. The sky still glowed with the sun's powerful hues of red and violet, but they too, soon faded. It was as if the sun was abandoning the sky; leaving while it could.

In the moonless darkness, lit only by the many thousands of sparkling stars, a sand storm began to blow outside of the compound. A massive thumping sound began. *Thump! Thump! Thump!*

With every powerful thump, the sand whirled faster. Vortices collected and twirled frantically before dispersing. The thumping became more rapid, until it was a steady drone. As it still increased speed, the air surrounding the facility rotated counter clockwise at speeds of nearly one hundred miles an hour as intense magnetic waves swept in a circular motion. The drone became a steady synchronous hum, and then it quieted down just as suddenly as it had started. The winds stopped, and the sand came to rest back on the ground.

All was quiet once again except for a low pitch mechanical hum that could literally be felt vibrating through the sand.

The nearly invisible shields surrounding the complex gradually became brighter as they were fed their maximum power. Lights, beacons and small radars that were shut off to save energy were re-activated once again.

The main Trexian reactor was now finally up and running.

Every structure in Grantex now had a light of some sort, glowing. Every structure except the sheds in the desert, one of which held the B-100 Revenant, which rested until she could be repaired and fight along side her sister to destroy the sub-station and complete the mission.

They were the world's last and only hope.

Four men held the key for the survival of the planet...

...but Michael Gates and Dustin Ford needed to break the lock.

CHAPTER 29 Breaking And Entering

"Approaching the inner gate," Dutch reported.

Unlike its formidable counterpart the *Wall*, the inner gate was a mere metal barrier, with two thin metal gates covering an opening equal to the size of the *Wall's* entrance. Flowing under the closed gates, through a twenty-foot clearing, like a trail of ants was a steady traffic of transports, fuel trucks, troop carriers and construction vehicles. They were traveling on a shiny twelve lane highway stretching from the main gate to the tower hangar.

Protecting this line of defense were two towers on both sides of the entrance. Each was about four stories tall and housed active radar seeking missiles and gatling-weapons. On the very top of the towers were two high-powered neon-helium lasers, designed to destroy any incoming missiles or small ships. One blast would annihilate the human aircraft.

"The gates are closed," Dutch began to configure the weapons.

"Well," Bishop dove at the left tower, "Let's knock on them."

As the F-202 closed on the poorly armed inner gate, it locked on its force shell cannon onto the left guardian tower.

In the dark of night, neither the Molluskan laser operator, nor the Aracteroid commander noticed the small human craft rushing straight at them yet. The Molluskan, leaning back in is chair, looked up through the glass bubbled ceiling and began to chatter gibberish and point wildly as it finally noticed the bright blue flashes coming from the darkness, but it was too late.

The entire glass bubble topping the left tower shattered as it was riddled with hundreds of twenty-millimeter force shells. Although the AIM-22 was designed for air combat, its fragmentizing warhead and infrared seeker made it ideal for the hot and fragile laser system. A single Hydra missile crashed into the laser itself, taking it out of commission.

The right tower began to fire its force cannons and radar seeking missiles at the F-202, as it was pulling up from its dive.

"Black us out! Now!" Bishop yelled to Dutch, as he noticed a string of missiles heading at them.

The cockpit lit up and the Lakota was violently thrown hard to the left as one missile impacted its right underside. The rest of the missiles with no radar signal to follow anymore, simply continued on their original course and barely missed the Lakota by a couple feet.

"Any damage?" Bishop asked harshly.

"No. The shield absorbed... Brake left! " Dutch shouted.

The Lakota broke hard to the left as a red beam of light blinked by it.

"This bastard's got an attitude problem!" Bishop yelled.

"Head at its base," Dutch ordered, "I'm going to pull the rug out from under its feet."

The F-202, although invisible to radar and infrared, could still be visually detected, and it was currently being searched for through the cross hairs of nearly every gunner in the right tower. Both towers began to fire flares into the air.

Instantly, the area was lit up and the stealth F-202 was visually spotted.

"Shit! Flares! They can see us!" Bishop shouted just as the first force shell struck the shielded canopy. The F-202 dodged and maneuvered its way through a tremendous hail of force shells, some hitting the forward shields and exploded, weakening the shields considerably. At dizzying speed, the F-202 dove at the base of the right tower. It began to fire its nose cannon, tearing holes into the metallic walls of the tower. As the F-202 drew ever closer, its force shells began to tear away entire panels of armor from the tower. VanDuinwyk watched with satisfaction as a giant hole appeared in the tower wall.

"Firing," he yelled over the roar of the air, engines and crashing force shells against the shields.

A Unicorn missile was fired at the gaping, smoldering hole, and the F-202 pulled up hard and to the right to avoid crashing into the tower.

The missile's cone came apart only fifty feet from the gaping rift in the tower's armor. The missile shot through the hole and the bomblets scattered into the towers bowels and then exploded. The result was spectacular: With a solid lurch, the base of the tower totally exploded, sending a wave of shrapnel out into the highway, shredding several vehicles on the spot. The tower began to collapse into the right section of the inner gate, where it obliterated itself while punching a huge hole in the gate itself, and giving the Lakota a way to get in.

Both Bishop's and VanDuinwyk's jaws dropped.

"I didn't expect it to do that!" Dutch stuttered.

"I love you man. " Bishop howled.

"Well, can't question a good thing, let's go." Dutch locked his weapons onto the barely damaged left turret.

Before flying into the rift in the gate, the F-202 strafed the left tower once again, peppering holes in its surface with holes. Once the Lakota had cleared the inner gate, it once again disappeared into the darkness.

CHAPTER 30 Master Puppet

It was nearly pitch black. Sand lazily blew over the desert floor, before the *Wall*. A large patch of sea-green glass, sand that had been melted by multiple nuclear blasts of the nomad missiles over twenty-four hours ago, spread out from the gate. The two former metal crushers had been reduced to crumpled piles of slag that remained just outside the gate where they had been destroyed.

The *Wall* itself was blackened and charred from the blasts, with some sections noticeably depressed inward. Only the gate itself was still pristine, having been retracted into the ground when the nomads struck. Though still impressive, the *Wall* was no longer impenetrable; three human ships had violated the towering structure. Six humans had pierced its mighty defenses and indeed, the mystique was gone.

A quiet rumble could be heard in the distance. From a quiet rumble it grew to a loud thundering roar. The sand was blown around, creating a dust storm as a ship descended from the sky. Its engines digging craters in the sand with their thrust. Only one hundred feet from the desert floor, the large four wheels descended from their cradles deep in the undercarriage of the ship. With a thundering jolt, the wheels met the sand. And the thrusters quieted down.

Aside from the menacing hum radiating from new arrival, all was again quiet.

After several minutes of protocol checks and security codes, the shield covering the gate to the *Wall* was lowered and the gate began to sink into the ground. When it was fully open, the huge ship rolled over the melted metal crushers, and into the compound. The gate's shield immediately closing behind it. The gate rose back into its position, sealing the compound.

The ship drove into the compound, past the Molluskan Barracks and through the only functional gate of the inner barrier. It drove past the cooling facility and through the main tower's perimeter gate. There, it waited for the tower's hanger doors to slid open before driving inside and parking side by side with the much larger MegaKore.

The Batteckery had landed.

One by one, a row of lights flickered on inside the massive hangar of the tower. The Batteckery and MegaKore were both basked in light.

As the Batteckery's hydraulic landing system lowered the body to the ground, steam swept across the floor of the enormous hanger. As the undercarriage met with the cold steel floor, a soft rumble was felt. A huge roll-top hangar door set on the left side slowly opened. Simultaneously, several ramps began to extend to the floor.

Standing at the loading dock where the ramps touched down was a perfect formal line of dressed up Molluskan. Across from them was a line of battle dressed Aracteroid. In the center was a green carpet extending all the way to the edge of the platform.

Krewtek waited at the foot of the carpet for his royal guest with Grackconn at his side, carrying his usual load of paperwork.

As each of the ramps reached out as far as possible, then slid horizontally inward until then converged to form one solid sloped platform from the opening in the ship to the floor. After several Molluskan and Aracteroid filed out to make their own lines and the green carpet was rolled out over the ramp, Non Risolm finally strutted out. For as long as this ceremony took, after seeing who it was for, it seemed hardly worth it.

Non Risolm was a short Trexian, about four and a half feet actually. He walked with a half strut, half limp. In fact he even dragged his left foot sometimes to impress others. His horns were stubby and stunted. In the center of his bulbous head was a very large eye. Too large. So large, in fact, he sometimes closed it half way to make it appear smaller. Risolm was a small and ugly Trexian.

Non Risolm's personality was less attractive. He was perpetually rude, irrational and a coward, who preferred to have others fight his battles, which he started thoughtlessly. After several failed assassination attempts, Non Risolm believed he was invulnerable. As he approached Krewtek, he felt that it was a shame that no one managed to kill the little bastard.

Krewtek smiled at his fellow Trexian as Risolm saluted him in a false show of respect.

"Welcome to Grantex Starport I," Krewtek said motioning Risolm to lower his arms. "I hope your trip was a pleasant one," he said almost sarcastically.

Risolm opened his large mouth. "The trip was *hell...*" he muttered, "the food was nauseating and your Molluskan are even stupider than I ever dared to imagine. As for the landing..."

"Very good, I'm happy you enjoyed it. Now come with me so we can talk business." Krewtek jovially cut him off. And began to walk towards the large doorway that led into the tower. Risolm had to run to catch up as they both exited the hanger. All who were left seemed to heave a heavy sigh of relief, except for the Molluskan who were oblivious, and only knew they were told to stand still.

Krewtek walked into his office and sat down in his chair. Non Risolm followed close behind but stopped at the doorway when he realized there was no chair in front of him. Krewtek loudly sighed and stared at

Risolm with a look of severe irritancy. "Now what the hell is wrong with you Risolm,"

Risolm opened his mouth again, "I refuse to go on with this meeting unless I have a chair, if that's too hard..."

"Shut the hell up and get in here. We're no longer in front of the subordinates, so I'm not going to put up with any of your whimpering," Krewtek snarled.

Non Risolm gasped, his eye opened all the way, exposing a yellow iris with a vertical pupil. "But, you... you can't talk..." he stammered.

"Yes, I can Risolm. And I will. It's been a hell of a week here on Earth," Krewtek's voice became slightly less hostile as he explained. "The reactor was late getting started, the humans have breached the compound in a brilliant offensive using our own damn technology, and at least two of the little bastards are running rampant within our facility! Our forces are dropping every time they attack, and to make matters worse, *Kimbett still lives!*"

"He's alive? I thought you guaranteed me he would be dead before I got here," Non Risolm whined.

"Shut up Risolm! The assassination failed, I'm sure you can relate to that!" Krewtek hissed. Risolm quickly snarled back.

"What to we do now?" Risolm said, shaken.

"My plans remain almost unchanged. However, in addition to keeping the crew of the MegaKore in line, you now also have to protect it from Kimbett."

"What do you propose?" Risolm asked calming down.

"I'll give you a security sequence that only you and I will know, as soon as your onboard, you have to seal everything off. Including the main computer. Only then will we be guaranteed that Kimbett will never get aboard, even if he's got someone on the inside," Krewtek said.

Non Risolm frowned at the mention of a security code. "What if the crew mutinies? What if they decide to torture me until I reveal..."

"Shut up," Krewtek cut him off apathetically, "I'll send a squad of my elite Molluskan troopers along with you. And in a day, Lieutenant Rycon will arrive and be your personal body guard."

"What makes you think this Rycon can be trusted," Risolm whined.

"You remember the ancient Trexian proverb: *There is no enemy like a traitor brother*," Krewtek stared of into space as he said this.

"Huh?" Was Risolm's response.

"Never mind. Now, let's go over the details," Krewtek said with a big sigh.

Krewtek hated Risolm as much as his subordinates, but Risolm had one characteristic all others lacked, he knew he could control him.

. . .

Sulfurous gases filled the metallic valley of pipes and equipment. Waves of heat radiated from below, creating mirages that rippled off in the horizon. On the crest was a green human-like creature, he smiled crookedly at the Molluskan working below. He looked up past the brownish column of haze rising from the valley to see the main tower, illuminated against the midnight sky. It was about fifty miles away, and at the rate Kimbett was moving, it would take him another day and a half to get there.

"I've got to buy some time," he said to himself.

The workers below were oblivious to the predator that watched them from far above. Some were unloading metal cubes from the metal crusher, others were operating the giant liquefier that produced the metal girders that still others attached to a cylindrical skeleton of a structure they were producing. It looked as if they working through the night to add another wing onto the construction plant. As they worked, Kimbett could hear intermittent Molluskan grunts.

"I hate Molluskan," he said in English with an American accent. With that he scrambled over the edge and disappeared into the valley below.

At the far left of the construction yard, unseen to the rest of the Molluskan workers, two workers chattered quietly to themselves as they worked. One was unloading from a large gray truck, bags of gray gelatin that, when doused with water, turned to a concrete like plastic. The other one was cutting the bags open and pouring the gelatin into a large foundation mold.

As the taller Molluskan dropped the bag of gray jelly, the smaller one told it to get two more. The tall Molluskan nodded stupidly, and walked off. As it began to walk towards the truck it noticed the pilot's hatch was open. It unholstered its small plasma weapon and cautiously walked around to the left side of the truck and peered inside the cab. The cab was entirely empty. Something tapped its shoulder, and it spun around with its weapon out.

Crack!

All its mind registered was the a sound as something threw its back against the side of the truck's hatch. It found itself looking at a horribly disfigured Kimbett. He was holding a high-powered riveter, used to bind metal girders together. It tried to move, but a dull pain burned from its chest, as it realized Kimbett had pinned it to the driver's side door. It raised its plasma gun to fire at Kimbett, who swatted it from the Molluskan's hand, taking two fingers with it.

"Thanks," he said, "sleepy time." he finished as he pointed the riveter at the Molluskan's head...

Crack!

The shorter Molluskan withdrew the silvery gray crescent shaped blade from its sheath, and cut the bag open. Grey jelly oozed from the slit carved into it, then it replaced the blade and grabbed the bag with both arms and turned it upside down, pouring the contents into the foundation mold. It whirled around as it heard something behind it approach.

It nearly jumped when it saw Admiral Kimbett standing behind it with a standard Trexian *dagger* plasma gun. Kimbett was about to fire, when the Molluskan, with lightning speed, withdrew its blade and slashed his wrist, knocking the plasma gun into the mold of gelatin. Kimbett grabbed the Molluskan's arm and threw his knee into its stomach. As it doubled over, it reached for its own plasma gun, but Kimbett smacked it from the Molluskan's hand and the plasma gun slid away.

The Molluskan uppercutted Kimbett, and Kimbett head butted the Molluskan after it sliced a gash in his abdomen. Both flew back from each other.

This was no ordinary Molluskan! Kimbett looked down at the wounds to his wrist and stomach and then stared at the creature in front of him. It looked like a normal Molluskan worker, with the large hard-hat and chest plate. But its eyes were not the typical empty black, this one's were glossy red, with puffy pink bags under them, and its skin was pale. It raised its blade and growled. Drool dripped from its tentacles. *The Molluskan was insane!*

Kimbett looked down and saw the plasma gun lying at his feet. He looked at the rabid Molluskan and smiled an evil smile as he kicked away. Thorns grew from the pores on his shoulders, hands, elbows and knees.

"All right asshole let's dance," he barked while walking towards the insane Molluskan, who was beckoning him to come closer.

The two suddenly charged each other, Kimbett leapt into the air and planted his foot in the center of the Molluskan's body. The Molluskan dropped its knife and jumped for the plasma gun. As it grabbed it, it was covered in thousands of tiny yellow spines. Kimbett threw his arm up for another volley, and the Molluskan got off a single shot at point blank range before it was hit again with Kimbett's thorns. It began to itch itself franticly before Kimbett threw his fist into its face and sent it down into the foundation mold. There it lay face up, motionless, up to three inches in gelatin.

"My *God*, what are they feeding you guys back at the Molluskan Barracks?" Kimbett said sarcastically as he looked at the smoking plasma burn on his shoulder. He leaned over and pulled the ignition card from the fallen Molluskan's belt, and head back towards the cargo truck.

Kimbett smiled with his few teeth, "Time to go for a little spin."

A group of ten Molluskan was working on the new wing. They scrambled about moving girders, and using the riveters to bolt them to other girders. None heard the sound of the engines until the truck rounded the corner; Kimbett behind the wheel.

Some Molluskan dove out of the way, some climbed the girders, but most just stood, shocked and stupid, as Kimbett hit them at nearly eighty miles an hour. Molluskan flew everywhere, some exploded upon impact, while others were tossed like rag dolls. Kimbett screamed as he rocketed down the metallic canyon, heading straight for the tower.

"Ready or not, here I come!" he howled.

. . .

There was no green carpet laid out for the Non at the MegaKore. Risolm and his squad of *decimator* toting Molluskan Troopers seemed insignificant to the gargantuan vehicle. As they approached the port side, they became aware that the airlocks below the main cargo bay were opening. Non Risolm at first though

Destarus might actually be sending out the respectful greeting party, he was half right.

Molluskan poured out of the hatches about fifty yards away. But they weren't bringing a green carpet. Instead, Non Risolm found himself surrounded by over one hundred MegaKore MTs. Risolm's own six MTs made angry Molluskan sounds while they pointed their weapons at the hoard surrounding them.

"Welcome Non Risolm," A voice came from the crowd.

"Show yourself. What is the meaning of this! I could have you executed for this show of disrespect!" Non Risolm shouted. As he did so, the ring of MTs parted and an old Aracteroid walked in, leaning on his staff.

"I'm sorry if you are disrespected Sir, but Admiral Krewtek gave us specific instructions to make your stay aboard the MegaKore as safe as possible. This is merely your escort," the Aracteroid said politely.

"Who the hell are you anyway?" Non Risolm crudely asked.

"I am Doctor Kailecko. Now if you will come with us, we can arrange a brief tour and show you your quarters." With that the doctor scrambled on his three operational legs.

"Non Risolm reluctantly followed, there were many questions on his mind. *Why was his escort pointing their weapons at him? Or why wasn't there a ceremony?* Risolm accepted that no matter what happened, he was better off within the walls of the most powerful and most feared battleship in existence. Boratus arrived at the massive battleship shortly after the short admiral had disappeared. As he approached, the MegaKore MTs paid him no attention.

As Non Risolm walked down the narrow corridors of the MegaKore en route to the bridge, he noticed that he had the crew's full attention. Molluskan stood in adjoining doorways and glared, Some Aracteroids walked by with their heads turned, some even let off a muffled hiss. But most of them simply stared at him with their four crimson eyes and drooled venom onto the floor. Risolm wasn't intimidated, he had lived most of his adult life with a price on his head.

As he reached the hatchway leading to the bridge, Risolm found that it wouldn't open, he began to beat on it with his fists. Kailecko pushed past the MTs and came beside the short Trexian. Non Risolm watched as Kailecko tapped in a security code. The door hissed open, and lead into the largest bridge Risolm had ever seen.

As he walked in he was in total awe. Fifty yards in front of him stood a thirty by sixty foot view screen that was set deep into the wall. Above Risolm were seven levels of balcony that surrounded the central bridge pit. In the pit itself was the captain's seat, twenty feet above Risolm, above the door he came in, was the Admiral's seat, accessible by two curved staircases. This is where Kimbett would have controlled not only the MegaKore, but as the flagship; the entire fleet. It was the seat of power, and it now sat vacant.

In the captain's chair sat a strange looking robotic character that faced the giant view screen that was currently showing a schematic of the Grantex compound. Kailecko scrambled over to the creature and whispered to it.

The creature raised its hand at the view screen and with a flash, it went dead. Then the robotic creature stood up and turned around. Strapped over its shoulder, was a very strange looking weapon. Non Risolm didn't know what Captain Destarus had looked like until now. Destarus walked over to Non Risolm and saluted.

"Admiral Risolm," Destarus began, "I am Captain Destarus. Welcome aboard the MegaKore Battle Ship. I hope your stay will be a healthy one."

"Why wouldn't it be Captain," Risolm snapped.

"Well, you see, we weren't told of your visit until two hours ago, and our Admirals on this ship seem to keep disappearing," Destarus said nastily.

"If you're referring to the traitor Kimbett, don't worry about it. My love is for the empire and nothing else," Risolm lied. His true love was for himself. "Now if you'll excuse me, I have been ordered to change the security codes on this ship."

"Why?" Destarus asked, not showing his concern.

"If the traitor Kimbett is not killed, he will surely end up here and we cannot permit this to happen," Risolm said arrogantly, "Besides, you don't need the codes for now anyway Captain Destarus. As you can see, we're not going anywhere." As he finished, he withdrew a small red cartridge.

Destarus quickly stepped forward, "You can't change the codes," He said, formidably covering the console with his metallic hand.

Risolm stepped two steps back, and Destarus became aware that six of Risolm's MTs pointed their weapons at him. Destarus looked at Kailecko who nodded his head at him, but Destarus shook his head, *Not yet! We have to wait for Kimbett* he seemed to say. Kailecko looked at the ground in defeat.

"Move Captain. Or I'll have you moved," Risolm said bluntly.

Destarus rolled his eye and stood aside as the short Trexian plugged a small red cartridge into the console. After a few minutes, the cartridge was removed and given to one of Risolm's body guards with orders to have it vaporized.

"Now," Risolm started, "The Navigation and tactical stations are locked off to everybody but me, as are most central computer functions. Any attempt to break into these systems can and will be punished by death," he began to pace back and forth as he spoke, "I know that there is a good possibility that the traitor Kimbett is on his way here. So we've taken an extra precaution: I've locked off all external hatchways, including the main cargo bay and all emergency and service hatches. In short, there is no way in or out," Risolm chuckled.

Destarus closed his eye. Had he lost the only chance he might of had? He didn't know. No wonder Krewtek had kept his plan to appoint Risolm the new Admiral secret. Kailecko sat back in the chair at the tactical station and glared at Risolm's MTs.

Risolm climbed the archway over the doors leading into the bridge and up to Kimbett's seat. There he sat and began to punch buttons randomly like a child given a new toy. His MTs walked up the stairs to the first level platform and took positions.

Destarus' hands were tied. He couldn't leave now if he wanted to.

Risolm continued to chuckle and play with the controls at the Admiral's station. Destarus let out an audible synthesized sigh.

A puppet now pulled the strings.

CHAPTER 31 Pest Control

Krewtek sat solemnly behind his desk with his face buried in his hands; the Trexian Admiral didn't have his usual evil grin, he didn't have his trademark happy, sadistic attitude. He was instead, seriously worried.

The room was unusually dark and gloomy, the luminous chart on the left wall was turned off, and his desk was cleared of all papers and tablets.

The screens behind his desk were black, and on his desk-screen was a frozen picture of a bloody wall in the gardens under the staircase to the garden tower. Written on the wall in yellow Aracteroid blood were Trexian glyphs that translated to: *It Begins*.

He now knew what happed to Bakkaraqu.

Krewtek had every reason to be worried, one of the biggest ones was that Kimbett was nowhere to be found. And Krewtek knew that his blood would probably be used to write the next message on a wall, unless he could act fast.

The dot eyeball on his desktop looked at him with detached concern, but other than that seemed very bored.

There was a knock at Krewtek's door. His head snapped up, and he reached for his *hellion* multi-barreled sidearm. His Molluskan bodyguard brought his gun up and waited for the order to fire, just as Krewtek had ordered him to. Krewtek unlocked his door by pressing a button on his desk.

"Enter," Krewtek said nervously as he switched off his desk-screen.

The door slid open and a cybernetic Molluskan walked in. Rycon, usually emotionless, seemed not to mind the two weapons pointing in his direction. His one living eye was utterly unrevealing, yet projected vast, deadly, intelligence.

The strange looking Molluskan walked in and closed the door behind him. Krewtek lowered his weapon, but the bodyguard still held his up, pointed at the new being in the room.

The strange Molluskan swept his camera from side to side, scanning the entire area, retrieving gigabytes of data, but ignoring most of it. It suddenly spoke.

Rycon raised his arms in respect, "I am at your service Admiral," he said in perfect synthesized Trexian, white tentacles twitching slightly while he spoke.

Krewtek motioned to his bodyguard to lower his weapon, which he did so dumbly and reluctantly. Krewtek locked the door.

"Ah, Lieutenant Rycon. How has the perimeter been since the attack?" Krewtek asked the cybernetic Molluskan.

Rycon immediately began, "There has been no sign of any humans since the attack. ^^ Boratus has repeatedly stated he is short on building materials, and needs to salvage the two metal crushers outside the gate."

"Impossible. The gate is not to be opened any more until the reinforcements arrive," Krewtek stated, "Besides, they've been melted down, you'd have to cut them out of the ground before somehow dragging them inside."

Rycon stood perfectly still, "Understood Sir,"

"Now, I have a special assignment for you Lieutenant." The Admiral said turning on the screen that again showed the words written in blood.

A slight humming vibration could be felt emanating from Rycon.

"I need your help here, Lieutenant." Krewtek began, "There is a traitor among us. A former Admiral of mine, you might have heard of him, his name is Kimbett."

The mechanical aperture in Rycon's artificial eye expanded, a small red light glowed from within it.

"I know of the former Admiral Kimbett, Sir," said Rycon.

"Well, he was responsible for letting the humans deactivate the gate shield at main gate and penetrate our mighty defenses. And I'm afraid he also is responsible for the death of Lieutenant Bakkaraqu and some of his officers, along with the destruction of fragile equipment at garden tower in the garden dome." Krewtek put his hands on his desk and interlocked his clawed fingers.

"You will find the traitor Kimbett..." Krewtek narrowed his eye, "and kill him," Krewtek seemed to elongate the Trexian equivalent of *kill.* "...before he reaches the MegaKore," he added under his breath.

Rycon wriggled his white tentacles, hinting surprise. "How can you be sure Kimbett is heading for the MegaKore battleship?" demonstrating his ultra-high audio sensory.

Krewtek didn't answer at first, after a long foreboding pause, he spoke, "Kimbett is a complete psychopath, but he isn't stupid. He knows the only way he can escape now is to reach the MegaKore,"

"I assume Captain Destarus is now in command of the MegaKore. Correct?" Rycon inquired.

"No, I don't believe Destarus is very trust worthy; he served under Kimbett before arriving here. So I have decided to hand command over to Admiral Risolm,"

Rycon became very quiet, after another longer pause, he spoke. "Non Risolm?" Rycon glared at Krewtek, "Why him?" Rycon's skin seemed to loose all moisture, at this moment he looked entirely machine.

"That is no concern of yours," Krewtek said coldly. "You have two days to complete this mission, if you can't find Kimbett, you will have to deal with me," Krewtek gave his trademark grin.

"Your excused," he finished.

Rycon saluted his superior and turned to leave.

"One more thing Lieutenant," Krewtek hissed. Rycon stopped but didn't turn around.

"You and Destarus are like brothers aren't you?" Krewtek's eye narrowed.

"We were both created on the Ko Ssevorg. The same engineers created us, Sir. But we are not brothers."

If Rycon would have turned around, he would have startled the Trexian Admiral, for his artificial eye was glowing crimson. Although Krewtek didn't know it, he had evoked an emotion not often experienced by Rycon: Anger.

Krewtek hit the unlock button, and seconds later, Rycon had departed.

The Molluskan bodyguard looked at Krewtek and made Molluskan noises. The little dotariak on his desk stared at him in what looked like disgust. The portrait of his Trexian Superiorness, Lord Kroyce, even seemed to be glaring at him.

"Not good... not good at all," Krewtek said quietly.

CHAPTER 32 Rycon

Unseen to the Molluskan patrolling the edges of the ravine, Gates sprinted from the parked forklift where he been hiding for several hours, to a metal crate, and then to a storage shed. There was a half moon tonight, enough to bask an eerie blue glow over the alien buildings and Earthly ground.

As he reached the shed he had found the coolant pump in, he stopped to catch his breath. Although breathing hard, Gates was capable of sprinting another mile if needed, for he knew he must reach the Revenant with his supplies if there was to be hope of repairing it. He poked his head outside the shed to see over one hundred and fifty gatling-gun toting Molluskan and armored Aracteroid that were patrolling the sides of the ravine. He realized that they somehow knew this was where he would try to cross.

Gates heard Molluskan chattering and immediately hid in the corner. In walked two large Molluskan troopers gabbing wildly as they worked together to tear open a thin metal box and remove two small clear bottles from it. Gates watched, dehydrated, as the Molluskan removed their helmets and drank the liquid obscenely. *Water!* Gates though. The two Molluskan finished off their bottles and threw them in the dark corner next to Gates, who picked up one of them and tried to shake what little water was left, into his mouth. He felt better.

On the eastern side, Rycon looked around angrily, yet emotionless.

Xo joined him.

"I am putting you in charge of the security forces Ensign." Rycon said plainly.

"May I ask why, Lieutenant?" Xo said, a little taken back by his new responsibility.

Rycon continued to scan the area without looking at Xo.

"No." he said simply.

Xo nodded, "Alright, I have it."

"You'll find everything you need in my office." Rycon added.

Xo again nodded as he unscrewed the lid on a metal thermos.

"Krewtek really screwed this one up huh, Rycon?" Xo said between sips of a hot beverage.

Rycon began... "He has made too many mistakes to ensure absolute success of the primary objectives of not only the first mission, but the mission following as well."

"You said it Lieutenant," Xo said with a mild chuckle before taking another sip.

"Kimbett is out here somewhere..." Rycon said looking around the base.

"Those humans are out here somewhere," Xo corrected, pointing nowhere in particular. "And they are our biggest problem right now."

"Kimbett is the problem," Rycon said flatly, "He will defiantly now attempt to gain control of the MegaKore and use it against us."

Xo shrugged. "So what? I'd feel better having him at the helm rather than Risolm, the *Instant Admiral.*"

Rycon said nothing.

"Besides, I don't think Kimbett is the traitor around here..." Xo said, his voice trailing off....

Rycon turned his head and with his organic eye, peered at Xo, who stared ahead. "You are implying Krewtek? What or who has he betrayed?"

"Well, let me put it this way: I don't believe Kimbett kidnapped Bakkaraqu, dragged him to the garden tower, and then killed him." Xo drank a large gulp of his hot beverage.

"You know too much for your own good Ensign..." Rycon surmised.

"The Aracteroid talk... they don't think a Molluskan can understand them... but I hear very well." Xo said, wiping his tentacles.

"So you say Kimbett was framed..." Rycon continued.

Xo sighed, "No Sir, I'm saying Bakkaraqu was hired by Krewtek to kill Kimbett and Kimbett ended up killing Bakkaraqu, that's what I'm saying." Xo drank the last of his thermos and put it in his pack.

"My mission is to track down and kill Kimbett. That is why you are taking over here. I will fulfill my mission," Rycon mindlessly droned.

"What will you say when your next mission is to kill one of your subordinates, or close friend, or even *me*. Will you fulfill your mission Sir?" Xo said calmly, yet sternly to his superior.

Rycon again said nothing, but continued to stared at Xo.

"You have to draw the line somewhere Lieutenant. Before *YOU* are labeled traitor and none of your brothers are left to save you," Xo said poetically as he jumped into a small jeep-like vehicle.

Rycon's eerie silence continued for another ten seconds.

"I'm going to the Molluskan Barracks, are you coming Sir?" Xo said, starting the engine.

"No. I am going to try to head the traitor off before he gets to the MegaKore," Rycon said flatly.

Xo said nothing, but his face showed only disappointment. He rode off into the sand towards the Molluskan Barracks.

Rycon walked towards the large bridge crossing the ravine.

Gates dove at the edge of the ravine, sliding to a halt only a foot from the group of pipes that draped over the edge and stretched across the chasm. He nervously looked around to see if he had been spotted. The Molluskan and Aracteroid scurried around completely oblivious to Gates. Spotlights and, no doubt, computer surveillance systems were looking everywhere, but they appeared to be more interested in the larger bridge. No one was watching the way Gates would cross.

Gates crawled out onto the collection of pipes and cables. He had been merely scared when crossing the first time, but was now terrified. In the dark, he had trouble seeing where the few handholds were on the smooth pipes.

With the half moon shining down on him, Gates began to crawl along the cables and as he did the pipes began to creak and groan. Gates and Ford had crossed this way once before and knew it could be done, but the shaking and creaking of the bridge seemed to change his mind. Never the less, he set out.

Rycon felt something. He polled his sensors to verify that he was alone, but to his surprise was not getting a straight answer from his augmentations. Rycon couldn't explain the sensation he was feeling. It was as if he was feeling the presence of another highly intelligent being. But the only other life forms on the bridge were about sixteen MTs, who certainly were not intelligent. Rycon ignored this feeling and continued to walk down the bridge when his infrared scanner, through the glare of the shields above, picked up an intermittent signature to his right. He looked over and stopped dead in his tracks.

Before Rycon, across nearly fifty yards of open space, was a human. It could barely be seen through the infrared interference from the shield above, but it was there, crawling on the utility bridge trying to get back to the desert. Rycon internally switched his vision to low-light level and instantly revealed the human in full detail... *this could not be real!*

He stared, stunned for a full second before his on-board computer system prompted him to take action, and he instantly raising both arms in the air and let out an ultra-loud computer synthesized Molluskan battle cry that filled the air. A second later, he locked his targeting system onto Gates, pointed his rocket launcher at him and fired.

Gates heard the yell and looked just in time to see fire erupt from the arm of a very strange Molluskan. In a mere second, Gates was on his feet and diving forward as the small foot long missile blazed behind him, only inches from the top of the small bridge and exploded into an airburst of shrapnel that luckily did not find him. As Gates landed on the bridge again, he slipped off the side. If not for the small cables running along side the larger pipes that he was holding on to, Gates would have fallen far below into the raging waters Hell's Mississippi, and never be seen again. He quickly scrambled on top of the bridge again.

Rycon had barely missed human, but wasn't planning to do it again. He reloaded his launcher with another antipersonnel rocket and aimed.

Gates had reached the western most support beam holding up the bridge, he quickly dropped down on the other side of the girder for cover.

Fire, again, erupted from Rycon's arm as a sleek white missile, flew from the rocket launcher, in a direct course with the support beam.

Gates gripped the metal pipes as hard as he could as the rocket impacted the other side of the support beam. The shock nearly catapulted Gates backwards, but he held on for dear life as burning metal scraps rained down on him from above. Another rocket hit the support tower, but Gates held on still. The support was dented, but not damaged badly. Designed to stand against the constant flow of water in the ravine, the sturdy support was also resistant to the weak anti-personnel warhead of the rocket.

Three more missiles struck the support beam, but Gates somehow held on as sparks and fire blew past him. Gates suddenly realized that there was silence. He figured either the strange Molluskan had given up or the explosions had made him deaf. After a couple of seconds, Gates could hear several distant Molluskan sounds again.

Rycon muttered angrily. *This human wouldn't die.*

The conical opening of his rocket launcher dilated to its largest setting. Rycon reached back, and grabbed the largest rocket in his pack; it took up half the space.

Gates pulled himself up over the edge to take a peek, but all he could barely make out was the strange molluskan pointing his launcher diagonally upward and firing a very large rocket ballistically into the air. The rocket sailed upward into the sky and nearly out of sight. Gates had merely a fraction of a second to duck again before the over-excited molluskan troopers began to fire their force-cannons, tearing holes in the bridge piping itself.

Bits of plastic and metal pelted Gates as the force shells ripped through the non-reinforced cables and pipes. The hail of bullets stopped when Rycon began roaring angrily for them to cease-fire. The bridge was now in very bad shape, its already shaken integrity was nearly destroyed as the mounts holding the pipes and cables to the support beam were severed or damaged by the gunfire. Gates knew that it would not survive another volley of shells.

As the large rocket reached seven hundred feet, it began to make a slow inverted dive and head back down to the surface. From a small conical lens in the front of the rocket, Rycon piloted the missile by wireless remote. By the time it was within a hundred feet of the surface, he could see the bridge dead ahead and the human two thirds across behind the support strut.

Gates heard a noise. Almost like a jet engine. He swiveled his head around and gasped as he realized that something was coming at him from behind, he knew it was the rocket.

Franticly, he though of his options:

Let go, fall in the water, and get sucked into the reactor. *Nope.*

Stay here, get blown to tiny pieces. *Nope.*

Before Gates could think of a third option, he found himself climbing up onto the piping and running among the force shells the trigger-happy Molluskan were firing.

Rycon growled, gritting the teeth he didn't have as he tried to turn his missile to intercept Gates' new anticipated position. Fifty feet away.

Gates felt a great lurch and was thrown off his feet. He landed hard on the large pipe that ran the length of the bridge and realized something: *The bridge was moving!*

The entire bridge began to sag dangerously, the metal cables began to snap one by one and the pipes began to slide amongst themselves. Gates tried to get up and run again but not before a tearing metal sound and the piping dropping from under his feet followed by an eruption of steam from one of the pipes. He reached for the white plastic covered cables before he lost his footing as the last big pipe tilted past forty-five degrees, broke free from the west side of the ravine, and fell to the raging waters below.

Screaming a mechanically synthesized scream, his artificial-eye blazing crimson, Rycon realized he would miss. The human had fallen too fast for the missile to correct course; the rocket narrowly missed the human and splashed into the waters below, exploding and sending a fine super-heated mist into the air.

Gates held onto the cables for his life; his swollen hand stung as his fingers clenched against the pull of his one hundred and seventy pound body and the sixty pound satchel. The cables were all that remained of the small utility bridge. Force shells whirred past him like snow in a blizzard. One grazed his arm, tearing away a large piece of skin and uniform. Another shot grazed his left armpit, sending a burning sensation through his chest and side. He felt the end would come soon, and at that time, one ripped through the cables forty feet behind him.

He felt his body drop from the sky, and as he fell continued to grasp the cables in a death-grip. The rocky cliff wall was zooming at him out of the darkness alarmingly.

Rycon aimed his rocket launcher at the swinging human but lost him as he swung behind the outcropping of rock at the cliff wall. Gates closed his eyes before slamming into the rock as another missile exploded into the cliffs behind him.

The Molluskan began to cheer in their infinite stupidity. Rycon reloaded as his artificial eye glared red and his color was the whitest it had ever been. He turned around and swung his rocket launcher into one of the cheering Molluskan, knocking it off the bridge. He then turned his launcher on one of the remaining Molluskan and fired, blowing it to pieces at point blank range.

"Stop!" Rycon growled.

The molluskan stopped and stared at him blankly.

"The human is not dead! I will kill him!" he said, and all of the Molluskan nodded.

"If you see his head, shoot it! And *DO NOT* use rockets!"

They nodded again.

"And if you shoot me, I'll kill all of you. Understand?!"

They nodded again in perfect unison. Rycon reloaded his rocket launcher with his last rocket and picked up a medium sized gatling-weapon left by the Molluskan that fell off the bridge.

He head for the west end of the bridge.

Gates had been the type of kid who went on all the scary rides at a carnival as a kid, but *never again!* He had just swung over a hundred feet on a plastic and metal cable over a river of certain death at a rocky cliff wall. Nothing could top it.

Gates tasted bile, blood and dirt, and found himself grasping desperately to the rocky cliff wall. Looking up, he saw a mere thirty feet to the top. Turning his head to his right, he was happy to see the rock bulge in the cliff wall, blocking the second bridge and the dreaded rocket Molluskan from his view, and him from theirs. Gates began to climb.

Rycon reached the sandy rock at the end of the bridge. He quickly turned left and ran along the edge of the ravine towards the human's last know position.

Gates could climb no further. The cable connected with a shiny metal conduit eight feet below the metal platform where the western end of the destroyed utility bridge used to rest. All he could do was try feebly to scale the smooth rock wall to freedom.

Gates was suddenly struck in the head by a black rubber hose. He looked up and his eyes opened as he saw the desperate face of Ford.

"Grab it!" Ford yelled.

"What the hell are you doing here?! I told you to wait back at the bomber!" Gates yelled up to Ford.

"I'm impatient! Now hurry the hell up!" Ford shook the hose.

Gates needed no further convincing; he grabbed the stolen coolant tubing and used it to climb the last eight feet. Ford's hand met with Gates' and he was pulled over the edge.

"We're being followed!" Gates grunted as he began to run from the ravine. "I know, follow me!" Ford yelled before they both jumped and rolled over a very large sand dune.

Before Rycon could reach the human, he watched as it was rescued by yet another human and they disappeared over a dune together. Rycon followed with a vengeance. As he sprinted over the dune he fired his last rocket from his launcher. The small missile sailed up into the sky, and lit up the sand as if it were high noon. The flare slowly descended on a parachute, casting eerie shadows across the dead landscape.

He began to look franticly, *where were they?* Rycon looked around for footprints, clothes, *anything!* But he could only see thousands of Molluskan footprints, as there were hundreds walking that area over the last week. *The humans had vanished!*

Rycon began to fire his force-cannon into the sand around him. Explosions rocked the desert floor as glowing red liquid sand shot through the air in wave after wave. After a tumultuous moment, Rycon ceased fire and watched for five minutes. All that could be heard was the distant humming of the reactor, and the flowing water of the ravine. Convinced that he had failed, Rycon walked away. The humans had gotten away.

"Ford. You alive?" Gates' voice sounded from under the sand.

"Jesus! What was that thing?" Ford responded.

"Can you move?" Gates asked.

"Not with your knee buried in my gut," Ford grunted.

Gates stood up out of the buried fox hole, and Ford followed quietly.

"How did you know there was a hole there?" Gates asked Ford.

"I dug it," Ford said as he started running westward, "...they never captured me at SEER school."

Both men ran back to the grounded Revenant.

Ford had only bruises and marveled at Gates' horrible condition.

"Jesus, who'd you gets in a fight with? Lucifer?"

God was on their side tonight.

CHAPTER 33 Taste Of Sweet Fear

January 18th, 2034

Krewtek stood quietly, staring at the abandoned truck. It was covered in white Molluskan blood and dented from the impact of the bodies it had hit. Draped over the hood was a dead Molluskan who's head was buried in the shattered windshield. A second Molluskan was hanging from the right cabin door. Krewtek stared into the dead Molluskan's black eyes. Sticking out of its forehead was a ten-inch rivet. Imbedded in its chest was a second rivet, pinning it to the opened truck door. Dried white blood oozed from its forehead and chest like sap from a tree.

A long silence endured.

Surrounding Krewtek were four squads of Molluskan body guards, Grackconn, Xo, Rycon, and the pale skinned, rabid Molluskan, covered in the Gel-Cement.

After a long silence, Xo spoke up, "Ya know, some times these damn worker-Molluskan go berserk and do things like this,"

"Ask the worker what happened," Krewtek said quietly to Rycon, without looking at him.

Xo looked astonished, "Ask the *worker?* You'd be better off getting an answer from the truck."

The rabid Molluskan's gaze shifted to Xo.

"This is an enhanced version of a Worker-Molluskan. Designed and bred for use on Earth," Grackconn explained.

Rycon nodded and spoke, "What attacked you K23?"

The rabid Molluskan turned and stared at Rycon, and began speaking in broken Trexian, "K23 be knocked out! K23 not know what teethy thing be?"

"Idiot Molluskan! Answers, not riddles!" Krewtek snarled.

The rabid Molluskan just glared at Krewtek hatefully, drool dripping from its tentacles.

"Sir... please, getting information from these things isn't an exact science Sir," Grakconn cautioned, "especially this new strain."

"Teeth? Maybe it means it was smiling. Wasn't Molluskan then; we can't smile," Xo noted.

"K23, What species was it? Trexian, Aracteroid, Maquiasan, Human, Thalkaloid..." Rycon asked.

"K23 see teethy green thing! Teethy thing throw itchies at K23. Knock K23 into pit!" The pale Molluskan stomped its feet hard.

Krewtek raised his head and stared, everyone was quiet.

"Maybe it was another human Sir, wearing war paint. Who knows how many are crawling around here." Grackconn interjected.

"It wasn't the humans. " Krewtek finally said, pulling a thorn out of K23's head and holding it up for all to see. "I should have known... Kimbett..."

"He is much closer than I had anticipated," Rycon said almost apologetically.

"You're responsible Rycon!" Krewtek howled, "You had one job! I ordered you to find him!"

Xo spoke up in Rycon's defense, "Kimbett knows us too well Admiral; he's always twelve steps ahead, you won't catch him unless you plan thirteen steps ahead."

"Xo is right Sir. I think it's obvious where he's heading," Grackconn interrupted.

Krewtek kicked the door of the truck.

"Now what about the two humans Rycon?" Krewtek asked, frustrated.

"Two different humans crossed the river. I nearly killed one, but it had luck in excess," Rycon said without showing his regret.

"My latest search of the desert has turned up no sign of the second ship, Sir," Grackconn added, "And, as you know, an hour ago, the Humans broke through the inner gate and are now heading for the tower."

"They're coming..." Rycon said ominously. "And with the MegaKore's stations locked off, its a sitting duck in its hangar."

"What are we going to do, Sir?" Xo asked.

Grackconn began again, "Yes Sir? What are we..."

"Quiet! All of you!" Krewtek shouted, closing his eye tight.

After a lengthy pause, he spoke.

"Rycon. Go to the MegaKore and make sure nobody allows Kimbett to enter, and inform Risolm that he must unlock the weapons and tactical station," Krewtek said.

"What about the helm, navigation and communication stations?" Rycon asked.

"They don't need those to defend themselves," Krewtek snapped back.

Rycon nodded.

"Xo. I want you to have a squad of troops ready for the Humans if and when my Dotariak find them."

"Yes Sir!" Xo said.

"Grackconn. I want you to stop searching the desert for the crashed ship, and start organizing a strike force of Aero attack fighters to hunt the airborne ship!" Krewtek ordered.

"But Sir! We don't have any Aero fighters, and we can't detect the enemy ship! We don't know where it is..." Grackconn whined.

"*Fool!* Use your head," Krewtek scolded, "we have over fifty Aeros stowed in the hangars of the Batteckery and the MegaKore."

Krewtek turned back to Rycon, "Inform Risolm that we'll need six Aeros from the MegaKore."

Rycon nodded again.

Krewtek turned back to Grackconn, "Take six more Aeros from the Batteckery."

"Yes Sir!" Grackconn said.

"And I want you to station this strike force outside the tower, near the power sub-station. If they make visual contact, they will have the human ship out numbered and outgunned," Krewtek said.

"Consider it done Sir!" Grackconn said obediently.

"Get out of here!" Krewtek barked.

With that, Rycon walked off towards his transport. Grackconn and Xo walked back to their troop carrier, followed by two of the Molluskan squads. The last two squads boarded their own transport and sat waiting for Krewtek.

Krewtek climbed in the truck sat in the drivers seat, noticing the red blood stains within the cabin. Krewtek looked at the interior of the pilot's pod, something caught his eye, something he had not noticed until now. Smeared on the dash board, in molluskan blood, were the English words: *I'm Coming!*

Krewtek swallowed hard.

CHAPTER 34 Family Reunion

Risolm entered his secret fourteen digit code and backed up from the airlock, waiting impatiently for the computer to recognize his code. Upon accepting the code, the computer opened the airlock leading outside. Risolm half expected Kimbett to bolt through the open door and grab him by the throat, but that was a silly thought; *how could he get here so fast.*

Standing outside was a cybernetic Molluskan.

"Permission to come..." Rycon tried to ask.

Risolm nodded his head violently, "Yes! Yes! Yes! Just get in here!"

Rycon stood still for a moment, "Aboard." He finished before walking in and looking around the hangar in apparent awe. He had never been aboard the MegaKore before, and he was shocked by the size of its hangar alone.

"Hurry, seal the damn door!" Risolm commanded to his bodyguards.

Risolm waited for the door to shut and latch before he even acknowledged Rycon's presence. Once the door was shut, Risolm turned to Rycon and smiled.

"Lieutenant Rycon. Nice to have you aboard," Risolm said snidely.

"Likewise Admiral," Rycon said without a drop of emotion in his electronic voice.

Rycon followed Risolm to the bridge. Upon entering the cavernous bridge, Rycon immediately focused on the being sitting in the captain's chair, with its back turned to him. The being stood and turned around, its blue eye dilating upon seeing Rycon.

Risolm spoke, "Captain Destarus, this here is Lieutenant..."

"Rycon," Destarus said, walking over.

The red glow in Rycon's eye faded to black, "It has been a very long time Captain."

"Yes it has Rycon," Destarus responded.

"Oh! You two know each other!" Risolm clapped his hands together. "Oh yes, I remember, you two are like... brothers." Risolm smiled. Destarus felt like bashing the short Trexian Admiral with his customized rifle, but thought against it... not the right time. Feeling similarly, Rycon wanted to blow Risolm's head off with a rocket.

"Sir. I've been instructed to give you this." Rycon handed Risolm a black cartridge, "On it are official orders to release the computer lock on the weapons, tactical, and communications stations, in case of an attack by the humans."

"Humans?" Destarus doubted this possibility.

"Krewtek also commands that you deploy six of your Aero fighters to his designated coordinates," Rycon continued. Non Risolm looked shocked.

"What's this all about," Destarus asked his sibling.

"The human ship has broken through the inner gate, and may be heading for us. We don't know," Rycon explained, "and not more than six hours ago, we found an abandoned truck, stolen by the traitor Kimbett, only fifty miles away."

Risolm's mouth opened.

Destarus chuckled too softly to be audible.

"With your permission Sir, I would like to oversee the deployment of the six Aeros," Rycon stated.

"Ya...yes!" Risolm stuttered, trembling at the thought of an encounter with Kimbett.

Rycon departed the bridge.

"I'm going to get something to eat," Destarus said, walking off. Doctor Kailecko, who was sitting at the powerless tactical station, followed him.

Risolm inserted the black cartridge into Destarus's computer station and unlocked the communications system. As soon as the procedure was complete, he opened a channel to Krewtek's office.

. . .

Destarus sat alone in the alien ward room. His hands were folded on the table in front of him. Soon, a lone Molluskan chef walked into the dining area and served him a bowl of gray and brown mush with a large spoon, a hard biscuit, and a mug of water; the standard Trexian meal. Destarus made no move to eat his food, instead he waited patiently.

Not more than five minutes passed when the double doors opened and Kailecko walked in. He sat at the table with Destarus. Kailecko looked around to see if they were alone, while feeling under the table for listening devices.

"I already checked," Destarus said ominously, referring to his built-in hardware designed to *hear* any radio signals and electronic emissions from hidden listening devices.

"Boratus is on his way, he barely made it in before Risolm locked the doors," Kailecko said.

Both quieted down as the Molluskan chef approached and served Kailecko's meal: a bowl of green and red vegetable mush with pink meat sprinkles, and a mug of sugar water; a standard Aracteroid meal. Kailecko began to eat with his claws. As the Molluskan grunted and left, they continued their conversation.

"How do you know this being?" Destarus asked.

Kailecko chewed and swallowed his food before answering, "I served with him once on Gisten and once on the Batteckery."

Destarus's left chest plate sprang aside and two mechanical claws emerged and grasped the bowl of mush.

"Do you trust him?" He asked while a black nozzle emerged from between the arms and began to suck up the gooey meal; this was how Destarus ate or drank his food. His digestive system was designed to make use of almost any organic compounds, though for the sake of his crew, he ate common foods.

Kailecko nodded, "With my life."

"We can't afford to be wrong on this one Kail," Destarus said, the miniature arms replacing his empty bowl on the table.

"I've known him for a long time. He's of the Brotherhood," Kailecko ate more of his salad.

The doors opened again and Boratus stomped in. Upon seeing the two at the table, he walked over, pulled up a chair and sat down. Although he was sitting, he still towered over the other two officers.

"Glad you could make it Lieutenant Boratus," Kailecko said, "this is Captain Destarus,"

Destarus nodded at the giant, "Kailecko tells me that in addition to construction work, you are also a computer technician."

"Yes Captain, I came up from the ranks. After being conscripted, I was trained to be an electronic maintenance officer. In fact, I am quite familiar with the systems within the MegaKore." Boratus said, displaying a hidden intellect inconsistent with his brute appearance.

"What do you know about the computer access locks," Destarus asked, getting right to the point.

Boratus was not surprised at the question at all, "From what I can tell Sir, it is a simple yet effective access block. The code is fourteen characters, but with over thirty characters from the Trexian alphabet to choose from, it could be over a million combinations..."

"Can you crack it?" Kailecko asked, sipping his water.

The Molluskan chef walked over to the table and deposited a plate with a blood-red, muscular, scale covered leg of some unfortunate animal and a large mug of salt water; a standard Maquiasan meal.

The Molluskan departed.

Boratus leaned back in his chair, causing it to groan in protest, "Anything can be cracked. It just takes time, and stealth. If you can keep security out of the computer room..."

"Can it be broken now?" Destarus asked, impatiently.

"Not without narrowing down the possibilities first, right now it would take years of systematic trial and error," Boratus said before seizing the leg with his claws and taking a huge bite out of it.

"Can we bypass the main computer? Manually patch in to..." Kailecko asked,

Boratus shook his head while chewing, "These systems are designed to run everything from the main computer; that's why they have so much shielding protecting the computer rooms. Isolating subsystems is possible, but would time... a lot of time."

"Bah! We can do nothing with that Rycon now lurking around anyway. He and those MTs Risolm brought aboard are going to make it next to impossible to tamper with the bridge computers," Kailecko said, sipping his water.

"What *is* Rycon anyway, I've never seen a Molluskan like that," Boratus said, changing the subject.

"He's called an Enhanced Molluskan. And he was built aboard the Ko Ssevorg research station before it was destroyed at the start of the Great Trexian War," Destarus said while placing the biscuit into his chest compartment.

"The Ko Ssevorg?" Boratus turned his head at Destarus, "I heard that is where you are from, Sir."

Destarus nodded, "Yes, Rycon was built by the same scientists and engineers who augmented me. When the Ko Ssevorg was destroyed, none of those scientists survived," as he said this, the biscuit was pulverized by a mechanical jaw inside his chest compartment, and then swallowed into the black nozzle.

"So you and him are brothers, of sorts. Can we trust him?" Boratus asked.

"Yes we are. And no we can not," Destarus inhaled his water and his chest compartment closed, "Rycon has hated me from the day I saved him from the jar he was in on the burning decks of the Ko Ssevorg."

"Why does he hate you?" Kailecko asked.

"I don't know, he's more machine than he is Molluskan, perhaps he wanted me to let him die," Destarus stared at the table, "maybe he has a reason to hate me,"

. . .

Kimbett leapt over the security fence surrounding the perimeter of the cryo-plant. Its tall buildings and warehouses were laid out before him. He looked around sharply to see if anything was in pursuit. Directly to the left of him was the main roadway into the tower hangar, back the other way, it lead to the Garden Barracks, Molluskan Barracks, and then finally, to the main gate. Currently, there were several vehicles rocketing up and down this sixteen lane highway.

"Need a vehicle, some vehicle... any vehicle..." Kimbett saw a couple more cars zoom by at very high speeds. The cryo-plant's main complex was only a few feet to the left of him; two black armored, unarmed, soldiers guarded its main doors.

"Sprinters," He muttered hatefully. The black armored, unarmed soldier was actually a completely robotic bipedal, auto-targeting, running bomb. A *true* smart bomb, the Sprinter bomb was designed to terrorize subordinate races by air-dropping them into cities. Once they would spot something, and identified it as a target, they would charge after it. Depending on the mode settings, they would grab the target with their powerful mechanical arms, and either detonate, or wait until the screams of the ensnared victim drew would-be rescuers closer and then detonate.

The Trexian had began phasing the expensive psychological weapons out of their inventories twenty years prior, and their numbers had dwindled to less than a thousand. But on Earth, there were only ten.

Kimbett hated Sprinters with a cold hatred. Mostly because he recognized that they could easily kill him, but also because they were machines; machines developed by a demented Trexian engineer who used death and fear to crush uprisings against their demented empire. Kimbett spat foamy saliva in their direction, and began to move.

As Kimbett slowly walked past the front of the building towards a loading vehicle. The Sprinters stood perfectly still. They had not *noticed* him yet, for surely every Sprinter by now had been programmed to recognize and destroy him. Kimbett walked closer and closer to the vehicle.

The main doors of the cryo-plant opened and an Aracteroid scurried out and walked along the concrete path until suddenly coming to a halt, its eyes widely staring at the green fugitive. Kimbett waved a gnarled hand at the Aracteroid and smiled with an ugly, twisted smile, before breaking into a full sprint towards the loading vehicle.

"Its Kimbett! Guards! Guards!" The Aracteroid howled, jumping up and down. The two Sprinters turned their heads before bursting from their positions into a dash straight towards him. Kimbett heard the building's alarms go off and could hear two pairs of heavy footsteps closing from behind him. As he reached the vehicle, the hatch swung open, and a Molluskan poked its head out. Kimbett immediately seized its throat, and it was sent flying from the cab. As Kimbett climbed into the vehicle, another Molluskan, also in the cab, snarled at Kimbett and shot him in the chest with its plasma gun. As smoke from Kimbett's flesh filled the cab, the Admiral hit the Molluskan in the face, and swatted the gun from its hand before throwing it through the door leading into the cargo section of the vehicle. Kimbett jumped into the driver's seat and his hand shot for the ignition card left on the dash. The footsteps were right outside the vehicle when the engine was activated and the tires squealed as the magnetic clutch was engaged causing the vehicle lurched forward.

The windshield shattered and several holes were punched in the fuselage as a tremendous explosion rocked the transport vehicle. One of the closest Sprinters detonated a mere three feet from the escaping transport. Kimbett fought, to keep the vehicle from tipping over on its side, as it rocked back and forth. As he looked through the spider-webbed windshield, Kimbett saw several silver armored troops emerging from all entrances and exits of the cryo-plant.

"Oh dear," Kimbett said bleakly as force shells tore up the dirt and plastic all around him, some tearing into transport. One shot through the cab and blew a large chunk of flesh off of Kimbett's right shoulder.

Kimbett screamed and turned a hard left, putting him on a perpendicular course with the super highway. The remaining Sprinter remained in hot pursuit. The transport roared across two lanes before the Sprinter was hit by a small transport going eighty miles an hour. The Sprinter exploded on impact, shattering the rear axle assembly of the transport. The small vehicle then careened across six lanes, dragging its rear end, until reaching the first lane of oncoming traffic where it collided with an eighteen-ton heavy-transporter, hauling two tankers of aircraft-fuel. The explosion sent a shock-wave that caused several smaller accidents.

Kimbett crossed eight more lanes and then turned sharply to the right, and was now heading towards the tower only fifty miles away. Behind him, more vehicles were crashing into the burning wreckages of the fuel truck and the many wrecks left in his wake. The Molluskan appeared in the doorway again, and was quickly hit in the face by the compartment door, which Kimbett slammed and locked.

. . .

"As for Kimbett," Boratus sipped his water, "Why are we waiting for him?"

Destarus looked at Boratus and his eye closed to a slit, "I've owed Kimbett my life to Kimbett several times. He's worth waiting for,"

Boratus nodded, "No disrespect Captain, but waiting is the worst thing we can do, especially for only one being."

"It is said that we have no one leader..." Destarus said, "while this is true, Kimbett is in the inner circle of the Brotherhood."

"He masterminded the Selok Rebellion," Kailecko said.

"He's done much more than any of us can know... even his mission here is part of his plan." Destarus explained.

Boratus sighed, "Look. All I'm saying, is that if we wait for Kimbett, it may be too late to take this ship and leave this place." Boratus downed the rest of his salt water.

"Regardless of what happens, we wait for Kimbett, Understand?" Destarus said flatly.

"No matter what," Kailecko added.

Boratus was silent.

"Look Boratus, understand this: the end of the Trexian Empire is coming... it has started... cracks exist in their foundation. Kimbett's efforts here will soon blow these cracks wide open." Destarus said in a hushed tone.

Boratus looked to Kailecko and then back to Destarus.

Kailecko spoke, "We need you Lieutenant. I know you took a big risk coming here, and now that you're stuck in here with us things have only gotten worse. But a time will come when our lives will depend on *you*,"

"Are you with us?" Destarus asked simply.

Boratus shook his head, "They took my home too..." he said, "Of course I'm with you Captain."

Destarus and Kailecko patted Boratus on the back and raised their hands and claws in a show of mutual respect. Although Destarus's mind was on Boratus, he was still devoting a lot of thought to something else. *Where are you Kimbett.*

. . .

Kimbett heard the high pitched whining sound above the roar of his engines. Two Dragonflies launched from the cryo-plant's hangars were approaching the renegade transport from behind. With absolutely no warning, the rear of the Transport exploded as a rocket tore into it. By some miracle, the vehicle held together.

In the cargo section of the transport, a Molluskan laid, buried under two feet soiled, dirt-caked, odorous Molluskan uniforms. It raised its head above the reeking gray and brown laundry, and gasped upon seeing that the entire rear section of the vehicle was missing. The floor in front of the Molluskan was missing, and the rear axle and drive train could been seen, along with the two gray spinning tires hugging the roadway below, which was moving at over eighty miles an hour. It gasped again when it saw the two Dragonflies approaching from the rear. It jumped up to its feet and began to pound on the door leading to the cab.

"Shit!" Kimbett shouted as force shells rained on the cab and pierced the metal roof of the transport. Some of them hit the engine, and it began to sputter. Black smoke poured from under the transport and Kimbett realized the transport was doomed when the internal sputtering and rough sounds could be heard from the engine as it began to fail.

Kimbett drove right, across five lanes until he was on the leftmost lane. Then he kicked open the left hatch, and amidst the rain of force shells, jumped out of the vehicle, his body slamming into the concrete at eighty five miles an hour. At first he slid, rubbing off any skin that touched the ground, then rolled violently. When his crumpled, gnarled body finally stopped, he was covered by a heap of dirty laundry that was flowing out of the rear of the transport.

The door was finally kicked open, and to its horror, the Molluskan realized that no one was driving the vehicle. It jumped behind the controls...

Kimbett had been lucky, as neither of the Dragonflies noticed him bail from the transport among the soiled uniforms. They both continued to attack the damaged transport. The Molluskan turned the transport around, and raced into oncoming traffic, dodging vehicle after vehicle. Conveniently, it was leading the Dragonflies away from the tower.

Kimbett got up and watched the transport drive off with both Dragonflies chasing it, unable to figure out why. He began to hobble to a pile of surplus pipes that were to be installed in the tower while it was under construction. After resting briefly, and picking the plastic shards from his bloody flesh, he resumed his journey to the tower.

. . .

"You promised me that he would be dead by now!" Risolm whined like a child.

"Silence! You pathetic excuse for an officer," Krewtek shouted.

Risolm was quiet.

"Now, as long as you keep all outside hatches sealed and locked. He can't get in," Krewtek explained.

"But what about Destarus? I bet him and his crew is conspiring to kill me right now! And if I unlock the tactical..."

"Be silent! " Krewtek demanded.

Risolm was quiet again.

"Just do as I say! Stay with your MT's at *all* times, and watch your back," Krewtek grit his teeth. "And dammit, Risolm, you *WILL* unlock the tactical and weapon's stations, understand?"

Risolm nodded his head feebly.

"Good..." The small screen flashed and went black.

Risolm walked out of the communications room, and onto the bridge. He felt like pouting.

. . .

Kimbett stood at the mouth of the Tower hangar. It was too dark to see the MegaKore, but he knew it was in there. He began to stagger into the hangar, leaving a trail of blood dots. If the MegaKore was where he left it, it would be at least fifteen hundred feet away, the length of fifteen football fields. After walking eight hundred feet, and with his eyes adjusted to the gloom, Kimbett could see the MegaKore towering above him.

"There's my baby!" Kimbett said with a near-toothless smile.

"Honey I'm home..." he muttered with a shattered grin.

CHAPTER 35 Mission Impossible

The power sub-station was little more than a large cylinder sticking up from the ground next to the Tower. On top of the small building was a gaping, circular hole with diameter two thirds of the building itself, serving as an exhaust port for the heat exchangers within. Inside the port was over a hundred metal girders, crisscrossing to form a protective mesh, to stop bombs, missiles or pieces of debris from accidentally falling into the magnet cooling chamber, damaging the fragile machinery inside, and causing a catastrophic chain reaction. The primary target of Operation Locksmith was this building.

Only eight miles away, on the other side of the Tower, was another problem, it was the reactor coolant facility, also called the cryo-plant. Along with the twelve hundred acres of warehouses, cooling towers, water towers, control centers and a massive network of pipes connected to each building, it also housed a considerable military base, almost the size of the Molluskan Barracks.

"Cryo-plant dead ahead," Dutch spoke into his headset, "should we attack, or hope they don't see us,

Bishop thought for a second, "if they see us, they'll put more aircraft in the air than we can handle. I think we should hit 'em, while we have the initiative."

Dutch nodded, "I'm with you,"

"How are we on weapons?" Bishop asked.

"One Unicorn cluster-missile, and five Hydra air-to-airs," Dutch listed off.

"Fuel..." Bishop said, looking at his gauges.

"I'd say we got one more good high-speed fight," Dutch offered.

"Alright then, turn on the gas, let's get some..." Bishop

Unlike the last bases the F-202 destroyed, the cryo-plant was truly massive. Its endless buildings and machinery could be seen stretching off out the shield at the edge of the compound. One area stood out among the rest of the gray metal buildings, it was a raised platform that contained twenty launch pads. In the center were four elevating platforms that could raise other aircraft from the underground hangars below the plant. There were currently eighteen aircraft parked on the platform. Just off to the left of the platform was another guardian tower, and next to it was a control tower, noticeable by the large windows at the top part of it.

"We'll have to go easy on our missiles and try to conserve," Bishop said, locking his nose cannon onto the aircraft control tower.

"No sweat, we'll just take the platform and towers, then it's the primary," Dutch said, transferring maximum power to the nose cannon.

"And after we blow the crap out of it and the shields fall, we'll fly the hell out of here," Bishop finished, "Let's go to work."

The F-202 flew at the cryo-plant's control tower and opened fire. The unarmed structure was immediately riddled with holes, shattering most of the windows in the control room, and no doubt, killing everything inside. It soon caught fire and began to burn.

"Two Dragonflies in the air!" Dutch reported.

As the Lakota flew over the launch pads, it fired its nose cannon, tearing up six aircraft in a single pass. Two more Dragonflies took off. The F-202 turned for another pass, and flew through a stream of force shells from the guardian tower. Bishop looked ahead to see four Dragonflies were closing from ahead.

"We've got to waist the platform fast or we're going to get our asses kicked," Dutch yelled over the crash of the shells.

Bishop passed over the platform again and fired two Hydras at the lowered elevator platform hoping they would seek a Dragonfly inside, but both missed the opening and impacted the platform, one blew apart another Dragonfly. As he pulled up, he let loose with the nose cannon, and managed to takeout one of the pursuing aircraft. The remaining three passed over them firing their own cannons and disintegrating the already weakened shields of the Lakota. The guardian tower continued to fire a steady stream of shells at the fast-moving Lakota using visual sighting only, as it was still radar invisible.

"One more pass. If I can't hit the damn thing, we're out of here!" Bishop said, turning the ship around.

"There all over us!" Dutch said as force shells flew by all around them, the guardian tower pummeled their forward shields and the Dragonflies ravaged the rear shields.

"Almost there..." Bishop said as he closed on the open elevator.

With a sudden flash, the shields around the F-202 shattered, and Force shells could be heard hitting the exposed hull.

"Now!" Bishop yelled as he fired one Hydra at the opening and pulled back the stick as hard as he could, sending the Lakota straight into the air, the Dragonflies in hot pursuit.

The Hydra miraculously found its way down through the opened elevator platform and exploded in one of the Dragonflies that was powering up. At first nothing happened, but then a massive fire erupted from under the platform as fuel and munitions exploded in a chain reaction. The platform shook violently and the left side sunk in the center and the remaining Dragonflies slid into the center pit where the elevator platform had once been. The entire area was then obscured with black smoke as the fires raged out of control.

With extreme difficulty, the Lakota managed to destroy the partially armed Dragonflies.

"They winged us..." Dutch said as the chameleon system flickered on and off intermittently.

Suddenly they slowed considerably. "Talk to me Dutch." Bishop said as the howl of the engines quieted and the airspeed dropped.

"We're out of ethanol," Dutch said, "Let us hope that was our last dogfight..."

As they resumed their course to the power sub-station Dutch nursed their shields back to full strength, but running the engines on electrical power only made them recharge at one third the normal recharge rate. As they cruised around to the other side of the Tower, they scanned for enemies, but there were none detected.

"I see it," Dutch suddenly yelled.

"So there it is. Our *Primary* target," Bishop said, with a sarcastic note.

"Do you think our Unicorn can penetrate the armor of the exhaust port?" Dutch asked, hopeful that Bishop would acknowledge.

"No. But I bet we can put some dents in it," Bishop responded.

"We have only one Unicorn, and one Hydra. And that's it," Dutch said bleakly.

"We'll have to make them count... Bandits! Nine O'clock low, Twelve O'clock, Three O'clock... *everywhere!*" Dutch began to yell.

The hidden Aero fighters began to rise from the ground as the F-202 Lakota was spotted, its damaged chameleon system failing to keep it concealed.

"Here goes!" Bishop shouted as he pulled the craft into a hard dive and accelerated towards the sub-station, wishing he had a few drops of ethanol left.

The force shells began to rain all over. Although the Aero fighter was designed for exo-atmospheric combat, it remained infinitely faster than the sluggish Lakota, and was much better armed. A missile rocked the rear shields of the F-202, nearly neutralizing them. Another one hit, and the shields fell. One more missile would destroy the human craft.

As the F-202 neared the sub station, Dutch aimed his laser designator at the exhaust port. The Lakota violently spun as a rocket hit its left engine.

"Holy shit!" Bishop shouted as the Lakota spun around 180 degrees, he squeezed the trigger of his stick and let loose a barrage of force shells.

Caught off guard, one of the Aero's following close behind dodged the stream of force shells and slammed into the Aero next to it.

The men in the F-202 watched in disbelief as two doomed Aeros head directly for the top of the sub-station. One crashed into the lip of the exhaust port, the other smashing through the protective mesh and into the cooling chamber. Liquid hydrogen, and water gushed from the damaged cloying cells and into the huge magnets that were at a temperature of roughly 1,000 degrees Fahrenheit. The result was the magnets shattering and sending burning fragments into the highly flammable hydrogen cooling cells.

The F-202 sped away as fast as it could move, force shells flittering around it. Seconds later, with a blinding flare of red light, the sub-station blew itself apart in an orange fireball. Seven of the pursuing Aeros were caught in the explosion and were never seen again. One emerged from the fire and fled the battle. The remaining two stayed hot on the Lakota's tail.

Force shells slammed into the rear of the Lakota, hitting its rocket engine but otherwise causing no damage. One shell went through the cockpit and punched an exit in the canopy, miraculously missing both men.

"Hold on VanDuinwyk!" Bishop said, as he raised flaps and engaged the airbrakes. The F-202 stopped to a hover, while the Aeros, which were incapable of hovering, continued on.

"Take the bastards out," Bishop commanded.

The Lakota fired its last Unicorn at the two craft. As the missile reached the two, it dispersed its bomblets and they in turn exploded into the Aeros. One blew up outright, but the second was only winged. The damaged Aero continued to fly until the F-202's nose cannon blew off its left wing. All of the fighters had been destroyed or driven off.

"My God! We did it! We took out the sub-station! We didn't need the Atlas!" Bishop howled.

Dutch wasn't smiling though.

"What's wrong?!" Bishop said, looking back.

Dutch was ghostly white, "The shields are still up!"

CHAPTER 36 Destiny's Handymen

Gates' trembling hand reached into the survival pack and retrieved the last two MREs. One was Vegetable Beef stew, and the other was good ol' Chicken noodle soup.

"And today we feast," Ford said semi-sarcastically.

"Vegetable Beef or Chicken Noodle," Gates gave Ford the choice.

"I'll take the Beef. It's the closest to a steak," Ford answered.

Gates placed his chicken noodle soup on the small chemical heater.

"Well, our foods cooking. We have to shut the reactor completely off and let it cool. Then, after we get the cooling system rebuilt, we can feed it coolant... if it is coolant. The weapon systems still have to be charged with the CO^2... one cylinder at a time." Gates said, walking to the hole in the Revenant. Gates spliced the pump's wires into the Revenant's power supply and quickly cycled the coolant system from on to off quickly. To his relief, the pump whirred to life for a moment.

"Thank God," Ford said without turning his head. His attention was focused on the carbon life support sash. Currently, all of its CO^2 cells were removed. Ford examined the complex circuitry on the back of the sash.

"Where did you find this thing again?" Ford asked.

"That's a story..." Gates said, sitting down next to him.

"Did you know there is red blood on the bottom of this thing. It almost looks like human blood."

"It's not human blood..." Gates said.

Ford said nothing, but instead looked at Gates, awaiting an answer.

"Ford, I ran into something," Gates paused, "I ran into a creature in the Garden Dome..." Gates looked at Ford, "And It spoke perfect American English. And it almost looked human."

"It looked human?" Ford asked.

"All except for the purple eyes, green skin, six fingers, razor sharp yellow teeth, and thorny vines from its palms," Gates smiled, "yeah, other than that it was spot on."

Ford stared, "You said it spoke to you,"

"It told me its name, but I can't remember what it was, and what it said that really made my stomach turn, it told me that this was really a construction fleet that set down here. And that the real soldiers were on their way."

Ford looked at Gates with astonishment. "It actually spoke to you?"

"Before it tried to kill me," Gates acknowledged. "But I kicked its ass. I sent it sky diving."

"What the hell was it?" Ford said, "I mean what do you think it was?"

"It looked like a walking plant. Maybe that's what it was, how the hell should I know? All I remember was something about a race called the Trexian, and they are calling the shots," Gates said, removing his chicken soup from the heater.

"So the Molluskan and Aracteroid are just the foot soldiers," Ford surmised.

"Yes. And these Trexians apparently are the leaders of this entire operation," Gates finished.

"Well, I met one of their finest. But it didn't say much to me," Ford said searching for a cigarette.

"Was it a Molluskan?" Gates asked, placing Ford's Veggie Beef Stew on the heater.

"Hell no," Ford scoffed, "It was some kind of four-armed crab with a very bad temper." Ford revealed the gash on his chest.

"That's nothing Ford, check this out." Gates showed Ford his neck, with all the cuts and bleeding holes.

"Yeah, well look at my boot," Ford said, showing his split boot tip.

"So, look at this!" Gates said, pulling back his cheek so Ford could see the missing molars that were knocked out of his head back at the Garden Dome.

Ford nodded with disgust. "You win."

Gates handed Ford his vegetable beef stew and they tapped their canteens together. *Cheers.*

Ford retrieved his cigarettes and took one of the last two left out of the pack, and began to look for his lighter. Ford searched every pocket, but came up empty. He sat back, with his eyes closed.

"Shit!" he suddenly said, "I left my damn lighter back at the crash site."

"Don't worry," Gates said raising the a portable blowtorch to Ford's cigarette, "you can use mine," he said as he lit Ford's cigarette with the blow torch.

"Nah, Gates..." Ford took in a deep breath from his cigarette and blew a cloud of gray smoke at the ceiling, "That thing was a gift from my father. Its my good luck charm; I've never flown a mission without it."

"Well you seem to be doing fine so far," Gates said, "you're still alive."

Ford nodded, but felt a loss. That lighter had lit a cigarette before and after every mission, until now.

"You know you never told me why you were already at Sanford Lake for months before we were. The Navy Cross... Purple Heart..." Ford prodded.

"I figured Drummond would have told you guys before we left," Gates paused, "I've been here before. A tower on the other end of this base."

"I thought as much. You went as a SEAL right?" Ford surmised.

Gates nodded, "We were the first Americans, I was the only survivor."

"I've heard the story... just rumors. So that was you." Ford said.

A long pause endured.

"You get some sleep," Gates said finishing off his chicken soup, "I'll stay up and work on refilling the reactor coolant."

Ford curled up and in less than five minutes, he was completely out.

Gates thought of Kimbett, he had the uneasy feeling that somehow, someway, he survived, and that he would be seeing him again. Gates felt uneasy about Kimbett's words: "There is evil that you could have never known lurking in that sky you look upon at night... death is out there, and is on its way here."

"What is out there?" Gates muttered, "Who the hell were you?"

. . .

Sunlight crept through the cracks under the window sill and spread across the ground. The sunlight was comforting to Gates, for he knew that this was his sun, the same sun that beat down on him when he used to play in his sandbox when he was a boy growing up in Arizona. Gates reached down and picked up a hand full of dirt. The dirt was lifeless. Nothing but loose dry sand with several smaller pebbles mixed in with it. Gates let the sand run through his fingers. Although the dirt seemed different, almost alien, to

Gates it was still Earth. This dirt had been labeled Mongol dirt, Chinese dirt and now Trexian dirt, but no matter what side of the border it rested on, the dirt was the Earth's.

Ford sat up.

"You're awake," Gates said quietly.

"How's the bird?" Ford asked, before squirting water into his mouth from his canteen.

"The coolant pump works, and the reactor is powering up. The computer should sound as soon as the reactor is ready. It should only be a couple more minutes," Gates said calmly. In reality, he half-expected the alien reactor to meltdown.

CHAPTER 37 Flash Point

Non Risolm walked in circles in front of Destarus. His single cyclopean eye darting back and forth erratically. His steps came unevenly, and sometimes even tripped on the grated floor of the bridge. Non Risolm was extremely worried... Non Risolm was terrified.

"Something troubles you, Admiral?" Destarus casually asked. If he had possessed a mouth, it would have bared every tooth with a giant grin.

"No, I'm fine, Captain Destarus," Non Risolm lied, "mind your own business!" he added a second later, trying to sound authoritative.

"What ever you say, Sir," Destarus said with an even more casual tone.

Destarus leaned back in his chair, content with the happenings around him. He knew exactly why Non Risolm was so nervous; not because the humans had succeeded in destroying the reactor-ignition tower outside the hangar, not because the reactor was late getting started and Rao Lok was nearly drained of energy and could no longer support the shield, and not even because of the reports of a large number of human forces approaching the *Wall*. No, the entire complex of terror stems from the knowledge that Kimbett is coming. After Bakkaraqu's failure to assassinate him, they were all doomed to the legendary Kimbett's wrath. He had made it through every barrier set before him, and Non Risolm knew that he was heading for the MegaKore and would not let anything stand in his way.

The door covering the exit on the left side of the bridge slid open. Non Risolm spun around, startled, and pulled his *hellion* out of its holster and pointed it at the dark doorway, nervously. In walked Rycon, and upon seeing the gun pointed at him, went into battle mode. His artificial eye narrowing into a little red dot. Rycon armed his rocket launcher, and now, at any second, could blow Non Risolm apart.

Non Risolm was now more terrified to see that he had threatened his own body guard, he put his weapon back in place and raised one hand, trying not to look nervous.

"Rycon, where... where have you been," Non Risolm said with a touch of authority.

Rycon didn't respond. He just stood there, motionless. The soft humming sound of his generators could be heard. The small red light in his camera seemed to burn into Non Risolm's soul. Rycon made no move.

After a long silence, the red glow in Rycon's camera went black, and the humming stopped. Rycon walked in, passing by Non Risolm but without saying a word. Instead he walked up the stairway leading to the higher platform surrounding the center pit, then stood silently between Doctor Kailecko, the Aracteroid surgeon, and one of Risolm's molluskan body guards, MT-Four.

Non Risolm felt uneasy, even a little angry, but wisely said nothing to Rycon. He could feel all eyes boring into him, except for Destarus who was silently working on one of his complex electrical equations out on his computer station. The dwarfed Trexian felt humiliated, and in despair turned to Destarus.

"Captain Destarus," he said spontaneously.

"Yeah, what do you want... Sir," Destarus replied without turning.

"Look at me when I talk to you," Non Risolm yelled.

Destarus turned.

Non Risolm now regretted his command, Destarus, who always gave a look of merely annoyance, now gave Non Risolm a look of hatred.

"I want... I mean..." Non Risolm was cut short by an alarm.

Destarus spun back around in his chair and punched a couple buttons.

"What's going on? What's happening? Somebody answer dammit!" Non Risolm pleaded nervously.

"Someone is trying to get in," said Destarus, while looking at Non Risolm.

"At... port side, 3A, on deck 1," Destarus added.

There was an immense silence. Rycon and Kailecko gave each other a look.

"Who is it?" Non Risolm heard himself say.

"Destarus looked back at the screen and punched a couple more buttons and then stood up as an image of Admiral Kimbett appeared on the main view screen directly in front of them.

"Oh Kroyce, help me," Non Risolm mumbled as his hearts nearly pounded their way out of his chest.

Destarus stared in awe at the screen before him, there was Kimbett. He was patiently standing in front of the airlock at 3A, looking at the camera that was now relaying the image to the main view screen, and smiling. *Kroyce, how could he be smiling?*

Kimbett didn't look the same though, he was missing his carbon life-support, his eyes were insane with rage, deep cuts scarred his body, and his face was riddled with holes. Kimbett however, maintained his smile, although it was missing most of its teeth.

"Let me in Destarus," Kimbett said with an all powerful voice.

Destarus looked at Non Risolm.

"Kill him! Activate the security field! Now! KILL HIM!" Non Risolm shouted as loud as he could at Destarus.

Destarus just looked at Non Risolm in defiance.

"What are you doing? Kill him!" Non Risolm yelled, confused.

Destarus made no move to do so.

"What's going on here?!" Non Risolm began to back up.

Destarus turned his back to Non Risolm.

Non Risolm began shake violently. "Trexians do not tolerate insubordination, I'm warning you."

Kailecko could sense the hostility, he gripped the ornamental ball on the top of his staff and turned it quietly, extending the spikes and exposing the blade at its base.

Rycon dilated his rocket port to its second largest setting. His electronic eye went red.

Boratus, who was four decks above the floor of the bridge pit, watched the events below and quietly moved closer to the edge of the balcony.

Destarus glared at Non Risolm, and shook his head before reaching down next to his seat.

Non Risolm reached for his *hellion*.

"*You will have to be punished!*" he blurted out just as Destarus spun around with the strange weapon he had seen when they first met. Non Risolm raised his weapon just as Destarus pulled the trigger. A bolt of white light arced out of the small spike in the front of his rifle, like a bolt of lightning, and burned through Non Risolm's right shoulder. The Trexian flew back into the wall behind him, the *hellion* flying from his hand.

The Molluskan troopers came into life. MT-Four, the one next to Rycon, fired upon Destarus. Destarus rolled behind the computer bank at his workstation, just as force shells plunged into the deck all around him. One of the Aracteroid officers sitting at his station was cut apart by a spray of force shells.

Rycon turned without warning and fired a rocket at MT-Four. The Molluskan exploded into a fiery ball of charred flesh and armor. All of Non Risolm's MT's began to open fire on everything that moved. MT-Two fired upon Rycon tearing off his mechanical leg before he dove behind the tactical station. Kailecko brought his staff down on MT-Five, but couldn't penetrate the armor, so the ninety six year old Aracteroid began to try to wrestle the *viper* from the trooper. Boratus came down on MT-Two from four decks above. Literally stomping it into the deck, and leaving two great depressions in the floor. Destarus began to fire at the MT-Three but the electrical bolt didn't seem to penetrate the Molluskan armor.

"Damn!" Destarus said as he was forced to take cover behind his ravaged computer bank.

Non Risolm was dazed but alive, his right arm was blackened and did not move. He began to search for his *hellion*.

Rycon raised his launcher over the tactical station and fired at MT-Six but missed and destroyed part of the wall behind it. Destarus's gun was kicked from his hand. He turned to see MT-Six pointing his *decimator* at Destarus. It was all over. Destarus watched with amazement as a rocket plunged into the MT, which exploded into fire, blasting Destarus with intense heat, Molluskan entrails, and shrapnel. Destarus raised his head to see Rycon staring at him, his launcher smoking.

Kailecko was wearing MT-Five down, the Molluskan was no match for an Aracteroid's endurance. The MT eventually fell down to the ground from exhaustion. Then Kailecko beat it repeatedly with his staff until it didn't move, picked up the *viper* and fired, tearing the Molluskan apart.

Non Risolm finally found his *hellion*. Upon grabbing it, he ran to the exit.

MT-Three raised his gun at Kailecko, and pulled the trigger. A two hundred pound metal girder that served as a rail was swung like a baseball bat, and struck the Molluskan, sending it flying into the a wall. Boratus swung again, this time cutting the Molluskan in two. Miraculously, any force shells didn't hit Kailecko.

MT-One had a superior position, on the upper decks it could sweep the entire bridge pit. It continued to fire at Destarus and Rycon, then at Boratus, then at Kailecko. Everyone was pinned down. Destarus tried to reach for his rifle, but his arm was nearly torn off by several force shells from MT-One's *viper* cannon.

"Somebody take him out!" Destarus ordered.

Rycon fired a rocket from behind his ravaged tactical station. But MT-One dodged out of the way. Kailecko was pinned down behind the communications station. Boratus was charging back upstairs to kill MT-One, but was again pinned down at the staircase.

MT-One armed the one of the missiles equipped on the side of his *viper* and aimed it at the tactical station.

Without warning, white liquid sprayed up from the very grating MT-One was standing on, formed into a white creature, and lifted the Molluskan up into the air. The *viper* dropped from the confused Molluskan's hands. The MT looked into the dead white eyes of its humanoid captor. Kicking and screaming, the Molluskan was carried to the edge of the balcony where he was thrown over just as Boratus reached the deck. The Molluskan screamed all the way down until landing on the navigation station, crushing the computer banks. Boratus stared in awe at the ghostly white creature, as it nodded to him before liquefying and splashing back into the deck.

All was quiet.

Destarus got up. With a look of total amazement. "Holy shit."

Rycon got up on one leg and looked at the destroyed bridge, smoke and Molluskan flesh was every where.

Destarus surveyed the area, "Where's Non Risolm!"

Rycon hopped over to the tactical station and pushed a couple buttons. But it was dead. Destarus ran to his computer station, which was also dead.

"Doesn't anything work?!" he was so excited he yelled it in his Trexian Spearixan dialect, which no-one understood.

Finally Destarus tried Kimbett's station, which had miraculously spared the onslaught. Covered in Molluskan blood and scorch marks, Destarus sat at the computer and brought up a map.

Non Risolm ran through the main corridor, en route to the Hanger. A MegaKore MT jumped in from of him, but was cut down by the armor piercing force shells from Non Risolm's compact, yet deadly *hellion* weapon. He fired at every living thing that happened to be in the corridor with him, even Molluskan and Aracteroids that weren't soldiers.

Destarus looked at the screen before him, it showed Non Risolm moving for the Hanger. Then he looked at the main view screen. Kimbett was gone. "Uhh... where is Kimbett?"

Rycon had already bolted out the door to catch Non Risolm, hopping on one leg and leaving a trail of black hydraulic fluid in his path. Boratus looked at Destarus. "Should I get him Captain?" Just then the ghostly white being arose from the grating in the floor and looked at Destarus.

Destarus turned and looked at creature.

"Relecite... You got something to add?" he asked, Relecite said nothing, but glided to the computer console and began to press keys. In a moment, the view changed to that of an airlock. Destarus turned to the screen, "No guys, if I'm right, Kimbett will beat all three of us to killing Non Risolm,"

They all watched the screen.

Non Risolm exploded into the Hanger, with his *hellion* sending waves of force shells everywhere. He ran for the first exit, 5C. Several MT's were bursting into the hangar at just about the same time, and opened fire on him. Sections of flooring exploded all around Non Risolm, and he dropped his the *hellion*. Non Risolm finally reached the airlock. He shut the gate just as a missile impacted it. He locked the gate and swung around to the external hatch. He then punched in his own special code, the one that Krewtek had personally given him. The Molluskan troopers beat on the gate, but to no avail, it was made to withstand rocket attacks. Water vapor condensed on every surface of the airlock, and a loud hissing roar filled the compartment as the airlock depressurized. Non Risolm laughed at the Molluskan, through the single centrally placed window he could see at least ten of them pounding on the door, along with the dreaded Rycon. Non Risolm had his back to external hatch.

Light flooded the airlock as the external hatch opened. The Molluskan stopped pounding and began to look at each other. One of them even dumbly gave a salute. Non Risolm turned very slowly and nearly died from the shock. Admiral Kimbett walked in with his thorns out.

"Nooooo!" Non Risolm yelled.

"I must have done something right in another life... Non Risolm!" Kimbett said to the cowering Trexian before him.

The molluskan watched the grisly scene through the central window, cheering and laughing, and then finally screaming in morbid delight as green Trexian blood splashed up against the window.

Poor Risolm, for once in his life, someone was happy to see him.

CHAPTER 38 Fruits Of Rebellion

Destarus looked down in disgust at the horribly disfigured MT's carcass before him. It was literally pressed into the deck, in its midsection was the huge footprint of Boratus. The bridge pit was crowded with MegaKore MTs and Aracteroid technicians. They worked to repair the severe damage done to just about every computer terminal in the bridge. Destarus motioned to one of the Aracteroids.

"Get a plasma cutter, this one will have to be cut out of the deck," he ordered, before sitting back down at his pulverized station, his holed chair creaking and groaning as he put his weight on it. "Well... shit," he said while looking around at the devastation all around him. Next to his station was a pile of white molluskan entrails. To his left was a gaping hole in the floor where a rocket had hit, ahead was the flattened MT stuck in the deck.

"Sir, Lieutenant Gris is dead," One of his technicians pointed to the perforated body of his former tactical officer.

Rycon hopped back onto the bridge on his one foot.

"Risolm is dead," he said with a mechanical tone. Destarus already knew.

"Where is Kimbett?" Destarus asked, turning around in his bullet ridden chair.

"I'm back home," Kimbett said, walking back onto his bridge.

Destarus stood up out of his chair and walked towards the admiral. Kimbett looked around at the damage, "Did I miss the party?"

All was quiet. All eyes were on Kimbett.

Without any further words, Kimbett walked up the stairs to his station above the bridge pit. He pressed the master intercom button on his undamaged console.

"This is the voice of Admiral Kimbett." His voice echoed in every corridor and room in the MegaKore. All of her crew was listening except for some of the less aware Molluskan.

"As most of you probably know, I am now an enemy of the Trexian Empire. But I'm sure that this doesn't surprise most of you. A wise friend of mine many years ago told me that most of those who have an IQ higher than a Molluskan end up as enemies of the empire at one time or another... now its finally my turn. They tried to make me disappear... but I still live." Kimbett continued, "I'm going to give you a chance, a chance that you've never had," Kimbett paused.

"I now control this ship. It is mine. Non Risolm is dead. It's likely that you all would be executed and replaced even if you were successful in recapturing the bridge. What I offer you are two options: You can fight me, fight for the masters who have enslaved your people. Or..." He paused again, "Or... You can resume your assignments aboard this ship under *my* command. And together we can join the revolution to destroy the Empire. I'm offering you a chance to fight for freedom! ...not just your own, but for all of us, all of the worlds under their thumb..."

"If you must fight me than fight and die well... but understand this: from this very minute, you are all free. The choice is yours. Our Revolution starts here!" Kimbett finished.

The MegaKore erupted with cheering. The bridge echoed with the cries of Molluskan and Aracteroid. Most of them had never dreamed of a chance to fight the Trexian. Even talking of a rebellion would mean execution, but now they had a chance. A chance to fight, the will to win, the courage to die. The cheering was an incredible sound, and lasted for minutes.

Destarus approached Kimbett, "Nice speech," he said.

"Thanks, I thought it up while waiting for Risolm to open the damn door, " Kimbett said.

Destarus looked at Kimbett, "What about holdouts? Do you trust..."

"Hell no," Kimbett interrupted, "we're not going to take the chance either. Where's Kailecko?"

"He's in medical, treating some of the wounded," Destarus pointed out.

"Captain, I want you to post your most trusted guards around all vital parts of the ship. Prepare a list of sixty-four of the least trustworthy members of the crew, and confine them to the brig.

"Yes Sir," Destarus acknowledged.

Kimbett smiled a crooked smile, and spoke into the intercom again. "All right then! Let's get the bastards together." Kimbett sat back in his chair and laughed, the cheering could still be heard echoing in every corridor.

Walking back down to the bridge-pit floor, Kimbett spotted Boratus, "You!", he then motioned to Rycon, "...and you, come here."

Boratus stomped over, "Yes Admiral," Rycon hopped over a moment later.

"This is Lieutenant Boratus Admiral, he's good with computers," Destarus said.

"Good... unlock the access blocks Lieutenant, I don't care how you do it," Kimbett ordered, his one functional eye staring down the taller Boratus.

"Yes sir!" Boratus said, departing.

He turned to the half-machine Molluskan, "Rycon I presume,"

"Yes Admiral," Rycon said flatly.

"Rycon turned against Non Risolm, Admiral." Destarus explained.

Kimbett slowly walked around the Molluskan, "But have you turned against the Trexian Empire?"

Rycon stared straight forward and after small delay, uttered a *yes*.

Destarus noticed for the first time, Rycon appeared alive.

"Yes Admiral... I would willingly die if it meant I could destroy the Trexian Empire," Rycon volunteered.

Kimbett stared at Rycon for a moment, and nodded to Destarus before walking away.

"You're our new tactical officer then. Take yourself to the machine shop and have that leg replaced," Destarus ordered.

Rycon nodded, "Yes Sir," and before leaving stopped at the barely damaged secondary tactical system console.

"Captain," Rycon motioned to Destarus.

Destarus walked over to the station and looked at the screen. Kimbett followed.

"I have an unidentified object heading straight at us."

. . .

"Well, that's it for our chameleon system," VanDuinwyk said morosely, as he shut off the damaged unit. It was history.

"We'll get there before they can get to us," Bishop said confidently.

Dutch's screen began to show signatures of several objects closing in on them from the west.

"Damn, their not wasting any time are they? I've got at least twenty eight bogies closing in on us, six o'clock low, twenty miles out," VanDuinwyk announced loudly.

Bishop let out a huge sigh, "They're from the cryo-plant! We must not have hit it hard enough,"

"Just as well...we did all we could do," VanDuinwyk said quietly, both men were silent.

. . .

Kimbett looked at Rycon's screen. *What are you running from?* Kimbett wondered.

"Sir, the object is being tracked by the cryo-plant's radar system," Rycon reported. Kimbett suddenly smiled. "It's not Trexian, it's that human ship!"

Rycon looked at Kimbett and nodded. "There are currently two entire squadrons of Dragonfly's heading to intercept."

. . .

"We're approaching the main hangar, Bishop," VanDuinwyk said, his eyes never leaving his screen.

"I can see it Dutch," Bishop said with a tone of exhilaration, "Where is the strongest power source?"

VanDuinwyk looked at his screen. "The walls of the tower are blocking my scan."

. . .

"Ready all battle stations! Go to alert one," Destarus commanded.

"Raising forward and rear shields, Sir," Rycon reported, pressing keys.

"Ready six of our Aeros, and have them standby for take off," Kimbett said.

Destarus blinked at his request.

"Sir, it's only one fighter with twenty-seven of our aircraft closing in on it." Destarus asked.

"Captain Destarus," Kimbett stared at his friend and smiled with only three teeth, "Do it now," he said flatly.

Destarus nodded, "Yes Sir. Rycon, ready six Aeros for launch."

. . .

"Here they come! Five O'clock low," Dutch yelled.

The Lakota suddenly dodged a wave of force shells from one of the Dragonfly's forty-millimeter cannons. Two Dragonfly's quickly closed in from the left and began to fire their weapons. The F-202 dove at the ground, then pulled hard to the left to avoid an missile fired from one of three more Dragonflies to join the chase. Behind them was an entire squadron of seven specialized *attack dragons*. Based on the Dragonfly design, the attack dragons carried more powerful ordinance and were much faster.

"They're all over us!" Dutch yelled.

Bishop looked at his screen. The opening to the hangar was only a mile away, and could be seen ahead. Lasers and force shells flew everywhere like snow in a blizzard. The F-202 somehow managed to avoid much of it, and its shields absorbed the rest.

"The hangar!" Dutch yelled as the F-202 Lakota dodged four missiles and turned hard to the left, into the dark rectangular opening of the hangar. The four missiles impacted the side of the tower and exploded throwing shrapnel into the decaying shields of the exhausted Lakota.

"We're not making it out of here alive Dutch!" Bishop shouted back, over the sputtering sounds of the force shells crashing into the weary shields.

"I know..." VanDuinwyk said quietly.

"I'm gonna ram this ship down this things throat!" Bishop howled. His face didn't display rage, but that of peace. *He was ready.*

. . .

"There it is," Destarus said, looking up at the main view screen.

Kimbett smiled, "Grab the human ship."

Destarus looked at Kimbett with a look of incomprehension. "Sir? Don't you mean, destroy the human ship?"

"No. I mean *grab* the human ship, as in, extend the tractor beam and lock onto it," Kimbett commanded.

The F-202 flew into the darkness. Closing in behind it were twenty-seven Trexian Dragonflies and attack dragons. They continued to fire their weapons. It was hopeless.

. . .

Destarus shook his head, "You're taking a big risk Admiral, Krewtek doesn't know we've taken over the MegaKore, but if we interfere..."

"I know risks Destarus. But things aren't always what they appear... we must act now," the look in Kimbett's eyes was that of determination. Destarus reluctantly nodded.

"Rycon, lock tractor beam two onto the Human," Destarus ordered.

. . .

"The strongest power source is dead ahead!" Dutch shouted into his headset over the crackling sound of the failing shields.

"What the hell is that?!" Bishop screamed as a blue spotlight, emanating from the darkness, suddenly fell upon the Lakota. Both Dutch and Bishop were nearly pitched through the canopy as the Lakota nearly came to a complete stop and was held in mid air by the tractor beam. Both engines continued to produce thrust, and the magic carpet drive was still working, but the Lakota did not move.

The hangar lights came on. Revealing the huge interior of the tower's hangar, and parked in the center, dominating all of it, was the MegaKore.

. . .

The Aracteroid squadron leader now saw the almighty MegaKore. It had the little human ship in its grasp.

"Good work MegaKore, but I believe we have the honors," The Aracteroid said to itself, as it locked a missile onto the helpless F-202 Lakota. Its claw was on the green launch button.

Both massive gatling-style guns on the hood of the MegaKore began to spew thousands of shells at the incoming Dragonflies.

"Kroyce! Hold your fire MegaKore!" The squadron leader said as he banked his craft hard to the starboard as force shells whizzed by. One of them clipped his right engine, blowing it into fiery shrapnel.

The force shells tore into another Dragonfly, tearing it to ribbons. Two more were obliterated by waves of force shells.

The squadron leader, who was missing an engine, was still airborne. "Retreat! Retreat! MegaKore is hostile and has superiority! Do not engage!"

The massive guns destroyed seven more Dragonflies. The remaining seventeen craft were in chaos, some were trying to retreat, others were trying to attack the MegaKore, still others were shooting at the F-202. All were panicking.

Two Dragonflies had a mid-air collision, while trying to avoid the force shells.

The MegaKore's left rocket pod fired a single missile that flew out toward a swarm of eight retreating Dragonflies. Within four hundred meters, it exploded, sending a cloud of small Pac-man shaped metal chips into the retreating craft. Five of them exploded in mid air, the other three were partially shredded and dove at the ground.

"What the hell is going on here?" Dutch's were eyes wide as they could get.

"Holy shit. Its destroying its own fighters!" Bishop pressed his head to the canopy and tried to see behind the F-202 Lakota.

"Emergency! Emergency! MegaKore has gone hostile! Repeat! MegaKore..." The squadron leader and his Dragonfly were riddled with holes as a newly launched MegaKore Aero fired its cannons at the crippled ship, which then burst into flames and fell the hangar floor.

The other five Aeros flew at the remaining six Dragonflies. One by one, the Dragonflies were picked off by the infinitely more maneuverable Aero fighters.

The entire fleet of twenty eight Dragonflies was destroyed in less than five minutes.

"Jesus. What is going on?" Bishop asked, bewildered, as the six Aeros thundered past the stationary F-202 Lakota and returned to the hangar on the port side of the MegaKore.

"Lock on our last two missiles," Bishop ordered.

"Locked on," Dutch said, as he locked the targeting computer onto the gigantic gun on the rear turret.

"Fire!" Bishop yelled.

The last unicorn missile dropped from its internal weapon's bay and rocketed away at the MegaKore for nearly four seconds before another blue spotlight shined at it. The tractor beam jolted it to a stop, before swinging it into the hangar wall, smashing it to pieces before it even armed.

"Fire again!" Bishop yelled.

The final hydra missile streaked at the MegaKore, but was cut down by a red laser that flashed for only a second from the hood of the MegaKore.

Bishop leaned his head back and exhaled, "That's it, we're history."

. . .

"Destarus. How good is your English?" Kimbett asked.

"Flawless," Destarus said in English.

Kimbett nodded, "Excellent, you do the honors..."

Destarus stared at his friend for a moment, "Honors?"

. . .

Both men's headsets crackled to life. Dutch and Bishop looked at each other and gulped. The crackling over the radio stopped and a voice replaced it.

"Attention pilots of the Human vehicle. Do not attempt to break free from our holding beam or we will destroy you."

The voice was synthesized. "If you attack us again, you will be destroyed,

"You are only alive because it is our wish that you live," the voice continued. "W will be transporting you and your vessel into our ship's hangar, I suggest you just sit back and relax for the ride." the crackling went dead.

Both of the human pilots were too stunned to talk. The Lakota began to move as it was being pulled towards the MegaKore.

"We can't allow this ship to fall into enemy hands," Dutch said calmly.

"I don't know..." Bishop spoke slowly, "...I'd say these guys are on a different team."

"Look. I don't know why they wasted their own jets and not us, but their intentions for us can't be good!" Dutch argued.

The Lakota was lowered in front of the hangar on the left side of the MegaKore. The hangar door slowly opened, revealing a black void behind it.

"So what are we going to do? Blow up the ship? Kill ourselves?" Bishop turned around in his seat and looked at Dutch.

Dutch was silent for a second, "No..." he said quietly.

Another tractor beam from inside the hangar locked onto the F-202, and the main tractor beam released. The ensnared Lakota began to move into the hangar.

"The way I see it, if they wanted us dead, we wouldn't be having this conversation right now," Bishop said, gulping.

Dutch didn't answer.

The F-202 Lakota was pulled all the way into the hangar, and the hangar doors closed behind it. All was black. The only thing that could be seen was the blue tractor beam that was emanating from a position about a hundred and sixty yards in front of the craft. After two minutes of flying, the Lakota stopped in mid air again. All was still black.

"Human ship. Lower your landing gear," The alien voice commanded over the radio.

Neither Dutch nor Bishop made any move to do so.

"I said lower... your... gear!" the voice thundered.

Dutch lowered the gear as instructed.

"Now hold on!" the voice said.

In a second, the tractor beam disappeared. It felt to the men as if the aircraft was floating for a second before falling nearly six feet onto the hangar floor. Shaking both men hard upon impact.

The voice came over the radio again, "Now. Shut off your reactor,"

"The hell with that!" Dutch yelled.

Bishop closed his eyes hard.

"Shut it off now, or we will shut it off for you," the voice said. It seemed to know English well.

"You shut it off, and we'll never get it started again," Dutch said, his eyes red with frustration and fear.

"We were screwed when the Chameleon went out on us," Bishop said, "Now we've got to survive. I'm shutting down the reactor."

Dutch sat back in his chair and exhaled loudly, as the humming sound of the Lakota's coolant pump slowed and stopped. Seconds later, the computer, radio and all other electrical instruments went dead. The Lakota was still.

The lights of the hangar flickered on. Totally surrounding the human aircraft were nearly two-hundred Molluskan troopers, and several of the strange weaponless black armored figures. Standing directly in front of the aircraft was a strange looking mechanical being. It had a large blue eye centered in helmet-covered head.

Destarus turned on his amplifier. And spoke very loudly to the men in the Lakota.

"End of the road Gentlemen. Get out," he yelled.

Bishop and Dutch, terrified, didn't react at first.

"Hey! I'm getting very impatient... now get out or I'll simply have my troops open your ship up the way they are trained to. You won't like it." Destarus threatened.

The top hatch of the F-202 Lakota opened and the two humans crawled out. After being in the air for over forty-eight hours both Bishop and VanDuinwyk were almost unable to move their legs. Bishop was the first to scamper to the deck of the hanger. As his feet met with the alien metal it gave off a loud thump that echoed within the massive room. Dutch jumped down a second later, his cramped legs collapsing beneath him. Both men limped around to the front of the F-202 Lakota and stood their defiantly.

Destarus, alone walked over to the two humans and stood only four feet in front of them.

"Proper introductions first. I am Captain Destarus," Destarus said. "And you are...?"

Neither of the men said a word.

"It doesn't matter," Destarus grunted a mechanical grunt, "My superior has decided to let you live for some reason. Too bad actually, I had other plans, but sometimes you just have to do what your told."

Still, both men were silent.

"Huh, still not going to talk to me?" Destarus nodded, "Take them," Destarus said in Trexian. A large group of Molluskan closed in on the two humans. Neither resisted.

. . .

The Green Dotariak eyeball strutted endlessly through the sand. Besides coming by the tracks of fellow Dotariak who were searching for the humans, and some debris from the crash, the eyeball, after two days, had come up with nothing except for a trench, some debris and a dead aracteroid. Sunburnt and thirsty, it uncapped its water pouch and discovered that it was nearly out of water. After recapping its pouch, the Dotariak set out on a new mission, *to find water!* It head in the direction of a string of storage sheds that probably still had water stored in them.

It continued to walk through the sand.

. . .

It was completely dark outside the circular field of light. Both men were bound back to back by a flexible metal cable. Both were sitting on a single metal table. A light shone down on them from above. Outside the light, Dutch could hear crackling noises. He could sense the presence of other creatures in the darkness, watching him.

The sound of a door sliding open could be heard, footsteps, and then the closing of a door. Bishop heard the footsteps of something approaching. His heart raced as something stepped out of the darkness and walked straight at him.

What Bishop saw was a grotesque bipedal humanoid figure completely green in color. Its face was a twisted mask of flesh, with one eye swollen shut and bleeding oily yellow fluid that streamed down its cheek. Although its mouth was closed, its lower lip hung open, revealing dark gums adorned with a single yellow tooth. A line of crumpled metal valves was implanted from its shoulder, across its chest, down to its hip. As it approached Bishop, he could hear its raspy breathing and smelled the stench of decayed flesh.

Kimbett reached out his gnarled six-fingered hand and seized Bishop by the throat, and forced his head up. Bishop's demeanor was calm, despite his terrific fear. The creature examined his throat and then moved his head and examined his face. He looked into Bishop's eyes and smiled a broken smile, with his three remaining teeth. His one visible eye was a reddish purple, swollen, and bloodshot.

After that the creature walked around to Dutch and examined him as well. Unlike Bishop, however, Dutch smiled arrogantly at the green alien. The creature grabbed Dutch by the wrist with its six fingered hand and studied his air force tattoo. It appeared to be highly fascinated with these humans. They were now showpieces; trophies of the war.

"I may have use for you..." Kimbett said in English.

Bishop and Dutch both began to sweat at hearing this thing speak in English, with its deep resonant voice, but remained silent. Kimbett walked over to the Bishop again and bend down, putting his face only inches from the human's face. Bishop could smell the alien Admiral's foul breath.

"You were willing to die trying to destroy them," Kimbett said coldly. Bishop said nothing.

Kimbett stood up straight and said something in Trexian to the guards that the humans could not see, and the left the room. Bishop and Dutch had no idea what to think.

. . .

Gates and Ford ran through the metallic hallway. They had heard the creature chasing them. Gates was exhausted, and he felt that he couldn't run anymore. His legs were about to give out. Down the hallway, they could see the Aracteroid now, and it was closing.

"Come on Gates!" Ford yelled, helping him along. There was a door in front of them, Gates hit the green button and it opened, he ran through and tripped. The door slid shut behind him, trapping Ford with the Aracteroid.

Gates stood up and beat on the door, but it did not open and all was quiet. He found himself in a circular room, with doors on all sides. They began to open, and creatures began to step out. The rocket-molluskan, the crab creature Ford described, the old white haired Aracteroid, the white liquid creature, and the large Molluskan in the film he had taken. He was surrounded, he began to turn around, feeling that something was behind him. He was seized by the throat and found himself looking into Kimbett's violet eyes. Kimbett growled and threw back his hand, from which spines grew.

"Die!" Kimbett shouted as he plunged his spiked fist into Gates' heart.

Gates sat up and screamed. He was alone, and it was dark.

He realized that he had been dreaming again; he found himself back in the shed.

"It was only a bad dream..." Ford's voice said, "...Human."

Human? Gates looked over his shoulder and Kimbett was right behind him. The thin tin wall of the shed suddenly exploded inward, and Rycon ran in and clubbed Gates across the face with his rocket launcher. As Gates recovered from the blow, Rycon fired a rocket directly at his face!

"Jesus!" Gates jumped straight off the ground, and immediately saw Ford. He backed away from him, shaking violently.

"You're awake now. It was only a bad dream," Ford said quietly.

Gates was sweating, and his heart was racing.

"Smile," Gates commanded.

"What? Ford said, instinctively smiling. Gates saw normal human teeth. He sighed and relaxed.

"We're almost out of here Mike, don't loose your marbles now," Ford said, slapping Gates' shoulder. Gates nodded. His skin was drenched with sweat.

Ford walked over to the windows and opened them up. Beautiful golden rays of sunlight poured into the shed. A rush of cool air blew in. The day was absolutely beautiful. Gates shook his head and got to his feet, retrieved a canteen and drank the last few drops of water.

Gates thought of the green eyed girl in the decontamination suit again. He began to imagine the rest of her body beneath that white suit. Gates was slow to admit to himself that he had fallen in love with those green eyes the second he had seen them. He wanted to live to see her again... he didn't even know her name.

The computer began to beep. Gates walked over and turned a valve open on the coolant cylinder and with a hiss, the coolant was rushed through the new coolant system. The reactor output began to climb. Twenty percent, thirty percent, forty percent and then higher. Gates emptied all three cylinders into the cooling system and the reactor was running and a healthy ninety-two percent.

"They did a good job when they named our bomber the B-100 *Revenant*." Ford said with a grin.

Gates looked puzzled. "What does that mean again?"

"A revenant is someone who comes back from the dead," Ford explained.

Gates returned the grin.

A gentle breeze blew through the shed.

"Well we will definitely live up to our name."

CHAPTER 39 Cleared For Takeoff

Gates cautiously pulled off the cap to the injector of the power cell. White vapor rose from the hole, before he plugged the negative power lead into it. After doing the same for the positive side, he cautiously rested the cell in its make-shift compartment, using Ford's camouflage utilities as a cushion. The cell fit perfectly in its new housing, Gates sighed heavily as he closed and locked the access panel.

Ford, who now wore his flight suit, was sitting patiently on the plastic shelf looking out the window. Although he looked relaxed, he was very anxious and alert.

"Ford," Gates reached his hand up, "Get me the one and a quarter inch wrench will ya',"

Ford walked over to the tool kit, picked up the appropriate wrench and stopped dead in his tracks.

Standing quietly in front of Ford was a small green irised eyeball, with a bag over one shoulder, and what looked like a telescope over the other. It looked as stunned as Ford. The eyeball dropped its gear and pointed at Ford.

Ford was in shock.

Then the eyeball pointed to the ground. The message was all too clear: *You're going down.* Ford's shock turned to rage as his defiance gained control.

"Die you little..." he threw the wrench at the eyeball, but it dodged away, and ran through a crack in the wall, back out into the desert.

Ford ran for the door, but was stopped by Gates. "Forget it. He's not worth it,"

"Not worth it? If he gets back to tell them about us, we're dead," Ford complained.

"Those little bastards are collective, which means the second he saw you, they already knew we were here," Gates heart accelerated as he realized what he had just said. Ford looked at him in utter confusion, then in determination.

"We don't have much time," Gates said, taking the wrench. Ford's face suddenly dropped. Gates turned and looked out the window. On the crest of the sand dune, stood four Molluskan troopers, their silvery armor gleaming brilliantly in the sun. Another eyeball could be seen sitting on one of the trooper's shoulders, pointing at them.

"Hurry!" Ford shouted to Gates.

Gates ran back to the coolant pump, and realized that Ford had grabbed the wrong wrench. Gates didn't think twice before pounding the bolts into their holes, using the nearby jack as a hammer. Ford jumped into his seat and started the engines. Slowly, to his relief, they began to hum into life.

Gates was hit by a blast of heat and sand as he passed the window. A missile had blown apart one their neighboring sheds. If Gates had looked out the window, he would have seen the eyeball, sitting on the attacker's shoulder, pounding on the Molluskan's helmet, and pointing in a frenzy at the shed Ford and Gates were in.

"I swear to God, if I make it out of here alive I'm going to ask that green eyed girl to marry me," Gates said as he picked himself up off of the sand.

Before Gates climbed into the top hatch, he noticed the bag and telescope that the eyeball left behind, for reasons he couldn't explain, he grabbed them. Upon jumping into his seat, Gates omitted his safety harness, and shouted to Ford: "Go! Go!"

The shed vibrated as the B-100's engines were suddenly fed the powerful ethanol-based fuel.

As the Molluskan trooper fired his missile, he was confused to see an explosion rock the shed, before his missile was even half way there. Following the explosion, was the B-100 Revenant, still with the large tires attached to its landing gear. The missile simultaneously impacted within the shed, creating a ball of fire directly behind the bomber. The Molluskan were stunned at the sight.

"Whoa!" Ford yelled, as the bomber dipped alarmingly towards the ground. "We didn't have time to take the damn wheels off," Gates observed. "Are you buckled up?" Ford asked. Gates looked at him curiously, "No, why?"

It didn't take long for the Molluskan to recover from the dazzling takeoff of the B-100. They quickly aimed their weapons at the bomber and fired. Force shells riddled unshielded metal of the fuselage. The B-100 suddenly turned on its left side, both left wheels slipping off the makeshift axles, dropped off the side and bounced on the sand. The Molluskan dropped to the ground or jumped out of the way. Flying overhead, the bomber rolled to the right side.

The Molluskan raised his *viper* force cannon, and leveled it on the escaping human bomber that was flying directly above him not higher than fifty feet. Before he could squeeze the grip, a large gray wheel came at him. The Molluskan screamed with out stretched arms seconds before the tire stomped it into the ground. The other tire collided with the rest of the squad, knocking them down like dominos, and sending the eyeball rolling to the sand.

It got up on its feet, and glared at the escaping craft. If it knew how, it would have given them the middle finger.

Ford pulled up. After, they had cleared five hundred feet, he hit the blue button that raised the shields. To his total amazement, they still actually worked.

"Are you hit?" Ford asked back to Gates.

"No, but this thing needs a lot of bondo work," Gates joked, looking at all the new holes in the fuselage, luckily none of the force shells hit any major system.

"Well, I think I might need some bondo," he said calmly.

"Gates' eyes widened. Where?" he leaned forward.

"In the leg, just a graze..." Ford said, gritting his teeth, "There's a purple heart..."

Gates nodded his head calmly and passed the medical kit to Ford. Who, with one hand on the collective stick, cut away the bloodied pant leg.

"How bad?" Gates asked concerned.

"I'll be all right, its going to be hard to use the left pedal though," Ford said while finishing the dressing on his upper thigh. Two inches further back, and Ford would never have to worry about perils of parenthood.

As the adrenaline faded both men were in awe that they were still alive, and actually airborne.

Gates looked at his screen, and grinned, "Aside from your leg, we have no major damage. chameleon system is working, and we have two nearly full fuel tanks to make it there in a hurry,"

Ford nodded.

"I didn't get into my G-suit..." Gates reported, noticing also that he hadn't even changed into his flight suit. Neither man wore his flight helmet.

Ford nodded again, "I'll try not to give you too many bumps,"

. . .

Admiral Bruin gazed across the desert. From left to right, all he could see was charred black sand, the sea-green glass formations of melted sand, and the two hulking masses of twisted metal that were once metal crushers. Standing before them, dented and beaten by a nuclear barrage, was the Trexian compound's main gate, *The Wall*. Although this barrier had been breached before, it was still a formidable obstacle. If Operation Locksmith failed, his mission was to attempt to destroy it in a full assault. Hours prior, he had received word that the sub-station, the primary target of Operation Locksmith was destroyed. To his horror the shields remained up. He could only imagine that intelligence had mistaken the sub-station's function. He had no idea of the fate of the men who had fought and sacrificed themselves to take out the wrong target. His stomach turned at the thought of the loss of such brave men, to such a futile cause. Their mission had been thrown together, and despite the logistic nightmare and record coordination between the different military branches, he honestly never believed the men had a chance.

For their sake, and for the sake of the world, Bruin was ready to die trying to destroy the barrier. General Sterling arrived at Bruin's side on the deck of the sky carrier.

"It's time Admiral," he said quietly.

Bruin turned his head to look at Sterling. "My father once told me that man's finest hour is found in born of disaster. I wonder if this will be our final hour,"

"I believe we were born to do this Chuck, its our time, its our finest hour..." Sterling said solemnly.

Bruin turned his head back to *The Wall*. "The fate of the world is in our hands,"

Both men were quiet for a moment.

"It's now, or never, Admiral," Sterling interrupted quietly.

"Lets do it," Bruin said before turning to the hatchway leading to the interior of the airship.

The mostly American, British, German, Australian, and Canadian fleet consisted of four sky carriers, 1310 aircraft, 2108 tanks, and more than 1,000,000 troops. Off of the coast were an additional 38 aegis cruisers and destroyers, two battleships carrying long range cruise missiles, and four aircraft carriers with an air wing of 92 aircraft a piece. This was the largest military assembly ever, and represented the bulk of the human race's modern warriors.

The fleet embarked on a journey to be remembered for all time, and what would be known as *The Battle of Shanghai*.

. . .

"My God," Was all Ford could say.

"My guess is, Dutch and Phil decided to have a little fun before going for the sub-station," Gates added later. Both men had to shout over the roar of the engines because neither had time to don their headset-equipped helmets before taking off. Both were looking over the charred smoking remains of buildings and wrecked vehicles. Molluskan could be seen scurrying over the wreckages.

"This was the Garden Barracks... hopefully they left us a clear path all the way there," Ford said.

Gates shook his head. "I'd be willing to bet that the Molluskan Barracks is sending fighters right now."

"Maybe, but as long as no one sees us we're as good as invisible," Ford rebutted.

Gates was about to say something, when both men spontaneously agreed that they would meet opposition. This was done as several force shells impacted the rear shields. Gates looked at his rear view camera to see a Dragonfly in pursuit.

"Where the hell did he come from?" Ford yelled as he rolled the Revenant out of the path of the oncoming force shells.

"Damn, I hate being right..." Gates complained.

"Can you get him?" Ford yelled back.

More force shells sailed by, some spattering against the rear shields.

"Tail gun is charged, but the tracking system has no power..." Gates yelled back.

"Take 30% off the shields and feed it into the rear defense system," Ford suggested before suddenly pulling straight up.

Gates was pulled back into his seat so hard he felt the blood rush out of his face.

"This bastard's trying to get a missile lock on us, Hurry!"

Gates began transferring power to the tracking system only to discover that the unit hadn't been hooked up correctly before their escape and was useless. He knew that Ford was too busy to care about this problem, and kept quiet. The shield flickered a bit and darkened as all 30% of the power was directed to the tail gun.

The Revenant dove at the ground to avoid the missile lock, but it was too late. Several alarms went off as the enemy craft fired a missile at the B-100. Just as the missile armed itself twenty feet away from the bomber, it was cut apart by the diamond-shaped force shells spit out by the twin barrels of the now operational tail gun.

"Missile down!" Gates yelled. "He's next..."

Unknown to Ford, Gates had spent days training on the tail gun long before Ford had even been selected to pilot the Revenant. The tail gun pointed at the patrol craft and fired. Its shield rippled as hundreds of force shells plowed into it, but it was undamaged. The patrol craft emitted a laser blast that hit the bomber's left engine, missing the unshielded exhaust port, and was absorbed by the weakening shield.

"Take his ass down!" Ford yelled while fighting with the controls.

Gates armed a missile and locked it onto the enemy craft's left pylon, where Gate could see a small force-cannon, a laser pod, and two large missiles attached. He launched the missile, and waited. The Dragonfly yawed to avoid the radar guided missile, but not quick enough. As it exploded, the warhead tore a large hole in the shield. The hole quickly began to seal, but not before several force shells flew in from the bomber's tail gun and ripped into the pylon, and one of the attached missiles.

The entire left pylon exploded with a ball of orange flames, and was then followed by a larger explosion as the left engine blew apart, sending shrapnel into the cockpit. The patrol craft spiraled alarmingly before diving at the ground and slamming into the surface.

"Take that you bastard!" Gates yelled.

"Way to go Gates!" Ford cheered. "I wondered where he came from?"

"Probably complements of the Molluskan Barracks," As Gates said this he remembered the F-202. "Hey Ford, see if you can reach Meridian-2."

Ford didn't reply as he finally reached for his auxiliary microphone and activated the cockpit speakers. He turned to the appropriate channel and hailed the F-202 Lakota. There was no response.

"Something is wrong. I can't raise Meridian-2," Ford's eyes closed.

"I'm not detecting any jamming, but they might not have line-of-sight to them," Gates said hopefully.

"Ya, maybe," Ford said morosely.

"Well if they're dead, they will be avenged when we blow the shit out of the tower," Gates glared at the looming tower only seven-hundred miles away.

"The only thing that stands in our way is the inner gate."

Gates began to calculate the distance given the obstacles. "We should reach the tower in under six hours, if we don't have to "

CHAPTER 40 Thorn In Your Side

Kimbett gritted what was left of his teeth hard as the probe was driven through the flesh in his arm. His arm exploded with inhuman pain as the probe suddenly struck something hard and stopped.

"Ah! You hit a bone! Can't you be a little more careful!" Kimbett yelled at the old Aracteroid.

Kimbett was sitting on a surgical table, in the MegaKore's medical station, with Doctor Kailecko. They were alone.

"Sorry Admiral, this is a deep one," Kailecko apologized, "Wait, I think I got it!"

Kailecko withdrew the bloody probe from Kimbett's arm, at the end of it was a lead slug. Kailecko dropped it in a pan, with seven other lead nine millimeter slugs.

"That makes eight," Kailecko shook his head, "What the hell did you get in a fight with?" he asked while examining the back of Kimbett's shoulder.

Kimbett smiled, exposing only three teeth, "Something I never expected to see here,"

"What the hell is that?" Kailecko said while feeling a lump in the flesh of back of Kimbett's head.

"What do you see Doc," Kimbett asked casually.

Kailecko took his scalpel and began to cut at the flesh above the lump. There were no anesthetics used. Kimbett winced slightly at the pain in the base of his skull as he heard a loud crunch.

"Got it," Kailecko said as he pulled a small piece of metal from Kimbett, and examined it. It had several alien symbols pressed into it.

"What do you make of this?" Kailecko said passing it to Kimbett.

Kimbett smiled, "Gates, Michael F, 603197187USN A POS" he read the dog tag aloud.

"It's Human? What was it doing in your head," Kailecko asked, while burning his head incision closed.

"I tangled with one of the little bastards in the garden," Kimbett said, spitting one of his teeth into the tray with the bullets. "Not only did it kick my ass, it managed to get out before Bakkaraqu got there to kill me,"

"Probably the same one that I ran into," Kailecko chuckled. "It didn't take that little bastard long to get away from me either,"

"I heard that Boratus ran into one of them too," Kimbett commented while Kailecko examined his wrist. It had a piece of gray plastic sticking out of it.

"Yes. And Rycon tried to catch up with it back at the canal bridge, and found the one we saw trying to cross," Kailecko said.

Kailecko looked thoughtful, "How many humans do you think are here?"

Kimbett stared at his scarred hand, "Only four. And we have two of them."

"How can you be so sure?" Kailecko asked.

"Because the last two are from the third ship. And they survived the crash," Kimbett said, looking at the tag.

"How did you learn their language anyway?" Kailecko asked.

Kimbett smiled. "I'll tell you..."

. . .

Destarus shook his head angrily. "No! You incompetent fools! I want the tactical station totally replaced!" He began to pace back and forth agitatedly.

The Molluskan trying to fix the hopelessly smashed tactical station spontaneously dropped their tools and wandered off. Destarus shook his head again.

"Worthless..." Destarus said under his proverbial breath.

The floor of the bridge pit was covered with cables, metallic scrap, bolts, screws, Molluskan guts, pieces of armor, smashed electronics and nearly a hundred red irised Dotariak, the MegaKore's own breed. Several Molluskan were busily repairing the damaged computer banks, alongside the Red Dotariak. A very large crustacean was busy cutting the floor panel with the Molluskan imbedded into it, out of the floor with a plasma cutter.

"Where's Rycon?" Destarus yelled.

Boratus finished cutting the Molluskan from the deck, and shut off his blowtorch.

"I think he went to the machine shop to replace his leg," Boratus said, removing a protective mask he used while cutting.

"I guarantee Krewtek already knows we just blew twenty eight of his planes to pieces." Destarus said, looking at the destruction all around him.

"Let *him* worry Captain, there is not a lot he can do to us, considering we are in possession of the biggest weapon on the planet," Boratus said calmly.

"We still don't have the codes to unlock the damn Navigation and Helm!" Destarus pointed out.

"I have a team down at the port where Risolm tried to escape, his fingers were bloody when he punched in the code," Boratus explained, "So we can check the buttons for his blood, and narrow down what buttons he pressed. From there we can systematically work out the code."

"I hope you can do this soon Boratus, I really do," Destarus pointed his finger at Boratus. "Now would somebody replace this damn chair!" he yelled, kicking his already holed chair, splitting it in two.

. . .

"I watched this place for nearly thirty years. I watched these humans..." Kimbett winced with extreme pain as Kailecko removed the plastic shard from his wrist. "Walked among them..." Kailecko examined the shard for a second, "Watched their... TV..."

"What the hell was this doing in your wrist?" Kailecko interrupted, holding up the gray piece of plastic, before dropping it into the pan.

"Oh, that's that Quick-Mold stuff the Molluskan use for foundations. Some new-breed Molluskan slashed me with a blade covered with the stuff," Kimbett said pointing to another shard in his gut.

"So you were part of the recon team here on Earth?" Kailecko asked while reaching for his pliers.

"I *was* the recon team," Kimbett spat another tooth into the metal pan.

"So you're the reason why we were expecting stone castles, spears and catapults instead of jet engines, nuclear warheads, and great big floating fortresses," Kailecko said with a smile, while jerking the jagged, crescent shaped piece of plastic from Kimbett's abdomen. Blood began to pour from the hole.

"Yup. I falsified the reports... the Trexian still believed the humans hadn't progressed in four hundred years up until they actually got here," Kimbett said with a grin.

"You knew this would happen!" Kailecko, astonished.

"Well... I hoped anyway. The only problem is that Krewtek wanted me and this ship to come to this planet with him," Kimbett said.

There was a short pause in the conversation as Kailecko removed the last piece of plastic debris.

"Well, all we have left are your life-support valve implants," Kailecko said pointing to the smashed, inoperative valves in Kimbett's upper torso. "What happened to your life support system?"

"I left on the tower in the Garden Dome," Kimbett spit out his last tooth, and smiled with no teeth.

"We'll have to use your spare," Kailecko said, ripping the first valve out of Kimbett's shoulder. The implant came out with a stringy tendril of flesh tethered to it. Kailecko reached for his scissors.

"So why are you doing this Kimbett?" Kailecko said, snipping the string of dark bloody flesh.

"You haven't heard my story yet?" Kimbett said with a humorless chuckle.

"I've heard stories... but I'd like to hear it from you Admiral. If that's all right with you of course." Kailecko said with genuine respect.

Kimbett nodded. "All right. They killed my people. We resisted, and we were punished accordingly. Or at least, that's what we were told. I was trained for fighting, while other survivors were used in medical experiments. The Trexian were fascinated by our ability to regenerate and photosynthesize."

Kailecko nodded, "That's how it happened to us too. Only our Shaman made a pact of peace. We would join their armies if they would leave our world alone. So far, they have. But we all know it's only a matter of time."

"And it's the same with Boratus's people from what I understand; his leaders struck some kind of deal," Kimbett said.

Kailecko ripped out another implant. "Destarus is the exception. He's a Trexian and he's against the empire."

"Yes but he's a Spearixan Trexian, he's probably the only one that isn't a slave," Kimbett winced as Kailecko ripped out another implant.

. . .

"Sir! Incoming message from the cryo-plant," One of the Aracteroid technicians yelled to Destarus, who was sitting in his new chair.

"What are you going to say?" Boratus asked.

"I'll make something up, try and buy us some time," Destarus said, taking a second to think of a good lie. "Go ahead," He then said.

The view screen flickered and then revealed a picture of an Aracteroid commander.

"Captain Destarus. Where are my Dragonflies?!" he asked casually.

Destarus' eye stared down at the ground. "It is to my severe regret to inform you that due to an apparent external weapons malfunction, your fleet has been destroyed."

The Aracteroid commander opened all four eyes as wide as they could get.

"My entire fleet..." It said, bewildered.

Destarus nodded, "Yes Commander. It was a terrible accident."

"What the hell happened!" The Aracteroid demanded.

"Well Commander, we're still investigating that," Destarus formulated a lie, "Apparently Non Risolm's computer lock-down confused our defense system into believing that all of your ships were the Human ship."

"Were the human's destroyed?" The commander asked, shaking its head.

"Yes Sir, in fact, everything in the air was destroyed," Destarus lied again.

"This is a total disaster! I want to speak to Non Risolm this second!" The commander shouted.

Destarus gulped a layer of mucus down his organic esophagus. "Uhh... I'm afraid he's down at the Main Computer Station, attempting to isolate the malfunction."

The Aracteroid wasn't impressed. "So what? Patch me in via intercom."

"I'm sorry, but all intercoms are off line, as are most of our computer systems while we try to track down the computer error," Destarus lied yet again.

"This is ridiculous! I want to talk to that little runt right now! Those were some of my best pilots!" The commander pounded its claws on its desk.

Destarus was running out of lies and patience, "I'm sorry Commander! But in case you weren't paying attention, he is unavailable at this time, when he becomes available, I'm sure he'll call you. Until then, you'll just have to wait. Destarus out!" With that Destarus closed the com channel. The view screen went black.

Destarus sighed a big sigh through his mechanical lungs.

"Do you think he bought it?" He asked Boratus.

"It's hard to say, but one thing is for sure, " Boratus looked directly at Destarus, "he will tell Krewtek that we slaughtered his Dragonflies, and Krewtek will want to talk to Risolm."

"And we'll be out of time," Destarus rubbed his eye.

Kimbett stood up. His body was an absolute mess, with bleeding holes and gashes over most of it. His hair began to shed off, until he was totally bald, and then his fingernails fell off, one by one.

"All right Admiral, the sun chamber is ready when you are," Kailecko said, putting on his protective eye-wear.

Kimbett walked over to the long silver cylinder and pushed a button on it. With a pressurized hiss, a door slid open, revealing the interior of the chamber. The interior of the Sun Chamber was designed specially for rapidly growing plant crops hydroponically, but now it would serve as a regeneration chamber for Kimbett, who stood, naked, in front of the open cylinder a second before walking in. The door slid closed and sealed.

“Okay Admiral, this should take only about an hour,” Kailecko’s voice echoed inside the chamber.

As the process began, mineral rich water rose up from the floor, until it was as high as Kimbett’s knees. At the same time, the cylinder was filling with carbon dioxide, and with a low buzzing sound, the light panel in the ceiling began to gain intensity until it was so bright no other features could be seen in the room. Kimbett sprouted thousands of leaves, to collect as much as the light as possible. His body surged with energy, as the mineral water soaked into his legs and spread throughout is body. Thousands of tiny black pores opened and closed on is skin, acting as stomata as the photosynthetic process began to pick up speed. Kimbett knelt down and drank some of the water, feeling it re-energize his damaged tissues. The feel of the light pouring down on him and the carbon filling his lungs caused him to throw back his head and laugh euphorically.

. . .

Krewtek’s flesh brow raised as he heard the Aracteroid commander’s report.

“So what about my Dragonflies? Those were my best pilots! Some one is responsible!” The Aracteroid glared at Krewtek.

“Captain Destarus and Risolm will be held responsible, all right?” Krewtek slammed his hands down on the desk.

“They better be...” The Aracteroid said slowly, its red, glistening eyes burning into the screen a second before it closed the com channel.

Krewtek sighed a big sigh. “I really don’t like that commander’s attitude.”

“At least we killed two more humans,” Xo said, standing in front of Krewtek’s desk.

“We only have two left, and their ship is badly damaged,” Grackconn said.

Krewtek looked up at his men. “Clear out. I have to tell Kroyce we have eliminated the human ship.”

Xo and Grackconn both saluted and walked out of the office.

Krewtek opened a channel with Kroyce.

. . .

Boratus and a team of Aracteroid technicians were sitting in the MegaKore’s Main Computer room, trying to figure out a fourteen digit access code, with thirty-eight possible digits for each of the fourteen.

The thirty-eight digits had been narrowed down to twelve, because only twelve buttons had Risolm’s bloody finger prints on them. The question was, which two were pressed twice, and in what order were they pressed. Two computer terminals had been disconnected from the main computer, and hot-wired to operate independently. They were used to attempt to access hundreds different locked terminals at the same time. Upon entering the wrong code three times, each terminal would be suspended for three minutes. Boratus had written a computer that selected which terminal to try the next possible code on in order to maximize the rate of codes.

The computer began to beep.

An Aracteroid sitting at the console among the jumble of wiring raised its head and stared at the screen excitedly. It immediately ran over to one of the minor computer terminals and punched in the 14-digit code and to its surprise, the computer accepted them. The Aracteroid scrawled down the numbers and jumped up, out of its chair.

“Sir! I think I’ve got it,” An Aracteroid ran up to Boratus, holding a writing pad with the code. Boratus snatched the paper from the Aracteroid.

"Excellent work Petty Officer." Boratus patted the Aracteroid on the shoulder with his gigantic claw.

Destarus stood up as Boratus entered the bridge with a piece of paper in his claw.

"Lieutenant," Destarus nodded.

"The code Sir," Boratus handed Destarus the access code to unlock the circuits controlling navigation and helm control.

"Excellent work," Destarus walked over to the replaced Helm station and tried to reboot the system. Upon requesting the code, Destarus entered the fourteen Trexian characters. The computer took only a fraction of a second to recognize the code and access was restored. Both the helm and Navigation systems rebooted.

Everyone on the bridge sighed a collective sigh.

Rycon, who was standing beside Destarus on his new leg, took the pad and walked to one of the new computer terminals and punched in the code.

"Sir. We have regained full use of our outer hatches and service ways," he said before taking his place behind the tactical station.

Readouts from the engine room show that the reactor control was restored to the chief engineer, Commander Relecite.

"Good job everyone, the ship is now truly ours," Destarus said.

"Incoming message from Krewtek's office, Sir," Rycon reported.

"This is it Captain," Boratus said.

Destarus nodded, "Now it's time to rattle our saber. Go ahead,"

The view screen flashed and then displayed the familiar face of Admiral Krewtek.

"Hey Krewtek, what do you want?" Destarus said without a shred of respect.

"Destarus? Where's Non Risolm?" Krewtek inquired.

"Non Risolm? Who's that..." Destarus was truly enjoying himself, "Oh yeah, the little dwarfed Golgenese midget? Oh yeah, haven't seen him..."

"Captain Destarus! What the is going..." Krewtek gasped, his eye bulged.

Destarus turned to see Kimbett walk onto the bridge with Risolm's head in his hand.

"Here he is, Sir," Kimbett raised the disembodied head of Risolm high in the air, before spiking it at the ground so hard it broke off a horn.

"You!" Krewtek gaped.

"Didn't expect to see me again did you, you double crossing bastard," Kimbett smiled at Krewtek with a full set of flawless yellow teeth. In fact, Kimbett no longer showed any scars what so ever, he had a new life support slung over his shoulder, even his hair was trimmed and neat. It was as if he hadn't even been scratched.

"No..." Krewtek fell out of his chair, terrified, his worst fears confirmed.

"That's what I thought." Kimbett smiled joyfully.

Krewtek, regaining his wits. "You'll never get past the security code!" Krewtek howled.

Kimbett laughed, "Oh really? Captain, the code please."

Destarus named off every Trexian character.

Krewtek said nothing.

"You tried to kill me Krewtek," Kimbett pointed at the view screen.

"My turn."

CHAPTER 41 Together We Stand

The sky carriers moved into their positions. They were just out of range of the giant force-cannons guns buried in the wall. All troops and land vehicles were spread out in a line behind the carriers. The time for battle grew near.

From the west, on the surface, behind the massive airborne assemblence of military might, a wave of steel swept across the sand and through the ruins of the Chinese city. Russian and Chinese tanks began to arrive. Hundreds of them, as well as troop carriers and supply vehicles. The entire Asian Confederation arrived for a battle. Who could have imagined they and NATO would be on the same side.

"Incoming message from the their commander Sir," The radioman at the communications terminal in the combat information center aboard the USS Kentucky informed Admiral Bruin.

"Put him on," Bruin said, sitting at his station.

One of the screens flickered on and showed the bearded face of General Sergei Loganov, his long time military rival.

"It is nice to make your acquaintance, Admiral," He said with a heavy Russian accent.

"Likewise General. At least, while we're not shooting at each other, Eh?" Bruin smiled.

Loganov smiled as well with a soft chuckle.

"It's good you guys showed up. We were about to start the fireworks without you," Bruin said.

"Do you think we would let you Yanks take all the credit for saving the world?" He said, laughing out loud. "Where do you want us..." Loganov paused, "Sir."

Bruin didn't trust the man he was talking to, but he had little choice, and it was far better that they fight the enemy with the combined armies, rather the Allies fight alone and take heavy losses while the Confederation sits it out.

"We're sending you our battle plan. When we give the word, unleash hell," Bruin said. Loganov saluted and the screen went black.

"Four continents are involved in this battle now, we damn well better win!" Bruin said.

The B-100 Revenant had run into no resistance on their way to the sub-station. With the compound shields still up, they figured the sub-station was still functional, and it was their intention to knock it out.

Gates gasped upon seeing the ravaged inner gate. Both of its gates were currently open, and hundreds of vehicles were swarming over the tower that had punctured one of them, attempting to clear the wreckage. In broad daylight, they flew through the gap, the chameleon system masking them from the damaged, but still functional left guardian tower. To both men's surprise, no shots were fired from either the tower or the crowd below.

Once inside the inner perimeter, they headed for the power-sub station. In less than half an hour, they had discovered the sub-station's fate.

"Jesus Christ!" Gates said, his eyes refusing to close, as he looked at the carnage below. The sub-station itself, had been blown apart. Everywhere, the ground was littered with crashed Trexian aircraft. Both Gates and Ford were scanning the ground for the F-202, but neither saw it down there.

"Maybe they left when they realized that waxing the sub-station didn't lower the shields." Gates said optimistically.

"No. They went for the Tower. They went to stop these bastards, they knew they couldn't leave," Ford said.

"Let's nuke the Tower!" Gates said.

"No. The gate to the tower is closed, and I read that the armor of its outer walls is far too tough," Ford said. "if only we could get inside..."

"Gates. I'm seeing at least fifty ships parked on pads around the cryogenics, cooling plant," Ford interrupted himself.

Gates looked down at his screen. The pads were full of triangular ships, not Dragonflies. "Those are fighters," he observed.

"We can't let them get airborne!" Ford said loudly.

Gates only nodded. "I'm arming the Atlas. We may not be able to complete this mission, but we'll go down with a bang!"

Ford agreed, and Gates began to punch in the arming safety codes for the Atlas nuclear bomb.

The fires on the landing platform had long since been extinguished. The damage to the underground hangar was extensive, but not irreparable, and it had already been repaired enough to be in working order. Currently there were twenty-two Aero fighters parked on the platform, along with twenty eight miniature autonomous fighters, and two Savaad bombers. The fighters, both robotic and manned, were the last ones left in the compound besides the thirty-four left in the hangars of the MegaKore. They were currently fueling up to launch a major assault against the MegaKore.

Krewtek's biggest mistake was to park them all together.

"Steady..." Gates cooed, his eye glued to the eye piece of the retractable bombardier scope.

The unseen bomber approached the airfield.

"Dropping!" Gates shouted, hitting the large red pickle switch. Ford immediately pulled up and banked hard to the right to avoid the fury that would be momentarily released. As the atlas fell, two wings extended from its sides, its curved nose was painted blue, with green continents. A huge cartoonish, happy face was scrawled in black on the 'Earth'. Below the crude happy face, written in bold white letters, the words *Have a Nice Day.* The Tieseler's crew may have been dweebs, but they had a sound sense of humor.

Through a camera mounted in the nose and an encrypted radio link, Gates controlled the bomb's trajectory by moving the stabilizers on the wings and tail fins. Through the camera, he could see the landing platform.

It drew closer, and closer.

He could see Molluskan scurrying around like ants. One of them, Gates decided, he would aim for.

Closer and closer....

Gates could now make out the Molluskan in minor detail. Some were just standing there, probably mumbling to themselves, some were loading ordinance onto the Aeros, some were operating fuel pumps.

Closer and closer...

Gates noticed a small insect-like thing with the Molluskan, it was an Aracteroid. With plenty of altitude, he corrected course to intercept.

Closer and closer...

By now, the bomb had been visible on radar for over fifteen seconds. Alarms had sounded, but there was no escape. The platform was approaching at a dizzying speed. Gates saw the Aracteroid look up, and through the blurry monochrome screen in the eyepiece was certain he could make out all four of its eyes wide with terror.

"Smile asshole," Gates quipped, "your on Atomic Hidden Video."

The BLN-88 Atlas was designed to plow into the target, and through any armor, and then explode in the interior; it was designed for the sub-station. The Aracteroid's brain only had a moment to contemplate the blue happy face with the human letters, before the bomb smashed through it and through the platform, continuing into the hangar, and straight through a Dragonfly below. The bomb landed below the wrecked Dragonfly and impacted the floor of the hangar, partially burying itself into the floor.

Through some unexplainable miracle, the camera lens remained intact, Gates watched, stunned and horrified, as Molluskan and Aracteroid crowded around the unexploded bomb.

"The damn thing was a dud!" Gates yelled, kicking the computer.

Ford flinched, "Shit."

The Molluskan snarled at the happy face. One of them broke from the crowd, ran up to the bomb, and kicked it. Gates' screen went black.

With a burning flash, the ground behind the bomber ignited into a plain of white fire. The white soon turned yellow, then orange, then red and finally faded. As the concussion caught up with the B-100, it sounded like a crack of thunder over the roar of the engines. No more.

From where they had dropped the bomb, six miles in any direction was blackened. Four miles in any direction was flattened, and for a two mile radius there was nothing! The base had been vaporized.

"Damn, what a rush," Ford screamed.

"Nothing made it off the ground, now we need to find a way into the tower," Gates said.

The B-100 Revenant was now flying around the tower.

"Maybe we can shoot our way in," Ford said, firing a couple round at the metal walls. They ricocheted off with a blue spark. "Nope. They've got some kind of a shield protecting..."

"Ford! The doors are opening," Gates interrupted.

"Well, well, well," Ford's brain could not think of anything else to say.

The giant sliding doors to the tower hangar opened slowly revealing nothing but stygian blackness behind them.

Both men waited for fighters, but none emerged.

"Either someone's going to come out, or they want us in," Ford said to Gates.

"I say we go in, just keep an eye out," Gates suggested.

"All right," Ford said reluctantly.

The Revenant turned into the hangar.

Ford was watching his scanner, "Gates! I'm reading an extremely powerful signature directly ahead. Levels are going off the scale..."

A blue beam shot out of the darkness and locked onto the bomber. Stopping it dead cold, just as it had done to the fighter.

Ford and Gate's were both nearly pitched through the canopy. Both engines, which were still running on ethanol fought to stay lit, before flaming out and switching to electrical.

"What the hell's going on?" Gates shouted.

The door behind them slowly slid shut, closing the last ray sunlight off. All was dark.

The radio suddenly crackled to life with an synthesized English voice: "All right humans, I'm getting tired of doing this; so just kindly shut off your reactor,"

Ford turned back in his seat to look at Gates, "We're in trouble,"

"I'm shutting it down," Gates said to Ford before powering down the reactor.

Ford was about to say something in protest but as the engines powered down, he realized any words were too late. They weren't going anywhere.

"The last ones had some trouble with that part," The voice said sarcastically.

"Others?" Gates asked.

"Now we know where Dutch and Phil went," Ford said.

The B-100 was taken into the hangar, but all was still black. Gates and Ford still had not actually seen the MegaKore.

"Continue to impress me, lower your gear," The voice commanded sarcastically.

"What gear? You idiot!" Gates yelled back over the radio.

The B-100 was dropped as the beam was released, and the bomber landed on its belly, with absolutely no shock absorption, shaking Ford and Gates violently.

"Now get out," The voice boomed from outside the ship rather than the radio. Gates and Ford both shook their heads.

"We've come this far..." Ford said.

Gates unbuckled his straps and began to get out. "I'm not worried..." he said, "we'd be long dead if they wanted us dead Dustin."

In pitch black, both men climbed out of the battered bomber. Ford winced as he put his weight on his wounded leg.

The lights flickered on, and Ford and Gates found themselves within a cavernous hangar bay surrounded by an army of silver armored Molluskan. An old aracteroid, a giant brown and orange crab and a metal-armored creature stood before them. Gates recognized the old Aracteroid, Ford, with horror, recognized the giant. But neither had ever seen the third creature. Boratus and Kailecko both instantly recognized the humans. Boratus growled at Ford.

Destarus spoke again, "So your the ones... you're the resilient humans who've been sabotaging the base and causing so much trouble..."

Gates nodded, "We just laid a nuke on your airbase too..." he said recklessly.

Ford, his fear evaporated by Gates' statement spoke, "and just who the hell are you?"

Destarus laughed a mechanical laugh, "You'll soon learn everything humans, come with me."

Unlike Dutch and Phil, they were not physically grabbed and carried away, they were merely escorted.

As they left the hangar, Gates turned to Ford and whispered: "That's the old spider thing I told you about,"

"That's the big crab I told *you* about," Ford whispered back.

They began to walk though a maze of corridors and stairwells. At every junction, there was a crowd of Molluskan and Aracteroid staring at the two humans.

. . .

Krewtek threw his head down on the table and screamed. When he raised his head, all of the veins in his skin were bulging and filled with light green oxygenated blood.

"Oh Kroyce! I'm going to be executed for this!" he beat his fist against the table, "Why! Why! Why!" he shouted, spittle spraying from his mouth.

"Sir. It only took out a third of the coolant plant, it's still cooling the reactor," Grackconn said, trying to be optimistic.

"No! You fool!" Krewtek picked up his Battle game-board and threw it at the Aracteroid, striking him in the head and sending him to the ground, clutching one of his eyes.

"Kimbett now owns the MegaKore! This is the worst thing that could happen! Not to mention, he is parked inside this damn tower! Do you know what he could do?" Krewtek threw his desk on the ground, dumping the resident eyeball onto the floor.

"And the humans!" Krewtek walked around to Grackconn, who was still on the ground.

"The humans that *YOU* failed to find!" he kicked the Aracteroid, "The humans *YOU* said were dead!" he savagely kicked him again, "The humans *YOU* said were not a threat!" he kicked the Aracteroid in the head, sending a spray of yellow droplets of blood into the air.

"Just! BLEW! UP! OUR! AIR FORCE! " He picked up Grackconn and threw him over the desk, where he collided with the chair and flopped to the ground. He didn't get up.

"You *DARE* to try to convince me that everything is okay," Krewtek said to the motionless Aracteroid. Yellow blood was dribbling from his ear.

"When this is all over, I'll have you burned alive. I swear I will," Krewtek said, still breathing hard. Grackconn still didn't move. Krewtek picked up his clipboard and tossed it at him.

The door opened, and Xo was standing in the doorway, silent.

"Now, Ensign Xo, I hope you have better news for me," Krewtek said smiling.

Xo didn't respond right away, he looked at Grackconn for a second, he still wasn't moving.

"I just came to inform you that we confirmed that both human ships were captured by Kimbett, and are aboard the MegaKore," Xo said plainly. His fingers were caressing the grip of the massive *pulverizer* twin force cannon slung from his shoulder.

Krewtek nodded, staring at the ground and began to laugh to himself. The laugh was somewhere between a genuine laugh and crying.

"Of course they are! Why not!?" he smiled and began to spin himself around and around, "and soon, the rest of them will be here and kill us all," Krewtek apparently had gone mad, he began to jump up and down and make force cannon noises with his mouth, "Putt, Putt, Putt!" he imitated.

"I swear..." Krewtek gulped, "You better pray there is a way out of this... or you're all coming with me..." Krewtek said breathing hard.

"Sir! Get control!" Xo shouted at Krewtek. Xo was almost at the point where he was willing to kill Krewtek. It seemed logical, Krewtek's body guard was nowhere to be seen.

Krewtek paused and calmed down, he was almost to the point of a mental breakdown, but was not quite there yet. He spoke calmly, "I'm going to the Batteckery, Xo. I want you to assemble what army you can and position it at the Molluskan Barracks. Hear me? I want *everything* at the Molluskan Barracks, its the only base we have left."

"Yes Sir," Xo said.

"Then..." Krewtek paced, "I will speak with Kimbett one last time, and see if I can at least get him to leave the compound. There's nothing we can do about him now. I'll have to blame everything on Risolm and hope they don't execute me anyway,"

Krewtek stopped pacing and went violent again, and kicked in one of the monitors on the wall behind his chair. Glass sprinkled on Grackconn's motionless body. With that, Krewtek scooped his yellow irised dot off the ground, walked over to his desk, and retrieved his *hellion* from a drawer, shut off the lights and left his office.

Xo walked over to Grackconn and picked him up. He was still breathing, but rich, yellow, arterial blood was flowing from his nose and ear. One of his eyes was also bleeding, and was tightly closed, the others were also closed.

"It's all right, my friend, I've got you." Xo's black eyes seemed to glisten in the darkness.

"You'll pay for this..." he said aloud, and regretted not killing Krewtek a moment ago.

CHAPTER 42 Enemy Of My Enemy

After a maze of corridors and stairwells Gates and Ford ended up at a small rectangular door. Destarus punched in the code and it slid open, they were pushed forward. Upon walking onto the enormous bridge, Gates and Ford were surrounded by a crowd of aliens and both instantly noticed two familiar faces before them; they were standing next to an empty chair, in front of a large blank view screen.

The two prisoners were escorted over to the other two human prisoners.

"It's nice to see you're still alive," Ford said in a low voice.

"My God... I thought you two were dead!" Dutch shook hands with Ford, fighting back his total glee.

"Believe me, its not like that wasn't an option," Gates said casually, looking around at the entire bridge. The catwalks above were packed with thousands of Molluskan and Aracteroid. Some were in armor, others were dressed in red and black uniforms. Gates keenly noticed that none of the uniforms bore the triangular Trexian insignia. He also noticed not one gun was pointed at him. In the crowd behind him, he noticed several familiar faces. The rocket-molluskan, the crab creature that Ford saw, the Aracteroid with the patch and monocle.

Gates looked at VanDuinwyk, "Where are we?"

Dutch looked over at Gates, "A ship... you wouldn't believe how big,"

"We blasted their airfield with the Atlas... it was too cool..." Ford said to Bishop, evoking a smile.

"We took out the sub-station, but the shields never fell," Bishop whispered back.

"That's because your intelligence is inferior," Destarus walked out of the crowd of Molluskan at the end of the bridge. "It was a reactor ignition complex, it had nothing to do with the shields, and since the reactor had already started, you accomplished nothing." he continued to walk towards the humans.

"It's nice to see that you all know each other. Now I would like to introduce you to the senior officers of the rebellious MegaKore battle ship." As Destarus finished his sentence, the rocket molluskan walked out.

"This is Lieutenant Rycon, who I'm sure you two have already met," Destarus said, pointing at Gates and Ford. Rycon stood side by side with Destarus. The Aracteroid walked out.

"This is Doctor Kailecko," Destarus said. The Aracteroid eyed Gates and nodded at him, standing at Destarus' side. The giant crab thing then stomped out.

"And this is here," Destarus said, looking up, "is Lieutenant Boratus." Boratus pointed at Ford and growled, all three yellow eyes staring at him from its armored head. Ford's heart fluttered, but he didn't show his fear. In front of Destarus, a stump of white jelly oozed up from the grated floor and molded into the white figure that Gates had run into. Its colorless, white irises constricted upon seeing Gates, it nodded at him.

"And this is our Chief Engineer, Commander Relecite," Destarus finished, "and I am Captain Destarus."

"So your the guy in charge?" Ford asked.

"No, not me..." Destarus said, laughing a mechanical laugh.

"I am," a voice rang out from behind Destarus. On a platform above where they had entered, a figure spoke from behind the shadows. Gates recognized the voice.

"Oh shit," Gates said, expecting this somehow.

The crowd parted and a green humanoid figure walked out, wearing something that resembled a black leathery jacket.

"The Weed," Gates said. Kimbett walked, past Destarus, and up to the humans.

"Admiral Kimbett... remember?" he said to Gates, his purple eyes boring into him.

"I remember you... Gates, Michael F, 603197187USN A POS" Kimbett recited from memory.

"So that's where my dog tags went," Gates said, unshaken.

"Yes. They were imbedded in my skull, along with two metal slugs you shot me with." Thorns grew from Kimbett's fist.

"I'm a bad shot, there should have been twelve rounds in your skull," Gates said bluntly, "I'll try again if you want, you look like a fast healer,"

"You wouldn't believe how fast," Kimbett replied in a low threatening tone.

"Just like a weed, you keep growing back," Gates smirked fearlessly.

Kimbett began to laugh, and it seemed as if in any second, he would kill Gates, but instead took several steps back.

"There's something I want you to see Gates, Michael F," Kimbett said, nodding at Destarus. The huge screen flashed and revealed a bulbous gray skinned ball with two horns and a crescent mouth, with a yellow eyeball above it. It was unlike anything any of the men had every seen before, yet looked similar in some ways to the alien Captain.

"Kimbett what are you doing?" Krewtek shouted in Trexian.

"This is your enemy, Gates, Michael F," Kimbett said to the humans, "Admiral Krewtek."

Gates looked at Krewtek and shook his head.

"That is one ugly bastard!" he said. Upon hearing, Kimbett laughed, Destarus translated to the crowd and they laughed as well.

Krewtek stared at the humans.

"So you ones," Krewtek said in broken English, "have destroyed many lives."

"Damn right!" Ford yelled.

"Why attacks we? We not here hurt you. We here protect," Krewtek pleaded, with a touch of artificial sincerity.

"Bullshit pal," Gates spoke, "I was one of your first visitors,"

Krewtek's eye narrowed.

"I have an offer for you Gates, Michael F," Kimbett interrupted, "and your friends."

"Kimbett liar! Trick you! Kimbett..." Krewtek suddenly went silent, but his mouth was still moving. Rycon had muted the volume.

"As you probably already noticed, we are no longer part of the Trexian Navy," Kimbett began.

"The *what* navy?" Dutch interrupted.

"The Trexian Navy." Kimbett pointed to Krewtek, "That's a Trexian,"

The *master species*, Gates thought.

"Anyway, we are parked under the shield generation tower, and Krewtek isn't stupid enough to try and fight us here. We know this. And it is our intention to leave this place with as little damage as possible,"

"What's your offer," Gates asked.

"This tower houses the main shield generator. You destroy it after we leave, so the shields lower and we can just fly out of this damn compound," Kimbett said.

"You'd just leave? Without destroying this compound?" Ford asked.

"No. As I understand it, your kind has a massive army mounted outside this compound, and when the shields drop, they will pour into this place and annihilate them for me," Kimbett explained. Bishop and Ford gave each other a look.

Gates gave a sly look, "Why not just blow it up yourselves?"

Kimbett sighed, "Don't argue with me Human, time is too short."

"All right," Gates said, "What if we refuse?"

Kimbett threw back his head and laughed, "Then I will kill you all where you stand and do it myself," A chorus of inhuman laughter followed as Destarus finished his translation to the crew.

Ford nudged Gates a little bit. He turned to see the bewildered faces of his brothers. Ford made a anxious face and gestured for Gates to accept.

Gates smiled, "All right Weed. You have yourself a deal."

Kimbett smiled, reaching out his hand. But Gates made no move to shake it.

"Always the wise human, Gates, Michael F," Kimbett lowered his hand. With lightning speed, he swung his fist into Gates' face, knocking him to the ground, with a bloody lip. Ford helped him up.

"I owed you that," Kimbett said, spitting a wad of mucus at Gates' feet.

Destarus turned to Boratus, "Re-arm their ships, and repair whatever damage you can,"

Gates stood up on his own and gently pushed Ford away. He stared at Kimbett and smiled, blood on his lower teeth.

"We'll meet again, Weed," Gates said hatefully, "I promise."

"Humans, accompany me to the hangar!" Destarus said, and Ford grabbed Gates and dragged him away.

Kimbett watched as Gates disappeared through the doorway.

"I'm counting on it," he said, then he nodded to Rycon to un-mute Krewtek, who had watched the entire transaction.

"Kimbett!" Krewtek's voice thundered over the screen. "I will give you one last chance! "

"I'm listening," Kimbett said.

"Give me the humans, and I'll let you roll out of here," Krewtek offered.

Kimbett shrugged, "Sure, why not. I'll accept."

Krewtek's eye widened. "You will?"

"Oh, yeah." Kimbett smiled evilly, "I'll give you the humans all right." Kimbett made a cut-throat gesture to Rycon, and Rycon closed the channel.

Krewtek's confused face flashed off the screen, as it went to black.

"I want those humans to be in the air in half an hour," Kimbett said to Boratus. Boratus saluted and stomped off towards the hangar.

Kimbett turned to Relecite, "I want to be rolling out from this hangar and be ready for atmospheric departure and planetary orbit within thirty minutes. No less," Relecite saluted, liquefied, and disappeared through the floor.

"Rycon. I want weapons and shields to be fully charged when we go to leave," Kimbett ordered and Rycon nodded.

. . .

As Xo drove his transport down the highway he barely dodged another transport that was heading the wrong way. There was a mass exodus from the Tower to the Molluskan Barracks, and at the same time, exactly half of Krewtek's ground army was positioning itself for an assault on the MegaKore as it leaves the Tower.

In the back seat of the transport, Lieutenant Grackconn slumped. He slowly regained consciousness.

"Whoa," he moaned, "where am I," he said, before coughing violently.

"We're going to the Molluskan Barracks, Sir," Xo said.

"Ensign Xo? He didn't get you too?" Grackconn sputtered blood up from his throat again. Krewtek had apparently damaged some of his abdominal organs.

Grackconn reached one of his claws up to his eye. "My eye hurts." Blood was still flowing from his eye.

"We'll get you to a medic, don't worry." Xo said, while dodging a wrecked fuel truck. He was now approaching the inner gate. The guardian tower was still blocking the roadway.

"Don't worry about me... Ensign... I'm all right..." Grackconn went unconscious again.

Xo turned off the road and drove around the wreckage of the tower and continued towards the Molluskan Barracks.

. . .

Boratus looked at Gates and began to speak in loud, bold syllables, Gates understood none of it.

"All right humans," Destarus began, "The holes in this bomber have been patched up. Your primitive weapons with ones you will need,"

"No shit?" Ford said, looking at the two absolutely huge white tubes replacing the missile pods.

Boratus began to speak again. Destarus translated.

"These missiles are special. You will need them to destroy the generator. The route to the generator will appear on the display that we have mounted in the aft cockpit of your bomber. The switch for your nuclear bomb will now fire your missiles. Do *not* hit that switch until you are in the field chamber, within the interior of the silver globe on top of the tower. You'll know when you're there. Once launched, the missiles will do the rest."

Gates nodded in acceptance.

"Also both ships have had their rocket engines replaced with our own variant," Boratus, through Destarus continued, "the fighter has been repaired and your stolen force cannon has been replaced with a better one. It will have to remain here and make sure nothing follows the bomber. We have equipped the fighter with four powerful missiles that are suitable for attacking groups of aircraft. I'm aware you took out most of their air force at the cryo-plant, but you'll still be outnumbered."

All four men stood there and stared at the improvements to their aircraft. Bishop stared at the four tubes that replaced the hydra pods on the Lakota.

Boratus stared at Ford, who fearlessly held out his hand to the giant, which cautiously approached and took what he offered. *What had you given it Ford?*

Boratus spoke words again.

"Good luck, he says," Destarus translated, "Now get the hell out of here. I say." Destarus added, giving a Trexian salute.

The humans just stared. Ford was the first to raise his hand, and soon all humans were saluting the American way, though Gates was the first to drop his.

Boratus stomped away, along with all other aliens. The men were alone.

"This is unbelievable," Bishop said.

Ford nodded, "I say we just get it done and get the hell out of here, we've done our part,"

"Just cover our asses while we do the deed," Gates said to Bishop.

Bishop smiled, "They're not getting by us, man."

The MegaKore's hangar door began to slowly open.

"We gotta run," Gates said, heading towards the bomber.

The men boarded their ships and readied themselves.

"What the hell did you give him?" Gates asked, grappling with his harness.

"A cigarette," Ford admitted.

Gates just looked at him.

"Hey. It's universal..." Ford said.

"Is your leg going to be alright on the petals?" Gates asked, powering up the reactor.

"I'll be fine, you just enjoy the ride and worry about hitting your switch," Ford joked.

Gates had no problem with that.

CHAPTER 43 The Four Horsemen

Krewtek sat in the captain's chair of the Batteckery, which was parked outside the Molluskan Barracks, which was the only military base left intact. He sat in the chair, alone. Not long ago, he had ordered everyone to clear the bridge. Word had gotten around about what had happened to Grackconn, and no one questioned his orders. Krewtek stared at the main screen, which displayed the tower.

"You know what to do," He said to the small yellow irised eyeball. It nodded.

. . .

Deep in the bowels of the MegaKore, red-irised dotariak marched through mazes of conduits running virtually over every inch of the ship. The red dotariak colony was the MegaKore's own variety; specifically engineered to maintain and repair the delicate machinery within spaces of the MegaKore too hard to reach by larger creatures. Sharing the MegaKore with the red dotariak, were a variety of other dotariak colonies. Blue dotariak were responsible for base maintenance. Green dotariak, were responsible for intelligence gathering and surveillance. Purple dotariak were designed to service and repair aircraft and light vehicles. Gray dotariak were garbage decomposers, which mindlessly ate discarded organic matter in the garbage dumps within the MegaKore. And finally, the Yellow dotariak were Krewtek's own personal breed. There were also minority groups such as orange, brown, white, pink and black, but there were none aboard the MegaKore.

Three dotariak stood in front of the main computer conduit. Two were yellow, one was green. The yellow were signing to the green. After a complex sentence of arm gestures, clicks and beeps, the yellow conveyed its message to the green. The green nodded and gave several of its own gestures. *It had agreed.*

Although the dotariak were a collective intelligence, different colonies could not communicate to either other directly.

The yellows walked over to the conduit and began chewing on the protective insulation. A red passing by stopped, noticing the two yellow dotariak chewing on *its* ship. It walked up to the eyeballs and seeing no reason to remove the insulation, tried to pull one of them off the conduit. The green ran up to the red and tore one of its antennae off. The two yellow both jumped off the conduit and proceeded to bite and scratch the red dotariak to death. Before dying it sent a distress signal to its brothers through its remaining antenna.

Another dotariak walked by and quickly realized something was wrong: It walked toward the dead dotariak and stared with its purple eye, and at the two yellow which had resumed eating away at the insulation. Two additional yellows rushed past the purple and joined in eating the insulation, and there were now three green dotariak. The purple signed to the green, asking simply: *Why?*

The green danced and gestured, communicating simply that they were helping the yellow dotariak *destroy the MegaKore*. It waved its paws, commanding the purple colony to join them. The purple rushed at the green dotariak and grabbed its arm, biting it off. It then proceeded to beat the second green with the dismembered arm until it was overrun and killed by three more greens rushing it.

It had begun.

. . .

"Shields at maximum Sir," Rycon reported.

Kimbett nodded to Destarus.

"Open the hangar doors," Destarus ordered.

Rycon punched in the sequence, but the doors didn't open. The lights to the hangar went dead.

"They've cut the power Sir," Rycon reported.

"Oh please," Kimbett said irritatedly, "Forward Batteries, remove the doors,"

The hangar doors suddenly exploded outward with a ball of fire as several four-foot-wide force shells plowed into them.

"Take out the access hatch," Kimbett ordered.

The MegaKore's massive turret turned towards the metal bubble in the ceiling, covering the service-way into the tower. A missile launched from the rack buried inside the turret. It exploded and completely shattered the metal bubble, exposing the entrance into the innards of the tower.

"The door's open. Sir," Destarus said.

"Launch the Humans," Kimbett then ordered.

. . .

Boratus heard the order to launch the humans over the intercom. He lifted his arms a couple times, signaling for the humans to leave.

"This is it," Ford said, adding power to the magic carpet, and lifting off of the floor. The F-202 Lakota was right behind them. They left the MegaKore hangar, and into the darkened tower hangar.

"That's a big ship," Gates mouth gaped. As he saw the MegaKore for the first time, the light streaming through the open hangar doors illuminated it. Its own hangar door began closing just after they cleared.

. . .

"Let's roll," Kimbett ordered.

"Rolling Sir," Destarus said.

The MegaKore rode out of the flames of the Hangar doorway, and over the ashes of the cryo-plant. The massive ship taxied onto the silver highway and head for the inner gate.

"No contacts Sir," Rycon reported.

Destarus nodded, "Figures, I bet we have a clear path,"

. . .

Twelve red dotariak poured into the area, and began attacking the green and yellow dotariak on the conduit. After a lengthy battle, the red managed to save the conduit, but too soon the yellow and green all over the ship began to rip up electronics.

The main computer conduit's insulation was gone, and half of the soft twenty-two karat gold wires had been chewed apart. An endless stream of dotariak, red, yellow, green and purple flooded into the area. The red and purple fought side by side to defend the damaged conduit, but were soon overtaken and the conduit was destroyed.

Other parts of the ship, the red came at the yellow and green wielding screwdrivers, and wrenches. The blue colony joined the Yellow and Green, but was tiny in numbers. The gray stayed neutral, only too happy to consume the dead bodies of those on either side.

The war began to escalate like a wave of water washing over the ship, as the dotariak communicated nearly instantaneously to other members of their colony, and they, in turn, relayed the messages onward.

Vital systems like the reactor control, central computer, weapons, navigation and the reactor itself became targets.

Unknown to Kimbett and his crew, a second battle was waged within the hull of the MegaKore.

. . .

As Xo reached the Molluskan Barracks he found it as he expected it: a panicked frenzy. Molluskan and Aracteroid were running about in a hurry. Thousands of Dragonfly aircraft were scattered everywhere. Ground units, such as sprinters, tanks, troop transports, brawlers, and antlions were everywhere. Even the remaining twelve metal crushers were being refitted for combat. Surrounding the base was over two hundred thousand MTs, and about fifty thousand armored Aracteroid. On the horizon, the Batteckery loomed.

Xo stopped one of his Molluskan and asked what was going on. It told him of the massive human army building up outside. As he turned back to Grackconn, he found Grackconn on his feet, limping and stumbling towards the Batteckery.

"Oh no you don't, Sir," Xo said, catching up to his comrade, "we need to get you to a doctor."

Grackconn twisted his way free from Xo's grasp, "Leave me alone Ensign, I'm fine."

Blood was still dribbling down his head, in fact Grackconn was not fine.

"Come on, get back here!" Xo shouted.

Grackconn turned, his three operable eyes staring into Xo's.

"You've got a battle to fight," he said, coughing up blood, "and so do I," he continued to walk.

Xo yelled his name once more, and Grackconn turned. They looked at each other, Xo knew it would be the last they spoke, and he couldn't think of what to say.

"I'm so sorry..." Grackconn coughed violently, blood dribbling from his mouth and nose, "...my friend."

"Me too..." Xo said quietly. Grackconn walked away towards the Batteckery.

Xo knew he was dying. He watched until Grackconn disappeared in the crowd of figures swarming over the pads.

Xo had hated his masters, and had questioned the mission. Now he questioned his own convictions.

I am a coward, he thought.

With Rycon probably killed in the MegaKore, he was alone.

"Sir," An aracteroid ran up to him, "As you ordered, six infantry divisions are formed; five Molluskan, one Aracteroid,"

Xo's mind snapped back to the situation at hand, "Have them equipped and ready to move."

The Aracteroid nodded in agreement, "Ready to move where Sir?"

Xo looked back to the tower, and then at the shields above,

"Everywhere,"

CHAPTER 44 Judgment Day

Gates hovered the Revenant side by side with the Lakota, in the empty tower hangar.

"Ready Meridian-3?" Bishop said.

"Ready Meridian-2," Gates responded.

"Go get 'em," Dutch radioed.

The bomber rocketed off and turned straight up the service way.

"You just cover our ass!" Ford radioed, before disappearing into the service way.

The F-202 Lakota turned to face the hangar doors.

. . .

Scores of the hovering Dragonflies swarmed all over the MegaKore, in a vein effort to destroy it. The giant tires of the MegaKore crushed the other vehicles on the road as it took up all twelve lanes of the highway. The first wave of Dragonflies was shot to pieces by point defense lasers and force cannon turrets on the MegaKore. It took no damage in the feeble assault. The MegaKore continued until reaching the closed doors of the inner gate, where it slowed to a stop. Although one of the huge doors was bashed in, the opening was too small.

Destarus pointed at the screen, "Rycon, fix it,"

The MegaKore fired its large turret gun. The one-hundred and fifty foot doors were both blown off their hinges and landed a half mile away. The MegaKore drove on, running over the fallen guardian tower.

"Sir! I've scanned the Tower and discovered a separate power signature traveling up the tower," A young Aracteroid said to Krewtek.

Krewtek frowned, "The Humans," He said.

"The MegaKore has passed beyond the inner gate and is heading down the highway, towards us!" The Aracteroid said a second later.

Krewtek looked at the young Aracteroid, "Tell them to divide the Dragonflies attacking the MegaKore into two divisions. Keep one attacking the MegaKore, have the others kill the humans."

. . .

Gates and Ford were both pressed back into their seats as gravity and G-forces combined forces as the bomber accelerated straight up the vertical access tunnel. The tunnel was well lit, but of inconsistent size. Ford felt nervous as the walls seemed to be closing in. To make things more challenging, catwalks and cables were strung between the walls of the corridor, which averaged the width of a high school cafeteria. A ceiling was approaching.

Gates stared intently at the black slate anchored to his navigation station.

"This alien-computer says to turn left into the smaller conduit," Gates said, staring at the small, colored 3-dimensional map on its screen.

Ford saw the small conduit and hesitated.

"It's tiny!" Ford said, decelerating.

"The computer says that's the way," Gates said.

Ford eased the large bomber into the small tunnel, and once in, gave some more thrust and continued onward.

. . .

"Bishop. Radar is picking up several vessels closing on that door," Dutch said calmly to Bishop.

"It's about time," he replied.

One by one, the Dragonflies entered the dark and vast hangar.

"Here they come, let's see if these alien weapons pay off," Bishop said, depressing the trigger in his stick.

Blue light erupted from the five barreled Trexian nose cannon as it spit out thousands of fifty-millimeter force shells in a single burst. The force of the cannon, pushed the hovering F-202 Lakota back a few feet before Bishop released the trigger and let out a gasp of exhilaration.

"Oh *hell* yeah," Bishop glowed, impressed with the new firepower. With a big grin, he depressed the trigger again. The Dragonflies were just within range of the human ship, when it began to fire wave upon wave of force shells. The first four Dragonflies were shot to pieces. Two more came within range, but were both peppered with force shells, and sent to the floor. A Dragonfly coming in from the door fired a missile. It flew at the stationary Lakota and closed half the distance before being torn apart by the steady hail of force shells.

Bishop threw back his head and laughed above the howl of the cannon, "Ha! Come get it assholes! I got a sack fulla quarters, and am gettin' the high-score tonight!" he howled.

. . .

The MegaKore drove by the decimated Garden Barracks.

"All right. The humans took care of this base for us Rycon, we can wait for the humans to take out the shields here," Destarus ordered.

Rycon took the throttle control and pushed it forward, but there was no reduction in speed. Rycon looked down and to his confusion, his station appeared dead. All of the lights and gauges were dark.

"What's the problem Rycon?" Kimbett said, getting out of his chair, walking down the stairs.

Rycon stared at the console, "I seem to have lost power to this station."

"Use the auxiliary station!" Destarus ordered running up to the dead station. Rycon got up and ran to the smaller station next to the wall.

The MegaKore continued to roll down the highway, a turn was approaching.

"The damn Molluskan forgot to hook something up again," Destarus said, removing the screws to the panel.

"Sir!" Rycon called to Kimbett, "The auxiliary station has just failed,"

"My station is inoperable too!" Kailecko shouted.

Kimbett ran his fingers through the thick mane on his head, "What the hell is going on here?"

Destarus removed the panel to see a yellow irised Dotariak with bulged cheeks, eating the wiring within the station.

"Kimbett we've got dotariak in the equipment!" Destarus yelled, smashing the dot with his metal fist.

Kimbett shot a annoyed look to Destarus, "So? They're always in the..."

"They're eating it!!" Destarus interrupted.

Kimbett's face dropped with the sudden realization, "...I missed something,"

. . .

"Signal the charge!" Bruin shouted from his perch on top of the control tower above the flight deck of the sky carrier USS Kentucky.

A chief petty officer acknowledged, "Aye Sir," and disappeared through the hatch.

It had begun.

The human ground force, was made up of the combined armies of many countries, but the bulk was made up of the Russians, British, Australians, Chinese and the United States. A wave of firepower began to move at *The Wall*. All four sky carriers rumbled to life, and began launching wave after wave of F-35 Joint Strike Fighters, and A-33 Anteaters. Wings of Chinese MiG-127s and Su-131s arrived and were armed with land-attack missiles. By this time, due to the genius of Tieseler's group, many of the U.S. aircraft were armed with weapons salvaged from the Trexian, such as lasers, force cannons, and missiles.

The Wall came to life as well. Its lasers and missile racks firing constantly, blowing apart several planes before they could fire a shot. Once within range, the human jets let loose with their weapons. Recognizing that *The Wall* had the supreme advantage with its weapon range, the airmen were ordered to close the distance as soon as possible and do as much damage as they could. Soon, tons of depleted uranium slugs, force shells, and warheads riddled the thick metal walls of the main gate. Slowly, the two massive gun ports dilated, and the massive gatling-style cannons protruded. The cannons opened fire and began to sweep the sand in front of the main gate with gigantic ring shaped force shells. They blew craters into the ground, and buried or smashed incoming land units.

Once all planes were dispatched, two carriers remained back, out of range of the main gate to be landing platforms, and refueling stations, the remaining two approached *The Wall* at a higher altitude and began to fire their 22-inch rail gun batteries.

. . .

The B-100 had long since cleared the small tunnel and now headed up the remaining length of the tower. The interior was now much larger, dark, and had one central cylinder traveling up the center with them.

"That must be some kind of big-ass electrical line," Ford said,

Gates looked at his screen, “Its kicking out one hell of a magnetic field... off the scale,”

Ford felt the heat radiating from his canopy, becoming aware of the extreme temperatures inside the tower, “lots of energy here,” he said.

“I’m interested in the thing it’s energizing,” Gates replied coldly.

As the B-100 Revenant continued its trek up the tower, it snagged a cable attached from the cylinder to the wall, snapping it. If not for the shields, it would have torn its engine nacelle off.

Gates looked at the alien navigation screen, and then looked ahead. Something was wrong. Directly in front of the B-100 Revenant was a silver, featureless wall. It was not supposed to be there.

“Through that wall is supposed to be the pedestal where the target’s supposed to be,” Gates explained.

“How am I supposed to get through it?” Ford asked, as the wall approached quickly.

“I don’t know...” Gates shouted, wide eyed, as the wall rushed at him.

“Good!” Ford said, squeezing the trigger on his stick. Though the Revenant had its original force cannon, it was enough to chew through the metal barrier and fill the air with sparks and liquid metal droplets. Ford didn’t released the trigger.

. . .

Behind the metal barrier, a circular pedestal spanning nearly a mile in diameter rested at the bottom of the interior of the globe. The barrier exploded upward for a moment before collapsing into the itself as the B-100 flew up out of the hole, and turned horizontal again. Ford could see a massive eerily lit chamber ahead as he accelerated.

“Where the hell are we again?” he asked.

Gates smiled, "Somewhere we were never supposed to be,"

The B-100 shot out from under the pedestal and into the cavernous empty space of the metal globe. Every hair on Ford's body instantly stood straight up. Gates' did the same.

"Radiation is high, let's not stick around," Gates reported. "...the static electricity reading is incredible!"

"This thing might run off of static. It looks like a Van De Graff generator," Ford said.

The walls of the globe flashed for a moment.

"What the hell was that?" Gates asked.

The Revenant slowed to a halt and turned around to face the center of the globe. The ship was basked in reddish-violet light as they faced the shield generator's element. On top of the pedestal was a pyramidal metal structure with thick towering spire extending straight up to the center of the globe. On top of the spire was an enormous huge transparent sphere nearly half a mile in diameter. Inside of it, moving, pulsating purple, red and blue arms of light reached out from a central black core. Massive bolts of white lightning periodically arced from the sphere to the interior walls globe, followed immediately by a loud crack of thunder.

"What... is... that?" Ford said in awe.

Gates smiled,

"That, my friend, is our new primary."

CHAPTER 45 Rolling Thunder

Kimbett looked, disbelieving, at Destarus. "What do you mean you can't stop us?"

"Our navigation is gone! They must have chewed the cables to the computer!" Destarus yelled, tearing the station apart.

"What exactly does that mean?" Kimbett asked.

Destarus looked at Kimbett bleakly, "If they got to the navigation computer itself, not only can we not stop this thing... we can't steer it, or take off for that matter."

"Sir! A second division of Dragonflies are closing," Rycon announced.

"You know what to do Lieutenant! Deal with them," Kimbett barked.

Rycon nodded and then looked at his dead panel. "Sir. Weapon's systems are still out!"

There was an audible hiss and crackling sound echoing around the MegaKore. Kimbett closed his eyes.

"Sir!" Rycon shouted.

"Let me guess!" Kimbett yelled, "We just lost the shields!"

Rycon nodded, "The rear shields have been deactivated,"

Kimbett kicked Destarus's station and punched the intercom.

"Boratus!" He shouted.

"Yes sir!" A voice came back over the intercom.

"Launch our Aeros and have them take out the Dragonflies!" Kimbett yelled.

"Sir. The hangar doors won't open," Boratus immediately responded.

Kimbett beat the wall with his fist.

"Boratus!" he resumed, "forget the doors! Take some of your men and hunt down the dotariak that are attacking the ship!"

Boratus paused, “Dotariak? Why would they...?”

“We don’t have time!” Kimbett yelled at the intercom.

“Yes Sir!” Boratus thundered back.

The MegaKore continued to thunder down the highway strip. The Dragonflies swarming all over it, firing into its exposed hull, weakening its thick armor with every missile impact, shell hit, and laser.

. . .

Like hornets pouring from a disturbed nest, Dragonflies began to spill from the opened doorway. The lone Lakota couldn’t destroy them quickly enough. As twenty-eight rushed in at the F-202, it was able to cut apart twelve before they reached it, the remaining sixteen began to attack. Amidst a curtain of force shells, the Lakota accelerated from its hover and began to take evasive action. As the lone human fighter battled eleven of them, five managed to slip by and head for the service way, obviously aware of the bomber’s ascent.

“There heading for the bomber!” Dutch shouted against the roar of the cannon.

“Arm one of those missiles they gave us,” Bishop ordered.

As the F-202 screamed past the service way, it fired four black missiles up into the metallic tunnel. Using an unknown method of guidance, three of them locked onto one of the Dragonflies, chasing it down and blowing it to shrapnel. The fourth missile hit the rear of a second Dragonfly, damaging its left engine. Unable to continued the climb, it flew back down the tunnel and was destroyed by the waiting Lakota. The remaining three Dragonflies were heading for the Revenant.

. . .

The A-33 Anteater was the successor of the A-10 thunderbolt. Designed primarily to destroy armored vehicles on the ground, it was also adept at removing the weapon turrets on top of *The Wall*. The hangar embedded in *The Wall* had opened and had launched four Aeros that had evaded the cryo-plant disaster. They were the only Trexian fighters left, and were hopelessly outnumbered.

The massive multi-barreled force-cannons were now rolling full force, pouring out round after round.

The USS Nevada, after sustaining multiple small arms hits, began to drift too low and was rocked with a direct hit from the huge force cannons; its unshielded hull was torn through like tin foil. The fifty armored vehicles and about half two thousand troops on board were either outright destroyed, or severely wounded. The shell punched an exit through aft end of the sky carrier, and following it was a plume of metal scrap, smoke and debris. The carrier began to slowly spiral alarmingly towards the surface before damage control teams aboard were able to inflate the emergency helium cells and slow its descent. The devastated USS Nevada was able to limp away from the battle and set down out of range of the big guns, where it was abandoned.

The USS Hawaii and USS Washington were close enough to be within range of the small weapons, but too high for the giant force cannons which did not have enough elevation, as they headed for *The Wall*'s main gate, both pounded away at the shields with their 22-inch rail guns and now guided rockets as well. The flagship, USS Kentucky loitered silently above, and continued to coordinate the battle.

. . .

The Molluskan operating the giant cannons were too busy firing at the sky carriers to notice the F-35 Joint Strike Fighter coming straight at them.

Captain Riggs was running his plane directly at the right force-cannon port. He fired his laser-guided Unicorn scatter-missiles, one after another.

The Molluskan controlling the right cannon point defense system locked his laser onto the first of the incoming missiles, but was killed by cannon-fire from a MiG-127 moments later. The remaining unicorn missiles released their munitions, sending their explosives to spray into the gap between the cannon's barrels and *The Wall*, taking out the protective shield. The Molluskan gun-operator, recovering from the shock of the explosions, began firing the giant ring shaped force shells at Riggs's incoming jet.

Riggs was firing his twenty-millimeter cannon when the giant force rings shot past him. One came straight at him, and he had no time to dodge. The F-35 was hit almost dead on by the ring, severing half of his left wing, but miraculously Riggs, and the rest of his plane, had survived. He ejected within seconds, but not before pointing the fuselage of his plane at the massive unprotected force cannon.

With the shields down, there was nothing to stop the F-35's burning wreckage, flying at nearly mach one, from flying into the unshielded gap and into the motor-bay beyond. The F-35's four Sandman bombs ignited, along with its nearly full tank of fuel; it was as good as a fifteen ton bomb. Explosions began to rumble from behind the force cannon, its revolving barrels came to a grinding halt, as smoke billowed out of. The cannon exploded, its six fifteen-foot wide barrels separating from the turret. With another larger blast, the entire cannon nosed forward and tumbled out of its slot to the sand below.

There was an immense cheering from the humans in the CIC, the command information center, of the USS Kentucky.

. . .

"We're going off the highway!" Destarus shouted.

"Maybe we can ignite the boosters on one side and use that to correct course..." Kailecko suggested.

"No good. If we can't shut them off again, we'd be worse off," Kimbett said, trying to fix the tactical station. His hand was covered in yellow jelly, from smashing dotariak.

"We would over turn, and end up flipping," Destarus said, completely disassembling his station.

The MegaKore was heading off of the road, and began to run over vehicles that were parked on the shoulder, smashing them flat with its large wheels.

"Sir. I can't arm the Pulsar missiles from our main pods. But from here I can lock them into position, and activate there jets," Kailecko said, operating one of the backup stations on the second level of the bridge.

"What are you telling me Kailecko?" Kimbett said, looking up at him.

Kailecko explained, "If I lock them into place, and activate the engines in only our left pod, it will push us slightly to the right and back onto the road, maybe buy us some time, Sir,"

The MegaKore clipped a radar station. Tearing off one of its gun turrets.

"Do it!" Kimbett ordered.

. . .

Boratus ran to the main computer router room. He found that Relecite was already there, spraying acid from his palms at the Yellow and Green dotariak. Boratus saw two Purple and Red dotariak on the ground. He raised his foot to stomp them, Relecite grabbed his arm and stared at him, shaking his head.

"They're good huh?" Boratus said as Relecite glided by him and out the door. Boratus followed.

. . .

The rockets in the left missile pod fired their engines. The exhaust pushing them towards the right, back on the road.

To Kailecko's horror, however, his station then went dead, and he was unable to shut them off. They finally stopped when their fuel ran out. The MegaKore had over corrected and they were now heading off the road on the other side, and directly towards the main construction plant of Grantex.

"Turn! Turn! Turn!" Kimbett yelled.

Kailecko hit his panel. "It's too late!"

The MegaKore smashed through the construction plant. First uprooting the crane, and then running straight through the concrete molds and then into the chemical tanks, and finally into the vehicle hangar and seven-story worker barracks, totally demolishing everything in its path. If not for its forward shields, it would have been severely damaged. The MegaKore turned back onto the road on its own, and was rebounding back and forth against the tiny twenty foot walls on both sides of either side of the highway.

The view screen suddenly went dead.

"Shit!" Kimbett got up, "Kailecko! I want you to repair this station right now."

"Yes Sir," Kailecko said, running down the stairs to the bridge pit again.

Kimbett went to Destarus's station, and began to try and raise the view screen.

"The Molluskan Barracks is..." Rycon paused, "we just lost all of our sensory, Sir," he said grimly. The crackling sound occurred again.

"And the front shields!" Rycon added a second later, with a touch of alarm unusual for him.

The MegaKore thundered past the Molluskan Barracks and the parked Batteckery. With the swarm of Dragonflies following it.

"Die you bastard!!" Krewtek said through gritted teeth, as he watched with satisfaction.

CHAPTER 46 Eye Of The Storm

"I'm reading at least one protective shield around it," Gates said.

Another bolt of lighting arced from one section of the globe to another.

"I hope these things work," Ford said, looking through the canopy at the large pods attached to both sides of his bomber.

"We'll know soon enough..." Gates said, "here goes!"

Gates paused for a second of silent prayer, "Firing!" He finally yelled, hitting the red pickle switch for the second time.

The B-100 was thrown backwards as both pods catapulted their missiles forward. Neither man actually saw the missiles, only a haze of gray smoke in their wake.

.

"Let's get the hell out of here!" Gates yelled over the roar.

Ford said nothing but hit the throttle. The bomber flew straight for the base of the pedestal where it had emerged.

Both missiles were on a direct course with the sphere. One missile suddenly pulled up and did a loop in the air, coming in far behind the first. As the first missile reached the first defensive shield, it detonated tearing a gaping hole.

The B-100 was flying down under the pedestal, Gates caught a glimpse of the explosion before disappearing from view. Ford flew towards the hole in which they came up. Ford pushed his collective stick forward, and the B-100 dove down the hole, forcing blood into both men's head as the negative G's mounted.

Gates grunted as he saw red, but the feeling soon passed.

"Sorry," Ford said apologetically.

"Meridian-2, if you guys can hear me, you better get the hell out of here! The shield generator is history!" Gates yelled into the radio.

A garbled but audible voice replied, "Roger that, Meridian-3. We are out of here," The F-202 ignored the last Dragonfly and head for the exit.

The second missile that looked much like a jet engine with wings flew its pre-programmed course through the breach in the shield. With nothing to stand in its way, the missile impacted the glass sphere, busting through it, and continued to fly until hitting the core in the center. With a muffled explosion, the thick glowing arms of ionized gas within the sphere faded a second before the ozone-rich atmosphere rushed into the sphere and mixed with the flammable gasses inside. The resulting explosion destroyed the sphere entirely. The lighting began to arc between the inside of the globe and the spire where the sphere had once been perched. The metal pyramid on the pedestal began to heat up. They began to turn white hot and melt.

The globe on top of the giant tower burst outward with a thunderous shudder. All beings outside who witnessed the tower's unexpected demise were in a state of shock momentarily. The shields over the compound thinned, turned a reddish shade of purple and gradually faded into nothingness.

. . .

Ford was traveling straight down when three Dragonflies zipped by the descending bomber.

"Where do they think they're going?" Gates asked.

The cylinder running through the center of the Tower began to successively explode, starting from the pedestal on top. All three of the Dragonflies slowed and turned around to chase the bomber. Behind them, higher up the tower, an explosion sent chunks of metal and debris raining down. One Dragonfly was cut in two by a falling metal support beam. The remaining two dove down the passage way. The cascading explosions continued down the tower, as the tower was melting from the top down.

"Gates, we got two tail-gaters," Ford said, as he was nervously piloting the bomber at a very fast speed down the narrow passageway.

Gates was already trying to remove the alien navigation computer from his console as it was blocking his screen. With a grunt he managed to overcome the strong adhesives and the pad came off with a tearing sound. He threw the pad under his console so gravity wouldn't send it forward into the diving Revenant.

Force shells spattered the rear of the Revenant as the closest Dragonfly began to fire.

"Uhh... Gates buddy..." Ford said, barely heard over the sound of the force shells hitting the shields.

"Patience young Jedi..." Gates while training his manual aiming reticle on the first Dragonfly. He squeezed the trigger and a stream of force shells flowed from the tail gun to the Dragonfly and it soon burst into flames as he shot through its central fuselage.

"Ha! One down!" Gates screamed.

"We're coming up on that narrow tunnel..." Ford said as his heart fluttered, "it's going to be close..."

As the B-100 shot through the narrow tunnel an explosion lit up Gates' display and the trailing Dragonfly disappeared behind a curtain of fire.

The Revenant exited the tunnel, a tongue of fire following it down into the larger interior of the tower. A burning jet engine emerged from the fire and continued the chase; it was all that was left of the last Dragonfly.

"We've got a problem! Burning piece of the enemy! Six O'clock!" Gates yelled, before opening fire at the gaining piece of debris with the tail gun. It had no effect.

Ford grit his teeth as he accelerated through the winding, dark passageway, expecting to scrape the walls and slam into a catwalk any second. Falling with a cloud of shrapnel, the burning engine followed close behind. The small opening into the tower hangar appeared in the distance just as Gates' display lit up. Ford held his breath as the walls of the tunnel racing by were basked in an orange glow; a massive wave of fire was heading straight at them from behind.

Gates' eyes widened, "Move this bucket!"

Ford didn't know how fast he could go and still be able to pull up before hitting the hangar floor, and prayed he was slow enough as they shot through the service tunnel entrance and into the hangar. As Ford pulled up, Gates felt the G forces pull the blood from his head and saw blackness creep into the corners of his eyes. No man had time to put on their G-suits before their escape.

The Revenant turned horizontal only two hundred feet from the smooth hangar floor. Behind them, the burning jet-engine and debris exploded into the floor of the hangar followed by a raging column of fire. The Revenant head for the destroyed hangar door.

All power systems of the tower began to overload: every light flashed and went dead, every cable and wire melted and every electronic circuit sizzled. A massive power surge was building up within the walls of the tower, and with no generator to turn the power into shields, there was no load to relieve such an energy buildup. The tower itself absorbed the energy; converting it to heat.

"Now we know why that green bastard didn't blow it up himself!" Ford said, sweat flowing from his brow.

Gates looked at the map of the facility, "Don't leave the compound, head for the inner gate!" he shouted.

"Why?" Ford asked, "the shields are down, we can circle around..."

Gates interrupted, "We need to put that inner gate between us and the tower."

Ford understood.

"I'm getting enormous readings...," Gates reported as they flew past the flattened cryo-plant air base.

Gates looked in his rear view camera and saw the paint boiling off the surface of the tower. In some spots it seemed to glow red. The Trexian symbol, decaled on the side exploded.

"Shit!" Gates said, "brace for impact!"

In the fashion of a volcanic eruption, the base of the tower exploded outward, sending a wave of fire several miles out. Ford managed to fly over the inner barrier just as the concussion wave swept over it, knocking part of the wall down. The chaotic air currents tossed the Revenant around like a windsock in a hurricane, but they soon subsided. The remainder of the tower quickly sank, each section exploding with the same ferocity as the base, until the shattered globe at the top disappeared into a black crater, covered by a cloud of choking black smoke.

"Holy shit we made it!" Ford announced.

Gates sighed a big breath of relief, but was not at ease.

CHAPTER 47 Reckless Driving

Kimbett ripped off the green plastic jacket to the 22-karat gold wires with his teeth, twisted them together and then threw the auxiliary switch to the main view screen. With a static blast, the screen came to life with computer checks and diagnostic data. It mostly read malfunctioning equipment all over the ship. Kimbett smiled at his successful repair. He quickly hit the forward viewer key. Kimbett's eyes opened as wide as they could, his smile turned to a cold frown.

"Destarus....! " Kimbett moaned, stunned. In front of him, as large as the view screen, was a giant metal wall, racing at them at over ninety miles an hour. The MegaKore was on a collision course with the *Wall's* main gate.

"Shields! Shields!" Destarus shouted. "Where are the damned shields?"

"Shields are inoperable Sir! The main regulator controls have been severed in engineering," Reported Kailecko.

"Use the auxiliary!" Destarus howled.

"Auxiliary shield controls not responding Sir!" One of the technicians shouted in reply.

"Dammit! Who's in Engineering?!" Destarus demanded.

"Boratus and Relecite" Kailecko responded.

. . .

In the Engineering section, the Green and Yellow dotariak colonies were destroying everything in sight. The Red and Purple colonies, although outnumbered, were trying as fast as they could to repair everything as quickly as possible and at the same time repel the enemy.

Relecite tore away an access panel to weapons control; staring at him were nearly thirty yellow dot, all gnawing away at the insulators covering the main targeting system's power cables. If they had gnawed completely through, they could have shorted out every weapons system aboard the MegaKore. Relecite, wasting no time, quickly sprayed down the panel with acid from the ducts on his hands. The dotariak were melted away in a foaming white froth.

Boratus kicked the door to the reactor room in. The dotariak had used a soldering torch to weld the door shut, but in wasn't effective against Boratus's brute strength. Before Boratus' eyes were literally millions of dotariak. They coated every surface of the room, including the reactor chamber itself. Red, Green, Yellow, and Purple dotariak were battling it out on the floor, which was awash with slippery yellow paste and countless dotariak bodies. While the some of the Yellow chewed into the walls to destroy the sensitive electronics behind them, others were using tiny drills to bore into computer screens and circuitry. One was using a plasma cutter to cut a rectangular hole into the reactor itself.

"No! " Boratus howled as he rushed inside, followed by several MegaKore MTs and Molluskan engineers and technicians. Boratus splattered the eyeball with the plasma torch, and began to destroy all Yellow and Green eyeballs in sight. One of the molluskan slipped on the dead dotariak littering the floor. The rest of the Molluskan joined in the stomping frenzy, they finally stopped the slaughter when the last yellow dotariak was crushed under one of their feet. The Red and Purple dotariak danced and jumped into the air before attempting to repair the reactor room's controls.

"Boratus! Relecite! Come in!" Destarus's voice boomed over the intercom.

"Go ahead!" Boratus said.

"Listen, We have a class one emergency here! We need shields right NOW!!"

. . .

Kailecko was able to restore partial tactical control to the MegaKore, that is, he could now fire the point defense lasers. Weak and inferior, the point defense laser system is designed to destroy incoming missiles and aircraft. They were practically useless against the enormous wall of metal the MegaKore was speeding at. Kailecko tried desperately to restore control to the rest of the weapons.

Kimbett ran to the smashed tactical station and lifted up one of the bent and dented consoles. Miraculously, the one computer screen Kimbett needed was not destroyed, in fact it still had power. It currently showed the shield status. Which was displaying a green diagram of the MegaKore and usually had a blue aura surrounding it to define the shield. There was no aura. Kimbett clenched his yellow teeth.

The MegaKore was getting closer...

. . .

A great column of fire rose into the air off in the distance, followed by bright flashes. A great mass of black smoke blocked out the western horizon.

"Their tower is goin' up! Check it out!" One of the enlisted men shouted from the railing on the deck above. Sterling looked up and was surprised to see what was left of the massive structure slip below the rising curtain of smoke forever.

"Admiral," Sterling spoke into the headset built into his Kevlar helmet,

"Go ahead General," the radio squawked back.

"Are you seeing what I am seeing out here?" Sterling said, a great sense of relief and surprise in his voice.

"Not only am I seeing it, listen to this," Admiral Bruin responded.

"...in your direction. Meridian-3 will follow." some familiar voice boomed over the radio.

"Roger that Meridian-2, glad to hear from you. Come on home, we got the signal fires lit." Bruin replied.

The Lakota survived!

"We'll keep an eye out for Meridian-3," Bruin finished.

So had the Revenant.

"Looks like Locksmith is a winner General, the shields are down," the admiral said.

. . .

"Where am I supposed to find the problem?!" Boratus complained, looking around at all the tangled messes of wiring, hanging from the walls and ceiling.

"It's in sector twenty-two on deck seven. Hurry!" Destarus's voice rang out.

"I'll be right there!" Boratus yelled while running out the door. One molluskan followed him. Boratus ran full speed at the stair well and slid down a support column all the way from deck twelve to deck seven. Then he ran to sector twenty-two. This was the computer section, the MegaKore's brain. Currently, no dotariak were in sight, but it was obvious that they were here, all the wiring for the computers were hanging out of the walls and sparks were fizzling out of the cracks in the monitors. The floor was warped and smoking, indicating a fire on the deck below.

Boratus felt anger in not seeing a swarm of yellow or green irised dotariak eating all this delicate hardware; it appeared as if he had missed all the action. Across the room was a metal door with the words *Main Shield Processor*. Boratus kicked open the door, expecting to find forty or fifty dotariak inside. Instead the room was barren.

The interior of the closet sized room was all shiny and metallic, the shield systems computers rested safely on the floor and shelf, protected in their bomb-proof and shock-absorbent metal cases. Boratus' eyes instantly locked onto the shelf where all the cables hook up into the main computer. On the shelf was a little yellow eyed dotariak glaring at him and in its clutches was one ribbon of wires; the ribbon that all commands to and from the shield computer must travel through. The ribbon was currently unplugged, one end in the left paw, and the other in its right.

Boratus's eyes narrowed. He ran at the eyeball with his claws in the air. The eyeball threw the connectors in the air and scurried to the end of the shelf and disappeared into an access port. Boratus ran at the port with his claw reached back, ready to smash through the tiny metal door and crush the eyeball hiding inside. His plan were cut short when the floor collapsed under his feet and he now dangled, by two claws, over a pit of sparks and smashed computer equipment below. Jagged shards of metal and live wires carrying thousands of volts littered the area below, there was no ground to speak of.

It was a trap.

The molluskan suddenly burst through the door and stopped dead in its tracks, it saw Boratus' two claws grasping at a girder that held up the solid part of the floor. It was even more confused as it saw several dotariak run from a small access port, over to Boratus' claws. Boratus looked up and instantly recognized the little yellow eyed one as the little bastard that unplugged the shield computer. The dotariak began chewing on the soft and vulnerable suction cups between the armor plates in his claws. Boratus screamed in agony as his own red blood trickled down his arm. With his lower two arms, he began to swing at the biting eyeballs.

The Molluskan walked over to the hole in the floor and looked mindlessly at Boratus. "What are you doing?!" Boratus yelled.

The Molluskan shrugged and grumbled a word that meant *I don't know.*

"Get over there to that shelf and plug that thing in!" Boratus howled. The eyeballs relentlessly chewing on the interior of his claws. Boratus tried to pull himself up, but he had nothing to grab onto. A fire suddenly broke out below him, it quickly turned into a blaze.

The Molluskan walked over to the shelf and picked a severed wire, then walked over to Boratus to show him.

"No! You fool! The ribbon of wires! THE RIBBON! " Boratus tried to motion with his other two hands.

The Molluskan walked over to the shelf and picked up both sides of the ribbon and tried to put them together. After a few tries, the pieces finally clicked into place. An eyeball walked over to the Molluskan and began jumping up and down hysterically, before it was flattened by the Molluskan's clenched fist.

. . .

Kimbett watched with a bewildered expression of a madman. The diagram of the MegaKore began to light up, showing that the shield grid was activated.

"Yes!" Kimbett yelled. He reached out a finger and pushed the forward shield button. And with a click the diagram showed the rear shields rise.

"No!" Kimbett clenched his teeth and pressed the button again, and again, but only the rear shields came on.

"Destarus! I can't get the damn shields to go forward! They only go aft!" Kimbett raved.

"What do you want me to do about it Kimbett!" Destarus said while tearing through the wiring to the auxiliary station of the bridge.

Kimbett didn't know why he kept yelling at Destarus, it was clear what was going on, Boratus had gotten something backwards. Kimbett theorized: This would mean that if he raised the aft shields, then the forward shields would go up!

Hope brushed Kimbett only for a second before he realized that the aft shield controls were pulverized.

. . .

"Boratus! Where are my damn forward shields, I only have aft!?" Kimbett's voice rang out over the intercom.

"Now what's wrong?" Boratus asked the molluskan. It shrugged.

"I'm only getting aft shields..." Kimbett said calmly, "and unless you idiots change that real soon, we're all going to DIE!"

"Shit! You plugged it in backwards!" Boratus yelled.

The molluskan looked at Boratus incomprehensibly.

"Fool! Unplug it! Now!" Boratus commanded.

. . .

Kimbett watched with horror as the aft shields disappeared. The wall was a mere thirty seconds away. It came, ominously, at them. Close enough to see the rivets in the metallic panels.

"If we hit the wall..." Rycon began.

"Don't let me down Boratus." Kimbett said quietly.

"...with our shields down..."

"Everybody brace for impact!" Destarus yelled.

"...we will not survive." Rycon finished. A dribble of sweat rolled down his white face.

Kailecko gasped.

"*PLUG IT IN YOU STUPID MINDLESS WORTHLESS PILE OF...*" Boratus erupted a stream of insults towards the Molluskan as it continued to franticly clash the two plugs together.

Click! Clack! Click! Snap...

. . .

Kimbett began, for only the second time in his life, to feel like he was at his final moment. Even as he was falling from the tower in the garden dome, he knew he would survive. Even as the sprinters charged him, and escape seemed impossible, he knew he would escape. But he didn't feel that now. Impact was in less than ten seconds, and nothing short of a miracle would prevent the MegaKore from hitting the main gate of *The Wall*. Its own shadow appeared to be on a collision course with them.

Less than five seconds.

In the corner of Kimbett's eye he saw the diagram light up, showing that the shields were again charged. This time the forward shield button blinked. Kimbett's eyes opened up as far as they could exposing his purple irises and black round pupils. With about two hundred feet between the MegaKore and the gate, he launched himself at the button.

. . .

With as much strength as he could muster, Boratus pulled himself up over the edge. He was almost high enough to get a leg up when he was thrown out of the hole, as the entire ship jolted violently and all went black.

. . .

General Sterling looked out over the battle field. Everywhere he saw explosions, the sound of jets flying overhead and below were deafening. Thundering sounds of the heavy artillery of his carrier added to the symphonic maelstrom of destruction. Sterling glanced at the main gate for just a second. So far, the forces of Earth had not been able to crack the mighty gate of *The Wall*, but had only managed to partially disarm it. Only one of its massive multi-barreled cannons remained. The shields were now down, and he had to make a decision: Do we pull back, and cross into the compound from a previously shielded alternate route, or do they keep fighting to pacify *The Wall* since all of their resources are there.

Before he could make up his mind, the decision was made for him.

With a silent flash, the gate suddenly exploded. Sterling's jaw dropped, as he watched the gate disintegrate and in its place was a large wall of fire. Through the flames, flying outward with the giant chunks of metal shrapnel was a giant machine. It was a gigantic red and black wheeled vehicle as large as two sky carriers, a blurry blue haze surrounded the front half of it. As it dove out of the wreckage of the gate, it left a trail of debris flying behind it like a comet.

It struck the earth, causing a small earthquake, and jack-knifed sideways, throwing a tidal wave of sand and rocks at the troops and equipment below. Sterling gripped the rails and had only a second to brace before the sky carrier was jolted by a massive wave of heat from the explosion only a mile away. The sky carrier's computer controlled variable-pitch engine nacelles rotated and provided thrust to counter the forces trying to up-end the massive floating ship. The General was thrown to the deck as the airship lurched violently. After a moment, the air calmed, and Sterling cautiously got to his feet and walked back to the rail. Several other men who raced to the railing to get a look at the MegaKore joined Sterling. Everybody watched, stunned.

There was no order to fire upon the alien craft.

. . .

All was black.

"Destarus?" Kimbett spoke.

At first he heard no noise.

“Is anybody still alive?” Kimbett asked the darkness.

“I’m here, Admiral,” Kailecko’s voice rang out of the void.

“Hit the emergency lights Kailecko,” Kimbett ordered.

The bridge was basked in a blue light. Only Kimbett and Kailecko were conscious, Destarus was draped over the railing surrounding the bridge pit. Kimbett jumped up onto his feet and walked over to Destarus, picked him up and laid him onto the ground. Kailecko hobbled over to him, yellow blood dribbling from his nasal holes. His eye patch had been torn from his head, revealing his exposed, gaping eye socket.

“He’s coming around,” Kailecko said, examining his Captain. Destarus opened his eye and began to stand, but Kailecko tried to push him back to the ground.

“I’m all right Kailecko.” He said pushing Kailecko aside. “We’re still alive...”

Rycon was just standing perfectly still. If Destarus didn’t know better, Rycon would have appeared totally shocked to still be alive.

“Rycon!” Kimbett spat some crimson blood on the floor, “Tell me we have enough power to fire our weapons.”

“We do Sir, batteries one and three are fully charged,” Rycon reported. Just as he was finished talking, the lights came back on. “The reactor is still operating at full capacity, although there is no external computer control over it. The last I checked, Commander Relecite was manually managing it while our Red dotariak repair the computer.

Kimbett nodded, "Do we have weapons control?"

. . .

"What the hell is it Sir?" A young soldier asked Sterling.

Should we attack? Sterling asked himself.

Sterling didn't couldn't answer his own question before *The Wall's* last massive force-cannon opened fire on the MegaKore. Bluish explosions rocked the already weakened shields of the battleship. In response, the large aft turret began to slowly rotate around and pointed at the force cannon port. There was a second long pause before the giant cannon mounted on the aft turret fired a single round into the port. The six barrels of the force cannon port were ripped apart from each other in a searing explosion. Another shot rang out from the cannon, impacting just below the wrecked force cannon, blowing a large chunk of metal out of the wall. The cannon again fired, this time into the hole below the port. Hidden explosions rippled throughout the interior of *The Wall*, and fire burst from every opening. The explosions intense enough to shake the Earth. The explosions gradually died down and great black columns of smoke poured from different parts of the mortally wounded alien barrier. All of the spotlights went dark, everything became still. *The Wall* had finally perished.

"I don't know what it is, but it seems to be on our side," a Naval Captain, one of the air-wing commanders said within earshot of Sterling.

Sterling smiled, "This is it. All units Attack!"

. . .

"Main gate has been neutralized Sir," Rycon reported.

"Excellent shooting Rycon," Kimbett looked cracked his knuckles nonchalantly.

Kailecko grunted, "Permission to head back to Medical and tend to our wounded."

Kimbett looked at Destarus, who nodded.

"Go ahead Doctor," Destarus answered.

"Are we capable of planetary orbit?" Kimbett asked.

"All systems seem to be functional except for the main computer," Destarus answered, "it seems like the Yellow and Green colonies had a party with it."

. . .

The red irises of the Red dotariaks dilated as the lights came on, standing with them were their allies, the Purple dotariak. The Green and Yellow colonies were closing in on the trapped group of Red and Purple. They were totally surrounded. All of the dotariak wielded small crowbars, wrenches, jagged metal scraps, or pieces of other dotariak. There were nearly a hundred Red and about forty Purple. But there were over a thousand Green dotariak and about fifteen hundred Yellow. There would be no escape.

The battle began. Dotariak rushed at each other and soon were locked in a frenzied hand-to-hand combat, stabbing and pulling each other apart. The Red and Purple dotariak were fighting valiantly, but futilely. The battle took place below the central heating system. With no warning, a small explosive tore a hole in the heating cells, spilling scalding water onto the fighting dotariak killing all of them. The Red dotariak had sacrificed there own for the destruction of the Yellow and Green colonies. Nearly all of the Green were killed. And less than one hundred Yellow dotariak were left alive aboard the MegaKore, and they would soon be hunted down and killed. The war within the walls of the MegaKore was over. The Red and Purple were victorious.

. . .

Krewtek's eye was green with anger and disappointment. He doubted that there could be any future for him in the eye of Kroyce. He had failed his mission. In the Trexian legends, the valiant Trexian hero always died defending his post, and defending his honor. Krewtek was fine with all of that except for the dying part. He instead boarded the Batteckery and was planning on escaping. Staying alive was his new mission.

The Batteckery lifted off from the Molluskan Barracks, and with no shields left to defend Grantex. There was no main gate left to stop the hoards of human war-machines from invading, and he was leaving everyone below to die in a bloody and futile battle. But in fact, he had no intention of allowing the humans to capture Grantex. He had one last responsibility to carry out.

The Batteckery lifted off the surface of the planet and began its hour long trek upward to an orbital position.

The still MegaKore rested silently outside the inactive main gate.

"Sir, Relecite reports that the yellow, blue and green dotariak colonies have been destroyed," Rycon reported.

"All right, let's get the hell out of here," Kimbett commanded.

"Engage thrusters. Rise to orbit," Destarus ordered.

Fire erupted from under the MegaKore. It began to lift off from the ground and head skyward. Before long, it disappeared. With the alien ship out of the way, the USS Kentucky began to approach the gate.

Sterling glared at the broken structure, “The music’s started, and the lights have dimmed... now it’s time to dance...” he muttered.

CHAPTER 48 Reversed Polarity

With the shields down, the human aircraft flew up and over the main gate and into the compound.

A trail of tanks, personnel carriers and supply trucks converged on the gaping hole punched in the main gate of *The Wall.* Although the hole in the main gate was huge, the only part of the hole that went all the way to ground level was a fifty-foot wide canyon of twisted metal. The first tanks to navigate through the treacherous metallic rift in the main gate were met with waiting Trexian ground forces. Dragonfly aircraft swarmed into the rift in the gate in an attempt to destroy the vulnerable column of slow vehicles. If they could block the rift with wreckages, the human ground forces could be stopped at the gate.

Force shells and rockets bombarded the ground vehicles, but detonated against the blue shields protecting the columns. An unarmed variation of the M1A1 Abrams tank now carried a shield generator; this was another last-minute addition from Richard Tieseler's group, and was proving successful. The leading vehicles exited the rift and closed the distance as soon as possible with their attackers.

The human vehicles would have been destroyed one by one by the superior Trexian firepower, but were spared as the precision 22-inch rail gun slugs from the sky carriers rained from above, hammering the enemy ground forces. All three remaining sky carriers had floated over the *The Wall* and into the base's perimeter and in turn attracted the wrath of the swarm of the Dragonflies. The chemical laser systems of the sky carriers lit up the sky as they blasted away at the shielded Dragonflies. Su-131s arrived in the sky carrier's defense and exacted a heavy toll on the slower Dragonfly aircraft, breaking up the assault.

The Trexian ground forces, slowly attrited from the withering assault from above began to retreat. Those that didn't were eventually overwhelmed by the sheer quantity of human firepower pouring through the gate.

A Trexian missile arched through the air at supersonic speeds, racing to the mustering group of human ground vehicles. After several laser hits, and a direct hit from an anti-air missile, it wildly veered off course. The sky lit up with an intense flash, followed by a great expanding ball of fire high in the air. A high-pressure wave of air slammed into the sky carriers and human aircraft. Smoke erupted from the USS Hawaii, and it slowly lost altitude.

"Are you alright Sir," a petty officer helped Sterling to his feet. His face felt sunburnt by the glare of the nuclear detonation.

Sterling looked up at the pink and white cloud and then at the young petty officer, who surprisingly showed no sign of fear.

"That was a nuke!" He reached down to grab his Kevlar helmet, and put it back on his head.

. . .

"We're losing altitude. Major structural failure, I don't think we're flying out of here Sir." The Captain of the Hawaii said over the radio.

Admiral Bruin beat his hands against his console in the CIC (combat information center) of the USS Kentucky.

"Drop your cargo, and try and get as much distance from here before you touch down." Bruin said.

The *cargo* Bruin was referring to was the Hawaii's two cargo containers that both held fifty tanks and armored personnel carriers.

"What was that missile's origin!?" Bruin barked.

"The Molluskan Barracks Sir!" A Lieutenant quickly responded.

Bruin got on the radio again, "All units, Mother Goose, watch your spacing and commence attack on the Molluskan Barracks! Close the distance as soon as you can!"

. . .

Both the USS Washington and the USS Kentucky dove to a lower altitude of eight hundred feet and head straight at the Molluskan Barracks. At this point, hundreds of tanks and armored vehicles were spread out ahead. The Trexian forces had fortified the Molluskan Barracks and waited for the humans to come in range. Soon, human aircraft arrived and the skies again lit up with a fury never seen before on Earth.

The battle was tremendous. The building itself was well armed. Its armored and shielded walls were studded with every weapon imaginable from particle lasers, and twelve-inch force cannons. Concrete tank traps, and four-foot spikes stuck out of the sand at its perimeter like the primitive defenses of Omaha Beach in World War II. Bombs and guided missiles rained on the shielded structure from the planes above and were responded to by waves of force shells and powerful lasers.

The human ground forces came within range of the Molluskan Barracks and a full ground war erupted. Armored personnel carriers spread out unloaded their infantry.

. . .

"Missile in the air!" a Lieutenant reported. Everyone in CIC inhaled. "Bearing... straight at us! Twenty seconds!"

Bruin gave no orders, as he watched the symbol displayed on his tactical screen approached the symbol for his flagship at an alarming speed. Live or die, he was proud of his men and women. He could see the fear in their faces, but they never wavered, never hesitated, and never panicked.

"Let 'em have it." He muttered.

The missile's electronics could detect the large slow moving target and was heading straight for it. Laser blasts from the Kentucky as well as those from the Washington chewed into the thin shields surrounding the weapon. It was in fact, not a nuclear weapon, but an anti-matter weapon. The warhead was made of a small quantity of anti-hydrocarbons, which were held inside of a force field. At the time of detonation, this force field was simply deactivated. The mixture of anti-matter and the matter of the weapon itself would mutually annihilate each other and release massive torrents of energy.

One laser penetrated the armored tip and sliced into the electronics beyond.

. . .

"Brace for impact!" The words came over the announcing system.

"Sir, please get inside!" A petty officer pleaded with Sterling, who ignored him as he watched the missile head straight at the Kentucky.

Sterling's eyes refused to shut as the missile approached and turned to a blur as it slammed into the upper bow of the USS Kentucky and sent a cloud of Kevlar and aluminum into the air. To Sterling's surprise, the missile ricocheted back into the air and continued off into the horizon. Thirty seconds later the horizon again lit up, but the detonation was much further away.

"It missed!" Someone shouted. Sterling hardly needed to brace for the concussion wave.

"We've been lucky up until now," Sterling spoke into his headset, "we need to destroy that missile launcher,"

Both remaining sky carriers landed momentarily, releasing their cargo modules before rising back into the air. The modules opened, and one hundred additional human armored vehicles joined the fray. The sky carriers continued to pound the Molluskan Barracks with their twenty-two inch rail guns. The human troops approached the perimeter of the base and were met by confused molluskan and Aracteroid, but the infantry's drive to the base was ground to a halt by the MTs.

The Barracks launched smaller missiles at the sky carriers, many of which were shot down. One missile was able to penetrate the USS Washington's anti-air defenses and impacted its starboard hanger bay, setting it ablaze and rupturing several helium gas cells. The airship maintained altitude as the damage control parties battled the blaze.

The enemy brawlers and other Trexian vehicles poured from the hangars of Molluskan Barracks and prevented the rush of human tanks and artillery from penetrating the perimeter. The superior anti-aircraft weaponry studding the building drove off most human aircraft.

. . .

The F-202 Lakota was approaching the Molluskan Barracks.

"Our mission is already complete," Dutch said, looking down at the battle.

"We're not done," Bishop said flatly, suddenly diving at the barracks.

"Our chameleon system is busted, and we're running on electrical," Dutch reminded Bishop.

Bishop nodded.

The Lakota suddenly rocketed forward, firing its new booster engine supplied by Kimbett. A trail of blue fire streamed behind the fighter, and in mere seconds had broken the sound barrier. The human fighter swooped down at the Molluskan Barracks and fired the remainder of its alien missiles at the roof of the building, inflicting severe damage. Like the original solid-fuel booster, the alien version could not be shut off once started, and they could not turn around for another pass. But the damage was done; the humans spontaneously rushed the defenses of the Molluskan and closed in. Bombs were planted on the Brawlers, grenades and mortars hailed on the heavy Trexian vehicles. Although the alien ground forces were technologically superior, they were totally outnumbered. The human infantry pressed on, and the mechanized infantry backed them up with tanks. Once within range, the tanks and rocket launchers began to join the carriers in their barrage of the building itself.

. . .

The B-100 flew past the destroyed Garden Barracks, and headed onward to the Molluskan barracks. Behind them was a huge black column of smoke. Their bomber had been through more than the designers could have thought of. The temperature of the explosion had boiled most of the B-100's black paint off, yielding a patchwork of chrome colored metal. The canopy was almost too foggy to see out of.

. . .

Sprinters, MTs, and Aracteroid flooded out of the barracks with other reinforcements and tried desperately to combat the humans. The western side of the Molluskan Barracks was the first to be reached by the soldiers. One of the doors had been barricaded, and had to be blown in by a C-4 charge. The soldiers began to flood into the building.

Inside, in the cramped, gloomy hallways of the Barracks there were battles ranging from close quarters shootouts and hand to hand combat. Lance Corporal Milan was currently using his M-20 rifle as a club against an armored Molluskan. His ammunition had run out long ago. He beat it over the helmet several times, warping his own rifle, but not the helmet. After a long time, the Molluskan's feet were knocked out from under it, Milan picked up a small plasma weapon from a nearby molluskan body and shot it until it stopped moving.

"Sir!" he yelled.

Major Brobyn was also there, be was currently in a knife fight with an Aracteroid. The Aracteroid swung its claws at Brobyn, but he dodged and slashed its upper left arm, crippling it. It lunged at Brobyn, but was struck across the head with Milan's M-20, sending it sprawling to the floor, unconscious.

"Let's move on, shall we? Sir," He said, throwing another plasma weapon to his commanding officer.

Brobyn caught the weapon and spoke into his headset. "Mother Goose, Liberty One, west wing is secured." With that he followed Milan onto the next section.

The entire eastern wing of the Molluskan Barracks exploded as its armor was pierced by a twenty-inch rail gun slug. The weapons of the Molluskan Barracks had either been destroyed, lost power, or had been commandeered by humans.

"Mother Goose, Liberty-Five," Sterling heard, "Barracks Hangar secured."

Brobyn kicked open the swinging door into a dark area. Before him were three Aracteroid manning computer equipment. They charged him but were cut apart by the marines who had emerged from behind him.

"Spread out!" Brobyn commanded, and four marines, including Milan secured the area. Through a large window, Brobyn could see a missile mounted in its launch tube. Although he couldn't see additional missiles, he guessed they were fed up through a subterranean magazine.

"Sir," Milan motioned to Brobyn, "Check this out,"

On the screen of the largest console was a live video of the USS Kentucky, with some sort of reticle targeting it.

. . .

"Mother Goose, Liberty One, missile launcher is secured," Sterling's radio barked, causing him to let out a sigh of relief. Sterling gave the order to cease fire on the Barracks, because of the danger of hitting his own men.

It was only a matter of time now.

Milan, Brobyn, and twelve others from his platoon kicked open the door to the control room of the Barracks to find it mostly deserted. Some Molluskan were still wandering around, and those that did not resist were captured. Most of the main strongholds of the Barracks were under human control, but there were over six hundred cube shaped cells that served as quarters for the Molluskan and Aracteroid, each was its own little pillbox. One by one the Molluskan quarters were systematically destroyed. In some cases, entire hallways were filled with rubble and bodies to block the human's advance. These rooms had to be broken into by boring through the walls separating them from neighboring cells. Most Molluskan, when reached were eager to surrender.

None of the Aracteroid surrendered, and all died fighting.

The wave of humans moved through the building, from the west wing all the way to the destroyed east wing. Humans poured down into the basements below the building finding literally thousands of unarmed Molluskan tending a huge hatchery where Molluskan were grown. All were captured without a fight.

The Molluskan and Aracteroid armies made there last stand in the Barracks Garden. Among the catwalks of the enormous hanging gardens, the Molluskan sniped at the intruders. They fought valiantly, but were soon overrun by the massive tidal flood of humans. Many human soldiers and marines by this time were carrying Trexian weapons.

Milan broke into the main tower. A spiral catwalk led up. He ran up cautiously, checking every corner for a Molluskan. Besides an occasional scurrying blue eyeball, he saw nothing. He continued his way to the top of the tower, where he was hit by a blast of fresh air.

Milan climbed the stairs and walked out onto the top of the tower. He withdrew *Old Glory*, which had been rolled up in his flak vest, and waved it on top of the tower. Nearly every breathing human in the compound, Russian, Chinese, Canadian, British, and American cheered. Brobyn came up right behind him.

"Mother Goose, Liberty One..." Brobyn paused, "The Molluskan Barracks has been secured."

Sterling closed his eyes. "Thank you." Bruin quietly whispered. Once word spread to them, the planes in the air did victory rolls, before landing back on their carriers.

At this time, the F-202 Lakota landed back on the deck of the USS Kentucky. Both pilots were received as heroes.

But it was still too early to celebrate.

CHAPTER 49 Fist Of Irony

Krewtek buried his face in his hands. From his safe position in the sky, he watched the Molluskan Barracks fall under Human control, and the remains of his army be crushed by sheer numbers of humans. The last military installation was taken, and the air force, and ground forces were in ashes. What was left of his MTs were either captured or killed. Grantex was lost, Krewtek's future was bleak. Kroyce would have him executed as a traitor, blaming the failed mission on him. Kimbett's betrayal, and theft of the MegaKore of course, would be also be blamed on him.

Krewtek chuckled nervously. "The bastards will probably say I was partners with him," he said quietly to himself.

The yellow dotariak on his shoulder rested quietly, with only a quarter of its colony aboard the Batteckery, its collective intelligence was only a quarter of what it had once been. No more games of the *Battle* would be played with it. It just sat, there, thoughtless. Krewtek turned to his young Aracteroid lieutenant, "Open a channel with the Rao Lok."

The young Aracteroid in turn ordered an older Aracteroid sitting at the controls to open a channel. Krewtek's duty as commander of the station was not yet over.

He began again, "Transmit Mission Abort codes... "

Both Aracteroids looked at each other in confusion.

Krewtek began to rattle off a twenty character long alphanumeric code.

Along the starboard side of the Rao Lok, two metal doors sank into the hull, and slid aside. From the opening, a mechanical scaffolding craned outward. At the end were two long, silver, cylindrical tubes, each at least a hundred feet long, and twenty feet in diameter. The crane articulated so that the tubes were pointing below, at Earth.

"Weapon armed," The older Aracteroid said.

The younger Aracteroid stuttered, "Sir... our own people are still down there..."

Krewtek exploded from his chair and punched the Aracteroid in the face, sending it to the ground.

"If I want your opinion!" he stood over the Aracteroid, "I'll ask for it!"

He swung around to the older Aracteroid. "Fire!" Krewtek yelled.

The rear end of both tubes erupted fire and two giant rockets were fired out. Both were anti-matter weapons of a massive size. One headed for the north pole, the other, for the south. Detonated together, on opposite sides of the Earth, would have the effect of shattering Earth's tectonic plates. Bacteria would be the only life to survive the geologic onslaught that would follow. The human race would be totally annihilated. Grantex would not fall into enemy hands, and Earth itself would not fall into enemy hands.

"I cannot weep for you," Krewtek recited a Trexian poem, "for my river of sorrow is dry, and my resolve great,"

The southern missile was suddenly shot out of the sky by a red beam of light. "Sir! Missile down! Missile down!" The older Aracteroid yelled.

"What!" Krewtek stood up out of his chair and watched the screen.

The northern missile, alone would be enough to wipe out the North America, Europe and Asia. As it raced for its destination, its on board sensors picked another object coming at it.

Krewtek watched helplessly as a rocket shot out of nowhere and intercepted the northern missile, both exploded in a brilliant anti-matter explosion.

"Who fired that rocket!" Krewtek demanded.

"Focusing in on that position now sir." The older Aracteroid said. The screen zoomed in on an area just above the Earth's horizon, there was a black space in the middle of the stars.

Krewtek gritted his teeth, "The MegaKore."

The MegaKore uncloaked. Unlike the human's chameleon system, the Trexian only had the technology to make their shields absorb all light, making them appear as a void in space.

"We're being hailed Sir!" The older Aracteroid announced.

"Put him on," Krewtek said, sitting back in his chair.

The screen displayed Admiral Kimbett, grinning typically.

"Well, well, well," Kimbett laughed, "How did I know you'd try that! Destroying an entire planet, now that's too evil..." Kimbett's face showed disgust, "... even for me."

"What are you going to do now? Attack me?" Krewtek said defiantly.

Kimbett nodded his head. "That's the idea," Behind Krewtek, the older Aracteroid could be heard moving around.

"You're a fool. You might kill me Kimbett, but I guarantee I'll tear into you with everything I have! And there aren't any repair bases where your going *rebel!*" Krewtek laughed.

"Let's dance!" Kimbett said closing the channel.

Krewtek turned.

"Fire all weapons! Take us to..." Krewtek stopped. The older Aracteroid was lying on the ground, its throat cut. In its seat was another Aracteroid. The shields around the Batteckery dropped, leaving it defenseless. The Aracteroid turned its head, its three operable eyes staring at Krewtek, its bloody mouth smiling.

"I found Kimbett for you... he's right there!" he rasped.

"Grackconn...." Krewtek said, his voice hollow. He suddenly withdrew his *hellion* and fired a burst into Grackconn's chest, knocking him out of the chair. He threw himself at the bloodied panel and tried to raise the shields.

. . .

"Lock on the central cannon," Kimbett ordered.

"Locked on," Rycon said.

"Powering up central cannon..." Kailecko reported.

Rycon watched the gauges, and finally said, "Central cannon is fully charged Sir."

. . .

The panel suddenly went dead. Krewtek, in a panic, tore off the maintenance panel, and found four dotariak chewing on the wiring inside, their purple irises looking at him.

"Nooo! " Krewtek yelled, throwing himself at the backup controls. Grackconn holding onto his feet. "You're coming with me Admiral!" Grackconn yelled.

. . .

"Fire!" Kimbett said, throwing his fist out at the screen.

The large central gun on the turret, fully charged, fired a one hundred and twenty foot force shell, traveling mach three through the frictionless space until crashing into the unshielded hull of the Batteckery, blowing its interior out as the force shell fragmented upon impact, tearing the ship in half. Its reactor exploded, but in the vacuum of space, only flashed for a second. The remaining rear hulk of the trashed Batteckery fell into Earth's atmosphere and began to burn up as it re-entered.

"Wow," Destarus said.

Kimbett looked at the dented dog tags from the human. "Gates, Michael F..." he said quietly.

"Shall we get out of here Sir?" Kailecko asked.

"We have to find some place safe so we can repair ourselves," Rycon said.

"If I can figure out how this thing works, we can make ourselves virtually invisible," Boratus said, holding up the stolen chameleon system from the B-100.

"Get on it, Boratus," Kimbett said sitting in his chair, for another five minutes he stared at the surface.

"Let's get out of here Destarus," He said, after a while.

The MegaKore rocketed off into the blackness it came from. Soon it was only a speck among the stars and then it was gone.

. . .

Deep, under the molten wreckage of the tower. In a small room, four Aracteroid, in silver radiation suits, operated and maintained the main reactor. Without the cryo-plant, there was no coolant flowing into the reactor. The river of water that was once flowing into the reactor, was now dry. The tower, which had absorbed seventy percent of the power generated was no longer there. The reactor itself was rising in temperature. Two Aracteroid were scrambling all over the control room, transferring power to this area, taking from that one, in a desperate attempt the stabilize the system. The other two managed the slow power-down of the reactor.

On a computer screen in the wall behind them, diagrams of the tower and reactor were shown. The tower was dark gray, since it was missing. The reactor was green, but in the center there was a red dot. It was slowly growing.

" Meridian-3! Come in Meridian-3!" Both men heard over the radio.

"Yeah! This is Meridian-3, go ahead," Gates responded.

"This is General Sterling," The voice replied.

"Hey! How's it goin' General?!" Ford said, smiling.

"Ford! Listen! There's no time! We're picking up the warning signs of a massive reactor meltdown, like nothing this planet has ever seen," Sterling shouted.

"Shit," Ford simply replied.

"All of our forces are pulling out, the USS Kentucky is just outside the main gate, if you can land, you'll make it," Sterling said. "Good luck Meridian-3."

Ford's face was white, "Roger that Sir,"

Gates rolled his eyes and shouted, "Son of a bitch!"

The B-100 Revenant was just passing over the smoldering Molluskan Barracks. An exodus of human ground vehicles was in progress below,"

. . .

In the room below the tower, all four Aracteroid were lying on the floor, dead. The entire room began to deform as temperatures soared over three thousand. The screen showed the reactor with the red dot covering all of it, and a white dot forming in the center. The screen suddenly went black, as a crack appeared down the center. And the room was enveloped in fire. A second later it was no longer there.

The sky behind the B-100 became white. Ford shielded his eyes as the back of the main gate turned bright white, and the blue sky appeared black as midnight. As the glare faded, a second sun was rising from a huge crater from behind the B-100. Gates watched, through the rear camera, as gaping maw opened mile after mile, sucking in more Earth. It was like staring into the gateway to hell. The ball of fire became a white cotton ball, and was expanding rapidly.

Ford realized that Kimbett said he had replaced the booster rocket. With a subtle prayer he slammed his fist onto the ignition, and to his total surprise, it fired. The bomber was rocketed forward, over the main gate, and out into the desert. The concussion wave reached out as far as the main gate and began to dissipate. After a few minutes, it had died down.

A massive magma-filled pit scarred the center of the alien compound, where the tower and cryo-plant had been. Gates and Ford both breathed the last sigh of relief. Shielded from the blast wave by the towering wall of the main gate, the USS Kentucky, USS Washington and damaged USS Hawaii had survived. The B-100 flew towards the Kentucky.

. . .

"We're alright Sir," Milan said to Brobyn, whose armored personnel carrier had been knocked on its side.

Upon exiting the vehicle, Milan was stunned to see a large Molluskan approaching with outstretched arms.

"Sir! Incoming trooper," he said, raising his M-20.

"Well, light 'em up Corporal!" Brobyn's voice boomed from inside of the APC.

Milan didn't fire as the Molluskan stopped. It reached up and removed its helmet, exposing its utterly alien face. Brobyn emerged from the APC, a pistol in his hand.

Xo looked fearlessly at the humans, “Suh wen dah,” he spoke.

Brobyn realized that he was surrounded by Molluskan.

“He wants us to surrender?” Milan asked excitedly.

Brobyn shook his head as hundreds of Molluskan lowered to one-knee, “He is surrendering to us.”

CHAPTER 50 Let It Rain

It was a phenomena that would baffle scientists for years. All the water vapor released in the reactor explosion, and the destruction of the cryo-plant had condensed into a massive super-cumulus. Massive torrents of rain poured down over the wreckage of the compound. Only half of the compound remained, the other half, from the inner gate, to the eastern perimeter, was now a gigantic crater, roughly six hundred feet deep and filled with cooling lava.

The B-100 Revenant flew under the fleet of giant sky carriers. And turned in a victory role. Under the gray clouds, on the decks of all carriers, men and women cheered. The B-100 landed on the deck of the USS Kentucky, and Gates popped open the hatch while Ford opened his canopy. Both men crawled out of their aircraft and were surrounded by a crowd of people. The rain was pouring down on them, but no one cared.

Ford withdrew his last cigarette, and frantically searched for his lighter, and then remembered he had lost it.

"Anyone got a light?!" he asked the crowd.

Gates produced the small canteen the eyeball had left, and from its pocket, Gates removed the Zippo lighter, with the old, blue, Ford truck painted on it.

"Gates!" Ford exclaimed, snatching the lighter from his hands. "Where did you...?" he stuttered.

Gates smiled, but didn't answer.

As Ford lit his cigarette, Bishop's huge arms embraced both him and Gates.

"Navy pukes! We did it!" he said, throwing back his head and laughing.

"No. You guys did it," Dutch said, shaking Gates' hand and then Ford's.

"We did it," Gates said, but in his mind he said something else, *The Weed did it.*

Under the shelter of an umbrella, Sterling and Bruin walked up Gates, Ford, Bishop and VanDuinwyk. The four men instantly stood straight up and saluted.

"Gentlemen," Bruin began simply, "The world is in your debt." he said extending his hand. Gates reached out his hand.

Sterling smiled, but couldn't find the words at first, "We thought you were dead," he said to Ford and Gates.

"We're glad you were wrong Sir," Ford said.

The elevator carried the Revenant into the internal hangar of the Kentucky, and Gates looked up to see the defeated main gate one last time before it disappeared from view.

. . .

Word of the Victory over Grantex swept the planet. Thousands of Chinese poured into Tiananmen square and cheered, holding up NATO and A.C. flags alike. In Paris, people crowded and cheered. In Moscow, thousands of proletariat workers left the factories and walked out into the streets screaming and shouting in total exhilaration. The entire country of the Unites States of America left work and walked out in the streets to party. In Times square, a man, a 3rd Class Petty Officer in the Navy, who had just gotten home since the NATO-A.C. armistice was signed, spontaneously walked up to a women he had never met before and embraced her in a deep kiss.

History had been made. The world would change fast now, faster than it had ever changed before. What it would change into was anyone's guess.

. . .

Gates sat on his bed. His chin resting on his palm.

Ford stabbed his fork at the tasteless green grape that was the last of his *lunch*.

All four pilots were in a white, bio-hazard room, level four restricted access.

"How long they'll keep us in here, Gates?" Ford said, the grape valiantly slipping away from his stabs.

"Until they determine we didn't catch any diseases," Gates said, bored out of his mind.

Ford finally seized the grape and brought it up to his mouth, and it slipped off his fork, and landed on the ground with a plop. The noises echoed ominously in the room.

"Man I'm the savior of the world, and I'm not eating steak right now... this is a travesty," Ford grumbled.

"Man, why don't they give us some real damn food?" Bishop asked, throwing down a month old Reader's Digest magazine.

"Well... The least I could expect is maybe a TV or a radio," VanDuinwyk said, "Maybe a Game Station with four controllers,"

"No flight sims!" Ford stipulated.

"Why? Because you're sick of flying or you're afraid I'd kick your ass," Bishop smirked at Ford.

Ford just shook his head.

At that time, the airlock hissed and opened. Another person in a full encapsulation suit walked in carrying a bag. Gates heart fluttered, only in his dreams had he imagined this moment. He instantly recognized her as the same woman that he had briefly met when he was last here. His eyes met with her emerald gaze for a moment. Gates was captivated.

"Gentlemen," She said began to speak, "I've brought you some things,"

She began to distribute new magazines, mail and various other objects. It was like Christmas.

She delivered a giant stack of mail to Bishop. Everyone looked at him.

"My daughter is in second grade, look's like her entire classroom wrote me," he said, happily opening up the first envelope.

She stopped by Ford and dropped off a post card.

"Dear Dusty..." He began to read. "I hope you're having fun in Sasebo, and remember to bring me back something Japanese!"

He laughed, "Better late than never I guess."

"So somebody finally decided to stop punishing us eh?" Gates said to the lady as she handed him a deck of playing cards. His eyes met hers again, and his heart began to race faster. He couldn't believe how damn attractive she was.

"Hey," he spoke up, "I'm Mike Gates," he said, extending his hand.

She smiled, "I know, Lieutenant."

Gates now looked completely embarrassed.

She reached out and shook his hand, "Dr. Celesta Patterson. It's a pleasure to meet you."

The other three men smiled and remained completely quiet.

"Celesta..." Gates began in a sincere tone, "...Will you marry me?"

All three of the other men's jaws dropped.

Celesta blushed and smiled. She looked into his eyes, and seemed to grip his hand tighter.

"No," She said with a grin.

All three other men closed their eyes simultaneously. "Ouch! Shot down..." Ford muttered.

Gates smiled confidently and nodded in defeat.

Celesta smiled mischievously, "But I will let you take me out to dinner,"

"Back in the air!" Ford quietly cheered.

"That is... if you're interested," She said, letting go of his hand.

"Yes... yes I am," Gates replied.

Celesta finished distributing the contents of the bag she was carrying and walked towards the airlock. Before she went through it, she looked back at Gates and smiled. He wasn't sure if it was his imagination or if actually saw her wink at him. The airlock closed and sealed.

Ford immediately ran over to Gates and slapped him on the shoulder.

"Yup. That's the Gates I know, bold but no brain," Ford said while laughing hysterically opening the deck of cards.

For the rest of the forty-eight hour decontamination period, the men joked and played cards.

They were only human.

The End

About The Author

Jeff Wilcox has been serving on active duty in the U.S. Navy since 1997. He began work on Flight of the Revenants in 1992, and completed the initial draft in 1996. He has plans for a series based on the novel as well as publishing an anthology of short stories. A 2004 graduate of the U.S. Naval Academy with a Bachelor of Science degree in computer science, Jeff also enjoys programming and has created several training programs for the Navy. He currently resides in Annapolis, MD.

Printed in the United States
28582LVS00001B/13